VERITY RED'S DIARY

VERITY RED'S DIARY

A STORY OF SURVIVING M.E.

Maria Mann

JANUS PUBLISHING COMPANY

London, England

First Published in Great Britain 2005 by
Janus Publishing Company Ltd.
105-107 Gloucester Place,
London W1U 6BY

www.januspublishing.co.uk

Reprinted 2007

**British Library Cataloguing-in-Publication Data
A catalogue record for this book
is available from the British Library**

ISBN 978-1-85756-630-7

Illustrations: Maria Mann
Cover Design: Nathan Cording

Printed and bound in Great Britain

CONTENTS

January	1
February	49
March	89
April	127
May	175
June	233
July	273
August	307
September	341
October	373
November	405
December	433

In memory of

Mum and Auntie Mary who would have loved to see this book in print. Hope there is a book shop in heaven. Also Rob's wife Bev, Rachel's mum Josie, little Jade now dancing with the angels, and Thom.

This book is dedicated to Nigel, Shauna, Seka Nikolich, the Toads and everyone who knows what it's like to have M.E.

Acknowledgments

A big thank you to everyone at Janus Books for making my dream a reality and presenting this book so beautifully. Special thanks to Rachel, Shauna and her parents, Auntie Jeanette and Gail Ronda (President of The National CFIDS Foundation, U.S.A.) for their enthusiasm, the M.E. Association for linking my web site (www.inter-netti.co.uk) to theirs, Theresa Coe (Action for M.E. editor of *InterAction*) for her help, John for support and help with info for illustrations, and David, Kim and Wendy for the encouraging words.

Cheers! To the girls at Kentec, especially, Cheryl for the loan of Monopoly, Charlotte for the loan of books and Allison for the loan of Nigel on the odd occasion during working hours. Also to Paul for his thoughtful card.

Heartfelt thanks to friends, family and Nigel's family who have been supportive over the years, to pen-friends for their wonderful letters and people from all over this country and America who have sent me e-mails.

I must not forget Dr. Jaqueline Bingham for her kindness, Matthew Manning and Seka Nikolich for their amazing healing powers and Sally for aromatherapy and being so understanding.

A whole book full of thank yous to Nigel for his brilliant internet skills, many hours spent typing and printing, his endless patience and sense of humour.

And last but not least, to my cats for warm furry love and beautiful muddy paw prints all over my manuscript.

January

Saturday 1st

9.26 a.m.   Big long yawn... mouth open *really* wide, like the huge ginger cat next door, Chris Evans, after a peaceful nap on his dustbin lid.

9.27 a.m.   Oooh! My head hurts. Hurts a lot. I can *feel* little men, like next door's gnomes, hitting me with their pointy axes.

9.28 a.m.   Scalp feels itchy too. *Must* have a bath and wash hair today.

9.29 a.m.   Only have energy to wallow in a hot bath full of Christmas smellies.

9.30 a.m.   Stretch legs and scratch behind left ear, like Chris Evans after a doze on a warm ~~purr~~ Peugeot bonnet. But do not bother licking between toes or twitching tail.

9.31 a.m.   Negative thought – no energy to wash hair so will have to endure scratching head like flea-ridden doggie. Positive thought – after scented bath, will have beautiful, sweet smelling armpits and feel wonderfully relaxed.

9.32 a.m.   Another great big yawn... like hippo in his bath after a long, hot, sweaty day in jungle.

9.33 a.m.   Bedroom looks cold and gloomy.

9.34 a.m.   Bedside clock is tick... tick... ticking my life away... every second I am closer to my death; the way I feel, that could be *very, very* soon.

9.35 a.m.   Notice thick layer of dust and cobweb on celestial bedside lamp. Also empty sherry glass and three foil mince pie cases full of purple, green and yellow Quality Street wrappers.

9.36 a.m.   Feel *really* fat and hopeless and hate self; like depressed hippo after fight with her boyfriend.

9.37 a.m.   Usual start to New Year.

9.39 a.m.   Do female hippos have boyfriends?

9.40 a.m.   Don't remember eating all those chocolates!

9.42 a.m.   Now I know why I had all those strange dreams last night: chocolate logs melting in a Victorian fireplace, holly leaves curling and burning, red berries turning black and wrinkling like raisins, a gold plastic 'Merry Christmas' melting and dripping like candle wax into soft grey ashes and old men with cream sherry faces, sitting on mince pie cushions with Sandeman port smiles.

9.43 a.m.   Why, *why* don't I ever dream about gorgeous hunky males driving me wild with desire and feeding me with Thornton's chocolates.

9.44 a.m.   Do lady hippos fall in love with gorgeous great hunks showing off their enormous wobbly bellies by the riverbank?

9.46 a.m.   Ben turns over, taking most of the bed covers with him. He's giggling in his sleep. What's he up to? Who is he with?

9.47 a.m.   Listen for clue... nothing.

                 Positive thought – probably having a fantastic time with me. Negative thought – he's with his other lady hippo, rolling about in the mud in the rainy season.

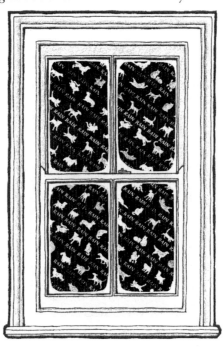

9.51 a.m. It's still raining cats and dogs.

9.54 a.m. Huge, long yawn... like extremely tired person. Lay awake half the night listening to the cats and dogs.

9.56 a.m. Ben turns over again, taking his enormous wobbly belly with him. He's happily snoring away last night's Christmas port and dreaming away the blue cheese; curled up in an untidy pile of limbs, duvet and pillows, like his discarded papers and clothes.

9.57 a.m. Wonder if I sleep in a tidy way, neatly folded up, making gentle feminine breathing noises.

9.58 a.m. Grab some bed covers for myself and try to go back to sleep.

9.59 a.m. Eyes tight shut; brain wide awake.

10.00 a.m. Don't want to get up till springtime.

10.02 a.m. Want to hibernate in a box in the wardrobe like next door's tortoise. He's a very old, thirty something tortoise, hasn't moved around much for the last few years and likes a little nibble on something tasty when he's in the mood; we have a lot in common.

10.04 a.m. Want to be a hedgehog but I'm too spineless.

10.05 a.m. Need bathroom.

10.06 a.m. Tempted to lie still and wet self.

10.08 a.m. Quiet outside, the world nursing a hangover from the festive season. Well, maybe not the 'whole' world, but quite a few people. Hundreds. Thousands.

10.10 a.m. We had hundreds and thousands on the trifle this Christmas. Of course, it's not in my special diet, so I had three bowlfuls; if you're going to be bad you might as well get stuck in and be really naughty, with blobs on.

10.12 a.m. Desperately need to go *NOW!* Need large Victorian chamber potty with flowers on. Need antique commode that looks like a chest of drawers, next to my bed. Need a big strong nurse to lift me onto it. Can't face dragging self out of warm smelly comforting place to cold bathroom. Can't face another year trekking to the toilet, attempting climbing expeditions up and down the stairs and the assault course round the kitchen. I can't face anything *ANYMORE.*
Pull pillow over head.
Pull covers over pillow over head.

10.14 a.m. Sit on toilet.

Ooooooh, Aaaaah, that's better. Here I go again, I've started another year; my natural bodily functions have forced me into it.

10.15 a.m. Can't be bothered to get off the toilet. Could sit here all day and have food and drink brought to me like a lazy king on his avocado green porcelain throne.

10.16 a.m. Pick up orange paper hat off floor and place neatly on head. Put on best regal expression.

10.17 a.m. Face drops into miserable, poverty-stricken peasant expression; the thought of another year sitting heavily on my shoulders like an elephant who's just eaten ten Christmas puddings – big fruity puddings with lots of booze in (like the old men down The Thirsty Tongue Tavern).

10.18 a.m. Can't move.

Elephant still sitting on shoulders.

Makes a change to sit in a different room anyway, gives one a different view on life even if an elephant's trunk is wrapped around one's face.

10.19 a.m. Drop toilet roll on floor – it rolls across bathroom like in Andrex advert. Expect small labrador puppy to burst in through door any minute.

Just sit and stare at pale green ecology toilet roll, now at other side of bathroom in dust under radiator. So many things in life are out of reach. Beyond my grasp. Unattainable.

10.20 a.m. Must think positive. Think positive. I will continue to hang on to my threads of sanity for another twelve months. I will. *I will. I really will try.*

Pull loose thread on sleeve of towelling dressing gown. Thread snaps. Oh bum! I'm even more batty than I was last year; living in my smelly bat cave, the world upside down, *and* I don't feel like writing any fang-you letters for my lovely-Christmas-presents. *And* I've got two birthdays coming up soon. *And* I don't want to think about cards or prezzies or wrapping paper for at least another month. Or two. Rest of year.

10.21 a.m. Still sitting on toilet counting the tiles around the bath. Thirty six. Count petals on flowers on tiles. Sixteen on each tile. Eyes working better than last year anyway, although I'm not positive about this. Last night I was admiring a beautiful brown moth in the kitchen, its wings many shades of brown and cream. On closer inspection, I found I had been talking to a bit of crusty baked potato skin. Creative brain cells working better though...

... her toothbrush looked sad and worn out, the bath towel frayed at the edges; the soap nearly all used up and out of shape...

Lean over and grab corner of toilet roll – now have different slant on life, and wet leg.

10.22 a.m. Shiver on edge of bath and pull tired old dressing gown tighter round self. Must get a grip on positive thinking this year; every time I start to feel down and think dark thoughts, I'll make a conscious effort to have bright happy thoughts.

10.23 a.m. Oh Lord! The world is a terrible place full of pain and suffering and pollution. My head is a terrible place full of pain and suffering and delusion. I'm going back to bed to hibernate till the weather is warmer.

10.24 a.m. Must wash hands, face and teeth first.
Ahhhh, Mmmmm warm water eases achy hands.

10.25 a.m. Stare in mirror.

... her face was as pale as puppy piddle...
... her face was as pale as the winter sky...
... her head felt as though one of Santa's reindeer had kicked her; she knew sitting on the roof on Christmas Eve had been a bad idea...

My hair! Ugh!

... her split ends had split up so many times, they were on the verge of divorce... tangled web of deceit... hair-brained scheme...

Eyes look horrible.

... her eyes were watery and bloodshot, she looked like she'd been crying all night; she hadn't, that was the night before...

10.26 a.m.   Find new pH-balanced eye zone revitalising cream, to soothe and refresh my delicate eye area, reduce fine lines and cure puffiness. It doesn't work but I may as well finish the tube. Press tube too hard and white liquid squirts across mirror Jackson Pollock style. Am tempted to complete work of art with blue shampoo, yellow hair conditioner and green toothpaste – to splash a little excitement into my life.

10.27 a.m.   Maybe not, will only have to clean up ~~mess~~ masterpiece and need energy for scrubbing teeth. Must go to dentist this year. When did I last visit that house of torture?

10.28 a.m.   I'm too ill to go; maybe next year. I need to avoid stress as much as possible and I'm sure visiting the dentist must be quite near bereavement and divorce (after all, you lose a tooth or a filling) in the Life's Worst Stresses list. That nice dentist left to go to Australia and the other one went back to Ireland so I don't know who'll be poking around in my mouth. I haven't had a toothache for years and I don't smile much so no-one sees my dirty teeth and I hardly see anyone anymore anyway; I missed the programme about ways of beating dental phobia and there was that article about the dentist who was sent to prison...

10.29 a.m.   Brush top set of teeth.
             Exhausted.

10.30 a.m.   Will clean lower set later.

10.31 a.m.   Sit on edge of bath again to recover.
             Thinking.

10.32 a.m.   Always have plenty of time to think, all day, all night if I want. Lucky, lucky me.

10.33 a.m.   Shall I go back to bed and stare at the ceiling (listening to the wind and rain) or sit downstairs and watch fruit rot (while umbrellas fly past the window)?
             Decisions, decisions – don't know how I cope with all this high-pressure responsibility.

10.40 a.m.   Slurp peppermint tea. Munch healthy Holland & Barrett

multi-grained toast. Enjoy Christmassy sitting room; jolly red Santa still smiling on Advent calendar, all the little windows open to reveal a drum, a bell, an angel, a trumpet. Christmas cards brighten up the mantlepiece and bookshelves: tiny churches nestle in white hills, snowmen with top hats and carrot noses grin with coal teeth, Santa and his reindeer fly over rooftops, teddies ride on sledges, a plump partridge sits in a pear tree looking a bit embarrassed, a startled kitten sits on a bed of poinsettia wishing it were curled up by the fire and a robin thinks the red bobble hat suits him perfectly. Fruit rots happily in the fruit bowl. Umbrellas fly past the window: black ones, spotty ones, tartan. Christmas tree fairy lights sparkle on red and gold tinsel and baubles; wooden trains and rocking horses rock gently as a lorry rumbles past making the house shake. Miniature chimes hanging from a star go ting... ting... ting.

10.41 a.m. Mustn't enjoy the scene too much; it has to be taken down soon. Well, it doesn't *have* to. I could be like that man who kept his Christmas tree and decorations up all year and the neighbours complained. Why can't people mind their own business and leave others alone?

10.43 a.m. Suppose we'd better take ours down; I've already got a reputation for being a bit weird. Oh why, *why* do all good things have to come to an end? *Everything* will go back to being dull and boring and grey and miserable and rainy.

10.44 a.m. It's going to be one of those years. Again. I know it. The toast fell out of my hand. Marg side down.

10.45 a.m. Think positive. I've got my recovery to look forward to.

10.46 a.m. But that could take years and years! Must count my blessings. But I'm always trying to count my blessings and I'm always losing count, I forget what I was thinking about and spiral into a pit of depression.

10.47 a.m. I should be grateful I'm still alive and able to attempt ~~suicide~~ counting my blessings, but it's hard to think straight when your thoughts go all curvy and threaten to drive you round the bend.

Can't think of any blessings today. Once I've eased into the New Year, it'll all come back to me. Chocolate helps. A lot.

10.48 a.m. That bag of chocolate money hanging on the tree looks enticing. It's fun peeling off the golden wrapper to find a picture underneath, neatly pressed into the deliciously divine and delectable little circular, coin-shaped piece of mouth-watering, creamy smooth, silky, sinful, sensual, irresistibly exciting ecstasy.

10.49 a.m. Experience chocolate high. Yesss! Brilliant!! My endorphins have been released and are joyfully swimming round my body like playful dolphins.

10.50 a.m. Eat more chocolate to prolong euphoria. Phenylethylamines are running around making my heart beat faster... I'm lustful... I'm passionate... I'm racing into the tunnel of love... oooooh... a near-death by chocolate experience.

10.51 a.m. WOW! I can see the light at the end of the tunnel now; one day I will recover, have lots of wonderful energy and make the most of every marvellous, pain free day. Life is for living to the full!!

10.52 a.m. Want to die.

Post-choc blues.

Press gold foil circles into neat little triangles. Not sure if I can face another year of being squeezed through the mangle of life, hung out to dry in the summer, then folded up and put away in the dark for winter. I'm already washed out enough.

10.54 a.m. Need more chocolate.

10.55 a.m. Maybe I'll sit here and eat myself to death with mince pies and Quality Street.

10.57 a.m. Eat satsumas and think healthy, happy thoughts enhanced by all that wonderful vitamin C. Will hide the Quality Street – never mind the quality, feel the pith.

10.59 a.m. Run out of healthy, happy thoughts.

11.00 a.m. Sky has darkened; the house looks spooky and my reflection in the mirror appears witchy. Stare out the window. It's raining bats and frogs now.

11.01 a.m. Party animals are still sleeping.

11.02 a.m. A man hurries down the street chatting into his mobile phone under a black umbrella; I suddenly feel the need for a fobile moan to a friend.

11.03 a.m. Am seeing Eileen on Monday. *That's* something to look forward to. Oh! There's *EastEnders* and *Coronation Street*, of course. Dear Eileen, my osteopath and friend and the only person in the world who seems to listen and understand me. Apart from Ben, when he's not transfixed by a TV screen, giant cheese sandwich, computer screen, attractive woman, his dinner, MicroMart, or fiddling with his little computer chess set. If I'm lucky, I might get two grunts and a 'No thanks' today. Perhaps I'll wander round the house dressed in nothing but three triangles of Dairylea, 'www dot' tattooed on my belly and a chess board drawn on my bum – it's big enough.

11.21 a.m. Hear Ben plod to bathroom.

11.22 a.m. Toilet flushes.

11.23 a.m. Grunt. Smoker's cough. Ben plods back to bed.

11.30 a.m. Stare out of window again. Rain has stopped. A Dawn French-type woman in a green anorak, calf-length navy skirt and sensible shoes is examining a mark on her car door. She rubs vigorously at it with a corner of a hankie.

11.31 a.m. Two small children ride along the path on their new bikes wearing bright new jackets and protective helmets in blues and reds and yellows, screaming with delight. Dad walks behind wearing old brown jacket and trousers and tired weary face. Feel sad.

11.32 a.m. Dawn French climbs into car, finds another corner of hankie and wipes off mascara smudges under her eyes.

11.33 a.m. Stare at trees.

... bare tree branches like veins sketched in charcoal on the palest blue water-colour sky...

11.35 a.m. Stare at bird.

... the seagull on the wet roof surveyed the street like an angry man looking for his wife at a party...

12.35 p.m. As I bite into a big lump of farmhouse cheddar on a cream cracker, an advert for Weight Watchers pops up on the TV screen. Change channel. Watch bit of cartoon. It's irritating, too full of action. Turn the sound down.

12.46 p.m. Nibble more nibbly things I shouldn't be nibbling, like hungry little mouse wrapped in white towelling dressing gown.

12.47 p.m. My claws need clipping.

12.50 p.m. Think I'll order a black dressing gown that doesn't need washing so often, from a catalogue.

1.00 p.m. The bell of All Saints' church strikes *one* in the distance. One single, solitary, lonely hour, all by itself, followed by cold minutes defrosting in the winter sunshine. Another day on its way out, leaving me behind. Alone.

... her boyfriend lay in bed, happily snoring, while she sat on the toilet feeling bloody miserable...

1.12 p.m. Sit in bath feeling fat and ugly.
Wish self a Hippo Nude Year.

1.14 p.m. Pick up mug of herb tea on the side of bath. Sip. Think positive: the mug is half full, not half empty. I will not let insensitive-comment-type people upset me anymore. Their words will wash over me like water off a fresh cauliflower's head.

1.15 p.m. Lie under bubbles listening to the birds and watching sunlight glow through golden liquid: Johnson's baby shampoo and the contents of a glass left by Ben last night – Glenfidditch Special Reserve Single Malt Scotch Whisky, first distilled on Christmas day, 1887, and produced exclusively with pure water drawn from the crystal clear Robbie Dhu springs close to the distillery. Its quality can be appreciated in the glass through its purity, elegant taste and long, lingering finish.
Lucky, lucky, lucky me, all this time to read the labels on everything; it's quite a hobby these days.
The whisky glass is a quarter full, not three quarters empty.

1.16 p.m. The shampoo bottle is nearly half full, not half empty.

My bath is more than half full and I'm soaking away my cares in aromatherapy, de-stress bath essence. Head feels better.

1.18 p.m.   Orangey aroma makes my nose tingle.

1.21 p.m.   Read back of essence bottle and try to convince self I'm feeling comforted and uplifted by the stress–relieving properties of mandarin, that I'm calmly harmonised by geranium and still reasonably sane. Most of the time.

1.25 p.m.   Wonder when the bath last enjoyed a good clean. Can't remember.

1.26 p.m.   Wiggle toes and fingers for daily workout.

1.27 p.m.   Worry about whether family and friends liked their presents; the tiny ant of doubt is always crawling up my neck, into my ear and nipping at my brain.

1.30 p.m.   Wish I hadn't ordered that joke present for Ben's brother Jeremy and his family. It all started last year when Jeremy left his Christmas shopping too late and gave all the family a Kit-Kat each wrapped in a cryptic note; I was really intrigued. We received Kit-Kat mugs a couple of weeks later, and last October when I saw a Kit-Kat tin full of fifty choccy bars and matching tea towel in a catalogue, I couldn't resist ordering it for him; thought it would give everyone a laugh! Unfortunately Kit-Kat is my favourite chocolate bar.

... she started hearing small sweet voices; was it angels, the beginning of Christmas stress or were they coming from the big red tin under the stairs...

Had to give the tin to a non-choc-loving male friend to look after; all the women I know love chocolate. I find it hard to believe non-choc-loving females exist and was amazed when I read about a woman who thought it was slimy and sickly; didn't know whether to think 'lucky cow', or feel sorry for her.

On Christmas Eve I wrapped up the tin and placed it under the tree with the other presents. The tree was near a hot radiator. Couldn't go to the family do, and Ben didn't say much about their reaction to my little joke, so my imagination ran wild. I bet all the chocolate bars were stuck together and Jeremy and his wife are on a New Year weight loss programme, the tin is too big to fit in any of their new pine kitchen cupboards, their son Alex is allergic to chocolate, the cat ate the chocolate, the cat was sick down the front of the posh stereo and they all hate me now and on top of it all, they gave us a brilliant present this year!

The little devil inside me wants to send Jeremy a Kit-Kat wrapper in a clip frame for his birthday.

1.36 p.m.	Bath water starting to cool. Let some out. Turn on hot tap and pour in more de-stress liquid ready for next set of worries.
1.39 p.m.	Must wear new Christmas socks with frogs on instead of stuffing them in the back of a drawer full of old bras and knickers, new bras and knickers too tight or scratchy to wear, black sexy underwear I never wear, shrunken socks tangled with sad tights and the thermal vests that looked quite feminine before the lace withered and fell off. Argh! Bath-too-hot-turn-off-tap.
1.40 p.m.	Massage achy shoulders with ocean soap.
1.42 p.m.	Must find an interesting photo (in focus), to put in the interesting arty photo frame from David. Must also find celestial candles to put in celestial candle holders. I know I've put them somewhere; sure I saw them the other day.
1.44 p.m.	Spot interesting bruise on leg. How did I get that?
1.45 p.m.	Massage feet with seaweed soap.
1.46 p.m.	Lie back with grumpy face, moving fins slightly like porcupine fish on seabed.
1.47 p.m.	Stare at nothing, like a sad prawn on a bed of lettuce.
1.48 p.m.	Plop seahorse bath pearl into water. Seahorse swims to bottom of the ocean.
1.49 p.m.	A turquoise crab and star fish dive in too; the packet did say, 'To liven up your bath time'.
1.50 p.m.	Tomorrow will try smelly bath fizzers (so Ben can tell his Mum how amazingly fizzy and beautifully scented they are) and bubble bath from Neal's Yard in the interesting blue bottle from Julia.
1.52 p.m.	Toenails need clipping.
1.55 p.m.	Today will put extra fruit on shopping list (so we can tell

Alex we're using the trendy chrome fruit holder), some batteries for the toy reindeer with singing voice and flashing red nose (to see if it sings and flashes its nose) and a hook so we can hang up the model hot air balloon (the brilliant present).

2.06 p.m.   Drag self out of bath like walrus suffering from tuskache.

3.15 p.m.   Hang up this year's slimline wildlife calendar – wish I were slim and having a wild life. Wash two plates.

3.20 p.m.   Knock leg on coffee table, ouch! Now I know how I got that bruise.

3.21 p.m.   Curl up on sofa, exhausted from all that thinking, bathing and housework.

Sunday 2nd

10.30 a.m.   Bad start to day. Spot another grey eyelash (possibly post-Christmas stress), worse than spotting a grey hair for some reason. Try to pull eyelash out but it holds on to my eyelid like a cat clinging onto a cushion it doesn't want to leave.

10.31 a.m.   My chin is pregnant with triplets – three big, bright-red spots (probably hormonal, possibly post-Christmas-munchies).

10.32 a.m.   Glare at spots with one aged eye and one thirty-something eye.

10.45 a.m.   Sniff Ben's Original Blend medium roasted ground coffee for a lift.

10.47 a.m.   Ben is sniffing a shirt to see if it's clean or not.

11.55 a.m.   Sit on toilet counting little perforations between two sheets of toilet roll (approx forty-seven).

1.34 p.m.   Lie in bath thinking about New Year resolutions.

1.35 p.m.   I'm not making any.

I've spent the last few years trying to give up all the things you're supposed to give up and doing all the things you're supposed to do when you have M.E., so if I make one teeny weeny resolution I think it will be to carry on as I am. But; I would really like to scream and scream *AND SCREAM* so loudly that all the windows crack, the wind blows the glass into the house, the neighbours think, 'She's having a bad day again, poor dear,' and the fresh air enlivens my spirit so much I laugh hysterically and bounce up and down on the sofa singing along to Abba!

Maybe I need a holiday this year. I fancy one of those boating holidays, snoozing to the rocking motion of the narrowboat while listening to water lapping against the riverbank. Bird song. Peace. Tranquillity. Gentle breeze on sun-warmed skin. Mmmm. Bliss. Watching kingfishers fishing, seven swans-a-swimming, six sailors sailing... five rubber rings... four drowning people, three lifeguards, two-oo muddy gloves and a pair of knickers in *pair* tree.

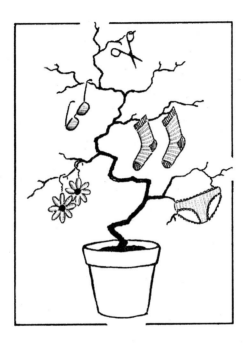

...she dreamt of waking up to a new painting in fresh greens outside her window every morning, instead of the same old boring scribble of grey-brown houses she had to endure day after day...

I deserve a holiday. I've been good. Huge pizza washed down with wine is no longer part of my Friday evening ritual. Big slurps of PG Tips with buttery Hi-Bran toast is no longer part of my morning ritual. It wasn't difficult to give up coping-with-work coffee (as I'm not working) and I'm no longer tempted by enormous doorstep creations full of interesting fillings from Sally's sandwich bar. But I do miss nibbling biscuits or chocolate bars, shopping-night cheesecake, after-a-bad-day ready-meals and *real tea*. I still want comforting chocolate and pizza and chips every day now; but it's lots of healthy fruit, veg, rice, beans and soya things for me these days (most days). I'm learning to enjoy herb tea (I really am) and drink litres of Irish mineral water; I imagine I'm pouring pure refreshing life into my body. It may help, you never know.

... she dreamed of the hills and valleys of Ireland...

I don't need my list of hangover cures any more, I've left it attached to the fridge with a Wallace and Gromit fridge magnet for Ben. I don't need it; I've promised myself I'll never need it again.

... one day he came home from work to find her lying on the floor, an empty bottle of Christmas sherry on the coffee table, an empty bottle of Christmas pudding brandy under the coffee table, a dirty glass on its side, six empty foil mince pie cases, a few crumbs and a screwed up cracker. A broken crayon lay in her hand, 'I CAN'T TAKE ANY MORE' scrawled on the wall. He could't believe it. She had stuck to her M.E. diet and hadn't touched a drop of alcohol in years...

Hangover Cures

Vitamin B complex	For shaky hands, crossed eyeballs and a complex.
Ginger or peppermint tea	For 'I can't face breakfast' tummy.
Nux Vomica (homeopathic)	For bloody awful headache. Interesting, but name makes me want to throw up. Drink lots of water instead and search house for painkillers.
Evening primrose oil and Vitamin C	Good for saving brain cells, boosting the immune system and lots of other things. Two giant capsules of E.P. oil and one giant tablet of Vitamin C if capable of swallowing.
Green tea	An antioxiwhatsname.
With honey	For energy to crawl across room.

Ben braved the icy winds this afternoon to buy Brussels sprouts, a packet of paracetamol and hair conditioner (I can live without food and water but not hair conditioner) from Mr. Patel round the corner. While he was out, I devoured a Mr. Kipling luxury deep-filled mince pie with a tablespoon of brandy cream (reserved for guests) and started on the Four Cheeses quiche. The healthy salad veg is going soft and wrinkly like me.

Monday 3rd

Dozed in a warm bath, cleansing my body, ready for my visit to Eileen; I didn't want her to suffer the smell of my sweaty armpits. Enjoyed the comforting sounds of hundreds of tiny bubbles popping around my ears as I inhaled essential oils of rosemary, lavender, lemon and pine. I should have felt invigorated, fresh and full of vitality. Well; I did manage to climb out of the bath and wrap a towel around myself and walk into the bedroom (an improvement on last year, when I had to lie on the floor for an hour to find the energy to wrap a towel around myself and walk out of the bathroom). Look forward to the day when I climb out of the bath, dry myself straight away and run to meet the day! Er, not exactly run; a pain-free plod will do.

Rang Z Cars to book a taxi to take me to the health clinic. Eileen's treatment relaxes me and helps my body to heal and balance itself; after a few minutes, my circulation starts to circulate, my memory and concentration improve and I'm able to enjoy a nice chat. Normally, conversation for more than a few minutes is exhausting (especially on the phone) so I look forward to my Monday appointments as much for the company as the treatment.

Sometimes I remind Ben I haven't spoken to anyone all day and perhaps he could spare *me* a few words after his talking-to-lots-of-other-people day. I fear one day he'll come home and say, 'Giv'us me grub, giv'us a shag and shuddup woman.'

Eileen, a small soft-spoken woman from Scotland, has lots of dark fluffy hair (like clouds gathering over the Highlands) and a bright smile (like the sun peeping out between the clouds). I could say here that when she laughs, her eyes sparkle like dew on heather and a tiny stream trickles down the nose of the mountain to gather in the long grass of the upper lip, but that would be going a bit too far.

When I first started seeing her, I felt like a complete write-off: my bodywork rusted and round the twist, my engine seized up and my windscreen shattered. My wheels had fallen off, my radiator overheated and everything was a mist because my fog lamps were broken.

Like a confident mechanic, Eileen does a few adjustments to my bodywork and I leave the clinic, pain free and relaxed; it doesn't last. My rear view has improved since starting the M.E. diet. But not much.

Had to cancel taxi to clinic – remembered Eileen wouldn't be working today.

Tuesday 4th

Slept like a chocolate log last night. Woke up feeling heavy and dark, and thought someone had stuck a plastic robin in my head. Felt lonely. Ben went back to work today; I'd become used to him sitting around playing with his little computer chess set. Blip.

I'm going to miss the sound of another person in the house: the click of the kettle switching off, footsteps on the stairs, the bathroom door being shut, the loo flushing, the distant sound of computer keys tapping away and a faint whiff of cigarette smoke drifting under the door. The little computer chess set. Blip.

But it's so cold and icy outside. I'm glad I'm curled up in the warm, surrounded by Christmas books and magazines, with the tree all sparkly in the lamplight. All is calm, all is bright and oh! my clothes are feeling tight.

This afternoon I read *Twenty Ways to Survive Christmas* (bit late now), an article about about self-healing and the first few pages of *Lords and Ladies* by Terry Pratchett (laughter is the best self-healing). I've been given a book on how to live with M.E. Don't want to live with M.E.; living with myself is hard enough. I want books with titles like *How to Recover from M. E. in a Week* or *The Secret of Recovery from Chronic Illness in Six Days*. I've read that this is a typical attitude of many people with M.E., who are often women in their thirties with a career and no time to be ill. So I'm typical and average. Huh. I wonder what my friends, Gail and Rose, really think of me. I wonder what everyone I know, or knew at work, or have met since I became ill, thinks of me. Judging by some comments, I'm a sad depressed layabout. Mmmm. They can think what they like but I know I'm not a couch potato, though sometimes my head feels like mash and my body like a bag of crisps that someone's just sat on.

Must stay calm, must stay cool or I'll never recover. Deep breath, deep breath. When Dad suggests I go swimming for the hundredth time, I must try to keep my temper and stop throwing mental axes at his head.

Gail gave me scented candles for Christmas to add to my collection. I've put them on the telly near the sitting room window so when I'm bored of looking out the window, I can pick them up one by one and smell their different scents. This relaxes me; my own personal aromatherapy. Rose sent me a bright orange aromatherapy candle. I don't know what feeling the smell is supposed to evoke but once I've stuck my nose on it, I don't want to take it off. Ben smokes a cigarette to calm himself down, I sit with a candle stuck on my nose; why not?

Candlelight is so restful. I light one with dinner every evening (a household candle from Safeways, not me posh ones). Before Christmas, I received five candles in the shape of different fruits (a free gift from a catalogue because I spent over thirty pounds). I'll put them in the trendy chrome fruit holder so it looks as if we always have fresh fruit on the table.

Power cuts never worry me.

Wednesday 5th

Goldshield have written to tell me New Year is always a happy time of year, sent details of their exciting new products at special low prices and informed me how to claim my free luxurious personal organiser. How lovely.

This afternoon I crawled slowly upstairs still wearing my winceyette pyjamas, dressing gown, woolly socks and woolly head; like a sloth I once saw on a nature programme. When I reached the top of the mountain, couldn't remember what I was looking for. Sat and wrote a poem (well, you do, don't you) then descended like a depressed sloth in the rain (my memory had not returned).

CLIMBING THE STAIRS

I'm trying to remember
What it was that I forgot
From the first step on the stairs
From the bottom to the top

No strength to go back down again
Back up the pain will burn
So I'll sit here quietly waiting
For my memory to return.

At the foot of the mountain, I remembered I'd wanted my telephone and address book; didn't have the energy to climb back up again so the phone call had to wait. Sat on the bottom step enjoying wonderful uplifting daydreams about a Stannah stairlift – I could travel up and down the stairs all day for fun and give little children rides!

Wrote a song to the tune of White Christmas.

I'm dreaming of a Stannah stairlift
So I won't have to climb the stair
May my days be restful, no flight
And the future a little more bright

Much later, made a short phone call to my parents but couldn't wish them a *happy* New Year because they're still together. Mum didn't sound too well; I expect she's been on her feet since December 1st. Dad bought her slippers for Christmas, a pretty apron and a can opener (not electric). Mum didn't say if she'd enjoyed her Doris Day double cassette. I did though – I listened to it three times and surprised myself by knowing most of the words. Now I tell myself, whatever will be will be, the future's not ours to see... I can't remember what I bought Dad; I expect he can't remember either. Was it a book? I wonder if there's a book entitled: *How to Listen and Be More Understanding Towards your Daughter.*

Feel like a sad, tearful child. Don't want Christmas decorations to come down. Don't! Don't! Don't! Want more chocolate money. Want to stroke Santa's reindeer. Want Christmas three times a year. Want big expensive present I can't have (Stannah stairlift). Want to be better. Sulk, sulk, sulk.

Ate six chocolates (Jeremy's fault for giving us Kit-Kat mugs, reminding me of choc every day), two mince pies and a piece of half-stale cheese on a nearly soft square cracker (Ben is on a diet and I hate to see waste). Wish I could exercise off seven hundred and fifty calories by moving my big toe up and down a few times.

Have worked out *The Insect Diet and Exercise Plan.* All you have to do is flap your arms a little or rub your hands together (washing movements) or crawl about a bit on the table. Nibble anything you fancy as long as it's small amounts and often (good for P.M.T.). Rest for long periods and breathe deeply, thinking about flowers and sunshine. Avoid the rolled up newspaper.

Thursday 6th

2.35 p.m. Started sadly undressing the Christmas tree. Removed the red and gold tinsel. Had a long rest. Removed baubles. Another long rest. Wooden decorations. Rest. Fairy lights and fairy from top of tree. Exhausted. Lay on floor. Stared at ceiling. Breathed in tree smell. Carpet like forest floor. Feet like green hedgehogs. Emergency food needed. Chocolate. Mince pies. Sherry. Continued to lie on floor surrounded by crumbs and Christmas. Burp. Smile.

6.25 p.m. Ben came home from work and said it was good to see I'd had a busy, enjoyable day. Later on, he carefully placed the boxes of decorations in a bigger box and tucked them in with tinsel to sleep till next Christmas. I asked if there was room for me. He asked if he could see me in the red sexy underwear he'd bought me for Christmas. I said I was tired after a busy day and anyway I'm too fat, hairy and smelly and the underwear needs a wash because someone probably tried it on in a changing room and didn't keep their knickers on. He said all that didn't matter, so I admitted I'm about to become a long-tailed lizard from Arizona (they've done away with sex and clone themselves). He said a whip-tongued lezzie called Sonia sounded interesting. I asked what he'd been getting up to on the internet lately.

Friday 7th

I miss the Christmas tree. Like me, the room has lost it's colour and sparkle. Dull. Grey. Gloom. Cold. Wet. Window. Yawn. Junkmail. Grunt. Bills. Groan. Gloom. Grey. Grant. Missed *EastEnders*. Herb tea. Sigh. Rain, rain, rain, rain, rain, rain, rain, rain, rain, rain, rain, rain, rain, rain.

Read through Christmas cards and had a giggle at the amusing ones. We should only send funny cards to each other at Christmas, like the one with a priest looking at the ground with dismay. The snow is sprinkled with green peas and the caption reads, 'He had hoped for peace on earth, but didn't like to complain.' Last year we received a card with reindeer falling out of the clouds and a couple walking in the snow; the caption read, 'Looks like rain dear.' Everyone needs cheering up, a bit of entertainment to ease the: 'What am I going to buy him? Will she like it? Can I afford it? Is that enough? Has she already got one? Will he like the colour? Is it the right size? Will she like the scent? Is he too old for Winnie-the-Pooh? Is she too young for a Spice Girls annual? Will this do for him *and* her? Are personalised mugs a good idea? Is an engraved cigarette lighter a good idea?' (Can't remember if she's given up or not!) 'What about a China mug and socks set? Or a sports tankard? Personalised Jack Daniels gift set? Britvic gift set? Baileys gift set? Surname origin certificate? Revolving photo frame? Bear figurines? Personalised throw? Dolphin tea light? Wizard wind chime? Charming octopus?' – *BRAIN ACHE!*

Just remembered another funny card, a cartoon of Mary riding on a donkey, pointing to the stable and complaining to Joseph that it's only got one star. Oh! and there's the one with Santa in his thermals – winter *draws* on, ha, ha.

When Ben comes home from the pub on Fridays, I like to guess what he's been drinking, how much he's drunk and where he's been; an effort to keep my sense of humour, my brain working and give me something to say. Sad, but true.

a) He falls into the room and crawls across the floor giggling: three pints of Speckled Hen at The Sticky Carpet Tavern, Slime Street.

b) He flops into a chair and tells me how marvellous I am and how fantastic he is: three pints of Bishop's Finger in The Frozen Crown, Coldhead Road.

c) Strides in with a big smile and tries to act sober: several glasses of red wine at Laura Ashtray's Wine Bar, Pricey Street.

d) He knows who I am but doesn't know who he is: many pints of Old Rodger at The Drum and Drunk–It down Drunkard Alley.

e) After countless glasses of wine at The Chinless Wine Bar, Spot Street, he tells me I'm wonderful but isn't sure who I am.

f) Too much Scrumpy Jack at The Smoky Throat Tavern down Coughitup Alley and he throws up.

If I've had a bad day, I don't have to make the effort to put on one of my brave faces. He doesn't notice how I'm feeling on a Friday. This is useful; I run out of brave faces sometimes.

Saturday 8th

This morning, Ben frowned at his bank statement, threw it on the I'll-sort-it-out-later pile, then read out a saying from his new diary:

> '**A Banker** – The person who lends you his umbrella
> when the sun is shining and wants it back the minute it rains.
> **Mark Twain.**'

This afternoon, he went healthy shopping at Holland & Barrett in the rain (without his umbrella) for healthy bread, healthy marge, soya milk, nuts and honey, vitamins and evening primrose oil capsules. When I read the back of my vitamin C bottle, I came across the glazing agent and had a brilliant idea. Next time my doctor is away and I have to see someone with an I-don't-believe-you expression, I'll say I think I've got H.P.C. Hydroxy Propylmethyl Cellulose. That'll give 'em something to chew on. It's even more of a mouthful than Myalgic Encephalomyelitis.

There's one doctor in particular who makes me *so mad* I'd like to tell him M.E. stands for Magic Encyclopaedia (a rare form of brain strain brought on by reading too many spell books). He already looks at me as if I'm a barmy old witch. Or I could give him a long list to annoy him.

LIST FOR DOCTOR

Manic Eat
Morbid Ennui
Maggoty Entrails
Madness Ensues
Mental Erosion
Memory End
Mad End
Misery Exacerbated
Misremember Eternally
Miserable & Exasperated
Massive Effort syndrome
Mysterious Elf syndrome
Misunderstood Entirely
Magic Encyclopaedia
Minimal Enthusiasm
Marriage Equivocal
Much Elm disease
Mostly Exhausted
Midriff Enlarged
Moody Eccentricity
Massive Ear syndrome
Maddening Exhaustion
Mammoth Effort disease
Mostly Expired syndrome
Mouldy Endocrine system
Mysterious Enchantment
Movement Excruciating
Maggoty Egg pollution
Mouldy Egg delusions
Miserable Existence
Muck Environment
Must Eat disorder
Misery's Envoy
Miss Enormous
Mostly Excusable
Missingself Esteem
Memory Equivocal
Monster Ensconced
Muchtoomuch Effort
Mad Elephant disorder
Magic Elephants bite us
Misanthropy Experienced
Misunderstood Eccentricity
Malingering Elephant disease
Myalgic Encephalo mackerel bite us

... today she decided she would tell Dr. Fahrt-Phace she was Mary Poppins and was suffering from supercalifragilisticexpialidocious... and demand a spoonful of sugar to help the medicine go down. Next visit, she would turn Dr. Frog-Face into a toad, after perfecting her special toad-in-the-whole body spell...

Early this evening, I noticed a very tall slim girl wearing a green raincoat hurry down the street holding a yellow umbrella over her head. The umbrella blew inside out; she looked like a buttercup bending in the wind.

Sunday 9th

Read my book about living with M.E. Yes, I'm taking my supplements; when I remember and manage to resist the urge to take them all in one go to get them out of the way. I'm relaxing; easy when I'm asleep (when I can sleep) and near impossible when I'm awake unless I glue a walkman to my ears and play relaxation tapes (I've heard so many times I'm bored of). Affirmations: I'm doing them now. I am calm and peaceful; I am healed and healthy; I love me (except when I hate myself for something I said five years ago, something I did fifteen years ago or something I didn't do twenty years ago). Oh dear! Oh Lord in Heaven! How have I managed to do so many stupid things in my short life? Why have I got all this time to remember them over and over? Why is it such an effort to recall the good, positive things I've done? Were there any? Yes of course there were. Must think hard... really miss working so hard that there's no time to think.

One thing I'm definitely *NOT* missing at this time of year is trailing around (like a little tug boat) after big-boring-ex-boyfriend at the Boat Show, Earls Court, London. Nor do I miss accompanying him to bike shows, sports shops, Brands Hatch, banger racing, hunting for the best surfing beaches while listening to the Beach Boys, sitting in the car listening to Olivia Newton John singing *Let's Get Physical* while he gets physical on a windsurfer in a gale force ten on a Cornish beach, freezing in a speedboat while he water skis, watching films with lots of car chasing or holding his little screwdriver when he needs assistance. But, I did get him into an art gallery once. Well, OK, I must admit, just inside the doorway. He glanced around the twelve foot square room (a tiny gallery on a cobbledy hill in Cornwall) then disappeared to look at antique bikes. Oh! and he peered in the window of a craft shop for nearly a whole minute; I expect there was a model bike or ship or something. I mustn't forget the wonderful polystyrene surfboard he presented me with for my birthday: a nice change from a box of Milk Tray from the Esso petrol station, given to me on his way to meet one of his other three girlfriends to play squash.

Ahhhhhh, hmmmm, THAT'S BETTER. Nothing like a good old rant.

I've just had a very enjoyable long bath recalling things I don't miss about other ex-boyfriends: splinters in tights and knickers when removed from washing machine (carpenter boyfriend); gut ache, watery eyes and freshly ironed clothes stinking of tobacco (chain-smoking, wine-making husband); ear ache and nervous twitch (drummer boyfriend); large bill for chocolate and tissues (heart-breaking, electric guitar-playing boyfriend); zinc white and cadmium yellow spots all over new black angora dress from Monsoon (artist boyfriend).

Written on the back of Ben's shaving foam are the words: 'If you are not happy with this product simply return it and we will cheerfully give you your money back'. If I marry again, it will be to a can of shaving foam. As long as I'm not pressurised into anything.

Our weird musician friend called round this evening after a cosmic wintry walk smoking interesting herbs. We drank herb tea in Kit-Kat mugs and I wished him a Hippy New Year.

Monday 10th

10.05 a.m. Wake up with a start!

Where am I? Where am I?

Why are the Beach Boys singing 'Surfin, U.S.A.' in my head?

10.06 a.m. Oh yes! Remember now; nightmare-beach-boyfriend flying past the window last night, whizzing up the street singing on a surfboard, flying down the street – waving on water skis, whistling on a windsurfer, smiling in a speedboat... next thing I know, I'm stranded on a cold empty beach, the wind whipping my hair across my face, waves crashing on pebbles. Beach boyfriend sails up to me and presents me with a box of Milk Tray. I open it, but it's full of pills and supplements so I tip them into the sand. Blue crabs crawl out of the sea, pick them up in their pincers and carry them back to Holland & Barrett on the hill. A giant green lobster taps me on the shoulder and I faint.

10.08 a.m. Lorry rumbles past house. Beach Boys are singing 'Good Vibrations' in my head.

10.10 a.m. Recall other dreams. Carpenter boyfriend making drum sticks for drummer boyfriend to hit me over the head with. Wine-making husband pouring red wine into a swimming pool and artist boyfriend mixing yellow and white paint with the wine. While I'm drowning in the swirly sickly pool, guitar boyfriend sweetly serenades me. Beach boyfriend surfs by and pushes my head under.

10.11 a.m. The chocolate dolphin saves me.

10.12 a.m. Fancy chocolate for breakfast.

Opened a packet of Safeway peppermint tea this morning and, as I peeled off the cellophane wrapper, the strong smell of After Eight mints caressed my nose. Oh hell! It's not fair; here I am resisting chocolate, trying to be calm and peaceful (with raging P.M.T.) and drinking herb tea. I'm sure I'd feel happier and more loving if I had a big beautiful box of chocolates every day.

My Medi-sin

Sunday   A box of After Eight mints (cold from the fridge).
Monday   Matchmakers (eleven feet of crispy knobbly chocolate).
Tuesday   Quality Street (with lots of purple ones).
Wednesday Huge box of those miniature chocolate bars.
Thursday   The round ones with gold wrapping in a handy see
through box.
Friday   Chocolate Orange (cold from the fridge).
Saturday   Matchmakers (orange flavour).
Valentine's Milk Tray, because the lady loves a second layer so
Day   she can eat the Praline Parfait, Hazelnut Heaven and
Montelimar before he does.
Birthday   Enormous box of Black Magic because the lady loves dark
chocolate best.
Christmas   Thorntons chocolates and Belgian chocolates because
the lady suddenly develops a taste for luxury.
Easter   A Maltesers Egg because the lady has suddenly developed
a large waistline.

Ben, if you are sneaking a look at my diary, please take note of the
above. WHAT ARE YOU DOING READING MY DIARY! I'll have a
selection of several from the list above if you feel guilty about reading
a lady's diary. I won't remember I've written this, so I'll just eat the
chocolates and say nothing, OK?

Saw Eileen tonight for my weekly bone crunch (toffee crunch,
nut crunch) and we talked about the herb teas we've tried: peppermint, rosehip, camomile, raspberry, nettle, fennel and lemon verbena.
Recently Eileen has tried a variety pack: mango and ginger, apple and
ginger, lemon and ginger, and mandarin and ginger. At
the weekend, Ben bought a selection of fruity infusions to excite my
taste buds: peach and passionfruit, blackcurrant and apple, strawberry
and mango. Lucky me.

Eileen said herb teas are an acquired taste; she is right. I told her
about how I've had to abandon my true love, Mr. Bournville Plain; she
was very sympathetic.

7.30p.m.   Started writing a song on the way home in the taxi...

Dark chocolate on white lace
A smear across my face
Chocolate on my teeth
Chocolate underneath
The pages of my book
Where you're not supposed to look
Chocolate everywhere
Even in my hair

I'm feasting on the biggest bar
My piggy eyes can find
I've eaten all my favourites
There's nothing left behind
I've got to have it now
And then I want some more
I've got to have it all the time
Coz chocolate I adore

Chocolate on my fingertips
And in between my toes
The carpets and the curtains
The end of my nose
Plain or milk
Or soft inside
It doesn't really matter
As long as there's lots of it
And my mouth it will enter

I'm feasting on the biggest bar
My piggy eyes can find
I've eaten all my favourites
There's nothing left behind
I've got to have it now
And then I want some more
I've got to have it all the time
Coz chocolate I adore.

9.30 p.m.	Better start doing my affirmations now – perhaps my sub-conscious will get the message one day. I am calm and peaceful; I'm getting better and better everyday; I love me; I love herb tea; I hate chocolate.
9.35 p.m.	Maybe I'll send my story of how I conquered chocoholism to *Weekly Wife*.
9.36 p.m.	Think I'm going to accidentally drop a Kit-Kat mug; after all, my grip isn't too good these days, nor is my eyesight.

Tuesday 11th

Dreamt about chocolate. Woke up craving Kit-Kat. My doctor should prescribe chocolate because...

a.) *Weekly Wife* says endorphins are produced during strenuous exercise and generate euphoria – I cannot exercise therefore I need chocolate more than most people, to keep me sane.

b.) Napoleon ate chocolate when he needed energy on military escapades – I *am* fighting a constant battle with the dreaded Myalgic-encephalo-monster, who keeps biting me and sucking the life out of my muscles.

c.) A traditional Aztec drink contained chocolate. An Aztec emperor once said the divine drink fights fatigue and builds up resistance.

d.) Chocolate contains high levels of phenol, a chemical that helps to reduce heart disease.

9.10 a.m.	Feel heartache thinking about Milk Tray and failed romances...
9.13 a.m.	Feel guilty. I've been thinking too many bad ex-boyfriend thoughts.
9.14 a.m.	Must think some good thoughts, root around for a few happy memories, dig up some good times. Don't want to become bitter old man-hater-type-woman with ~~peppermint~~ permanent misery lines etched into face.
9.15 a.m.	Ummm... Errrr... think... think... oh dear... can't think of any... oh yes... there was that time... no, he was lying... there was the romantic candlelit dinner... but he spoilt it... ahhhh... there was the... too naughty to write down... just lust... ummm... carpenter boyfriend made a shelf for my

30

nick-nacks and bought me nice-knickers... but they were more for him really... and the shelf fell down... beach boyfriend gave me a single red rose for Valentines Day... errrr... remember it was plastic... he said the real ones were too expensive, then went out and bought a Range Rover with a trailer to tow his speedboat... chain-smoker-husband was pleased with his hot dinners and clean house... but was always cold towards me and wanted dirty talk... must try harder to remember good things... hard work... think... think... think...

9.17 a.m.   Must have liked *something* about these men... yes... yes... I'm remembering... I can feel a good thought creeping into my mind... slowly... but surely... like a slug up a drainpipe... a hungry caterpillar up a cabbage stalk... beach boyfriend liked dogs and took his mum's Alsatians for walkies in the park... drummer boyfriend bought wild bird seed for the wild birdies... artist boyfriend loved painting pussies... ex-husband got up to a lot of fishy things but at least three of them were in a tank... and Ben? We're still together of course, but what did I see in him?... errrmm... oh yes... I was impressed he was a strict vegetarian and he fell for my huge vegeburgers, something firm and wholesome to get his teeth into; they cemented our relationship perfectly. We've taken a lot of knocks and broken down a few barriers since then; the foundations are a bit rocky but most of the time we find a balance. He's used to my looking a bit of a site but we're building a future.

9.35a.m.   Opened a couple of thank you-for-my-lovely-Christmas-gift letters. What's the matter with me? I just don't seem to be able to get round to doing mine this year. Everyone will start thinking I'm a thoughtless, ungrateful old cow. No; of course they won't. They'll just think I'm exhausted after Christmas and everything; but they might.

1.30 p.m.   Grazed on last night's greens for lunch and read a fascinating article on the subject of the paranormal, a field I'm interested in.

2.00 p.m.   Read about tea (another field I'm interested in). Discovered the tannin in normal tea prevents the body absorbing vital minerals from food, herb teas enhance the body's natural functions and nettle tea cleanses the body of toxins. The taste of nettle tea reminds me of cold chicken soup, I'd rather do what Eileen recommends to cleanse the body: three cups of Epsom salts in a warm bath with no soap (or no soup as I told a friend) and soak for not more than twenty minutes. The only drawback is you feel like a vegetable.

Peppermint tea boosts digestion, dandelion is a diuretic and a laxative (I don't need it), dandelion clears up spots (I do need it). Raspberry strengthens the womb tissues for smoother contractions: I must tell my sister – her baby is due in four days. Raspberry also soothes a sore throat; perhaps I'll send some to the delivery room.

Ben did the Tuesday shopping after work. Between the bananas and bread, I found a small bar of Galaxy. He's my wonderful, wonderful, thoughtful, caring, marvellous hero. What would I do without him (has he been reading my diary, the nosy pig?).

Wednesday 12th

10.14 a.m.   PANIC! PANIC!
             What day is it?! Oh God! I really can't remember!
10.15 a.m.   I'm losing my memory, I'll never find it again. My marbles have rolled under the sofa and disappeared into the dark dusty world of Lost Things.
10.16 a.m.   Where is the TV mag?! That'll give me a clue.
10.17 a.m.   Can't find it anywhere. Oh bum, bother, b...
10.18 a.m.   Is it Wednesday or Thursday? Saturday and Sunday are easy to remember as Ben is around and I still get the Monday morning feeling on Mondays (back to long week working hard at keeping sane). But by Wednesday or Thursday...
10.19 a.m.   Bend down on hands and knees and squint at tiny Wed above digital time on video recorder.
10.20 a.m.   Can't get up again. Notice Galaxy wrapper. Of course, it was shopping night last night!
10.21 a.m.   Pick bits off dirty carpet.

10.22 a.m. Draw *wed* in dust on TV screen.

10.23 a.m. Decide to cross days off on calendar.

10.24 a.m. Little bit of tinsel stuck between carpet and skirting board twinkles and smiles at me. I smile back – there will be other Christmases.

Ben rang my sister. She took ages to answer the phone because she was busy cleaning the house and singing along to 'Baby Love' by the Supremes. She said yesterday she had bumped into a chest of drawers, so she now has a bump on her 'bump'.

... the small life inside her was now programmed to love Motown music and be afraid of things that go bump in the night...

All this lying about is making me *so* creative.

GOODBYE M.E.

Don't drink tea or coffee
I take herbal tea
I'm going to recover
From this thing they call M.E.
No G and T with ice
Don't want to pay the price
It's camomile for me you know
And raspberry's quite nice
Peppermint for digestion
Rosehip, Vitamin C
Hello healthy
Goodbye M.E.

Thursday 13th

1.05 p.m. Rang Mum to wish her a happy birthday; I knew she'd be having one if Dad were out. Mum wanted to know how I was and became annoyed with me when I said I was OK. She wanted to know how I *really* was so she had something to tell the neighbours. If I tell her how I *really* am she becomes worried and upset, so I try to tell her the truth, but sounding happy and positive with it. It never works.

1.15 p.m.	It didn't work. I'm really stressed again – looking foward to my Monday treatment.
2.05 p.m.	Stood in front of the bathroom mirror and slapped Simple moisturiser on my face. I like Simple products, they are not tested on animals, perfumed or coloured, 'Just kind'. I wish more people were like that.

Peered at my lines and wrinkles: those four are the doctors who didn't believe I had M.E., those three are family who inferred my illness was all in the mind, those two are the pain of M.E. and this one is too much time to look in the mirror.

Felt brave. Looked at myself naked in the wardrobe mirror; big mistake! Turned sideways; even worse... I'm just like the *before* in 'before and after' pictures... I will not do this again in bright daylight. Next time (if there is a next time) it will be late at night, one bedside lamp on and when my eyes are too tired to see properly. Perhaps if I put on the uplifting sexy red underwear... perhaps not, red underwear R.I.P. in back of drawer.

Now I have time to care for my skin... all... this... time... Had a positive thought session; it nearly worked. I'm glad I'm plain. It must be awful to be beautiful and have to watch your looks fade, like an apple left to dry out on a window sill. I'd hate to look like Claudia What's-her-name. I'm getting good at positive thinking *and* lying to myself.

Friday 14th

A tall, dark and ugly man came round to read the electricity meter. His glasses steamed up when he entered the house, due to cold weather and warm house, not the sight of me looking hot and sexy.

Received one of my M.E. journals. Had a good read. Had a good headache. Read about other sufferers who are much worse than I. Had a good cry. Felt better. Smoothed essential aromatherapy de-stress hand and nail cream (with mandarin and geranium) into my hands. Mmmmmm... fabulous fragrant smell. My nose felt de-stressed.

Ben staggered in from the pub tonight, holding his head; he'd been pecked by a few Speckled Hens in The Smoky Throat Tavern down Coughitup Alley.

Saturday 15th

My sister's baby is due any time. Now I know what she got up to with a *friend* she went on holiday with last spring. A man has got my sister pregnant and I haven't met him yet! I didn't really expect him to call round and introduce himself as the culprit who put a bun in my sister's oven. It just seems strange, that's all. He works abroad a lot, so I'll let him off.

Ben bought Stork margarine. I didn't get the joke; my brain still isn't working too well.

Sunday 16th

Exciting day. Leafed through the TV guide. Lots of programmes about hospitals and war and murder and the news in between with more lovely war and hospitals and murder. Then, at the end of the news, there's a cheery bit. *Don't worry, everyone. Although there's lots of pain and suffering and misery in the world, a green cat was spotted in Devon.* This Friday, couples will be fighting on *Riki Lake*. Kawon dates Tanisha but he really wants Cherita, but Cherita's already 'kickin it' with Tanisha! Can't wait.

Weekly Wife was just as riveting: 'I Shot the Man I Love Because He Called Me Mrs. Blobby'; 'At War with the Germs' and 'Know your Spots': spots near your ears and on the neck mean you're run-down, red lumps on the forehead mean constipation and bad digestion, small hard lumps are undigested fats (yeast infection or candida), red spots around the jaw-line are usually hormonal and white puffy inflammations mean too much acid-causing food or an allergic reaction. Absobloodylutely fascinating.

My parents visited. Dad said how well I looked. Secretly took a painkiller and put on a smile. Mum went on as usual: was I eating, was I taking exercise, the terrible things on the news, my sister is overdue, my brother hasn't been to visit them lately, was I eating, was I taking exercise. I put on the *Action for M.E.* video about the basics of therapy and illness management. Mum looked worried. Dad snored all the way through. When they left, I put my head in a cupboard and screamed. Didn't warn Ben I was going to scream; he dropped a Kit-Kat mug. It bounced. I swore.

Monday 17th

10.46 a.m. Wear odd socks to be daring – one blue sock with frogs on, one green sock with sheep on.

10.47 a.m. Feel a bit odd.

10.49 a.m. A bit unbalanced.
One foot hopping from lily-pad into pond, one foot leaping over fences into green fields.

10.51 a.m. Decide to wear matching socks with hearts and flowers.

10.53 a.m. Ahhhh... much better, feel peace and love and more balanced.

Tonight I told Eileen that my sister is about to give birth and during my treatment she said I had all the signs of going into labour (and where did I get *those* socks!?). I've always been good at sympathy pains: when Mum had her varicose veins removed, I could hardly walk for a week; when a carpenter friend chopped the end of his finger off, my hand ached like hell and when Dad went into hospital with his haemorrhoids...

Tuesday 18th

Sat on the toilet listening to the rain. Watched raindrops piddling down the pane.

Ben has bought different coloured loo roll (orange instead of green) and a new brand of toothpaste (green instead of white). He's so thoughtful. I'd told him I needed a change and a little excitement in my life. Maybe next week he'll buy kitchen roll with a flowery pattern instead of a leafy pattern, or four tins of beans instead of three.

As he unpacked the shopping, I searched through the carrier bags; there was no Galaxy in the infinity of Safeway space.

I was sympathy nest-building today and asked Ben to ring Mark to see how Gina is doing. She is going to be induced if the baby doesn't (in her words) hatch out soon; what has she been hiding in her Dorothy Perkins dungarees?

... the small life inside her moved what it thought were its wings...

Oh dear! Oh Lord! Oh dear Lord God in Heaven above sitting on yer big white, fluffy, three-piece suite with matching carpet and curtains, please don't let the baby die or be deformed or ill, don't let my sister die, let it be round the right way, pop out easily, and don't let it have a big head like my brother (I mean BIG not *big*). Don't let the car break down on the way to the hospital or be involved in an accident. Don't let the hospital burn down. What if the baby strangles itself with the cord? What if my sister strangles her boyfriend during labour? They never could agree on a name for the baby.

I am calm and peaceful, healed and healthy; I love me, I love herb tea, I hate chocolate, I'd hate to look like Claudia What's-her-name; I will wear matching socks, the baby will be fine, the baby will be fine.

Wednesday 19th

8.05 a.m.   Hooray! There's a message on the answering machine from Mum; I have a healthy nephew, Matthew.

8.05 p.m.   Ben rings Mum for details. Although my sister had a difficult time, she's fine. Bet that's not what she'd say.

8.35 p.m.   Draw a smiley face on the bathroom mirror with a make-up pencil.

8.36 p.m.   Get a bit carried away. Draw smiley flowers on bathroom cabinet, squidge a toothpaste face in the sink and squirt a big green shampoo fish in the bath. Boredom is turning me into a vandal: it'll be tomato sauce on the kitchen walls next.

8.40 p.m.   Sit on side of bath feeling creative...

... she longed to run into the office where she used to work and splash black ink all over the nice and neat B.H.S. skirts of the women sitting at their nice and neat computers. That would give them something to moan about...

9.00 p.m.   Wish I were at the hospital.

9.01 p.m.   Fed up.

Thursday 20th

Ben washed away the shampoo fish and toothpaste face when he had his bath and shave. The smiley face on the mirror is still there, the smiley flowers too.

I'm glad Gina has decided to call her son Matthew. I don't think much of these unusual names like Fabian (sounds like a self-adhesive shelf-covering) or Kola (fizzy drink) or Milo (sounds like something you sunbathe on). Maybe I'm just boring and old-fashioned. Quite like some of the names Gina's friends have given their sons: Freddie and Frank, Harry and Henry. I imagine toddlers in tiny tweed jackets and caps, smoking sugar pipes. Not sure about Harold though, can't help remembering *Steptoe and Son*. And Henry brings to mind a rather well-fed little boy with lots of girlfriends.

One of the women where I used to work named her children Merlin and Tabitha; great time they're going to have at school! Her cats were Michael and Thomas; the dog, Lucy.

I like groovy sixties names like Saffron and Shona: plastic flowers, mummy's beads and shawls. Daisy and Poppy: mummy's little flower fairies practising their ballet steps in the garden. Lucy and Peter: adventures in Narnia and Neverland. Emma and Emily: mummy's floaty dresses and tiny feet just fitting into the toe of giant shoes, heels scraping on the path. Sometimes I watch little Charlotte run up and down the street in her trainers and combats with her brother's toy machine gun. Pity we have to grow up fast and learn about war and things.

Fancied watching an old-fashioned black and white film this afternoon (when I say watch, I mean mostly listen, eyes not up to flickering screen for long), the dialogue and music can be so restful; sometimes I'm lulled off to sleep for a while.

Today there was a choice between *The Ride to Hangman's Tree, Death Drums along the River* or yet another war drama. War, war, bloody war, lest we forget. I've spent many an hour feeling sad for our soldiers and the plight of those in other countries, but I've too much time to think now; I don't need reminding. I avoid the news. Sometimes I catch a bit of a nature programme, but it's not long before man's hunting or polluting is mentioned and that's me miserable for hours. Must stop switching on the box in moments of mad boredom. Wish I were a mindless moron who didn't care about anything. No, I don't. Yes, I do. Sometimes.

Too ill to travel to the hospital in Chatham.

Really fed up.

Friday 21st

A Land's End catalogue arrived today. They're out of my price range but I enjoy looking at the clothes, especially the interesting names for the colours. Quite fancied the drifter crew in pale celery or light driftwood, the broadcloth blouse in wild mushroom, jewelneck sweater (butterscotch or garnet), fine gauge V-neck cardigan (cappuccino) and wrap-around skirt in sesame or blue ink. Quite fancied the male model wearing the men's fine jersey birdseye jacquard polo too, but his pose was laughable.

I could do with a new-all-weather-type-decent-jacket; so could Ben. The women's pile-lined field coat looks cosy in light walnut or khaki. The goretex jacket has got a hood though. Mmmm... that three-layer parka looks the best buy, but the price – oh dear! Ben will look good in the TR series parka (dusty spruce or dark stone). Hmmm... think dusty spruce will match his eyes. Maybe we should have matching jackets to make our friends cringe.

Really like the cashmere crew sweater in pearl grey, it looks so soft and comforting like my old woolly cardi. The V-neck tunic sweater would cover my bum nicely; not in white though, English lavender I think, to keep me calm and peaceful. Mum likes lavender. Had a little chat with her on the phone this morning. She said she'd wanted the new arrival in the family to be called Christian but she's quite happy with Matthew as it *sounds* Christian. Now that we have a Matthew, Mark and John in the family, I expect, if I had a boy, Mum would insist I call him Luke, for the full set of Evangelists. She's over the moon with the new star of the family, her first grandchild, and I'm relieved the spotlight has been taken off me.

I want to go to Mothercare.

I can't go to Mothercare.

Very fed up.

Wiped smile off smiley face from bathroom mirror.

Saturday 22nd

Big beautiful day. Welcome to your new baby boy blue sky. Next door's hedge bounces in the breeze.

Ben came home from the shops with his I've-done-well face on, an enormous blue fluffy bunny, baby bibs (blue teddy motif) a baby boy card (various shades of blue) and he even remembered the wrapping paper. When I was working, I nearly always forgot the wrapping paper during my lunchtime whiz around the shops. If I did remember, I'd end up with 'Happy Wedding Anniversary' paper for a recently divorced friend's birthday present (because I liked the colour and pattern).

Told Ben what a good boy he was in my Mrs. Merton voice; he assumed his Malcolm pose. Mark brought Matthew and Mummy home today.

Everyone's seen new baby except me.

Everyone's met Mark except me.

Exceptionally fed up!

... she drew a sad face in the condensation on the bathroom window...

Sunday 23rd

Curled up on the sofa and read all about how to hide a Christmas tummy with six stylish solutions (hid tummy with cushion), twelve ways to stay slim and sexy all year long (polished off pack of brown rolls, Ben's lunch in the week) and how to make the most of the January sales.

I miss wandering around the shops, NOW HALF ORIGINAL PRICE! UNBEATABLE BARGAIN! CHECK OUT INSIDE FOR MORE AMAZING OFFERS! YOURS FOR ONLY £99.99! FREE DELIVERY! till my feet ache. I miss making a massive saving on a huge reduction, or wasting my money on four for the price of two products I'll never use, a pair of size ten jeans that will never see the light of day again and a top that doesn't suit me, but was reduced *three* times!

Very exceptionally sulkily fed up!

... she drew a sad face in the dust on the telly...
... she made a sad face with the crumbs on her plate...
... she made a sad face...

Monday 24th

Woke up feeling guilty about eating Ben's delicious brown rolls. Punished myself by only having one slice of toast for breakfast.

A gardening catalogue arrived; if I'm lucky this summer, I'll have energy to help Ben mow the lawn (snip off six blades of grass with nail scissors). Quite fancied the Feng Shui wind chimes (with ceramic discs), the verdigris heron (a statue cast in brass that captures the heron's natural elegance) and the Sammy Seagulls (to bring seaside charm to any garden or rooftop, made from steel and hand-painted on both sides in beach hut colours). Remember once pointing out to a friend a delightful dove statue on the pointy bit of a roof; as she looked up, it flew away.

Spoke to Mark briefly on the phone this evening. He said he'll bring Mum and baby round to visit me when Gina's up to it and told me he was present at the birth. I'm impressed! Sounds like he's still in shock. He's in for another shock when he meets me.

My postnatal depression has lifted a little now: Eileen's treatment helped. I told her I felt like a sheet of lifeless boring wrapping paper as I lay flat on her workbench; she asked me if I wanted to be rolled or folded. On the way home in the taxi, I breathed on the window and drew a big smiley face. The driver told me to stop vandalising his car.

Ben said he'd been taken out to lunch today. He didn't say with whom or what they ate or anything.

I am not worried.

Tuesday 25th

A photo of tired-but-happy-mum-and-sleepy-new-born-baby arrived today and made me smile like a slice of watermelon. Felt inspired to attempt a Madonna and child type sketch, in biro on a notepad. The floor soon became littered with screwed-up balls of paper and my hands started to ache a lot (eyes crossed and neck seized) so I gave up – Matthew's tie-dye all in one looked too sixties anyway.

Gina has tie-dyed all her second-hand baby clothes with purple dye so I've got a groovy nephew now. She doesn't seem to be suffering from postnatal depression. I think I'm having it for her. That's what sisters are for.

Ben said he had lunch 'out' again today; I bet he's met an amazingly confident, attractive, rich woman who buys him a huge lunch. I'm the amazingly huge, poor, ugly woman who stole his lunch.

Late tonight I placed the mum and baby photo (need more clip frames) on the bookcase and noticed a packet of paracetamol on Gina's shelf in the background; we take the same brand of pain killers – how nice!

Wednesday 26th

10.28 a.m. Under pile of junk mail and boring looking envelopes, I spy a cream envelope with flowers on.

10.29 a.m. Recognise tiny hand-writing slanting to the right, postmark Nottingham. Rose. First class stamp – urgent news maybe.

10.51 a.m. Curl up on sofa with peppermint tea and toast.

10.52 a.m. Open letter and read all about husband number four at the birth of baby number eight.

Sometimes, I wish Rose didn't write about things in such great detail, but her letters are always full of life and never dull; I love them. If she's not on the verge of divorce she's pregnant again or three of the kids are ill, she's ill, back together with husband, argument with in-laws, separated, on a diet, pregnant and had to stop diet, divorced, about to give birth, argument with ex-husband over child maintenance and ex-mother-in-law over who's having the kids for the summer holidays. Married again, separated again, one of the kids is in hospital, back with husband, pregnant again, stopped diet, divorced, kids ill, fallen in love with doctor, fallen out of love with doctor, one of the kids has had a fall at school. New boyfriend, pregnant, getting married, Victoria has discovered boys.

Victoria, my God-daughter, is a teenager now and I don't know what to say to her anymore. I must stop sending her Victoria Plum and My Little Pony birthday cards. What do groovy Godmothers do these days? Send a copy of *New Woman* with a packet of condoms tucked inside and a note saying, 'Be careful now dear and be home by midnight; we don't want to look like a pumpkin now do we, before we sit our G.C.S.E.s!?!'

Thursday 27th

Very exhausted after a night of nightmares. A rich, attractive woman in a *brown Rolls* Royce knocked me down and every time I crawled up out of the gutter, she knocked me down again. Her hair was clean and very shiny. My hair was stuck to my head.

Tried to write a letter to Rose. Couldn't think of anything interesting or entertaining to tell her so I wrote a short letter about how my health is improving, I've got an interesting bruise on my right knee, Ben's got a cold, I'm growing my fringe and I washed four whole plates and some cutlery yesterday.

Sealed the envelope then remembered that I'd forgotten to mention my sister has had a baby boy. Will tell her about him in my next letter answering all the sort of questions Rose likes to ask. Boy or girl? Name? Time and place of birth? Weight? Normal or Caesarean? Were forceps used? Any stitches or drugs? Any unusual birth marks? Any unusual stretch marks? How much weight gain and saggy flesh? Time in labour? Breast or bottle feed? Did the doctor have a nice bum? Has my sister got a sore bum? Did she cook the afterbirth? Was the father present at the birth? Does my sister know who the father is? Have I seen the baby yet? Will she have him Christened? Who will the Godparents be? Has she planned any more children?

There was a lot of shouting and the sound of kids screaming outside. I looked at the clock; it was going-home time. The parents were making more noise than the children; I'll never swear at my children like that. Will I ever be able to have children?

I'd like a budgie, or a rabbit or some fish but I don't like to see any creature trapped in a cage or a tank – I know how it must feel. Maybe we could have a Battersea doggie. No, I'm not up to walkies yet. We could give a home to a homeless moggie from the cat protection people; cats are very restful, calm and peaceful... mmmm...

... her house was full of cats, sleeping and grooming, paws and whiskers twitching on every chair and window ledge; calm and peaceful and knowing...

Recently, I've noticed a man who lives a few doors away taking his new boxer puppy for a walk at lunchtimes – such a joyful playful little creature (the dog not the man). Talk about people looking like their pets! I'm *SO* tempted to get my camera out.

I remember someone describing a woman to me as having a face like a boxer dog chewing a wasp, or was it a bulldog? Can't remember. They must have met my ex-mother-in-law. I'm not joking.

Friday 28th

Ben hammered on the front door early this evening; he couldn't find his front door key. He didn't go to the pub tonight or eat much dinner and had an early night. *On a Friday!?*

Perhaps liquid lunches with attractive, rich woman are affecting him. Just happened to glance at his shirt collar, in case a close colleague had brushed past him wearing a lot of lipstick: it's difficult to remove. Did I detect a faint whiff of perfume, the stinky sort advertised in those expensive glossy magazines? Checked his pockets for loose change (*not* lipstick or a bit of paper with a telephone number or a bill for flowers or chocolates). I just didn't want a pound coin or something clattering around the washing machine.

I remember once coming across a lipstick in an ex-boyfriend's carrier bag along with his drumsticks and percussion bits, after a gig at the local pub. He said some girl had asked him to look after it for her (heavy, cumbersome things, those lipsticks). I wasn't worried; judging by the colour and the state of it she was a right old tart, all lipstick and no knickers.

Have decided the lunchtime lady is probably a tart too. Not worried. Too much time to think. Sure I smelt expensive perfume though. No, I'm not. I am calm and peaceful. I am, I am, I am. Not.

Yes I am.

Saturday 29th

The rain arrived: the thunder clapped enthusiastically, hailstones can-canned across the window ledge wearing rainbow skirts. Umbrellas marched to the beat all the way down the street.

Weird musician friend came round. He stood on the doorstep like an enormous raven who'd just hopped out of the bird bath, glasses at an angle on the end of his beak. He shook his umbrella before he entered the house.

... the raven shook his tail feathers...

Ben gave him strong black coffee in a Kit-Kat mug. George (his latest name) told us all about the Quakers (his latest religion). He takes it all so seriously, I couldn't help asking him if he was getting his oats. As he glared at me, lightning flashed and for a moment I thought I was in a horror movie.

His feathers ruffled, George didn't stay long. He flew out the door, jacket flapping, squawking something about my soul being answerable to God alone, and blasphemy. Oh! Christ, we won't see him for weeks now and I'm going to feel guilty for days. Really hate feeling guilty.

Ben doesn't look guilty about anything. He bought me flowers and chocolates and agreed to do a bit more round the house and help with the cooking. He's so thoughtful; I've been imagining things.

A glass of red wine or two in the weekday evenings is helping to relieve my pain, give me the energy to talk, prepare a simple dinner, smile and not let on how I've been feeling all day. By the weekend, I can't lift an eyelash. Have admitted this to Ben and he's been terribly understanding; we may have chips a lot, but I don't care. I need to rest more and recover. I'm very practised at staring out of the window, at the wall, the ceiling and my fingernails – practice makes insanely perfect.

It's so frustrating, sitting at home all day and not being able to whiz around cleaning, and I'm still not used to bits on the carpet piling up for weeks. A dirty kitchen surface is like an itch needing to be scratched. I'm trying *very hard* to learn not to scratch my itches so much. Must admit though, sometimes I have a *bloomin'* good scratch – can't help it. When I lie about in awful pain for days afterwards, I keep telling myself it was worth it. Not so sure lately. Thank God we don't wear clothes that need ironing, have a washing machine and a tumble drier. But I could do with help loading the clothes in and out again. Ben is going to do his own washing now, his jeans are *so heavy* when they're wet. When I'm dragging them out of the machine, I feel like I'm delivering a baby hippo, then I need to lie down for ages nursing achy muscles and craving a cigar. I suggested he wore leggings (after all, men used to in Elizabethan times) but he didn't seem too keen, even when I told him he had great legs and should show them off.

Must try to be like the little ant I befriended last summer, turn over a new leaf and carry on as best I can. I don't worry so much about the state of the house when Ben's bachelor friends visit but when Jeremy, whose wife keeps their house spotless, or Gail and Gareth (artistic-palace-type-home) come round, I panic. Look at the state of the bathroom basin! The bath! The toilet! The kitchen floor! The carpet of dust! I keep hearing my mothers voice, 'If the place is a mess the woman is blamed.' It must be etched on my brain along with, 'Never get married or have children.'

Sometimes when I'm bored and restless, I turn the lights down low and light a big, blue candle. When there's a pond of hot blue around the wick, I stick used matches in the wax, light them and watch them burn down. Pointy black spikes of wood sticking out of the blue look like breakers on the beach in the moonlight. Very relaxing. I hear my father telling me not to play with matches, the occult or the naughty boy down the road.

Sunday 30th

Very worried. I'm boring. I know I am. Nobody's actually told me to my face how dull I've become, but I bet they're all thinking I'm as boring as a closed chemist on a cold wet Sunday afternoon in Lewisham. There I go again; I had to think of a chemist... pills... painkillers. All I seem to talk about (when I talk) is the latest natural remedy, a new supplement (to help me move my right foot in front of my left foot a little more each day), the weather (is it colder today or is it just me) or something really sad I read about some sick person (comforting, for some reason). Anyway, I've started leafing through the *Reader's Digest* and *Nature* magazines at the clinic on Mondays in an effort to become more interesting and have something to say, if I can remember what I've read.

Started telling Ben about the breeding habits of sea turtles, the hunting habits of spotted dolphins and did he know the bottle-nosed dolphin has eighty-eight to a hundred sharp conical teeth to grasp fish, then swallows the fish whole. Nodding and trying to look interested, he dived into his studio to swim away to the depths of computer land, muttering something about optimising his hard drive.

A couple of hours later, I stuck my head round the door to ask if he wanted a cup of coffee and inform him that the pink river dolphin has tiny eyes that are of little use in its murky water habitat. He ignored me as he sat in a sea of smoke, the screen flickering like a lighthouse on his mesmerised face. I wandered away muttering something about computers giving you eyestrain and knowing how the pink river dolphin feels.

The windows whined to be cleaned, the kitchen wept grimy tears (it wasn't looking its best), the washing-up sulked, the plates felt used and the carpet fibres groaned from the depths of deep depression.

Outside, a car door slammed. A dog barked. The wind growled and threatened to blow the house down.

... she climbed back under the bedclothes, covered her ears and tried to think calming, peaceful thoughts: sea turtles swimming thousands of miles in deep dark oceans and dolphins leaping in tropical waters. She longed to be with them...

Monday 31st

Wow! We've got kitchen roll with a new wave pattern on. Now I have ~~incentive~~ a positive motivational influence to polish half a glass and three inches square of window pane.

Didn't have the energy to wash or dress or visit Eileen (I've overdone it again) but felt a desperate need for some fresh air. Wore Ben's thick dressing gown over mine, his scarf, my hat and his gloves (with all that weight, I could hardly move) and stood in the garden for a few minutes. Dead leaves on the path were the colour of chocolate covered in bloom. *Weekly Wife* says bloom is the white film that can sometimes be found on chocolate that has been exposed to heat. The heat causes some of the fat in the chocolate to melt and rise to the surface where it sets as a white film when the chocolate cools. Mmm... interesting.

A blackbird on the lawn with a large, orange beak brought to mind the toucan in the Guinness posters; a black and white kitten sitting on the leaves on the path watching the blackbird reminded me of the Felix cat food advert; and my reflection in the window reminded me of a blue towelling Mr. Blobby. Chris Evans crouched on his dustbin lid twitching his ginger tail; he's always got his eye on the little birds. A few birds circled high in the cold grey-blue sky, like vultures over a corpse. I didn't think I looked *that* ill.

Tonight I saw a baby romper suit in my Art Room catalogue from the Museum of Modern Art in Los Angeles. Must order it for little Matthew.

Tuesday 1st

I've done it! I've done it! Yessss! I've survived the first month of the year. Only eleven months to go and I'll have another whole year of wonderful learning experience under my belt. I will award myself a certificate with a fancy border and important-looking writing like the one Eileen has framed on her wall at the clinic.

Only three hundred and thirty something days to go. Three hundred and thirsty for a decent drink days to go. *Must stay positive.* Only about eight thousand hours, wintry showers, millions of raindrops dripping on flowers. *I will stay positive and write better poetry.* Hundreds of headaches. Twenty eight million seconds to remember the past. Four hundred and eighty thousand minutes to try and forget. Four *hungry* and *atey* thousand miserable minutes longing for pizza and chocolate. Must hide that calculator.

During this year, I'll pump enough blood around my body to fill several swimming pools, shed three layers of skin and produce enough saliva to fill a bath. Ugh. Not to mention what my kidneys, pancreas, digestion, hair and nails will get up to. I expect I'll pour hundreds of pints of herb tea down my throat and empty gallons of aromatherapy baths down the drain. Wow! Great! I'm going to have a really busy year after all. Don't know whether to laugh or cry. Must hide *Weekly Wife*.

... she decided the only way to survive the year was to have pizzas delivered every evening to her door, by Pepé, the cute pizza boy. Supreme pizzas in giant boxes, cut up into neat little sections so she didn't have even to pick up a knife, just open the box. She would create her own perfect pizzas with extra toppings: hundreds of green peppers, thousands of onions, millions of mushrooms and sweetcorn niblets. The more she ate, the slimmer she would get. That would be a perfect pizza!

The Thorntons man would arrive in his Thorntons van (brown and cream, with 'Chocolate Heaven Since 1911' written on the side) at 9 p.m. on the dot. Wearing a Pierce Brosnan smile and a smart brown uniform, he would present Madam with a beautifully wrapped parcel, crimson with a tartan bow, containing a large selection of Thorntons finest...

Tried to hide the Kit-Kat mugs again today; one glance at the red and white logo and I still crave a choccie-covered biscuit. Told Ben the black keys on his Yamaha keyboard looked like Kit-Kat bars in black wrappers. He said he would play me some black wrap music. I was not amused.

... she painted the black keys chocolate brown and the lid of his grand piano red and white. It was then he knew, for sure, there was no hope for her... but she knew she was fine; all she needed was a break from the world...

Ben has been finding the mugs, even though I've tried hiding them in saucepans (with the lid on) in the oven or at the back of the fridge (behind the soya milk) with leftover gravy in. He likes to use them when Jeremy pops round for an afternoon of computer chat.

Computerish is a foreign language to me. When I hear Ben requesting a floppy disk over the phone or advising his mates to format their hard drive, de-fragment their hard disk or boot up from their floppy, I'm tempted (in moments of mad boredom) to grab the phone and ask an unsuspecting male (in my best deep, husky voice) how his floppy disk is doing and would he like a hard one. I haven't yet. But I might.

Andrew sent an e-mail tonight:

Hello Ben,

Thanks for agreeing to help with my recording problems. What is happening is that, though in audio mode I seem to be able to record things ok, when in midi mode I can only get sounds from the general midi bank. I thought at first it was a problem with the settings on my synth but I've noticed that I'm not even getting volume changes from the synth. Maybe the G.M. info is coming from the sound-card (a Guillemot Maxi ISIS) and either that is overriding the synth's input of midi info or for some reason Cubase is ignoring the synth in midi mode. I am completely confused so any help you can give me would be fantastic.

Yours, Andrew.

I'm beginning to feel behind the times and dumb not knowing anything about computers. Software suggests to me a warm woolly jacket for the machine, perhaps in com-pewter grey.

Think I'll tell Ben the ice in the fridge needs de-fragmenting; he might listen. Words like defrost, dust and washing-up are foreign to him. Maybe I'll attract his attention if I begin all my sentences with www dot.

Wednesday 2nd

Found a sachet of Badedas (revitalising bath gelée with extract of horse chestnut) in an old glossy magazine full of advertisements and sad models; all glossy lips and anorexic hips, freezing on beaches with nipples like pips. The writing on the sachet informed me that if I poured the contents under hot running water, I would step into a dream and afterwards 'things' would happen. Does anyone believe this?

After my bath, I had nothing better to do than wait anyway. The doorbell rang.

... she opened the front door and there he was, Mr. Darcy on a chestnut horse, his wet shirt clinging to his chest after a swim in the lake. Thank God, she had just stepped out of a scented bath into a long floaty dress. She smiled her Miss Elizabeth Bennet smile...

A skinny delivery boy chewing gum leered at my goose-bumps as I signed for next door's parcel. Oh well! Could have been worse: Dale Winton waiting to whisk me off in a supermarket trolley to have lunch with Paul Daniels.

I need a little magic in my life.

... she vigorously rubbed the teapot; there was bubbling, then a sound like a Coke can being opened, a high-pitched giggle, and out popped Lady Camomile Anthemis Nobilis – Lady Camo to her friends, Mrs. C, the tea lady, in her grandson's magic circle. She apologised for being a bit late, off her trolley, and only having enough time to grant one wish before she hurried home to feed the rabbits and doves, and dragon needed walkies...

Watched a repeat of one of my favourite films (wore sunglasses and had frequent breaks from watching screen), *The Witches of Eastwick*. I've seen the film three times already, so while I rested my eyes I was able to put mental pictures to sounds. Imagined Gail, Rose and myself as the three witches (I still miss girly nights out). Gail was Cher making the booby dolls (she goes to pottery evening class); I was Susan Sarandon setting fire to my cello (I used to sing); Rose had to be Michelle Pfffeiffffer making lots of babies.

Went to bed thinking about Jack Nicholson's wonderfully wicked smile with a mug of warm soya milk and *Sourcery* by Terry Pratchett, for a little magic in my life... now, what was Jack's name in the film? Something beginning with D... or R something, Darryl Van...

Thursday 3rd
Horn. That was it. Darryl Van Horne. The smiling devil.

... Devillia smiled at her reflection in the mirror as she applied the bright red lipstick. An evil thought formed in her mind like a bruise waiting to surface and turn purple. Startled and fascinated, she watched as tiny horns appeared between strands of blonde hair on her head like the first shoots of spring; they

grew as long, black and curved as her fingernails.

The red dress fitted a treat, her handbag and stilettos matching the horns perfectly. On an impulse, she sprayed Wild and Wanton on her wrists and behind her ears, patted her horns, smiled like Joan Collins and teetered into the night to be naughty...

Psychologists claim that we can cope with even the most difficult situations if we smile more. Lifting the corners of your mouth sends a message to your brain to release serotonin (happy hormone); this in turn keeps you calm and peaceful by stopping the release of cortisol (stress hormone). So I smiled in the bath, smiled at my reflection in the bath taps, the mirror and a spoon; my mouth smiled but my face remained dormant. I need two tiny pixies sitting on my cheekbones with miniature fishing rods holding up each side of my mouth.

Put on a French and Saunders video, had a good laugh but had a good headache too. Opened a bottle of mineral water, poured myself a glass and talked to the glass because we shouldn't bottle things up, but try to talk more. The glass was a good listener.

Oh, well. I should think myself lucky. I can walk into the kitchen and pour myself a glass of water (even if the two-litre bottles are difficult to pick up and open). The Serengeti wildebeest often find their drink at the river interrupted by a twenty-foot crocodile with massive jaws. And he isn't smiling.

Must have an early night so I can handle situations better; lack of sleep will encourage stress.

Friday 4th

Crawled off to bed early last night only to find myself chased by headless wildebeest and fat smiling crocodiles with big shiny teeth. Wendy of *Weekly Wife* (wearing her favourite casual outfit with the addition of a striped waistcoat for that trendy layered look) appeared riding a camel and informed me that if I stopped cancelling my dentist appointments, I would be able to smile more. All my teeth fell out into a Kit-Kat mug sitting in the washing-up bowl full of dirty water. I fell into the water; bits of onion and tomato seeds were floating on the surface. A little red devil perched on the tap laughing hysterically.

10.06 a.m. Wake up picking bits of imaginary onion and tomato seeds out of my eyes.

10.07 a.m. Think about tomato seeds – they'll grow anywhere. A boyfriend once told me he met an old man who used to work at a sewage treatment place. Apparently, tomato plants grew on the sewage and the tomatoes were very tasty! We were eating salad at the time.

10.09 a.m. Drag self out of bed and into bathroom.

10.10 a.m. Sit on toilet thinking about growing tomatoes. Ben's sister-in-law, Lina, throws tomatoes out of the kitchen window; they grow into splendid tomato plants. She comes from the Philippines and that's how they grow tomatoes out there. They don't pop down to Homebase for a nice little plant and a gro-bag.

10.11 a.m. Did we have tomatoes last night?

10.12 a.m. Resist urge to look in toilet...

10.15 a.m. Shuffle to kitchen.

10.16 a.m. Grin at sparrows. They fly away.

10.31 a.m. Break favourite mug (unfortunately not a red and white one) while making my bleary-eyed breakfast.

10.32 a.m. Wrap up pieces in kitchen roll and place them in plastic carrier bag, being careful not to cut self.

10.35 a.m. Throw the lot in bin, followed by contents of Ben's ash tray, scrapings from last night's dinner plates (with tomato seeds) and a few smelly, slimy-stemmed, dead flowers.

10.38 a.m. Ugh. Really tired now.

11.34 a.m. Remember article about M.E. in *Weekly Wife* I meant to cut out and keep.

Dear God,
Please can I have my memory back?
Lots of love, xxx

11.37 a.m. Attempting to avoid slimy stems covered with congealed food and fag ash, I pull at the corner of the magazine. It's damp. It tears.

11.38 a.m Don't handle situation very well. I am not smiling, laughing, talking or sleeping enough.

1.25 p.m.	Curl up to watch fifties film – *Tea and Sympathy*.
1.42 p.m.	Deborah Kerr is gliding across the screen looking tragic and serene in a tight posh frock. I'm flopped on the sofa, looking more tragic in a baggy old sweatshirt, shrunken leggings and threadbare thermal socks.
2.05 p.m.	Wish I were enjoying real tea and real sympathy right now.
2.20 p.m.	A tart in a café is perched on a bar stool smoking a cigarette. She has a thin waist, high pointy boobs and a low sexy voice.
2.21 p.m.	Daydream about smoking three boxes of Benson & Hedges to keep me calm and peaceful.
3.30 p.m.	Sniff. Sniff. Sniff. Blow nose. Wipe eyes.
3.32 p.m.	Recall end of film and one of the lines in the letter the teacher writes to the young boy – 'Dreadful experiences; if they don't kill us, they make us strong.'
3.46 p.m.	Continue stress-relieving therapy with some exercise. Wiggle toes on right foot, wiggle toes on left foot.
3.48 p.m.	Tense and relax muscles of knee on right leg, tense and relax muscles of knee on left leg.
3.50 p.m.	Move eyes from right to left a few times; eyelids collapse with exhaustion.
3.51 p.m.	Breathe slowly and deeply.
3.52 p.m.	Fall asleep and dream about exercising in a gym (lifting giant red tomatoes) feeling incredibly full of life and energetic. Then I'm rolling tomatoes at a bowling alley, and when I've won the game, I play snooker with coloured tomatoes; the cue is a giant cucumber. I laugh a lot.
4.29 p.m.	Wake up. Cry a bit.

Ben came home late after a night at The Thirsty Tongue Tavern, Slurpit Street, with Bill and Rick. He crawled straight up the stairs to bed and fell asleep. He looked very un-stressed; must have been all that talking, laughing, exercising (lifting pints) and breathing deeply at Toyah behind the bar, in her size sixteen top from Top Shop.

I've noticed he's made his lunchtime rolls all week, is eating all his dinner like a good boy and has stopped being so attentive, *so* maybe everything's back to normal.

Saturday 5th

Or is it? Maybe not; he was grinning and giggling in his sleep last night. I tried hard to make sense of his mumblings... loverleeedonstollp... salrightyerrrm... redlippppssssdonyeaa... knoooo...

Threw a squishy tomato out the kitchen window, Filipino style. A chilly wind flew back in my face. It's hard to believe it's cold outside when you're indoors in the warm, the afternoon sun is shining brightly pretending it's summer, daffodil leaves are shooting up through the lawn and tiny lime green leaves on the rose bush (illuminated by sunlight) flutter in the breeze.

A blackbird danced on the lawn to the birdy song. I thought of springtime and suspicion... fresh new-born life and yellow daffodils... red jealousy and lipstick... tulip glasses on a romantic table (I'm not sitting at)... the end of winter and the beginning of doubt.

Mark rang; he will bring mum and baby round to visit tomorrow. *I'm ever-so-excited!* I expect Gina will have warned him that I'm the overemotional sort, likely to go all soppy and teary over Matthew. Must control my feelings and breathe deeply (difficult when M.E. turns you into an emotional wreck).

I used to go on diets when I was younger and it annoyed my sister when I was slim, so she may have said I'm a diet freak too. Think I'll answer the door with chocolate round my chops and a big smelly bag of chips in my hand! Maybe not, might upset Matthew's tiny baby smell buds. Oooh! I can't wait.

My *little* sister is taller, wider and louder than I. She loves to boss me about and I take it because I'm such a wimp. I think she senses I'm weaker since I became ill and has taken advantage of the situation; although I love my sister, I ~~hate~~ dislike her a lot sometimes. She supports Greenpeace, keeps two big dogs and has adopted a whale. I support Action for M.E., the M.E. Association, the R.S.P.C.A., have two little spots and recently adopted a spider.

Sam, the spider, lives in the corner of the kitchen window. I compliment him on his web building and he makes sure I take my supplements every morning. Sometimes I rescue a fly from his web and he doesn't talk to me for days, but we always make up in the end. Sam heard Ben talk about searching the web. He's very curious about the giant web site that lives in the computer in www dot land.

Sunday 6th

Watch clouds drift by... high in a February sky... a Viking ship sails behind a dinosaur with a fat tummy... a tiger leaps, roaring... like in a Salvador Dali painting... seconds tick by... tick... tick... tick... the tiger's head breaks off and disintegrates... minutes tick by... a turtle with a white shell and dark underbelly swims above a grey cloud shaped like a ghost from the *Ghostbusters* film... an hour ticks by... *Ghostbusters* tune in head... a pixie with long arms and legs dances between fluffy mountains... time ticks softly by... blue sky... blue for a baby boy... all this time to look at shapes in the sky... I've never seen a turtle or a tiger in the clouds before... lucky me... that reminds me... Tigger... where's that gift catalogue... think I might order the personalised Winnie-the-Pooh rug for Matthew... I love the Tigger slippers... wish they were made for grown-ups... must get well so I can work again and spoil my little nephew... Winnie-the-Pooh first songs... Thomas The Tank Engine... Postman Pat and his black and white cat... much more fun than adult books...

When Mark arrived with mum and baby, I managed to control my emotions, just. He is so beautiful: beautiful eyes, beautiful fingers, beautiful toes, beautiful finger nails and beautiful skin (Matthew, not Mark). Mark is a quiet eco-friendly type, very tall, thin and fair; he sways from side to side like a tree in autumn about to lose its leaves. I think he's younger than my sister; I didn't like to ask. I was waiting for her to tell him to sit and give me his paw; I expect she's already got him trained to obey her commands.

After they went home, I felt inspired to write one of those sentimental poems *Weekly Wife* loves to print.

A LITTLE BOY

Oh what joy
A little boy
Today at last
We meet
Such tiny hands
And fingernails
I want to hold your feet
I've been trying

Not to worry
But these few days
I've missed her
But now I am
So thrilled to have
A nephew
And a sister.

Did I really write that?

Monday 7th

Two hours and twenty three minutes cloud watching with rests in between. A baby elephant holds on to the tail of a sperm whale who is chasing a sausage dog... and a fluffy teapot... the handle breaks off and floats away... a family of hedgehogs... mummy... daddy... baby... think of Matthew... can't wait to see him again.

Eileen unlocked the annoying-little-sister comments and premenstrual tension in my muscles, tied my neck in a knot and wrapped my ankles round my waist; that's what it felt like anyway. We talked about the seventies and the clothes we wore; chain belts and love beads, how we used to enjoy *The Good Life, Man About The House* and *The Liver Birds.* Eileen wondered whatever happened to *The Likely Lads* and admitted to dressing up like a Bay City Roller. I admitted to wearing David Bowie make-up. Neither of us admitted to singing along with Donny Osmond's 'Puppy Love'. Did I really balance on *lemon* yellow platform shoes under *lime* green flares with an *orange* shirt! I probably thought I looked fruity.

The taxi driver who brought me home from the clinic today wore old misery grey clothes. He complained about the traffic, the weather, the wife, the children and the dog. I didn't give him a tip, so now he has something else to complain about.

Tuesday 8th

9.36 a.m.   Find Orvis clothes catalogue under this morning's post, wearing spring colours and a plastic see-through jacket (the catalogue, not me).

9.37 a.m.   Oooh, I like the Thousand Flowers broomstick skirt (slender-looking column of crinkle pleats that swirl out gracefully when you move, in a blizzard of little pink and ivory flowers on deep blue) much prettier than jeans for broomstick joyriding.

9.39 a.m. The Water Colour crinkle skirt is lovely too (almost lighter than air, a soft floral on a crinkled rayon georgette over a cotton lining). I could drift around the house looking all romantic on Valentine's Day.

9.43 a.m. Mmmm, the Seacoast sweater looks cheerful with coastal scenes on the front, back and sleeves – in shades of blue for sea and sky, white waves, seagulls and yachts, a beach hut and a lighthouse (so evocative of days by the seashore, you can almost feel the cool ocean breeze and hear the gentle beat of the surf). I want it! Must get well so I can go to work and afford it. I'm sure if I had a jumper like that, I'd feel more calm and peaceful; maybe they'll have a summer sale.

10.46 a.m. Watch end of *This Morning with Richard and Judy*, featuring naughty dresses for Valentine's night.

10.47 a.m. Sulk. Want to wear a slinky backless number and go out and get legless.

10.50 a.m. Watch start of news; feel suicidal for two minutes.

11.55 a.m. Bath.

12.45 p.m. Curl up with hot water bottle to ease monthly pains.

12.48 p.m. Read about natural remedies for period pain in *Weekly Wife*. Regular exercise – can't do that. Hot water bottle – got that. Warm bath – done that. Yoga – can stretch a tiny bit, but not today. Massage improves blood flow – have energy to rub tired right eye only today. Camomile and ginger tea improves circulation – we've got camomile but I can't make myself like it today.

2.14 p.m. The seventies-type clothes Eileen and I were laughing about are on the 'Simply Wearable' page! Feel old. Wendy says you can have a lot of fun mixing and matching checks with stripes. I bet she wears sensible skirts, shoes and jackets in black, and keeps sensible things in a large handbag.

Wednesday 9th

Went to my eleven-thirty appointment at the doctor's surgery (didn't see sexy Coke-swigging window cleaner) to collect my three-monthly certificate to send to the D.H.S.S. so I can continue to receive my incapacity pennies so I can eat and keep warm so I can continue to stay alive enough to visit the doctor again.

My doctor was wearing a sensible maroon cardigan and a smile to match; I wore a washed out sweatshirt and face to match. Although she is sympathetic, I always feel a need to mention some improvement in my symptoms so she has something to write down. Maybe subconsciously one feels intimidated by the memory of school reports. Doctors *do* often have a school-masterly or mistressy way about them.

I'm terrified of sounding pathetic, misery-gutish, hypochondriacish, layaboutish, or silly-anxious-female-ish (a symptom of the way some doctors have treated me, I think). Although I have to say, having read about the symptoms of lots of other illnesses, it must be terribly hard for a medical person to diagnose this illness if they haven't had any experience of it before.

The stress after visiting a doctor continues for weeks, locked in my muscles (especially if my doctor is away and I have to see another one – male doctors are usually the worst), then the stress of the thought of the next visit begins. So how is one supposed to recover from this illness, what with family and friends not understanding and stress being the main factor keeping one ill and the house always looks dirty and my hair always needs washing and I really want to be well but people keep asking me what I'm doing to help myself as if I were a child and am I going swimming and that bloody doctor asking me if I'm doing any GARDENING!

I remember writing to a friend's young soldier son when he was in the medical bit (whatever it was called) in the Gulf War. He spent a lot of time picking up parts of dead bodies from all over the place and throwing them on to a truck. I remember him as a sweet lad in pyjamas; makes me want to cry my eyes out. Anyway, he described himself as a 'desert turd' in his letters. Now I want to describe myself as a pavement pooh and I feel *like shit* and I wish I could say that to a doctor instead of being so *bloody polite* and careful what I say in case they put me in mental hospital.

Feel *MUCH* better now I've got that off my chest.

Thursday 10th

The sun is bright. The sky is blue. In a meadow full of daisies, little children play ring-o-roses. Round and round, singing and laughing. They all fall down and the sky turns black.

10.06 a.m.   Woke up feeling fresh as a daisy under a cow pat. To cheer myself up, I decided to make Ben a colourful collage-type Valentine's card (over the next few days) as a thank you for cooking the evening meals lately (even though we've had a lot of chips). Now I'm getting more rest, I'm feeling a little better. I'm learning to love dust and the mites are having a ball dirty dancing all over the house. I don't care; it's music to my ears. And I'm not feeling jealous or suspicious; it's bad for me. I am loving and calm and understanding and peaceful about everybody and everything. I am not dwelling on past miseries so my immune system is rejoicing and the tiny cells in my body are finding renewed happiness.

1.35 p.m.   Start making Valentine card.

1.36 p.m.   Carefully cut out two heart shapes from a model's pink jumper in *Weekly Wife* with nail scissors.

1.38 p.m.   Cut head off model in pink jumper.

1.39 p.m.   Find picture of flowery bedspread. Cut out two more hearts.

1.40 p.m.   Wonder if he's still seeing *her.*

5.36 p.m.   Scratch eyes out of a couple of baking potatoes.

5.37 p.m.   Wonder if she's size eight and blonde like the model in the pink jumper.

5.38 p.m.   Screw up severed head of model in pink jumper.

6.07 p.m.   Hide scissors, glue, bits of magazine and headless model under the sofa.

6.08 p.m.   Ben won't notice.

Friday 11th

1.33 p.m.   Flick through TV mag and find gifts page.

1.35 p.m.   Snip round photo of heart-shaped chocolate box and three foil-wrapped chocolates.

1.36 p.m.   Mouth waters.

1.37 p.m.   Cut out cuddly red devil, Cupid's ale, Happy heart and Love candles.

1.44 p.m.   Rest and recall a romantic picnic by the river, feeding the ducks, laughing, making plans; he gently wipes a bit of coleslaw off my lower lip.

1.45 p.m.   Try to have more happy romantic thoughts – chocolate melting in my mouth would make it easier... rich... smooth... creamy... sensual...

1.48 p.m.   Cheer self up reading other people's miserable stories: *'We Divorced on Valentine's Day', 'Our Romantic Day Was a Washout', 'Our Valentine Fiasco'.*

1.57 p.m.   Find Valentine gift page in *Weekly Wife*. Cut out love-heart champagne glasses, single red rose in gift wrap, square heart candles and a pink daisy.

2.20 p.m.   Flick through gift catalogue and come across music box with bear sitting on top. Carefully cut it out – similar to a romantic gift I bought Ben when we first met.

2.25 p.m.   Rest – hands a little achy.

2.26 p.m.   Romantic memories: walking in silent world of snow in the moonlight, sharing a bag of chips on a cold winter's walk through town.

2.28 p.m.   Tearful. Why do things have to go wrong. I want to be a time traveller like Doctor Who. I want to relive happy moments. Will I ever be well enough to walk in the snow again or dance on the beach at midnight?

2.30 p.m.   *... he drew a heart in the sand and they watched the tide wash it away... when she arrived home, she found the delicate shell in her pocket had broken into five pieces...*

2.31 p.m.   Lots of tears. Lots of snot. Use up four pieces of kitchen roll with butterfly pattern on.

2.49 p.m.   I want to fly away... nobody loves me.

3.11 p.m.   Cut off heads of models in *Top Ten Tops to tempt him*.

3.12 p.m.   Feel better.

3.13 p.m.   Maybe I was an executioner in a past life. What a horrible thought, ugh, I'll have nightmares tonight.

3.15 p.m.   Wendy says brunettes should be wearing cool blue or ice pink; we should all be listening to great tunes on the Marks & Spencer 'Loving You' CD, wearing Aveda's most popular fragrance, 'Love' (made from pure flower and plant essences) or enhancing our pheromones with Philosophy's 'Falling in Love' (a clear odourless liquid with synthetic pheromones that promote self-confidence).

3.16 p.m.   Wearing silk or satin, or trotting around the house in nothing but his shirt and wearing your hair up (necks are appealing)

	is supposed to relight his fire. You need a fire when you're freezing to death.
3.18 p.m.	Romantic memory: we fell about laughing when we couldn't find the car in the multi-storey car park.
3.19 p.m.	We giggled in the corner of a restaurant because we were too merry to read the menu...
3.21 p.m.	He used to kiss my nose.
3.23 p.m.	Pile of comfort food on large plate.
4.05 p.m.	Glue two hearts, the cuddly red devil, Cupid's ale and candles onto piece of A4 black card.
4.15 p.m.	Wear glue on nose and heart on sleeve.
6.00 p.m.	Positive thought: I'll make heart-shaped vegeburgers on the fourteenth, find the pink candles, something fluffy and feminine to wear, wash my hair *and* present him with the best Valentine card he's ever received!

Ben stumbled in through the front door clutching his little Indian take-away after an evening with Bill, Rick, Rob and Bob the Slob at The Smuggler's Socks, Cheesy Street.

Ben:	Did you hear about the man who overdosed on curry powder?
Me:	No.
Ben:	He's in a korma.
Me:	He! He! He! Ha! Ha! Ha!

The smell drifting out of the foil containers was too much for me; my taste buds woke up and dribbled. I toddled off to bed to rest but hundreds of biryani and bhajee smell monsters galloped up the stairs after me. The dreaded tikka masala tribe and greatly feared vindaloo warriors captured my nostrils and dragged me back downstairs. It was no good, I had to surrender, even though I knew the guilt monster would devour me tomorrow.

When Ben had piled up his man-sized plate, I sat on the floor beside him with my dainty teaspoon, scooping up samples of each vegetable sludge with a few grains of rice. The spoonfuls got bigger without my noticing. I commented that it is not uncommon to see a remora fish suctioned to the body of a dolphin, picking up a few scraps of food quite harmlessly.

Ben asked me what I was doing with all the bits of paper under the sofa and why was I wearing nothing but that old shirt? I'd catch my death...

I tried to look all alluring and pouted but didn't realise I had cauliflower bhajee on my chin. When he staggered off to bed, I ate a whole garlic nan bread. Burp.

Sneeze.

Saturday 12th

The guilt monster had a great time tearing me to pieces this morning. Vindaloo warriors sniggered from behind the toilet.

In the kitchen, a biryani smell monster snuffled around inside the rubbish bin; the lid raised ever so slightly, one orange eyeball peeped out and followed me round the room. I pretended not to notice, opened the fridge door and was about to pick up the soya milk when a bhajee snake wrapped itself tightly around my wrist and tried to pull me towards the bowl of leftovers. But this morning I was strong.

Two lemon lettuce lizards scuttled over Ben's boots and hid behind the cooker. He looked down, blinked, frowned, then asked me again what I was doing with all the bits of paper under the sofa (I wasn't under the sofa). I said I was cutting out articles to stick on the kitchen cupboards, a plausible excuse: I've already decorated one cupboard door with the benefits of evening primrose oil, herbs and honey, garlic and ginkgo biloba, nuts and seeds.

Ben has pinned up leaflets from the local Chinese, pizza and Indian take-away. I try not to notice them. He carried his weekly hangover to the health shop this morning; sometimes, it's so heavy he has to stay in bed weighed down by beer monsters sitting on his stomach, then we have to eat normal bread and marge all week. I never complain! The assistants at Holland & Barrett must wonder why he always looks so unhealthy when he eats such a healthy diet!!

I hope he remembered to buy me Valentine chocolate.

... she wandered around the house as lonely as a trolley in a car park, her chocolate-sensitive nose sniffing the cupboards like a drug policeman's sniffer dog...

She wandered lonely as a trolley
And a stick without its lolly
But not as lonely as Auntie Nelly
When she hasn't got her telly

While the bedroom filled with manly snore and smells, I crept downstairs in the early hours to do a bit more cutting and gluing. Before long, the whole floor was covered in colourful pieces of paper and heads of models. Thought of confetti and Valentine weddings. If I were still married, today would have been my fourteenth wedding anniversary; we wanted to marry on Valentine's Day but so did everyone else and we were at the back of the queue. Wonder if ex-husband ever remembers and feels sad. I have a feeling he does. Oh God! It's hard to feel cheerful at 4 a.m. unless you are plastered and stuck to a gorgeous man who thinks you're evershow-luverlee-n-beauuutiful and gets down on one knee to ask, 'Will you carry me?'

Sunday 13th

1.35 p.m.   Sat on the edge of the bath thinking. Chocolates appeared in my mind's eye, nestled in a plastic tray in the pleasure part of my brain. The heart-shaped cup was empty; I held the Strawberry Fayre. I bit into the chocolate and stared lustfully at the other half (not half-heartedly). My hand moved without my permission towards Hazelnut Heaven and before long I experienced the joy of ~~Carnal~~ Caramel Kiss, Truffle Charm and a Praline Parfait. After the Coffee Calypso, I revelled in Eastern Delight.

1.37 p.m.   I should be entertaining healthy herbal thoughts for as long as possible. Three seconds.

1.38 p.m.   Hope I will be able to indulge tomorrow. If not, I will buy a choc treat on Monday and share it with Eileen. If she hasn't got a boyfriend at the moment, or has one and is at that he's-not-as-nice-as-I-thought-he-was stage, we can have a good old man moan together. I'll start it, I'm in the mood, haven't had a good man moan for months. If I get it out of my system, I'll be a lovely person again for a while until the next lot of niggles builds up and needs to escape. Gossip. I always hated the gossips at work; thought I was above all that, but I could really do with a bit of scandal to spice up my life now.

When I finally finished the Valentine card, the birds were chirping and soft early morning light was kissing the window pane good morning. I signed the card with careful lovingly spaced x x xs in the shape of a heart and kissed the day goodnight.

Monday 14th

Slept in a world of sweet endless romance, sailing down a river with the man of my dreams in a world of rose petal pinks and white swans on lilac blue waters. Then woke up to reality.

Still in a sort of dreamy lilac mood, I wandered downstairs to see if Ben had remembered...

Yes! Brilliant! Two wonderful cards, envelopes in marshmallow pink and randy red.

A large square crimson parcel, beautifully Thorntons wrapped with a bow and golden heart-shaped tag, sat on a *CLEAN* coffee table with no dirty mugs or full ashtray or discarded letters in sight *AND* fresh flowers! For a moment, I was in shock. Then I felt like a child holding one of those Devonshire ice-creams coated in double cream with two chocolate flakes, my only worry, the colour of my spade didn't match my bucket.

Breathed in the scent of sweet pea and had lots of loving forgiving thoughts towards my man, especially after eating half a box of chocolates whilst opening my cards: a romantic bear holding a heart, and a naughty one. Both were signed the same (a heart with a question mark inside). Just for a second, I hoped there was a secret admirer lurking somewhere. Hmph.

I was floating around happily in the bedroom on a cloud in chocolate heaven and humming to Stevie Wonder who had called to say he loved me, when I saw *it* on the carpet. At first *it* was just a piece of folded paper, then words and numbers; *it* grew rapidly into a reason to commit grievous-bodily-something.

Bitch! Temptress! Cow! Cow! Cow! I'll cut her heart out and stick skewers in her eyeballs. No, hang on, she sounds desperate, I feel sorry for her. No I don't. Bloody tart! Oh God, who is she?!

'Please ring soon' and a telephone number were written in round childish writing, the exclamation marks artistically heart shaped. So, he's found a younger version of me, has he?!!! I'll shove his chocolates down his throat (death by chocolate). No I won't, I'll finish them off to give me the energy to strangle him. Haven't got the energy, even with a mouth full of chocolate. I know, I'll poison him. No, I'll make him feel guilty. No, I'll wait till I'm better, then take sweet revenge. Bad idea. That could take years. *SHE'S* probably chasing *HIM* anyway and he's not interested. He's flattered. Bless him. Maybe I'll kill him anyway, just in case I'm wrong.

> *... she wrote, HELL HATH NO FURY on all the walls in blood red lipstick...*

While waiting to see Eileen, I leafed through magazines in an attempt to calm myself down. Principal Hotels were advertising a special offer on romantic weekend breaks... 'For you and your loved one; make sure you take some loving time with your partner this spring'. The Manor House Hotel, Moretonhampstead, Devon, looked wonderful: a Jacobean-style mansion with impressive views, oak panelling and glorious log fires. I fancied The Royal York in York too, with it's sweeping staircase and chandeliers. The Keswick Country House Hotel in Cumbria, a beautiful old English house offering Victorian splendour and standing in private landscaped gardens, sent me into a wonderful daydream...

...candlelight and champagne, fine cuisine and frolicking in a four-poster bed wearing my Victorian nightdress from Past Times catalogue (I'll have my wicked way then smother him in his sleep with a feather pillow, or stab him with one of those old swords hung on the walls of posh houses).

Eileen said Saint Valentine was celibate so all this meaningless commercialism exploiting our need to feel loved and show affection was quite ridiculous *and* Thorntons made the most of it writing silly messages on chocolate hearts and it's not just cards and chocolates any more, the card shops are selling...

Guessed she hadn't received a card from boyfriend or admirer so thought it best not to mention how thrilled I was with my *two* cards and mountain of chocolates, in case she crunched my bones more vigorously than usual. Felt guilty. I should be sharing my cards and chocs with her. Started a good man moan; cheered us both up lots.

The taxi-man was so late picking me up tonight I thought he'd forgotten all about me. Rang Z Cars and as usual a woman said, 'He's on his way,' in a squeaky couldn't-care-less voice. Where from? Lands End! I hoped I wouldn't get the same driver who brought me to the clinic. There seem to be four types of drivers: Mr. Cheerful-Chatty (sometimes flirty), Mr. Quiet and Gentlemanly (opens the door and treats you like a lady), Mr. Miserable-as-Sin (hates the effin job, other drivers and his passengers) and Mr. Aggressive ex-racing driver (often young or Italian).

Mr. Miserable picked me up again, worst luck. Couldn't imagine him buying anyone a waste-of-effin-money Valentine card. Couldn't imagine anyone buying him one either. But could imagine him having a sad, worry-worn wife, with sore hands from years of hand washing clothes, chopping vegetables and scrubbing floors (I want to give her a hug, I expect she hasn't had one for twenty-five years). His eldest daughter married young to the first man who showed her affection, even though he was an ex-convict three times over and ugly with one brain cell. His youngest son is a ~~heron~~ heroin addict and now lives on the street, stealing from his mother to pay for his habit. *Must stop thinking too much.* Thirteen people attempt suicide every day in this country. *Must think calm and peaceful thoughts.* Every two minutes, someone in Britain has a heart attack. Every two minutes! How many people a day is that? Hundreds! Oh dear! Oh Lord! Everyone is so stressed! I'm so stressed! I hope Mr. Cheerful-Chatty picks me up next week so I can restore my will to live.

Saved Ben one chocolate (the one I dropped on the carpet and brushed the fluff off) and showed him the piece of paper. He laughed. Hmmm. No sign of guilt. The note was given to him by young Welsh temptress Delyth at work. She had asked him to pass it to his mate Simon when no-one was looking. He'd forgotten. I said, 'I thought it was probably meant for someone else,' as I laughed in a carefree laid-back way like Basil in *Fawlty Towers*.

He put the note in his pocket and nipped upstairs to make a phone call. Have written number down, to check another time, just to put my mind at rest. Am very trusting really. Did not listen to phone call. Am practising being a trusting girlfriend. Heard him say, 'Yes... er no.... yes... OK..... you know I do... see you tomorrow... bye.'

Wish I hadn't eaten all those chocolates. I'm a horrible fat pig. Mustn't use that word, I love pigs and cows. Sheep too. I bet Mr. Miserable-as-Sin eats steak with the blood dripping out and slaughters his own chickens.

After dinner (heart-shaped vegeburgers by candlelight) we watched a historical romance starring Helena Bonham-Carter with the caterpillar eyebrows. I was just feeling all cosy and contented when my man announced he is going out for an Indian tomorrow night; he loved his Valentine card. There is a party on Saturday night (he has to go to because an old friend will be there he hasn't seen for years); how lovely I look tonight and Bill wants to meet him for lunch on Sunday.

Feel historical (old and quietly hysterical). Hope he's not meeting his Welsh-rare-bit-on-the-side! Oh-no-oh-no-oh-no!! I must GET WELL SOON – like the messages on all those cards I received years ago!

... She left the cards up on the mantelpiece; they had cobwebs on them now...

Tuesday 15th

Sat staring out of the bedroom window. A young woman wandered down the street wearing a silly expression, holding a pink umbrella covered in red love hearts over her head. Her long, floaty skirt, in this season's romantic red, flapped round her slim ankles, her valentine pink shoes clicked on the path. One of the high pointy heels stuck in a crack in the pavement and she almost tripped over. One day, she'll come down to earth with a huge bump, twisting one of her swollen, pregnant ankles, one hand full of shopping bags, the other gripping a broken blue umbrella.

Turned up the radio and sang-along-a-little with the Spice Girls, but what I want, what *I really, really* want, is to go to the party on Saturday night. I can't go to the party on Saturday night. I want to wear a party dress and party shoes. I can't go clothes shopping. I miss you Dorothy Perkins, I miss you Miss Selfridge. I miss sailing around in Monsoon and River Island, landing on the sunny beach wear, searching for tiger prints, snake skin or something pretty and floral.

THE PARTY

My friend had a party
But I couldn't go
I was very disappointed
I didn't let it show

The pages of this week's *Tempt Your Taste Buds with Tara* were covered with mouth-watering photographs of sweet and savoury pancakes; I felt a comfort-eating session coming on.

Today, Shrove Tuesday, it's traditional to stuff your face anyway in some cultures: sometimes as much as twelve meals a day! I suppose that's because it's the beginning of Lent, a time of abstinence, and pancakes are designed to use up the dairy products left in the kitchen. We gave up sugar and cake and biscuits when I lived with Mum and Dad; Gina and I never did go back to drinking tea with sugar.

Found the largest potato in the world, rinsed it, thought about *the note,* scratched a couple of eyes out, stabbed the skin a few times and threw it in the oven. Exhausted.

Devoured a lump of Ben's cheese, a packet of pistachio nuts, half a can of cold chick peas and a banana (ate around mouldy bits) while watching *EastEnders* and the end of a depressing programme about something awful.

Stood at the window. A group of teenage girls were all dressed up and going out to enjoy themselves; I expect they were hoping to meet the boyfriend of their dreams. Waited for the potato of my dreams to cook.

... she asked Mr. Potato if he were going to be much longer. He told her to 'Stop fussing, Woman', he was too old to rush about and these things take time; he could be hours, he wasn't the young potato he used to be in his Army days. He still missed his spuddies and their old patch in the rain of King Edward... during the war...

Cut a cross in the potato and filled it with lots of margarine mixed with a clove of garlic.

... he was very cut up about having to go away to war and missed Flora terribly. But it was almost worth the heartache when he returned and they were reunited; him in his smart crisp uniform and Flora wearing the yellow dress, melting in his arms...

I had just stuffed an enormous forkful of potato into my mouth when an advert for Weight Watchers popped up on the telly (again). Turned it off. Remembered my stars, 'You'll bite off more than you can chew, given half the chance.'

Sam Spider was annoyed by the heat in the kitchen and my eating habits so he disappeared into a little hideout unknown to me to dream about lady spiders in www dot land.

Ben said he felt ill when he came home after his Indian meal so we both lay in bed with gurgling tummies. He smelt of Indian restaurant and smoke and booze. I breathed garlic on him, ha! ha!

Wednesday 16th

Ash Wednesday. Feel grey. I don't want to be reminded of the days I had to go to church in the middle of the week and have ashes rubbed on my forehead by a priest; really scared me when I was little. God! It was bad enough being forced to stare (for a whole hour) at a life-sized statue of a man dying on a cross and dripping with blood every Sunday. I try to avoid staring at the large thorns on our rose bushes; when I do, I feel terribly sad.

Haven't worn my cross and chain for twenty years. I will hang it on a rose bush and wait for a jackdaw or a magpie to fly down and steal it. The bird will probably take it to a nest in a church tower and on the way drop it on the head of a young girl as she hurries to Sunday mass (just as she says a little prayer to say sorry to Jesus for being late). She will see this as a sign of forgiveness from the heavens and decide to become a bride of Christ and after years of effort helping others less fortunate than herself, she will die of a terrible stress-related illness and it will be all my fault.

Thorns. Ashes. They give me nothing but bad memories. Death of a friend. Cleaning out fire grate in the marital home. Burnt-out houses on the news. Forest fires. The carpet in The Sticky Carpet Tavern, Slime Street. My old boss at British Gas; I knew he'd been checking my work when there was a pile of ash by my desk first thing in the morning. If there was ash on *his* forehead, it meant he had collapsed on his desk, drunk again after lunch.

Bad day.

Thursday 17th

Accidentally knocked Ben's ashtray on the floor and left it there, in loving memory of my old boss. He marched in through the front door tonight (Ben, not my boss) and put his foot in it. I told him about the megapode in Australia, a bird that lays its eggs in mounds of warm volcanic ash to incubate. He said, 'Some birds will get laid anywhere warm and comfortable,' then he mentioned the new girl at work. All the men were saying how clever she was on the computer; the women, what beautiful hair and clothes. The jealousy monster sat on my head and made me frown; I couldn't shake him off. Asked Ben what he thought of the wonderful computer whiz-woman... 'Face like a Friday funeral, figure like two coffee beans on a coffin.' That's alright then.

Friday 18th

Stared moodily at my reflection in the mirror and wondered if plucking my eyebrows would bring some life into my eyeballs.

When did I last dress up? I want to look my best again. I'm good at looking my worst now; I have it down to a fine art. Sometimes I lie around with dirty hair, smelly armpits, grubby nails and hairy legs; but who cares, no-one sees me. At least going to the clinic once a week is an excuse to trim nails, depilate, wash my hair and make myself smell fabulously fragrant, even if the effort nearly kills me.

Ben doesn't make any comment about how I look. He may be going off me. He probably feels as if he sleeps with a piece of flabby lettuce or a meal left in the oven for days, dried up with no flavour and not very saucy. He'll enjoy a break from me on Saturday evening.

Tonight I brushed my hair till the grease shone and squeezed a spot on my nose (good and red and sore-looking). Blew my nose so hard my eyes became beautifully bloodshot and finally I looked exactly how I felt. I think I'll paint my face green, shave off my eyebrows and cut off my eyelashes. Then perhaps people will stop telling me how well I look.

Ben went on a pub crawl with Bill and Bob the Slob to The Fisherman's Armpit in Sniffit Street, Laura Ashtray's Wine Bar and The Sticky Carpet Tavern, Slime Street. When he came home, he didn't notice how I looked or smelt.

Saturday 19th

Holland & Barrett day.

Ben often chats to one of the woman at the health shop. Her sons's had M.E. for about four years (handy having a mum working in a health shop). Joyce has been very helpful and they compare notes. Today she told Ben about a doctor in Maidstone who was very cruel to her son when he first became ill. Months later, this same doctor developed M.E. himself and had to give up work. I know I shouldn't say this... best story I've heard in ages!

7.40 p.m.　　Ben rushes out the door wearing his new groovy turquoise shirt from Top Man, worn over jeans to look cool (hide beer belly). The smell of Shagemall after-shave runs after him crying, 'Wait for me.'

7.42 p.m.　　Ben returns to collect his forgotten bring-a-bottle giant bottle of Maison Rouge. Remembers I exist. Gives me a peck on cheek, asks me not to wait up and says, 'There's a little something in the fridge behind the mayonnaise that might cheer you up.'

7.45 p.m.　　Urge to open front door and call Ben to come back with giant bottle of wine and share it with me.

7.46 p.m.　　Urge to scream, 'Don't go!' out of bedroom window.

7.47 p.m.　　Am grown up now and must act in sensible, mature manner. Anyway, don't want to appear more pathetic than I already am. Sulk.

7.48 p.m.　　Head for the fridge to locate a little something behind the reduced-cal mayonnaise. Great! hundreds-of-cal bar of Bournville Plain. Eat three squares and think about how thoughtful my man is. Eat three more squares followed by loving caring thoughts about my man needing a break from the horror of living with a chronically sick person. After three more squares, decide not to feel jealous at the thought of his spending the evening with attractive women wearing party dresses.

7.50 p.m.　　God, I'm really jealous!

7.52 p.m.　　Ben will arrive at party soon.

7.53 p.m.　　Wonder if he's there yet.

7.54 p.m.　　Stand at window. Pick up scented candles and sniff them one by one. Watch talking and laughing couples going somewhere together, two by two.

7.56 p.m.　　Listen till their voices fade into the night. Breathe on the window and draw a sad face.

7.58 p.m.　　Need a whole suitcase of chocolate.

8.00 p.m.　　Plan comfort food for the evening.

8.01 p.m.　　Large baking potato in oven.

Forget to prick skin.

8.02 p.m.   Take potato out of oven, stab it a lot and cut off bad bits.

8.03 p.m.   Hope potatoes don't feel pain.

Hope I'm not going slowly insane.

Ben will be at the party now.

8.04 p.m.   Very tired. Remember *the* telephone number.

8.05 p.m.   Tear up number – I'm being mature and trusting tonight. Throw bits of paper in bin with used tea bags and potato peel. Empty Ben's ashtray over top so not tempted to fish bits of paper out of bin later.

8.10 p.m.   Plan entertainment to go with comfort eating.

8.15 p.m.   Watch *Stars in Their Eyes*. Eat bag of pistachio nuts and feel nervous for contestants.

8.16 p.m.   Munch, munch, munch.

8.17 p.m.   Wonder what Ben is doing.

8.18 p.m.   Admire dress singer is wearing and decide I need new clothes.

8.19 p.m.   Admit I need a bigger size.

8.20 p.m.   Add up all the calories I have consumed so far today.

8.21 p.m.   Hate myself.

8.22 p.m.   Wonder how many calories I use up while adding up my calories.

8.25 p.m.   Eat more chocolate.

8.29 p.m.   Fish bits of paper out of bin.

8.30 p.m.   Join bits of paper together but *the* number is illegible due to three wet tea bags. Feel sick due to smell of fag ash.

8.31 p.m.   Wonder if Ben is offering a light to a beautiful intelligent woman, or *her*.

8.32 p.m.   Hope she blows smoke in his face.

8.32 p.m.   Hope she gets lots of wrinkles from smoking too much and puts on weight when she tries to give up.

8.33 p.m.   Still trying to work out *the* number. Is that a 3 or an 8, a 2 or a 7? Just can't decide or decipher. This is fate! I'm being punished for all my jealous untrusting thoughts in the past. I will die alone surrounded by empty boxes of herbal tea and potato peelings.

8.34 p.m.   Wouldn't know what to say if I did speak to the Welsh temptress anyway. I'm too much of a wimp to come straight out and say, 'Look you, are you seeing my man, lusty leek features, yes or no?'

8.35 p.m.	Have missed one of the contestants on *Stars in Their Eyes*; now I won't be able to vote properly!
8.45 p.m.	Decide Matthew Kelly is lovely.
8.46 p.m.	Take Ben's brown-rolls-for-work out of freezer for late-night comfort snack.
8.47 p.m.	Nibble end of frozen roll like a starving rodent in the wild.
8.50 p.m.	Lie on sofa and enjoy Scottish singer. Remember Eileen is going to Scotland soon and has promised to bring me back a vegetarian haggis; I expect the ingredients include the insides of slaughtered vegetables.
8.51 p.m.	I'm going insane.
8.55 p.m.	Pour myself a cold, refreshing glass of Sainsbury's Glen Mor mineral water, all the way from the Scottish Highlands. Read on label that it's a natural partner to whisky, 'Uisge-Beatha'– the water of life.
9.00 p.m.	Feel sad that only one contestant wins *Stars in Their Eyes*.
9.01 p.m.	Wonder if any of the losing contestants try to kill themselves.
9.02 p.m.	Remember Abba's song 'The Winner Takes It All'.
9.03 p.m.	Remember third of a bottle of Scotch whisky in back of cupboard. Decide to put on 'Abba's Greatest Hits' and haff ma oan wee parrrteee!
9.05 p.m.	Wonder if Ben is drunk yet.
9.10 p.m.	If I mix whisky with pure natural mineral water, it will be half healthy.

... Mr. Mineral-Water sprang from a wee place near the village of Kiltarlity and had the time of his life mixing with a selection of the finest malts, their delicate sweet character seducing his taste buds...

9.15 p.m.	I bet everyone at the party has shiny hair, bright eyes and sparkling conversation. Don't care; I have a shiny glass full of bright sparkling drink.
9.16 p.m.	Sip refreshing Scottish liquid and sing along with Abba, 'Money money money... it's a rich man's world...'
9.25 p.m.	Stare at clock.
9.30 p.m.	Drag self out of chair to check potato.
9.31 p.m.	Potato not ready yet.

9.32 p.m.	Switch kettle on for cuppa-soup.
9.33 p.m.	Burn tongue.
9.33 p.m.	Swear.
9.34 p.m.	Abba is singing, 'Does your mother know?'
9.36 p.m.	Wonder if Ben is enjoying triangles of quiche, cheese straws and little tasty things on sticks (skinny model-type women) or *her* offering herself on a plate (if there's mayonnaise, he'll have a little bit on the side).
9.37 p.m.	Cut lump off Ben's cheese. Shove in roll without bothering to butter it. Shove in mouth. Yum!
9.40 p.m.	Stare at clock.
9.42 p.m.	Imagine everyone at party full of energy, talking and giggling, drinking and smoking, dancing and flirting.
9.43 p.m.	The music will be so loud they will have to press against each other to hear what's being said.
9.44 p.m.	Wonder who Ben is im-pressing.
9.45 p.m.	Think I'm going to kill myself.
9.46 p.m.	Think I'll take all my clothes off, stand in the rain and freeze to death.
9.47 p.m.	No. Can't be bothered. Too much effort.
10.00 p.m.	Remember potato.
10.03 p.m.	More marge than potato to prevent burning tongue again and produce feelings of comfort.
10.04 p.m.	Burn tongue again.
10.05 p.m.	Calorie monster sits on the fridge tutting and shaking his head.
10.20 p.m.	V. full tummy.
	V. woozy head.
10.22 p.m.	Stare at clock.
10.25 p.m.	Start thinking again.
	In full-woozy way.
10.26 p.m.	Jealousy monster curls up on sofa beside me and whispers in my ear. Cover ears; he doesn't know what he's talking about.
10.28 p.m.	Abba is singing, 'Knowing me, knowing you... ah haaah... there is nothing we can do.'
10.30 p.m.	Bits all over carpet start to annoy me.
10.31 p.m.	Crawl on carpet and pick up five bits. Mutter in drunken Scottish fashion like Rab C. Nesbitt.

10.33 p.m.   Lie on floor feeling sick.

10.34 p.m.   Mustn't be sick. No energy to clear it up.

10.45 p.m.   Abba is singing 'One of us is lonely... staring at the ceiling wishing she was somewhere else instead.'

11.25 p.m.   Still on floor. Wiggling toes to 'Dancing Queen'. My party is in full swing. I bet no-one at Ben's party is having such a fantastic time as I.

11.26 p.m.   Hope they all have achy feet from dancing and standing around in the kitchen.

11.30 p.m.   Pick up jealousy monster by the ears and throw him out the front door.

11.31 p.m.   Jealousy monster shouts through the letter box, 'You know I'm right!'

11.32 p.m.   Finish whisky and do a little Highland fling while lying on the floor (can be done, sort of).

11.35 p.m.   Roll a coaster across the floor.

12.20 a.m.   Still on floor singing, 'Gimme Gimme Gimme a man after midnight.'

12.25 a.m.   Crawl to kitchen.

12.27 a.m.   Force self to drink lots of water, take lots of vitamin C and evening primrose oil so I'm not dead tomorrow.

12.40 a.m.   Kitchen floor looks dirtier close up.

12.41 a.m.   Spot two evening primrose capsules under fridge door, a shrivelled pea and something with mould on under the cooker.

12.45 a.m.   Flick dried up pea between the legs of chair. Goal! Sam stands up in his web and cheers.

12.46 a.m.   Watch woodlouse crawl across my slipper.

12.47 a.m.   Say hello to woodlouse.

12.48 a.m.   Wonder if woodlice get upset when they see a dead friend.

12.48 a.m.   Wonder if woodlice have friends.

12.49 a.m.   Ask woodlouse if he knows he is a terrestrial isopod with a flat elliptical segmented body.
Woodlouse asks me if I'm aware that I'm an alcoholic biped of the family hominidae.

1.00 a.m.   Need to go to loo.

1.01 a.m.   No energy to go upstairs.
Think I'll sit in a puddle.

1.05 a.m.   Might drown woodlouse.

1.06 a.m.	Think I'm going to wet myself.
	I will be insane and incontinent.
1.07 a.m.	Mustn't laugh or really will wet self.
1.08 a.m.	Mustn't cry.
1.10 a.m.	If I don't *go* very soon there will be a yellow river running across the kitchen floor, the primrose oil capsules will float on it. At least it will be an excuse to clean floor; urine has lots of germ killers in it.
1.12 a.m.	Sit on loo singing.
	Ahhhh... relief.
	Surprising how much liquid the body can hold.
1.13 a.m.	Waterloo... do-be-do... do-be-do... do-be-do.
1.30 a.m.	Lie on bed looking at feet. Wonder when Ben is coming home.
1.32 a.m.	Toenails need cutting.
1.33 a.m.	Can't find nail scissors. Find lost tweezers and clogged up mascara.
1.34 a.m.	Attempt ~~suicide~~ to pluck eyebrows, to improve looks.
1.35 a.m.	Stab eye.
1.37 a.m.	Jealousy monster calls down chimney, 'He's not home yet, is he?'
2.00 a.m.	Feel sad. Feel sorry for self.
2.05 a.m.	Stare at clock.
2.15 a.m.	Sit on bath wearing tired dressing gown.
2.16 a.m.	Must buy new toothbrush.
2.17 a.m.	Must put new loo roll out.
2.18 a.m.	Must water droopy plant.
2.25 a.m.	Stare out of window at noisy drunken youths. A girl falls over in her platform boots and sits on path giggling.
2.30 a.m.	Hope Ben isn't lying drunk in a gutter somewhere, or a bed with some girl in platform shoes.
2.32 a.m.	Or on a platform somewhere, waiting to catch train as far away from me as possible.
2.42 a.m.	Sound of taxi outside.
2.45 a.m.	Sound of Ben having problems letting himself in.
2.46 a.m.	Sound of thunder.
	Tapping on door.
2.47 a.m.	Hammering on door.
2.48 a.m.	Decide to let him in.

Soggy-party-man with lopsided smile informs me he's had a dreffull time coz muzic ferry loud and he couldn't hear himself speak.

2.49 a.m.   Jealousy monster sits on his shoulder, sniggers and says, 'That's why he came home early, isn't it?'

2.50 a.m.   Shut J. monster in wardrobe.

3.00 a.m.   Can't get Abba songs out of head.

3.30 a.m.   Panadol Night.

Sunday 20th

Woke up feeling sane and sober. Pity.

Ben went out unshaven in yesterday's crumpled clothes to meet Bill at The Smuggler's Socks in Cheesy Street.

Bill is an artist who always wears grey and brown to match his grey and brown bed-sit, which is more grey than brown (possible camouflage so landlord cannot find him on rent-collecting day). He likes dust, smoking interesting herbs, eating bananas, interesting women, painting nude women, women smoking, women eating bananas and painting interesting nude women who are smoking or eating bananas. The ashtray in his bed-sit is a modern sculpture of dog ends, cigarette packets, matchboxes and banana skins carefully balanced: the Tate Gallery would love it. He could entitle the piece, 'A Balance Between Health and Sickness' or simply, 'Ashtray'. I can see it all now, little Japanese people will take lots of state-of-the-art photos and make miniature copies when they get home. Americans will comment that the artist must have had a *nice day* and what a *neat* idea.

I imagine Bill with a fag in his mouth, paintbrush in one hand and a banana in the other; wonder if he juggles them.

Still can't get Abba songs out of my head.

Monday 21st

Mr. Cheerful-Chatty taxi man picked me up this afternoon and brightened up my dull February Monday.

Today I was 100% cotton, had a 40° bath and, as I lay on Eileen's ironing board, she switched the setting on her steam iron to hot. I enjoyed my creases being gently smoothed out, including cuffs, collar and waistband above my belly button.

Eileen was Miss-Cheerful-Chatty. We talked about Bill; we've never seen him looking bright and cheerful. His moods are brown and grey, like his clothes and bed-sit. She recalled the days she lived in a bed-sit in the same house as he on the London Road. Bill still lives there. We think he's been there for a hundred years; we're not sure...

Eileen hasn't modelled for Bill's paintings but she used to model for life-drawing classes and quite enjoyed it, even though it was hard work keeping still in awkward poses. A few years ago, I bumped into one of my old art college tutors in Safeway and he asked me if I'd like to model for the local art college. I saw him stare at my breasts; it put me off. I asked if there were any jobs going for teaching art; there weren't.

I may only be fit for part-time work when I'm more recovered so I'm considering the modelling, but I'm not sure. I've heard it pays well. I've had a bit of experience (posed fully clothed for friends at college) but I don't think I want to show off my saggy body or hairy bits now. OK, diary, I'll admit it, I'm just not brave enough; I don't feel *reclined* to be an artist's model.

Leafing through *Reader's Digest* at the clinic, I saw pictures of Australian tribeswomen. My breasts are beginning to look like theirs; must start to wear a bra around the house.

Ben was singing, 'Money, Money, Money' in the bath tonight. He's caught Abba-itis from me.

Tuesday 22nd

Picked up this morning's post and spotted a bright green envelope amongst the boring brown and white ones, my name and address written in black curly writing: Artie Auntie from Yorkshire. Great!

Auntie's notes about her adventures abroad are always wonderfully detailed, interesting and colourful. Today, I found a small sketch enclosed of a château in France, drawn with ink and coloured pencils on a piece of cardboard. The note on the back had crimson dots splashed across it: the visit to the vineyard must have been fruitful!

With her last letter, Auntie sent a sketch of the rooftops of Haworth, Brontë country, near where she lives. The one before that showed gondolas on the canals of Venice. I have quite a collection now. One day I'll put them in those handy clip frames. One day I'll do all those things I've been meaning to do, one day.

Replied to Auntie's letter. Tried to think of colourful interesting things to say, leaving out the bad bits.

> Dear Artie Auntie,
>
> Thanks for your beautiful sketch and letter. Good to know you enjoyed your break in France. Sorry to hear about Uncle Keith; hope he gets well soon.
> I'm still seeing an osteopath once a week – gets me out of the house and gives me something to look forward to, as well as the benefit of the treatment. Ben is fine. He uses a computer at his workplace now and quite enjoys it.
> We've been trying out different herbal teas from our local health shop recently. The boxes look very colourful piled up next to the bread bin: nettle tea in pale green, lemon verbena in

pale yellow and the peppermint tea box in lime green. The orange, pink and purple fruit teas are sitting on the bread bin.

Doctor Stewart's Botanical Tea (No. VII Peppermint) has particularly good packaging, a soft yellow background with detailed colour illustrations of berries, flowers and leaves. The London Herb & Spice Company's design on their peppermint tea box is very good too: green and black leaf shapes on a lemony-orangey background, black lettering, and a drawing of a cup and saucer surrounded by a mint plant, in various shades of green.

Must go and put the kettle on now.

Lots of love,
Artie Niece x x
P.S. As you can see, I drink a lot of peppermint tea!
P.P.S. Have you tried it?
P.P.P.S. To be honest, at this moment, I'd love a chat with you over a coffee in the Tate Gallery – airing our views on Monet, Matisse and Millais; Seurat, Stubbs and Surrealism; Caneletto, Chagall, ~~Cannelloni~~ ~~Cappucinno~~ Carpaccio and that strange-looking man, over there, in the corner: the one with the floppy purple hat and paint-splattered waistcoat.

Wednesday 23rd

Didn't feel too bad today. The sun was shining and spring waited patiently round the corner, but I resisted the urge to catch up with this and that.

Washed my hair with acacia honey shampoo, the sweet fragrance reminding me of grandmother's garden, full of roses and sweet pea. Enjoyed a long aromatherapy bath using oils of *anthemis nobilis* (camomile) and *lavandula augustifolia* (lavender) to soothe and relax me. Calm and peaceful thoughts filled my mind while I smoothed Dove soap over my body and watched the sun sparkle on frosted glass.

Lay on the bed sniffing the acacia honey shampoo bottle to take me back to sunny afternoons in Grandma Molly's garden. I could see the colours of the flowers (like a Victorian water-colour) and almost remember what it felt like to be a child, skipping happily down the garden path, full of life and questions.

Piled my hair up, brushed mascara on my lashes, wore my best leggings and favourite blue jumper. Looked better. Felt better. Ben said I looked great. Felt happy. Then he said my shell-like ears were my best feature. Think I'll grow my fringe over my face, shave off the rest of my hair and wear dangly earrings to enhance the beauty of my lobes – I may start a trend. All this lying about is making me *so* creative.

Thursday 24th

Sat near the window creatively snipping off my split ends. Afternoon sunshine filtered through the curtains in such a way that I could see each tiny individual hair clearly. Snip, snip, snip; very relaxing. The women at the office where I used to work would be disgusted if they could see me now. I'm tempted to put the clippings in an envelope and send it to them with the message: 'Here are some cutting replies to all those nasty little comments'.

Friday 25th

The weather had M.E. The sky, washed out and a little blue, suffered unexpected southerly winds late afternoon.

Goldshield wrote to me with even more ways to discover *BETTER HEALTH* including their expanded Centural range for a demanding busy lifestyle. I will receive a *FREE*, very useful, *SEVEN DAY PILL TIDY AND ORGANISER* if I simply return the enclosed order form in a pre-paid envelope within seven days. Each compartment in the *PILL TIDY* is clearly marked and I will never have to worry about missing a day again. It's so simple and practical, I'll wonder how I ever managed without it! Couldn't see anything for flatulence, so I didn't bother.

Ben came home smelling herbal from The Hairy Hippy in Kaftan Street. He has recovered from Abba-itis but I've still got it... 'Can you hear the drums, Fernando...'

Saturday 26th

'There was something in the air that night, the stars were bright...'

Ace catalogue sent me details of their MAD MARCH SALE!! Lots of great savings with up to 50% off!!! Do I really want to think about Christmas paper and cards yet? No. I'd like to order the personalised stool with pencil-shaped legs in red, yellow, green and blue – if I had a small bum. Maybe I'll write to Santa asking for one. I expect he'll reply with details of the nearest Weight Watchers. The icing stencils look fun, for the day when I have the energy to bake a cake; the lap desk looks useful, but a cushion will do for now.

Received a postcard of a cat sitting on a harbour wall in Cornwall; Gail escapes to the West Country every few months with husband Gareth to recover from the stress of art directing in London. I've never seen Gail dressed in a colour: she always wears black and white and lives in a designer house with her black and white cat, Escher. I look forward to her postcards (often black and white). She's always up to something new, like Artie Auntie. I did something new and creative today: arranged the crumbs on my plate in a flower pattern with my finger and placed a button in the middle of the petals. I won't bother to tell anyone.

Sunday 27th

... she dreamt of Cornish beaches; riding a white horse in the blue sea, wearing a white dress under a blue sky, the wind as fresh as the taste of white toothpaste with a blue stripe...

When will I be well enough to travel to Cornwall again? I'm fed up with all the holiday adverts and Wendy's handy hints on where to go, how to pack my case and what to wear this summer.

I am calm and peaceful, I am healed and healthy, I love me. I am drinking mineral water on a beach in a stripy deck chair listening to the waves and the seagulls. I hate chocolate; I'd hate to be Claudia What's-her-name. My socks are matching so I'm balanced.

Sounds very windy outside; March winds have arrived early to get a good seat. I know when it's really windy: the petals on my material sunflowers in the fireplace flutter and the sash window rattles.

Monday 28th

2.05 p.m.   Lie on stomach in bath, floating on elbows for a change.
Recall programme last night showing underwater view in

swimming pool of very pregnant mummies to be. Turn over on back – too uncomfortable.

6.04 p.m.   Eileen and I talk about Scotland.

6.05 p.m.   Close eyes and imagine staying in a castle, waited on by servants till I recovered from M.E. – portcullis down, drawbridge up and surrounded by a deep moat. A crowd of family and doctors try to get in but I cannot hear their cries of, 'Pull yourself together!' behind the thick stone walls of my tower. I will let my hair down (Rapunzel-style) when I feel like it.

6.45 p.m.   Ask Mr. Aggressive ex-racing-driver-taxi-man to run me up to Scotland; we could be there in the time it takes to say, 'Hide ya haggis, Morag.'

7.17 p.m.   *Must* have a cup of coffee; the smell of Eileen's Nescafé drove me *mad* this afternoon.

7.19 p.m.   Sip from a delicate Dove Espresso china cup, featuring a Picasso sketch – prezzie from Artie Auntie.

7.20 p.m.   Leaf through *Matisse in Nice*, enjoying the colourful paintings, for full arty effect.

11.30 p.m.   Still feeling restless and nervy; caffeine stays in the system for nine hours so I should be OK by four thirty in the morning. Five hours to go.

11.36 p.m.   Feel inspired by Picasso and Matisse; think I'll make pretty dove patterns on the bathroom mirror with Truly Red lipstick and bright yellow hair conditioner.

11.37 p.m.   Maybe not.

MARCH

Tuesday 1st

Oedipus was asked, 'What walks on four legs in the morning, on two in the afternoon and three in the evening?'

The answer he gave was, 'a man' – who crawls on all fours as an infant and is supported by a stick in old age.

I asked Ben, 'What walks on two legs in the morning and crawls on all fours in the afternoon?'

He answered, 'You.'

Crawled across the carpet to squint at the video recorder and check which day it was. (Oops! Thought it was a Wednesday.) Crawled back to the sofa, nibbled a little more toast, then tucked my legs and wings in to make myself more comfortable – *THE INSECT DIET AND EXERCISE PLAN...*

Brillee-*ANT!* Wonder-*FLEA!* Marve-*LOUSE!* I'm two months closer to my certificate of endurance. I have survived *two whole months* without trying to kill myself or one of my family or a doctor. I'm almost completely immune to the Kit-Kat mugs; they are useful red and white drinking vessels. I am calm and peaceful more than once a week. Well, I was last week anyway.

I want to go to Scotland, I've always fancied a holiday in the Highlands. Why didn't I make the effort when I was well? *WHEN* (I'm not saying *if* any more) I'm well, I will do all the things I just sat and daydreamed about (I don't expect that'll include playing a leading romantic role with Colin Firth though).

A scene in the garden made my heart smile. A blackbird, as black as this morning's burnt toast, was hopping on the rain-washed lawn; daffodils, as yellow as last night's sweetcorn, hung their heads in shame, their yellow dresses were drenched.

Blackbird like
My toast
Daffodils
In a host
Can't decide
When I think of spring
What I like the most

I know:
Easter eggs

Springtime is the land awakening. March winds are the morning yawn.
Lewis Grizzard

Springtime; time to cut the hedge. March winds are last night's veg.
Me

Yellow Chinamen, dressed in green, nodding on the lawn.
Me

Noticed the young leaves on the rose bush near the kitchen window have more colour and shape now.
Unlike me.

Wednesday 2nd

Rain. Wind. Rain. Wind. Rain. Rain. Rain. A little girl and her mum had difficulty holding onto their umbrellas.

Couldn't be bothered to comb the tangles out of my mad March hair this morning; I'm wearing a style to match the season – the windswept overgrown hedge look. I am so in tune with nature these days.

I remember the women I once saw at the Glastonbury pop festival behind the food tent. They were close to nature, and to the vegeburger mix. As they bent over plastic washing-up bowls, mulching the burger mix with their hands, their long hair dangled and sweat dripped from their hairy armpits into the ingredients.

Couldn't face vegeburgers tonight.

Thursday 3rd

A Betterware catalogue flew in through the letter box and landed on the mat. The wind blew, threatening to huff and puff and blow the house down. I was a little piggy raiding the fridge for breakfast.

Read the catalogue while I munched and enjoyed a good laugh at the picture of a woman (smartly dressed with high heels on her new shoes) smiling happily as she dusted the hard-to-reach-areas with a multi-angle telescopic duster and joyfully cleaned the floor with her new aqua-mop *with* handle. Mmmm, perhaps we need a sink freshener or an astro-soft broom *with* handle or a flexible vacuum hose. The Futura Super Sweep carpet sweeper looked really exciting!

Suddenly, the house looked and felt grubby all over. Decided I must try to do a tiny bit of cleaning each day but felt tired just thinking about it. *Weekly Wife* says by spring-cleaning, we are brushing the cobwebs from our lives (hope Sam hasn't read this) and trying to reorder our thoughts and direction, ready to face new challenges. Oh! Well, looks like I'll have to spend the rest of the year going nowhere, my head covered in cobwebs and spiders for earrings.

In Victorian times, on one set week in the year, the whole house had a spring-clean, mostly to get rid of the effects of coal fires during the winter. We have central heating so the house can't look *that* bad. I will forget that Ben smokes, sometimes like an old Victorian chimney.

Friday 4th

There was a strange smell in the house this morning like something had died and was rotting quietly in a corner somewhere; thought maybe I'd died and when I looked in the mirror there would be no reflection, like the couple in the ghostly film *Beetlejuice.*

Sometimes I wake up amazed that I'm still alive. Sometimes I think the sheer effort of trying to keep my sanity will kill me. Sometimes I'm too exhausted to be amazed or think about anything... sometimes. Anyway, I'm not worried about the smell. I expect the rubbish needs putting out.

10.05 a.m. Brewed peppermint tea in a Kit-Kat mug. I'm not thinking about chocolate. I am cured. (Until the P.M.T. monster grabs me in his jaws – he's already got me cornered.)

10.07 a.m. Sniff Ben's coffee jar for a lift.

10.10 a.m. Stare out of window at woman with heavy shopping bags and worried face.

10.13 a.m. Recall being married.

10.14 a.m. Try to forget.

10.15 a.m. The spring-cleaning monster is standing in the kitchen. She is wearing flowery slippers, a frilly forties-style apron, pink Marigold gloves and an up-tight perm. Arms folded, chin tucked in, she raises her eyebrows at the overflowing washing-up bowl – disapproving mother-in-law style. She sniffs, then vanishes. I know she'll be waiting in the bathroom with a bulgy-eyed expression of horror.

10.25 a.m. Ignore spring-cleaning monster in bathroom.

10.26 a.m. Headache.

10.45 a.m. Wash hair with acacia honey shampoo and massage head.

10.50 a.m. Expend so much energy trying to extract acacia honey conditioner from bottle, give up and wrap hair in towel.

10.55 a.m. Will have a lot of trouble trying to comb out tangled hair now.

11.00 a.m. Pull out grey hair, peeping out from under towel.

11.01 a.m. Pluck eyebrow.

11.02 a.m. Pick tooth.

11.03 a.m. Hold hands in basin of warm water to ease pain.

11.05 a.m Sit on edge of bath and think.

11.06 a.m. Must stand on bathroom scales to frighten self into diet.

11.07 a.m. Maybe tomorrow.

11.08 a.m. Won't eat much today.

11.09 a.m. Stare at old make-up and hair scrunchies in wicker basket.

Dear body,
Please get well soon so we
can go shopping in
The Body Shop and treat ourselves.
Me xxx

11.15 a.m. Lie on bed sniffing shampoo bottle and thinking of grand-mother's garden – fragrant flowery thoughts.

11.19 a.m. Wish ceiling was covered in wonderful arty paintings. Wish all ceilings in house were covered in paintings. Maybe ceiling painting was invented by someone who was ill and had to lie down a lot.

11.20 a.m. Think of Sistine Chapel.

11.21 a.m. Maybe I should give Michelangelo a call.

11.25 a.m. Listen to birds singing.

11.26 a.m. Listen to traffic.

11.27 a.m. Try not to listen to sad thoughts.

11.28 a.m. Stare at tangled hair in mirror – looks quite fashionable really!

11.29 a.m. Gather hair to back of head with black velvet scrunchie – even better!

11.30 a.m. Will wear slimming black today.

11.40 a.m. Pity all black clothes look grey.

11.56 a.m. Boxer puppy, down the road, is barking in his garden.

12.05 p.m. Spring-clean four-inch circle on bedroom window so I can see clearly what man over road is doing in his garden. I'm a nosy neighbour now.

12.07 p.m. Boxer puppy is being taken for his lunchtime walkies. He's quite big now and stands like a very solid antique (Queen Anne) coffee table.

12.09 p.m. Sun is shining brightly. Women are wearing lighter-coloured clothes.

12.20 p.m. Dog and master return with carrier bag.

12.21 p.m.   Wonder what is in carrier bag. My nosy neighbourness is going to extremes; one day I'll find myself calling out the window, asking passers by what they've just bought, how much it cost, can they buy me a Kit-Kat next time and post it through the letter box please – I'll leave the money under the stone hedgehog.

12.25 p.m.   Hear clink as Mr. Boxer-face plonks carrier bag on step while opening his front door.

12.26 p.m.   Wonder if he's an alcoholic; he does lurch a bit.

12.27 p.m.   Will watch out for signs of cruelty to dog.

12.28 p.m.   Must have R.S.P.C.A. telephone number handy, just in case.

12.30 p.m.   Must stop watching *Animal Rescue*.
That poor little dog the other week, and the fox, and the duck. And that poor little pony and the badger and the kittens...

1.25 p.m.   Have just spent nearly a whole hour enduring sad thoughts. Will go mad if I don't turn on TV to take my mind off terrible plight of many animals all over the world.

1.40 p.m.   *Neighbours.*

1.51 p.m.   Eat banana.

2.00 p.m.   Not very cheered up.

2.05 p.m.   *Jerry Springer* – even more depressing.

2.10 p.m.   Spring-clean top of telly with bit of tissue.

2.15 p.m.   Stare at clouds and try to think positive.

2.30 p.m.   Long warm aromatherapy bath with seaweed soap. Long think about the seaside and summer holidays and footprints in the sand.

2.36 p.m.   Stare at feet.

2.40 p.m.   Three teardrops drip in bath.

2.44 p.m.   Watch fly crawl about on outside of window pane.

3.05 p.m.   Spring-clean half a tap. Pull face at reflection in tap.

3.14 p.m.   Lie exhausted on bathroom floor wrapped in towel.

3.15 p.m.   Think about Scotland.

3.20 p.m.   Love mountains.

3.21 p.m.   Love mountains of mashed potato.

3.22 p.m.   The clouds today are like mountains of old grey mashed potato, forgotten in the back of the fridge. Think about

	mash and gravy. No energy to mash potatoes – will start using instant mash, tastes like the real thing anyway.
3.26 p.m.	Love mash and gravy. Think about streams flowing down mountains.
4.15 p.m.	Spring-clean spots off middle of bathroom mirror.
4.20 p.m.	Sit on toilet sniffing acacia honey shampoo bottle again. I am calm and peaceful. I am Flora the Roman goddess of flowers, the garden, spring, the embodiment of all nature, queen of all plant life...
4.21 p.m.	Sniff acacia conditioner. I honour all growing things; I celebrate the beauty of spring, new life in my soul and the world around me. I am the flourishing one.
4.22 p.m.	Flush toilet. I am the flushing one.
4.30 p.m.	Stare at spring happening in back garden.
5.00 p.m.	Pick two bits of something off carpet. One bit looks like a crushed spider, hope it's not my friend Sam.
5.02 p.m.	Half fill kettle to save energy.
5.03 p.m.	**MR. KETTLE**

Wish I were like you, Mr. Kettle
You never run out of steam
Last night I was running and laughing
Woke up and it was a dream

5.06 p.m.	Do not butter toast to save energy.
5.07 p.m.	Lie on sofa to save energy.
5.08 p.m.	*Home and Away.*
5.15 p.m.	Rub de-stress geranium and mandarin handcream into tired hands. Mmmm, lovely smell.
5.30 p.m.	Read article about reincarnation in *Weekly Wife.*
5.36 p.m.	I must have been a sniffer dog in my past life.
5.37 p.m.	Hope I had a kind master or mistress.
5.45 p.m.	Stare at clock.
5.46 p.m.	Feel as low as Auntie Sarah's sunken sponge on Uncle Sidney's sixtieth.
5.50 p.m.	*Weekly Wife* surveys show that more people attempt suicide during early spring than at any other time of the year.

6.00 p.m.	Chris Evans (the ginger presenter, not the ginger cat) on Channel Four cheers me up.
6.10 p.m.	Watching one of the bands, I recall the hairy armpit women of Glastonbury. That's me off vegeburgers again.
7.05 p.m.	Do a bit of washing-up. Clothes, sheets and towels need washing too; they will soon be crawling downstairs with the curtains and piling themselves into the washing machine. I wish they would.
7.10 p.m.	Wish I were a man with a wife who loved to cook and clean and take care of me.
7.11 p.m.	Notice ladybird on wood-chip wallpaper.
7.12 p.m.	It's not a ladybird (or ladybug, as the Americans say). It's bigger, and instead of a red coat with black buttons, it's wearing a grey mac with yellow buttons – a big mac on chips, ha, ha.
7.13 p.m.	Tell bug to tuck its wings in properly and stop fidgeting.
7.14 p.m.	Find old postcard and a glass, rescue bug and return it to the wild.
7.15 p.m.	Eat cold leftovers in fridge (my stars were right: Cosmic Colin said I've got a lot on my plate at the moment). If Ben brings chips home after pub tonight, I'll help him eat his leftovers too (will stand on bathroom scales in a couple of weeks' time).
7.20 p.m.	Notice the walking antique coffee table is out again, wagging his tail. This time with a chap who looks like the younger brother of Mr. Boxer-face.
7.21 p.m.	Wonder if he's living with them (Mr. Boxer-face and Mrs. Sheepdog with shaggy blonde perm) or just staying for a while. Maybe he's left his wife or is on the run from the police.
7.35 p.m.	Brother of Mr. Boxer-face returns with very happy looking coffee table.
7.36 p.m.	Cheer up a lot.
7.40 p.m.	Wish people wouldn't ring and not leave a message on the answering machine; I like to know whom I'm ignoring.
7.41 p.m.	Dial 1471. Number withheld. Sulk.
7.42 p.m.	Spring-clean phone with my sleeve.
8.05 p.m.	Forgot to watch *Coronation Street*.

8.06 p.m.	Very moody – don't know what's happening with Deirdre or Spider now. I like eco-friendly, animal-friendly Spider; he reminds me of Shaggy in *Scooby Doo*.
8.36 p.m.	Want to be at pub with Ben and his mates.
8.40 p.m.	Cooker looks like it hasn't been cleaned for fifty years.
9.40 p.m.	Bored and lonely. Pour glass of red wine and hope Ben brings home chips.
10.00 p.m.	Much better.
	Put on Abba tape.
10.15 p.m.	Oh! No! I'll be suffering from Abba-itis all weekend – too late now.
10.20 p.m.	Lie on floor wiggling toes, mouth moving a bit to music at chorus time... 'Dancing Queen... feel the beat of the tambourine... oh yeaaah!'
11.25 p.m.	Ben returns from the deepest, darkest depths of The Blacksmith's Armpit in Sweat Street and sees me lying on the floor.
11.30 p.m.	He lies down beside me and plonks a large bag of hot chips on my tummy. We laugh.
11.31 p.m.	Warm my achy hands on bag of chips and breathe in chippy smell.
Ben:	Why do you look so ill and wiped out?
Me:	I've been spring-cleaning.
Ben:	What, all day?
Me:	No, I had an aromatherapy bath with essence of bergamot to refresh and enliven, and vetiver to stimulate and energise.
Ben	Didn't work did it.
Me:	No.
Ben:	Never mind.
Me:	Whose telephone number is that written on your hand?
Ben:	It's an RS Components stock code, twelve-volt D.P.C.O. relay.
J. Monster:	Oh yeah?

Saturday 5th

The clouds gathered like used tea bags in a sieve about to drip all over the kitchen floor. My bat mobile spun round in the draught from the old sash window. Sam scuttled into a crack in the woodwork. The wind whistled like a tired old man. I had rainy-pre-menstrual-thundering thoughts.

Remembered it was my brother's birthday. I'll make him a card tomorrow and send it first class on Monday; hope there's a stamp left in my purse. Peter has helped me more than anyone in my family. He rarely visits, never phones or pressures me to get well soon. His girlfriend, Lisa, is physically handicapped and he's had a lot of health problems himself over the years, so I expect he understands what it's like to be ill for a long time. Hard to tell with brothers sometimes, maybe he just hates me from the days when I was horrible big sister.

Stared out of window feeling horribly creative.

...Mr. Windergale played draughts with Miss Gentle Breeze. They chased each other under the great door of the gothic mansion and through the long corridors. It was his move; he lifted the bed covers on the four poster. She found him mind blowing...

Sunday 6th

Before I dragged myself out of bed this morning (brain kicking and screaming to be left in the bat cave and monthly pains digging into me like a grave digger plunging a fork into dead, hard soil), I turned over to watch the second hand marching precisely round the face of my bedside clock, like the steps of a child treading on the gaps between paving slabs, not missing one, all the way to school... step... step... tick... tick... tick... **one**... **two**... **three**... what am I doing this... **four**... I feel my life slowly ticking away... tick... tick.... **five**... more minutes and I'll get up... I'm so tired... I'm not interested in... **six**... anymore... I'm not interesting anymore.... this is hell... I want to be in... **seven**... I smell toast... if I don't get up soon, all the bread will have gone... Ben will have... **eight**... it all... tick... tick... time... time... a stitch in time saves... **nine**... times nine is... eighty-one... I feel eighty-one... I can feel myself getting older... getting older by the second... memory is failing... I've forgo... **ten**... what day it is... quiet outside... must be Sunday... tick... tick... when I was... **eleven**... it was so much easier to jump out of bed into my uniform and shovel down porridge ready to walk to school, avoiding the cracks in the pavement... step... step... tick... tick... tick... the second hand moves like the pointer in the hand of the heartless

teacher... you will learn... this... this... this... and this class... **twelve**...
tick... tick... march... march... March... wind... howl... hide...

*... she hid under the bed covers listening to the gale outside, one day she
would spring out of bed again and smile at the world...*

A draught broke Sam Spider's web. He made another one. I made a
card for Peter using a gift catalogue from Cancer Research. Cutting
out lots of miniature photos of birthday cards, I made a collage. The
tiny coloured squares and rectangles looked quite effective on black
card; a fish (Peter is Pisces), a bicycle (he rides a bicycle), balloons,
cakes with candles and a cartoon of a little girl with a baby's-cot-mobile
on her head. The caption read: 'Abigail felt totally up to the minute
with her hands-free mobile.'

Saw a few things I wanted in the catalogue and thought I might
order some birthday cards (I expect I'll like about three out of a pack
of twenty). The beach hut bath mat looked bright and colourful and
cheerful (I could enjoy looking at it while I'm sitting on the toilet). I
envisaged the beach hut bathroom cabinet on the wall above the
basin, but wasn't sure about the jolly sailor wall hooks.

Had a bleak moment when I came across the smart rattan desk
accessories, woven on strong metal frames. I suddenly saw my in-tray at
British Gas hidden under mountains of paperwork, overflowing and
filling half the office, waiting for me to return and sort it all out...
somebody opens a window and the papers fly out into the street and I
have to run around picking them up and spend ten years catching up
on my backlog – with no pay.

Tried to remember the last gas main project I worked on before
I became ill; couldn't remember a thing. I miss the office at Christmas.
I only miss three or four of my colleagues, wonder how they are doing.
Paul and Michael's little boys must be school age now. I hope Clare-
Marie found a boyfriend. Wonder if Ron still has his spotty dogs, if
soppy Sally's husband found out about her affairs and Mandy had
another baby. I miss excited mummies-to-be bringing their strange
black and white scan photos into work: 'That bit's his head, that's his
arm, that's a foot.' Miss the wedding photos: 'That's me mum and dad,
that's me bruvver and 'is wife, that's me cousin, that's me uvver
cousin.' Miss the holiday photos: 'That's me an' 'im on the beach

lookin' like lobsters, that's some weird ruins we went to, borin' they
was but 'e said they was really intrestin.'

My black and white photos of villages in Southern Ireland never
went down too well with the sun-worshipping typists. Wonder if the
dreadful Mrs. Pond has retired now and given the younger women a
break from her insane jealousy. Wonder if Jackie is happy now. I
expect Tracy has remarried and Keith still takes his little girls to the
Brownies.

The wind blew the garden fence down. Ben put it up again. A
gale brought our weird musician friend flying round... his straw-
coloured hair the wildest haystack. A Bhuddist today, Dharma was
impressed I'd befriended a spider.

He slumped his scarecrow body (stuffed with the problems of
the world and riddled with worm-like worries wriggling in the fibres
of his mould-green jumper) on our sofa. Sometimes he wears ashen
grey, or deep and meaningful blue, but usually depression black. He
never smiles; I think he tries to on special occasions but his sulky
mouth above a stubborn chin can't quite manage it. His winter-blue
eyes would never join in anyway; they're a million miles away searching for something somewhere. Now and then they come in to land
above a very serious large nose and *look* at you, if he thinks you've
got something interesting to say; then he'll stare at you with the
bright-eyed intensity of a hawk pin-pointing dinner, pouncing on
your every word, not letting go till you've satisfied his curiosity, or
tearing you to pieces if you anger him. Sometimes he just flies
away... if you're lucky.

I have a few small scars; mostly after using an incorrect musical
phrase in his presence, making a light-hearted joke about a dead serious composer he greatly admires, or his latest dead serious religion.
He's musically brilliant though, a joy (maybe not quite the right word)
to work with. He was a pleasure (no, not the right word either) to
musically create with, playing keyboards in my band when I used to
sing (still really miss preforming).

Monday 7th

Spent a lot of time wall-watching this afternoon. The *Dawn Mist* woodchip paper reminded me of rice pudding; sweet, creamy, delicious,
beautifully lumpy, mouth-watering creamed rice.

Later, I imagined I was a tiny insect walking on the wall and all the lumps were endless hills in a never-ending dry desert. I died of thirst. Tiny micro-vultures ate my flesh. Microscopic armies marched...

... the B&Q army marched over Tornpaper Mountain to defend the damplands of Lower Magnolia. The Do-It-All army of Upper Magnolia were out to conquer all for the giant spider king Arakhenaton. Neither army had heard of the Texas Territorials, who planned to rename Upper and Lower Magnolia the Brilliant Whitelands, with the help of Dulux, the god of all things bright and beautiful.

Somewhere on the outskirts, near Carpetland, Captain Mainwaring of Homebase held a board meeting. The troops gathered and Corporal Jones told everyone not to panic...

Stared at the blank television screen. What a gloomy-greeny-grey. Stagnant pond colour; still, lifeless, in the middle of Grime Wood. It will dry up in the hot weather and cease to exist. Noone will notice. Noone will care. Except the creatures that once lived in it – now homeless or dead from thirst.

I am calm and peaceful, healed and healthy. I love me; I love herb tea; I hate chocolate; I'd hate to be a supermodel. My socks match so I'm balanced; I am not lusting after creamed rice but I am ever so thirsty.

Counted the rain drops as they trickled down the window pane. Had no energy to get a drink so I contemplated opening the window and holding my tongue under the raindrops, quenching my thirst like a capuchin monkey licking water off leaves in the dry season. Counted the seconds between the lightning and the thunder so I could tell how far away the storm was. Listened to the wind whistling like the ghost of a tired old man and thought spooky thoughts. Felt scared and had to force myself to make a mug of calming camomile tea, the taste reminding me of wet grass; not that I used to eat wet grass, but I know what I mean. Maybe I was a horse in my past life and that's why I enjoy the Hay diet, ha, ha.

Dr. Hay is an unfortunate name for a chap who invented a diet. Could have been worse though, Dr. Vomit; but then again, he could have written a diet with Dr. Goodall and called it The V.G. Diet Plan and everyone would say, 'That sounds like a Very Good diet.'

Told Eileen I was a stagnant pond with a need to eat woodchip paper; it's possible I was a horse or a sniffer dog in my past life. I have an urge to murder a family member at P.M.T. time and I'm trying to stay calm and peaceful so I can get well soon but it's really, really hard. She laughed and suggested a diet of rice paper, a trip to the vet, or a visit to the counsellor at the clinic.

Eileen enjoyed her trip to Scotland and brought me back a brilliant bonny present from the Canny Scots Shop, Gretna Service Area on the M74 – a hand-made vegetarian haggis by Macsween of Edinburgh! The tasty-sounding ingredients include: oatmeal, lentils, turnips, onions, carrots, mushrooms and three types of nuts (peanuts, almonds and walnuts). Yum! Written on the carrier bag in olde worlde writing is

---

"Haste Ye Back"

I will ask her to... when I feel a haggis craving coming on. So, she was at Gretna Green huh! Must look on her wedding ring finger next week.

When Eileen opened her drawer to find the appointments book, I spotted two wee tartan packages: Scottish macaroon and Walker's crisp and crumbly pure butter shortbread mounds. Eating for two?

On the way home, Mr. Cheerful-chatty-sometimes-flirty-taxi-man asked me if I got up to anything exciting at the weekend. I said, 'Oh yes, on Saturday I had marmalade instead of honey on my multi-grain toast, started a new bottle of herby shampoo and on Sunday I went on a long adventure into the deep dark depths of handbag land. I discovered a shiny pound coin, an ancient Kit-Kat wrapper and a receipt for three items: hair conditioner, handcream and lip salve – essential items when you're getting old and dried up.' He didn't know what to say, so he laughed and told me I needed to get out more.

Sam Spider noticed *website: http://www.gretnagreen.com* written on the carrier bag as he nonchalantly crawled by, on his way to visit his lascivious lady spider friend with long legs all the way up to her cephalothorax.

Tuesday 8th

Like rain it sounded till it curved
And then I knew 'twas wind
Emily Dickinson

March winds did a better job of blowing the fence down. A page from a newspaper flew across the street and landed on a car windscreen. A crisp packet tap-danced along the gutter. Leaves fluttered like hands of little children waving goodbye to auntie. Ben said he'd put up a new fence at the weekend and hammered a stick into the ground to hold the old one up for now.

Wednesday 9th

Cold in the earth, and fifteen wild Decembers
From those brown hills have melted into Spring.
Emily Brontë

The fence blew down again. When Ben came home, he ignored it and had one of my calming herb teas; it didn't work. He disappeared into www dot land and it wasn't long before smoke drifted out from under the door.

A blackbird, black as a Monday depression, eyes as bright as yellow street lamps, flew under the bush at the end of the garden with his prize lump of bread. He pecked. And pecked. I watched the prize lump become small raffle ticket gifts.

... three sparrows hurried across the village hall to the stage to claim their winnings. A sad snail said he nearly had the right number but even if he won, some bird would try and pick him up on his way to collect it...

Thursday 10th

I really like daffodils, they are yellow
and very very pretty.
Emily (aged ten)

I wandered ~~lonely~~ down the garden path when the sunlight came out to play on the lawn. Next door's purple, yellow and white crocuses trembled in a row, like children on stage in a Nativity play. Their garden is neat and tidy; our garden is wild and overgrown, and in need of a makeover: a little blusher here, a touch of colour there, a good pluck and all over trim.

Ben lay in the bath tonight reading *Private Eye* and didn't mention the fence. I lay on the bath mat staring up at the woodchip ceiling, trying not to think of creamed rice, while Ben read out the funny bits. We laughed.

It made a pleasant change to look at a different ceiling; I know all the ceilings in this house very well indeed. I've thought of hanging up more mobiles or asking Ben to stick posters and beer mats on the ceiling, like in the olde worlde pub I used to go to in the village of West Farleigh. It was really cosy with comfortable armchairs, warm lamplight and walls covered in arty paintings. There were pickled eggs on the bar. Pickled old men waited for another packet of peanuts to be purchased so they could see more of the bimbo baring her bits in a bikini. Cosy couples giggled and whispered in corners. Married couples ignored each other and tried to make conversation with other couples.

Ben used to hang out in the public bar with his mates. An old juke box played 'Stairway To Heaven', 'House of the Rising Sun', 'Sultans of Swing', 'Strawberry Fields'... bar billiards, shove ha'penny and an ancient video arcade game added to the character. The carpet had a lot of character too.

It's a Beefeater restaurant now with the same atmosphere as MacDonald's on a Saturday afternoon.

Friday 11th

11.46 a.m. Open *Weekly Wife*. Read 'The Busy Woman's Firm and Tone Plan'. Turn page over.

11.47 a.m. 'Step by Step Cookery': 'Brandy Alexander, a delicious and convenient finale to your dinner party. This rich chocolate pie can be turned...' Turn page quickly and repeat affirmations.

11.48 a.m. The Easter issue of *Weekly Wife* is going to be hell. I just know it!

11.49 a.m. Read about pollution on our beaches, the dangers of steroids, cruelty to animals and 'Dear Sue: We said our last goodbye... Where did I go wrong... I've lost everything.'

11.58 a.m. Tearful. These mags should include free tissues and a bar of choccy to help you through them.

11.59 a.m. There's a free sachet: some sort of beauty treatment.
I will be sad and beautiful and interesting.

2.36 p.m. Wash pale face.

2.40 p.m. Gently smooth super-hydrating triple-action anti-wrinkle,
anti-UV ageing positive action fluid with moisturising
agents over my cheeks, chin and forehead.

2.43 p.m. Massage soothing extracts of something, nourishing
extracts of something else and natural extracts of passion-
flower over my eyes.

2.44 p.m. I can see the start of lasting confidence, a soft youthful
complexion, freedom from multiple fine lines, multiple
orgasms, multiple dermolipids and multiple fatigue from
all this face massaging.

2.46 p.m. All the positive triple-action and multiple-active agents
running about on my face would make a good *James Bond*
film.

3.44 p.m. Rummage through bathroom cabinet, crammed full of old
bottles, jars, pots and tubes I'll never use again. Must have
a clear-out one day...

Ben went down The Gold Finger in Bond Street with Rob and Bob the
Slob who are forty-something guitarists (still think they are twenty-
something rock stars) and play in a local band, Black Pizza. Rob wears
faded pop-concert T-shirts from the seventies when he's not wearing
jumpers lovingly knitted by his wife Bev, with musical notes and treble
clefs on. She knits matching ones for their blonde twins, Debbie and
Harry.

Bob the Slob is single, with a girlfriend in every pub. Tracy in The
Thirsty Tongue Tavern, Nicole in The Frog and Beret Bar and Fiona
in The Fizz and Nipple Wine Bar to name a few. He wears his belly outside his jeans and bits of chip in his beard, but he has charm and a
smile as wide as a crocodile who's just eaten someone's Kentucky Fried
Chicken and the 'someone'... for afters. He calls his pet rats the Spice
Girls and his tarantula Tina Turner. I wonder if she struts up and down
her tank singing, 'What's love got to do, got to do with it?'... swinging
her cephalothorax.

Saturday 12th

Ben spent the afternoon putting up a new fence. I supplied him with calming herb teas he didn't want.

Strange nightmares tortured me last night (what's new). Hundreds of tiny James Bonds were chased by the dreaded dermo-lipids, spots exploded everywhere and deep multiple cracks appeared in the sun-baked earth. Suddenly there was a blinding white flash! *Vogue* magazine were taking shots of me first thing in the morning for 'How to live with a face like yours!', 'How to beat the bathroom blues!' and 'What Do you look like!'

The nightmares continued. I climbed endless rope ladders in the sky with a heavy mud face-pack weighing me down. James Bond tried to rescue me but bits of face pack cracked and fell onto his head and knocked him out. Somehow I reached the top of the ladder and started picking my way across grated chocolate on a mountain-sized slice of gâteau. I slipped, fell, and found myself trapped in a creamy, curly bit with a cherry on top.

Is this a sign of my inner struggle for health, are there chocolate crumbs on my pillow or did I tuck me blankets in too tightly again.

Ben complained of backache and didn't feel like computering or cooking tonight so we had a Chinese take-away, watched telly and enjoyed an interesting, long, thought provoking conversation.

Me:	That's *him* isn't it?
Ben:	Who?
Me:	Umm you know er... he was in that sitcom in the seventies, or maybe it was the early eighties.
Ben:	Oh yes, whatsit-thingummy-doodah.
Me:	The one with Penny and... er...
Ben:	Vince.
Me:	Yes, Vince! That was his name; I used to fancy him.
Ben:	Nice mushrooms in this sauce... mmmm.
Me:	Mmm, tasty beansprouts, what sauce is that?
Ben:	Black bean... can you pass the eggy rice?
Me:	Mmm...munch...munch.
Ben:	Thought I saw him on a train the other day.
Me:	Wha... really?
Ben:	No, not exactly *on* the train. He was grinning out of *Hello*

magazine on the seat next to me, or was it *Alright* magazine, you know, one of those with lots of big, flashy photos, celeb lies and gossip and posh people posing at parties. Mr. Henry Palmolive-Tomcatson with his girlfriend Miss Honour de Shag Pile, pictured above.

Me: He always did like a bit of young fluff, the old goat.

Ben: He'll walk all over her.

Me: Miss May de Forcbe Withyou, pictured below right.

Ben: At Sci-Fi Fashion Show.

Me: Munch, munch, munch, Janet de Maincourse Withrelish.

Ben: Munch, munch, ha-ha, cough, cough, cough.

Me: Derwent de Wrongway Down.

Ben: Cough, cough.

Me: Waste of money those magazines.

Ben: Yeah.

Me: Er... can you get me *Hello*, just something to look at, I won't have to read much so it'll save on eye-muscle-energy.

Ben: OK.

Me: Yes, that one will do if they've run out of *Hello*.

Ben: What?

Me: I don't like Vince in this programme; he's all serious and bossy. I keep waiting for him to make a joke. It's so annoying, a bit like Julie Andrews trying to play a sexy part. How *could* she do that to us Mary Poppins fans!

Ben: Didn't he make a record?

Me: Yes, dreadful, something about dancing with a captain... crunch, crunch.

Ben: Slurp... awful record, bet you sang along to it though.

Me: Might have.

Ben: He's knocking on a bit now, isn't he?

Me: I keep expecting Penny to appear... what *was* his name in real life?

Ben: Didn't he used to call her Pen?

Me: Oh yes, and she had that awful mother. I really liked his mother though!

Ben: Nice noodles.

Me: Mmm.

Ben: Wasn't he in *Cats*?

Me:	I think so, but I've never seen it.
Ben:	Munch, munch, crunch, crunch.
Me:	I don't fancy him any more.
Ben:	What *is* his name?
Me:	What *was* that programme?
Ben:	Isn't that...
Me:	Yes, Cindy from *EastEnders*; she's looking old now too.
Ben:	Weird to see her in something else; I keep expecting to see Ian appear, scowling in a chipshop doorway.
Me:	Ha, ha, yes.
Ben:	That Greek bloke she's talking to, wasn't he in...
Me:	Yes! The one with Sharon and Tracy.
Ben:	That was really good. I liked Doreen, the nosy next door neighbour.
Me:	Yeah, brilliant. A couple of times when they filmed outside Maidstone prison, you could see my ex-boyfriend's mother's house in County Road and the corner shop where I bought chocolate on the way home from work when I had a flat in Boxley Road.
Ben:	I've been in that shop and the pub up the road.
Me:	Oh, yes. I forgot about the pub. Not a very memorable pub. I remember spending a birthday there, talking to my ex's mother. Not a very memorable birthday.
Ben:	Munch, munch, munch... slurp.
Me:	My ex said he used to watch me wander up the road past the prison, weighed down with Safeway carrier bags (probably full of cat food and coleslaw) before we got together. He must have seen me chomping through a Topic or a Kit-Kat or Chocolate Buttons or a Bounty bar or a Flake or a *20 percent extra* Mars Bar on a bad day. How embarrassing.
Ben:	I recognise that actress.
Me:	She was a maid in that period-drama-type-series thing. Susan Hampshire was in it and this other maid was hanged for murder, the one who is in *Coronation Street* now.
Ben:	I know! *The Grand*.
Me:	Yes! That was it. That girl (who was a maid in *The Grand* with the one who got hanged who is in *Coro* now) is the daughter

(in real life) of the skinny, tarty woman in *Coro* who was married to the Irish chap who drank a lot... can't remember...

Ben: Jim McDonald.

Me: That's him!... What was I saying?

Ben: You've missed the end.

Me Oh...

Munch...

Crunch...

Ben: Paul Nicholas!!!

Sunday 13th

Enjoyed a Scottish Sunday lunch: vege – haggis and veg washed down with Glen Mor mineral water from the Highlands and Lulu in an *Ab Fab* video.

Weird musician friend called round about three o'clock. Ben stood, fag in mouth (with his Billy Connolly in-a-temper look) daring the fence to fall down and weird musician friend (Dharma) did a Highland fling on the path, avoiding any insects or snails. Ben made him a sandwich and I asked if he knew which side his bread was Bhudda'd.

Had a long rest on the bed and later joined the lads, who were listening to the Scottish band Capercaillie and drinking Glenfidditch single malt. We talked about past lives and music and whisky, music and mountains, music and reincarnation and whisky.

W. M. Friend: I was a composer in a past life, I'm sure of it.

Me: I want to be a thin compulsive eater in my next life.

Ben: Don't you know someone who's had hypnosis and discovered their past life?

Me: Yes, Eileen. Her name was Isobel and, do you know, the name suits her!

W. M. Friend: Really?

Me: Mm spookee, eh!

W. M. Friend: What's the name of this band?

Me: Capercaillie.

W. M. Friend: Capa-what!?

Ben: Here's the CD.

W. M. Friend: What's it mean?

Me: Ah... the capercaillie is a large, old-world black grouse... a horse of the wood.

Ben: (Slurps whisky) A horse in a wood?

Me: A very small, feathery horse!

W. M. Friend: Caperrrrcailllieee.

Me: Drrrrambuiee.

W. M. Friend: *Dram* means drink and *buidh* means pleasing in Gaelic.

Ben: (Lying on the floor) Yesh... a very pleashing drink, mate!

W. M. Friend: (Dancing round room) This is a very groovy track; what's it called?

Me: Alasdair Mhic Cholla Ghasda.

W. M. Friend: Oh.

Ben: He's not going to ask what it means.

Me: Good, I haven't got a clue.

W. M. Friend: (Grabbing my hand) Come'n dance.

Me: (Getting up and wiggling a bit) Co ni mire rium!

W. M. Friend: Eh?

Me: Will you flirt with me?

W. M. Friend: Yeah.

Me: Oh, goody, ha, ha, ha.

W. M. Friend: (Draining his glass) Let's all go to Scotland!

Ben: And climb a wee mountain.

Me: I'm about to climb a mountain for a wee.

W. M. Friend: Let's climb right to the top!

Me: Top up anyone?

Ben: Yep, right to the top!

W. M. Friend: (Collapsed on sofa) Drrraaamm.... buidhhh..... drrrramm........ bhuddahh.........

Ben: There's a horsee...in the woodahh...

Me: I feel a wee verse comin' on!

There's a Bhudda
In the wood a
Capercaillie
In the fern
If you're not used
To Drambuie
Then your wee throat
It will burn

Monday 14th

Rain. Rain. Rain. Rain. Rain. Rain. Rain. Rain. Rain.

Rain. Rain. Rain. Rain. Rain. Rain. Rain. Rain. Rain.

Rain. Rain. Rain. Rain. Rain. Rain. Rain. Rain. Rain.

Rain. Rain. Rain. Rain. Rain. Rain. Rain. Rain. Rain.

Rain. Rain. Rain. Rain. Rain. Rain. Rain. Rain. Rain.

People passed by with umbrellas braced against the wind. I watched the clouds: gunmetal grey clouds, shooting across the sky. I saw puddles in the pavement: gunmetal grey pavement. I looked at the faces of the people: grim mental grey looking people... a man shot his wife with a dark glance.

A large, jolly-looking lady with an equally large, bright umbrella, the colours of the rainbow, bounced by. I laughed and snapped out of my wet-weather mood.

Found a small collection of hair and beauty sachets saved from *Weekly Wife* (waste not, want not). Decided to *do* something with my mad March hair and washed it with shampoo that reaches parts others don't; I wonder if it contains lager. (I had a beer rinse at The Sticky Carpet Tavern once, made my hair really shiny!)

Massaged Timotei rich replenishing conditioner with almond milk for creamy soft supple silkiness into my scalp. Felt very tired. Lay on the bath mat to let conditioner do its job. After a rinse, I flopped on to the bed and daydreamed.

... she awoke to find herself wandering through long grass, watching the sun sparkle on a stream by a watermill in Ireland; her hair long and flowing, beautifully cut and blonde...

Eileen had trouble treating my head. It kept slipping out of her hands: my hair was *so* shiny and *so* conditioned. Afterwards, I slipped next door to see the counsellor, Georgie (I need to know if I'm going mad).

Too tired to write any more. Just remembered it was Mother's day yesterday.

Tuesday 15th

Rang Mum. She was out. Forgot to ring again. Rang Interflora. Mum needs cheering up.

Weekly Wife... 'Step by Step cookery: Chocolate profiterole ring, choux pastry filled with brandy-flavoured whipped cream and covered in rich chocolate...' WHY do I torture myself!

When I met the counsellor last night I resisted the urge to sing, 'Hey there! Georgie girl' and ask her if she were always window shopping but never stopping to buy (love those old Seekers songs).

As Georgie bounded down the corridor to greet me, her glossy brown perm flopped on her shoulders like springer spaniel ears. She smiled at me with excitable eyes and lots of big shiny teeth; I resisted the urge to ask for her paw.

I was ordered to *sit* then watched her padding around her kennel-sized room sniffing and muttering about being all in a tizz. Finally, curling up in a large old leather chair, she barked at me *never* to turn up late or drunk and informed me I had to sign a contract for five more sessions. Felt like a lazy, pathetic drunk who couldn't make a commitment before we even started... have noticed she has a lot of male clients.

Eileen's treatment had made me rather dozy so I started to drift off a bit until Georgie barked, 'How do you rate your sex life in terms of percentages?' Did I ask for shock treatment? Do I look mad? Can my nerves take this stress? And there was I thinking counsellors were kind, understanding, sensitive types, unlike a lot of doctors I've met. I told her my sex life was 100 percent good and tried to hide my long nose in a tissue; I wasn't going to tell the truth and set myself up for the next question: 'Do tell me about the other 90 percent dear.' It was obvious she wasn't sure whether to believe me, but I know my illness is the reason for any problems and I didn't want to get into a detailed discussion with her, especially with her insensitive approach. The torture continued and ended with orders to write down my dreams for next week's session.

As I left, feeling shattered, tail between my legs, I noticed a collection of ~~root~~ rude vegetables on the window sill and a print of a painting by Beryl Cook: a lady in stockings and suspenders. Closing the door behind me, I heard her moaning on the phone; she must have had a bone to pick with someone. I think Georgie is barking mad.

This is good. Makes me feel quite sane. Woof!

I told Ben my counsellor thinks he's a 100 percent lover and she is looking forward to meeting him. He said he was sorry but he would have to work late the next five Monday evenings.

Wednesday 16th

It's light at six o'clock in the evenings now; summer is hiding round the corner but she's not ready to come out yet.

Capital Radio played sunny sounds from the eighties today, reminding me of the days when I sang and danced and got drunk at parties; I didn't know what was waiting around life's corner. I saw a clairvoyant in those days. Anne somebody. She predicted a few things correctly about my twenties and when she came to my thirties she went all quiet and said nothing. Now I know why. I'm glad she didn't tell me what was in store for me; but maybe if she had, I could have taken things easier. I don't know. You can't change what is going to happen, what is meant to be, can you?

What was I talking about? Oh yes, Capital Radio. I listened to a few songs but had to turn the radio off: Chris Tarrant's voice got on my nerves. A lot.

I don't listen to the radio much these days. I'm fed up with getting up to turn off the news or resisting the urge to dance to good tunes or wanting to cry at sad ones and wishing I weren't such a stupid, emotional old bag. I'm tired (fed up with that word too) of silence and noisy thoughts in my brain. Wish I had a little switch on my ear so I could simply turn a thought off. Think I'll have the radio on low and turn it up at good bits. I'll dance with my hands, like the ninety-year-old conductor who can't lift his arms anymore but has some movement left in his long bony fingers. He can only just hear the music and nods his head a little, his mind hearing Beethoven instead of Boyzone. He is the only man in the nursing home, surrounded by ladies in waiting, to die. There's a television always on in the room; an audience applauds a game show; he hears *his* audience, takes a bow, and slowly falls out of his chair.

Saw the end of a programme about people with disabilities. I'm so very, very lucky I had a life before I became ill. Had a little cry for those people. Felt better.

I want to stand on a Scottish mountain in a long velvety cloak, the wind in my hair, looking tragic yet beautiful like the women in

Renaissance paintings or a Scottish widow. Then have a wee dram o'whisky in The Spit and Sporran to drroon ma sorrows.

Found an interesting-looking carrot in the vegetable rack and carefully arranged it on the work surface with two tomatoes at one end. Ben said the counselling is having a bad effect on me. By the time he flopped into bed he was too tired to live up to his new reputation; I was too tired to care.

Thursday 17th

A perfect sunshine blue St. Patrick's green day.

Sat on the garden bench drying my hair by sunlight for the first time this year. Lifted my face to the sun, breathed deeply and thought tranquil, beatific, celestial thoughts to boost my immune system.

Recalled the St. Patrick's day parades in London, wearing my shamrock and eating Auntie Mary's fairy cakes with green icing on. Green icing fascinated me when I was small. I love green.

I LOVE GREEN

The green of hills and trees
Sprout, broccoli and peas
The triangles in Quality Street
Peppermint foot cream for your feet
The colour of bottles of gin
The foil they wrap Aero in

GREEN

Green candle in a holder
A paint stain on your shoulder
The felt pen in my hand
The seaweed on the sand
The green upon a duck
A sham-a-rock for luck
Icing on Mary's cake
Grass you left in the rake
The blossoming of spring
The emerald in my ring

... think I'm going on a bit too much. Julie Andrews, eat your heart out.

Saw my first bumble bee of the year and found a family of woodlice under an ancient pair of gardening gloves on the window ledge. I don't know how I handle all this excitement. We're using kitchen roll with a new flowery springtime pattern on too!

Friday 18th

Stood at the kitchen window clutching my mug of peppermint tea and watched the greenfinches feeding. I forgot to put them in my verse and I can't think of anything to rhyme with finches anyway.

As Ben crawled in through the front door tonight, he said he had seen Georgie at The Fizz and Nipple Wine Bar down Sipit Street on a girls' night out. After several medium drys and a fizzy white, she winked at him *and* she wasn't wearing a bra under her see-through top.

Saw my first ant of the year.

Saturday 19th

A sunny Holland & Barrett day.

2.00 p.m.   Sit outside crunching my healthy health shop treats, watching mother birds feeding their babies and using Ben's fence as a toilet (the birds, not me).

2.45 p.m.   A surprise phone call from Dave and Nicky. It's 3.45 a.m. in New Zealand. Strange to talk to friends on the other side of the world who have just come back from late night partying. They are delighted with the jars of Marmite we sent them and invite us to stay at their new home in Christchurch. We'd love to, one day, when I'm well and earning lots of money.

4.00 p.m.   Scribble kiwi fruit on next week's shopping list.

4.15 p.m.   Daydream about a holiday in New Zealand.

4.20 p.m.   The Kinks are singing 'I'm so tired, tired of waiting' on local BBC radio.

5.30 p.m.

Me: I'd like to see a koala bear. One of my tutors at college had one as a pet before she came to England. She said it cried

	tears when she told it off.
Ben:	Really?
Me:	Yes!... I'd love to see kangaroos and kiwi too.
Ben:	Are kiwi like those birds you see on Penguin books? Oh, no. I mean puffins.
Me:	Look on the shoe polish tin under the stairs, dear.

Sunday 20th

Endured Kiwi and Aussie nightmares all night long. Kangaroos jumped on my head, kiwi pecked in my ears and koala bears sat weeping in eucalyptus trees. Woke up tearful with a thumping headache and an urge to polish my boots.

My head hurts. My life hurts. My past hurts. My boots need polishing. My parents dropped in. I looked like a dropout. They didn't stay long.

Monday 21st

Tonight's counselling session was what I expected and worse. Last week, I mentioned my art college training and a book I own about Salvador Dali. My first mistake. Georgie asked to see it this week.

The book is large (cushion-size) and very heavy, with many sections showing drawings and paintings on the subject of religion, mysticism and all sorts. *It just happened* to fall open on her ample lap at the erotic section full of huge colourful paintings with naughty bits in. I nearly died. *WHY, WHY, WHY* me, Lord?

Georgie eagerly studied the paintings (I was waiting for her to wag her tail and start panting) and asked me which one was my favourite. My pink face laughed nervously. I hadn't even studied them myself, *HONESTLY!* Well, all right just a teeny bit. I find a lot of Dali's paintings rather disturbing, with all his insects, entrails, blood, war and crucifixion! Georgie smiled and acted as though she'd found a whole pile of skeletons in my cupboard. Her eyes widened. She fidgeted. I tried to draw her attention to the pictures I preferred: the *Metamorphosis of Narcissus,* the clever sketches of Dali's wife and the strange lonely paintings with crutches (the wooden sort for support) melting watches and telephones.

This didn't work.

The torture continued as she nipped at me with sharp-toothed questions. I threw a metaphorical stick; she ran after it but sniffed at it and wandered off to follow a more interesting male scent.

Considered throwing up to distract her.

I remembered to bring my W. H. Smith's recycled notepad full of the past week's dreams. My second mistake. Georgie said some of my nightmares were like Dali paintings (this is true, but only the lonely ones) and wanted to know if I'd had any naughty ones. I said I hadn't and hid my nose in a tissue again: I wasn't going to tell her about the dream where I sat on Margate beach eating a chocolate novelty willy. She'd have really got her teeth into that, and probably asked me if I had bitten, chewed or sucked the end till the novelty wore off.

In many of my dreams, I am caring for small children and animals; apparently this means I'm really caring for myself. After a while, I felt relieved I'd thrown her off the scent. For the time being.

On my way home, the sight of trees, their branches weighed down with marshmallow blossoms, lightened my spirits.

Mr. Miserable-as-sin-taxi-man was coughing and grumbling so I thought I'd make a bit of cheery conversation. I asked him if he had a frog jumping about in his throat, made a comment about the rain washing the blossom away, and wasn't it a shame. He turned his grimy little head towards me and gave me an is-that-all-you've-got-to-worry-about-you-stupid-little-cow sort of look. Hope he chokes to death on a big fat warty toad.

Over dinner (veggie toad in the hole) I told Ben how I nearly died a second time when Georgie started naming all the naughty private parts she found in the Dali paintings.

Ben: Did she say that 'V' word?

Me: Yes.

Ben: Do you need a new jar of *Regina* Royal Jelly capsules?

Me: Ha! Ha! Yes, please. She kept saying that horrible word for willy beginning with 'P' too and pointing at the naked men.

Ben: What, plonker?

Me: No, you know, Dennis with a 'P' and one 'N'.

Ben: Are you going back next week?

Me: Don't know.

Ben: Let's have a look at that book.

Me: Take it, I never want to see it again.

Ben: Hmmm, can't see what she got so excited about.

Me: Nor can I.

Ben: Oh dear, yes I can.

Me: Oh no! I forgot about *those* pictures, it's so many years since I looked at the book.

Ben: Hey, look at this! She's sniffing his...

Me: Oh, God, no wonder Georgie...

Ben: And that statue of a woman is squirting milk out of her...

Me: I can't bear to look, turn the page quickly, *please!*

Ben: This one's good isn't it?

Me: Yes, yes, brilliant sketch of his wife, Gala.

Ben: *LOOK AT THAT!*

Me: *WOW*, can't believe the detail... the colours... amazing...

Ben: Are that couple having a...

Me: Er–yes.

Ben: No wonder...

Me: I know. Please don't remind me.

Ben: Why has he painted that weird body full of drawers?

Me: I don't know. Something about secrets locked inside us maybe.

Ben: He says here, 'How do you expect my enemies, my friends, and the public in general to understand the meaning of the images that appear suddenly and which I reproduce in my pictures, when I myself, who am the one who makes them, I don't understand them either?'

Me: And he says here, 'I have therefore constantly followed the

	classical way, while still experimenting in a parallel direction.'
Ben:	'...Thus the mystical substance, by its high density and immobility, reaches an objective, pre-explosive state in a paroxysm. And matter becomes energy through dematerialisation, or spiritualisation.'
Me:	Does go on a bit, doesn't he?
Ben:	Bit of a nutter.
Me:	Very brilliant, talented nutter! I expect being a gay Catholic, married to a woman in the early nineteen hundreds, sent him a bit...
Ben:	Yeah, look at that painting of a dead rat dripping with blood in a baby's mouth and the entrails being dragged out of that body.
Me:	Mmm, very nice. No wonder Georgie kept giving me strange looks with her eyes all bulgy!!
Ben:	What's this?
Me:	*Still Life by Moonlight.*
Ben:	Are you sure?
Me:	No.
Ben:	Says here, 'I believe that I am the saviour of modern art, the only one who can sublimate, integrate, and rationalize, in an imperial manner and with beauty, all the revolutionary experiences of modern times.'
Me:	Oh. Nice to be confident.
Later	
Me:	Did you know Henri de Toulouse-Lautrec was a descendant of French aristocracy and died in his mother's castle at the age of thirty-six?
Ben:	No, I thought all those old artists died in poverty.
Even later	
Me:	Do you remember that chocolate willy you bought me at Margate and I tried to eat it on the train without the other passengers noticing because I just *had* to have chocolate.
Ben:	Yeah, you bit the end off thinking it was hollow and would be easily gobbled up, but it was solid.
Me:	I had a lot of trouble trying to eat it without moving my mouth too much, while giggling and avoiding Miss Disaproval's glare over *Weekly Knitting.*

Ben: The other passengers looked really interested in the view out of the window or their kneecaps.

Pause

Ben: We'll go to Margate when you're better.

Me: Yeah, maybe next summer.

Ben: Or the one after that.

Me: Or the one after that.

Tuesday 22nd

A health psychologist at Sheffield Hallam University claims that more light enters the pineal gland in the brain as the days get longer; this lifts our mood and makes us feel more energetic, enthusiastic and creative.

> **Dear God,**
> **Please make my pineal gland work better and I promise to use my creative talents more.**
> **Love, me x x x**
>
> **P.S. Instead of being ~~bloody~~ oops! miserable at P.M.T. time I will attempt to harness my wonderful pre-menstrual forces for creative endeavour; i.e. lots of miserable poetry and maybe a book, before my brain shrivels up like a dried walnut found behind the sofa six months after Christmas.**
>
> **P.P.S. Please make my neck, hands and eyes better so I can: paint pictures instead of wasting my time, create a beautiful herb garden instead of staring at a dried up lawn all summer and cook fantastic gourmet meals using my herbs creatively and enthusiastically, e.g. a swirl of cream and a sprig of basil on tomato soup, chives as an attractive garnish on salads, mint on potatoes (parsley to disguise my smelly garlicky breath) and, if I'm feeling very adventurous, lemon variegated thyme on fruit salads.**

I'm looking forward to my appointment with a doctor in Tunbridge Wells tomorrow. I've waited months and months to see her. A friend of a friend with M.E. said this doctor helped her a lot in the past. Feeling quite excited.

After my bath I lay on the bathroom floor with a towel under my head and recalled past experiences with doctors. Gave myself a headache. Remembered being dismissed from my job. Remembered ringing into work to tell my colleagues I thought I had M.E. Remembered hearing them calling out, 'Yuppie Flu', and laughing.

I could do with a Cadbury's Cream Egg now. Soon the shops will be jam-packed with chocolate eggs, always a difficult time of year for me. I feel like a smoker who's given up smoking and suddenly the shops are full of enormous glossy colourful tempting packets of cigarettes with bunnies and chicks on. Luckily, I only see the window display in the mini-market on Mondays, but I can feel all that chocolate out there just waiting to be unwrapped and consumed. The delightfully-exciting-alluring smell as you unfold the foil... the egg falls apart to reveal treasure in a cellophane casket... the snap as you break pieces off... some thick... some thin... you save some for later... but later is never far away...

Wednesday 23rd

Anger.   *Frustration.*   Pain.   Pain.   *Frustration.*   *Anger.*
Pain.   Pain.   *Anger.*   *Frustration.*   Pain.   Pain.   *Anger.*
Frustration.   Pain.   Pain.   Pain.   *Anger.*   *Anger.*   Pain.
Pain.   *Frustration.*   *Frustration.*   Pain.   Pain.   Anger.

Thursday 24th

8.00 a.m.	So alone.
9.00 a.m	Zombie.
10.00 a.m.	Numb.
11.00 a.m.	Eyes stare at nothing.
12.00 noon	Brain blank.
1.00 p.m.	I'll never speak again.
2.00 p.m.	I'll never move again.
3.00 p.m.	I've had it with life.
4.00 p.m.	I'm finished.
5.00 p.m.	Done for.

6.00 p.m.	I give up.
7.00 p.m.	Ask Ben to buy red wine, Bournville Plain and six Cadbury's Cream Eggs from corner shop.
8.00 p.m.	Need the iron anyway.

Friday 25th

Saturday 26th

> *It's such a little thing to weep*
> *So short a thing to sigh...*
> **Emily Dickinson**

> *I weep huge, heavy buckets of tears*
> *I sigh big, long, noisy sighs*
> **Me**

Think I will write a will.

Sunday 27th

I leave everything to Ben.

Watch Charles Bronson for half an hour in *Death Wish II*.

Monday 28th

Cancelled counselling session: couldn't face more torture. Didn't cancel osteopath session, and Eileen released all my tense, achy muscles. Told her about being treated (yet again) like a silly schoolgirl by ~~witch bitch~~ doctor; she was sympathetic. Felt much better. Bought the biggest Easter egg I could find for Ben at the stores next door.

Tore up suicide note.

Tuesday 29th

Awoke to find the garden having a dress rehearsal for April showers.

> *... everything had to be perfect for the big night; the daffodil dancers practised in the West End of the garden, bent with exhaustion and dripping with sweat...*

Tried not to think about the egg-shaped thing in a box I've hidden from myself. Received a nice letter from Artie Auntie. Had a nice read of 'I Lost Everything' in *Weekly Wife*. Had a nice cry. Somebody died in *Neighbours*. Another little cry. A dog was put down in *Pet Rescue*. Used five pieces of kitchen roll with leaf pattern on. Stole three of Ben's cigarettes and smoked them.

Wednesday 30th

Very pale, puffy eyed and coughing with a bad taste in my mouth, I looked extra ~~terrestrial~~ terrible first thing. So did the kitchen. Decided I could do something about the kitchen and accidentally broke Sam Spider's web in the process. Overdid it again. Sam said it served me right. Something cried out, 'Eat me, eat me, eat me,' from the back of the cupboard.

Thursday 31st

The other day my stars said the wonderful spring equinox that lights up my sign is not to be ignored and it's the beginning of a radiant period for me, when my confidence swells and creativity shines through all I do. Well, there's nothing radiant about my periods and it's my belly that swells, not my confidence, but my creativity will shine if I polish up my writing skills.

Wrote lots of miserable murderous poetry this afternoon. Blamed P.M.T. Ate Ben's Easter egg, all the chocolates inside, and enjoyed a wonderful chocolate high singing along to the Bee Gees... 'Staying alive, staying alive'. Experienced post-choc-blues: worried I might become a murderer. Don't want to go to prison; I'm already imprisoned in my body. Watched Sam Spider make a new web. *He* never gives up.

Ben has been working late quite a lot recently, he looks extra tired and has been catching the bus home from the train station instead of walking. Tonight, he complained about the fat, domineering, gossipy old woman he often ends up sitting next to on the bus. I said he's lucky he wasn't in the sea millions of years ago when the Megaladon, a gigantic shark the size of a Greyhound bus, dominated the ocean. He said she is much, *much* more threatening.

Miserable Murderous Poetry – without a title:

I want to kill my doctor
He won't listen to me
Don't know how many times I've told him
I think I have M.E.
I want to kill my doctor
Want him to feel my pain
Listen and take notice
Of the things I have to say
I want to kill my doctor
And when he's good and dead
He will have paid the price
For the tears that I have shed

———————

I want to kill
My boyfriend
Why is he
Working late
Is he very busy
Or has he got

A date
I want to kill
My boyfriend
And when
He's dead and gone
I'll discover
I've got it all
Wrong

———————

I want to kill myself
I can't stand the pain
Sleeping in my body
Snoring in my brain
I want to kill myself
And when I'm good
And dead
I'll never know
If I could have
Recovered
And continued
To burn my toast
And I will be a very
A very very
Sad ghost

SAD GHOST

Standing in the doorway
Sitting on a chair
It really doesn't matter
He won't know I'm there
Wailing like a banshee
Cobwebs in my hair
Weeping like a willow
Nobody will care
He won't know I'm there

Have started my herb garden, sort of; there's a garlic bulb sprouting in the vegetable rack.

Friday 1st

9.00 a.m.   Another morning. Another month. Same me. Same M.E. Same room. Same clock, second hand ticking tirelessly... tick... tick... tick... like a long, thin, white, pointy-nailed finger... tap... tap... tap... on a cauldron... one frog, one snail, one puppy dog's tail; that's what little boyfriends are made of. Two birds peck at the overgrown herb garden... peck... peck... peck... water drips from cottage eaves after April rain... drip... drip... drip... the witch's garden has survived another storm... I've survived *three months* of the year... I've survived three minutes of wakefulness today... tick... tick... tick... a big warty toad jumps into the pond – plop!

9.20 a.m.   Still feel a bit weird after last night's dreams... Ben's fence was made of dark, milk and white chocolate mingled together in a swirly wood pattern. I broke off small sections, munched through two panels and was about to start another when the police arrested me for murder, then charged me with mega-chocolate consumption. It was a bit silly of them to put me behind chocolate bars (dreams are like that). I ate my way out of prison, felt too sick to escape and lay suffering in smelly, miserable, rat-infested squalor. Woke up, but didn't feel much different.

9.25 a.m.   Must ask Ben to help me take the sheets off the bed and put them in washing machine. He wouldn't notice if they weren't changed for a year. I don't think men have a sense of smell; if the kitchen sink were full of rotting bananas, I'm sure he'd say something like, 'Is that a new perfume you're wearing dear?'

9.30 a.m.   Herb tea in Kit-Kat mug, toast and neighbourhood watch. Nothing interesting yet.

9.35 a.m.   Watch trees moving in wind and have a creative attack. (I hate the name of that programme *Art Attack* – *Which Craft* sounds much better!)

> *... she watched trees bending in the wind; the leaves, like budding artists displaying their talents against a background of ever-changing blues and greys, enjoying the natural light and the birds who pose for them every day...*

9.45 a.m.   Tear up miserable poetry in case someone sees it and I end up in mental hospital or prison.

10.00 a.m. Can't believe my toenails are long again. I'm sure I cut them only a few days ago. They are supposed to grow at half the speed of fingernails but I think it's the other way round with me.

10.10 a.m. Cut toenails.

10.12 a.m. Cut fingernails.

10.15 a.m. Arrange toenails and fingernails in flower petal pattern on coffee table, toast crumbs in middle.

10.16 a.m. Arrange Ben's fags in the ashtray in a flower pattern. Use a match so don't have to touch smelly ash.

10.17 a.m. Sneeze and blow ash everywhere.

10.19 a.m. Still sitting and looking at ashy mess; what would palace-type-home friends say if they could see me now? What would me muvver say?

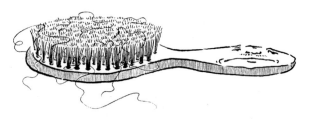

10.20 a.m. Run fingers through horrible, greasy hair. Don't know if I'll have energy to wash it today.

10.21 a.m. Brush grease through hair – ugh.

10.22 a.m. Sad old hair brush needs a wash.

10.23 a.m. Promise hair brush I'll wash it one day.

10.25 a.m. A knock on the front door. Peer out of window and see big blue delivery van. See big, tanned delivery man and interesting-looking parcel. Get excited (about parcel, not man, although man quite attractive).

10.26 a.m. Wrap head in towel to hide dirty hair and give illusion I've just washed it (this will also explain why I took so long to answer the door). Sometimes I put on an exasperated look to add to the effect, so caller thinks I'm a dynamic, energetic, enterprising career woman with lots to do on my day off. But it's a bit embarrassing when the caller apologises profusely for disturbing my ablutions; so I smile brightly and say it's perfectly all right and they go away thinking, 'What a nice woman,' and I feel good for five seconds before removing towel from head and greasy hair flops round face and all illusion evaporates like steam from the kettle.

10.27 a.m. Man apologises for disturbing my hair wash. Man has attractive voice and smile. Wish I didn't look so awful with soup stain on sweatshirt and sore red spot on left cheek.

10.28 a.m. Sign for parcel.
Man winks at me.
Go weak at knees.
Manage to flutter half an eyelash.
Parcel is for next door neighbour.
Sulk.
Bored.
P.M.T.

10.29 a.m. Want to know what's in parcel. Maybe if I open it and seal it up again nicely, neighbour won't notice – but probably will.

10.30 a.m. Rattle parcel a bit. If I rattle parcel a lot, might break contents and will have to check contents are OK.

10.31 a.m. Start to tear off corner of tape on side of parcel.

Tear looks bad.

Panic.

10.33 a.m. Look for sellotape to hide evidence of tampering with neighbour's property.

10.35 a.m. Only one inch of sellotape left (still unable to think in centimetres). Swear.

10.40 a.m. Must send off for something so I can receive a parcel. Must try to wash hair more around possible day of delivery. Must notice soup stains on clothes before answering door. Must have spot concealer always at the ready.

10.46 a.m. Leaf through Goldshield catalogue. Hmmm, rather low on evening primrose oil capsules at the moment.

10.48 a.m. Ah hah! Remember where there's a roll of sellotape.

10.49 a.m. Hooray! Injured parcel patched up.

10.50 a.m. Parcel still looks bad. Hope neighbour doesn't complain to Express Deliveries.

10.51 a.m. Hope neighbour has problems with eyesight. Feel guilty for having such a bad thought. Will go blind prematurely for my sins.

10.53 a.m. See something sad on TV. Turn off TV. Have been punished for my sins. Read TV mag: what's so good about Good Friday, death on a cross and everything?

10.55 a.m. Feel very grim for two minutes.

10.57 a.m. Pick up *Weekly Wife* and see something good about Good Friday: hot cross buns, of course! The best buy is Waitrose white hot cross buns, 280 cals/100g, 89p for six. They are good-sized buns with a nice moist texture and sticky topping, lovely zesty flavour, lots of plump juicy fruit and a perfect blend of spices.

Asda's buns are a disappointment, with too much sticky gunge on top, too doughy, heavy and dry. Marks and Spencer buns aren't all that hot either; the strong citrus peel and spice flavours dominate and the texture is a bit on the dry side. Gosh! This is all terribly interesting.

10.58 a.m. Mouth is watering.

Sainsburys are a close runner-up to Waitrose with an excellent blend of fruits and a light texture. There you go.

10.59 a.m. When Ben emerges from computer land, I will say

www dot to capture his attention, then tell him I've just been reading about the brilliant new diet for M.E. sufferers: it helps us gain energy and happiness for a day. Lots of hot cross buns *and* I simply must start today!

11.00 a.m. Just *have* to read about the best buy in Easter eggs. Celebrations by Mars comes out top: a huge Galaxy chocolate egg with a bag of Mars favourites inside. Expensive at £4.99 but good value for money.

The Thornton's Easter egg is ideal for chocoholics: thick and rich, like some men I've met. You can have a message printed on the egg but there are no goodies inside, which can be a big disappointment, like some other men...

11.05 a.m. Ben emerges from computer land. He seems to spend more and more time on his computer these days; I'm sure he loves her more than me, it doesn't take much to turn her on and she does everything he requests. I overheard him talking computerish the other evening:

'Can I drag that onto the desktop?'

'You can choose what you want to be displayed.'

'Can I enter my login?'

I didn't mean to overhear, just happened to be passing the keyhole. Well, I *am* so tired sometimes, I simply *have* to crawl to the bathroom.

11.07 a.m. Ben says he'll pick up some buns at Mr. P's shop when he nips out to see Bill later.

When's later?

Want buns now.

Must stay patient, am like a bored, naughty child. What is the matter with me? Must get well soon so I can run down to the shops in a desperate, pathetic way for emergency comfort goodies like I used to. Hate having to rely on someone else, will never get used to it. I know this is not positive thinking, but don't care at the moment. Have one-track mind: sweet, sticky, spicy, doughy, hot, buttery, buns, buns, buns and more buns!

11.09 a.m. Ben says he's worried about Bill, who is rather down at the moment, and is painting *The Sea of Suicide*.

11.10 a.m. Can't he see I'm down in the depths too and need my sticky buns now!?

11.11 a.m. Drag self to kitchen to toast bit of stale bread.

11.20 a.m. Half watch *Richard and Judy* with eyes almost closed and sound low: gossip and celebrity guests, healthy recipes and expert medical advice. *Yawn*.

12.30 p.m. Half watch the seventies sitcom, *Bewitched*. The music always takes me back to childhood dreams of becoming a witch, a mermaid or a ballet dancer; no wonder I never had a successful career. Maybe I should have trained to be a midwife who delivers babies underwater to the serene melodies of Tchaikovsky's *Swan Lake*.

12.31 p.m. Recall going to see a psychic/clairvoyant at our local theatre. Most of the audience were women, and many looked like Samantha's mother and grandmother in *Bewitched*. I found the audience much more entertaining than the show! You had to be there of course.

12.32 p.m. There's a new tabby kitten called Tabitha down our street; wonder if the mother cat wiggles her nose. Samantha would be a good name for a rabbit. Think I'd like a large, cuddly rabbit with floppy ears for a pet.

12.33 p.m. *Fatal Attraction* is on this week; mustn't forget to watch it.

12.34 p.m. Wash three plates and a sharp knife.

12.40 p.m. Ben says he has to go away next weekend for a works exhibition in Birmingham. He's bought new underwear and Bad Boy aftershave.

12.41 p.m. Sharp knife needs sharpening.

12.45 p.m. Sit and pick bits of white tissue off clean (dark-coloured) washing. So lucky to have time to sit and pick bits of tissue off clean washing. In my well days, I'd have been annoyed if I discovered I'd left a tissue in with my dirty clothes. But now things have changed, I have time for a long leisurely pick, pick, pick. Aarrgh!

1.00 p.m. Listened to *Shortland Street* while picking bits of white tissue out of black leggings.

1.15 p.m. Must write to friends in Kiwi Land.

1.30 p.m. Start letter to Dave and Nicky, but they have such exciting showbiz lives, I don't know what to say without sounding horribly boring and dull. I expect somebody picks bits of tissue out of their clothes for them – or a trained kiwi.

1.40 p.m. Screw up letter. Tape *Neighbours*.

1.55 p.m. Realise I've been taping *Neighbours* over part two of a very brilliant, intriguing drama for the last fifteen minutes. Curse my appalling memory.

2.00 p.m. Glare at video recorder with face like Grant Mitchell on a bad day at the Queen Vic. When is there a good day?

2.15 p.m. Can't believe I've started actually having dreams about characters in *Coronation Street*, *EastEnders* and *Neighbours*. Am not writing down the dreams neatly in W. H. Smith's recycled notepad ready for counselling. Georgie will only think I'm a very sad person as well as a Dali-type weirdo with a wonderful sex life. She doesn't understand how exhausted I feel all the time and may tell me to get a life and I'll try to strangle her and she'll have me admitted to mental hospital where they might not let me watch *EastEnders* or *Coronation Street* and I might die.

2.45 p.m. Ben appears, then disappears to the bathroom. While sitting on the loo, he calls out that he's nipping out to see Bill for an hour. Have translated this to three hours. Really will die if I don't have sticky buns in my mouth to calm me down.

3.05 p.m. More neighbour watching. A middle-aged woman in a navy blue jacket, navy skirt, navy shoes and tights (for that unbroken slimming look) is unlocking her car door. She throws her navy handbag in the front seat and takes off her jacket to reveal a navy cardigan over a sensible white blouse. I can't help wondering if she is wearing navy blue knickers and a sensible white bra. Oh dear! I'm turning into a pervert *and* a murderer.

3.13p.m.   Mr. Boxer-face is taking antique coffee table for walkies. Watch his waggy tail, bouncy gait and doggy face that looks like it's laughing with happiness.

Haven't seen brother of Mr. Boxer-face recently; maybe he's returned to his wife or works abroad now or he's back in prison or a grotty bed-sit or he's met a wild Welsh woman who's whisked him off to the mountains to wander in wellies in all weathers among woolly sheep and wonder wearily whether it will all wind up in wedlock.

3.15 p.m.   All the www dots floating around the house are affecting me.

3.16 p.m.   Ben bought wellies recently.

3.17 p.m.   Will ask Ben why he bought wellies.

3.18 p.m.   Tabitha tabby kitten is hiding under a car. Hope my dear old tabby cat is happy in cat heaven, curled up on a fluffy cloud with warm sun on her fur. Still miss her.

Dear God,
When I die, please can I go to animal heaven to be with Pinky and Perky, Lucky, Sasha, Tanya, Bugsy, Pepper, Blue Blue, Horis and Claudia. Don't fancy human heaven, might bump into someone who made my life hell.
P.S. If I'm reincarnated I'd like to be a fly on the wall so I can whiz all over the place and listen to interesting conversation and never be bored again, like now.
Love me x x x

3.21 p.m.	Wonder where my neglected old wellies are.
3.22 p.m.	*The wind whistled on the wet wintry Wednesday morning. Wendy sat on a wall under the weeping willow and wound her watch while waiting for William.*
3.23 p.m.	**Dear God,**

I've changed my mind Don't want to come back as a fly. Have remembered those awful Vapona strips (people who use them should have their hands and feet super-glued to the wall and see how they like it) and rolled up newspapers and plants with teeth Also, I've had to cope with enough ~~shit~~ situations that stink in my life, thank you.
P.S. I'd like to be a faithful dog, preferably belonging to a Mr. Darcy type. I would allow him to pat, stroke and kiss me as much as he liked.

3.26 p.m.	Mmmm, better stop before I get too excited.
3.27 p.m.	Ben returns with twelve hot cross buns, ten Benson & Hedges and a can of fizzy drink. Bill wasn't in.
3.28 p.m.	Two buns under grill. One in my mouth.
3.29 p.m.	Ben disappears into computer land.
3.32 p.m.	Enjoy *Neighbours* on video with face full of hot cross bun and marge dripping down chin on to sweatshirt.
4.00 p.m.	Looks like people across road are going away. Just a weekend trip, judging by the number of suitcases; wish I were going with them. Where are they going, taking three pairs of wellies, fishing rods and buckets, two blue cool boxes and a large yellow umbrella? Their car is the colour of purple fruit Polos.
4.03 p.m.	Sulk. Want to sit and comfort-eat whole packet of fruit Polos. Don't care if teeth rot and fall out – already look like haggard old witch with straggly hair and sinister stare.
4.06 p.m.	Read stars. Cosmic Colin says I must seek out serene or historic places over the Easter break. Stately homes, castles or cathedrals will sustain me spiritually.
	Will need wellies if it rains a lot and grounds are muddy.

4.15 p.m.	Feel ill after eating too many hot cross buns. Fed up, want to visit spiritual places.
4.30 p.m.	Say a little prayer as I soak in a ylang ylang, patchouli and orange bath to sustain my spirituality and sensuality.
4.35 p.m.	Ylang ylang, patchouli and orange is working. Imagine I'm being naughty in a grand house for a whole weekend and being chased up a wide ornate staircase, screaming with laughter, by handsome delivery man wearing only wellies and little denim shorts. He has a large parcel for me. Snooty ancestors frown down at us from their gilt-framed repose.
4.36 p.m.	Maybe I'll tell Georgie I've been up to all these shenanigans; she's gagging for a bit of excitement.
5.00 p.m.	Watch cold tap dripping. Drip. Drip. Drip.

Waiting to recover from M.E. is like being very thirsty on a hot day and holding a glass under a dripping tap, a tap that drips once every eleven seconds (I counted). They are small drips. Very small drips. Driplets. My sister could have given birth to triplets in January. One baby is hard enough, twins must be very tiring, more than two... exhausted just thinking about it.

When I was young, my parents grew a lot of fruit and vegetables. I used to hate topping and tailing black-currants for jam. It seemed to take forever to fill a small bowl. I'd rather top'n'tail blackcurrants now, than wait to recover from M.E. This waiting is like:

Waiting for Christmas when you are six.

Waiting for part two, in three week's time.

Waiting on the N.H.S...

Waiting...

In the queue at Wooley's on Christmas Eve.

At the service till when it's pouring with rain.

The ladies loo at the theatre.

Waiting for it to cool down.

Waiting for your money back.

Waiting for the dentist's drill to stop.

Waiting for that letter.

Waiting for that phone call.

Waiting for him to say sorry.

Waiting for her to say sorry.

Waiting for the right moment to tell him.

Waiting for a doctor to believe you have M.E.

Waiting for the ink to dry.

Waiting for pigs to fly.

Add all these together. Sit and watch paint dry. With a headache. The paint is brilliant white. And the tap is dripping... drip, drip, drip.

6.00 p.m.   Wonder if there's any more hot cross buns left.

Saturday 2nd

Three Easter cards arrived with this morning's post. There were two religious scenes (a church, a cross, daffs, tulips or crocuses featuring somewhere) from my parents and Ben's mum. The painting on the front of Artie Auntie's card was a delicate water-colour of purple pansies.

Stood wearily at the kitchen window (monthly cramps killing me) warming my hands on a mug of raspberry tea (should have been crocus or daffodil flavour) watching an April shower. The sun came out and sparkled brightly on the dustbin lid. Ben watched the sun sparkle on his new fence. Sam Spider isn't talking to me.

Shuffled into the sitting room to gaze out the window where I knew I'd see a rainbow... millions of drops of water... illuminated by the sun to make a spectacular light show... bright beautiful vibrant colours... a bow on Mother Nature's present to us... the gift of life. Watched the rainbow softly fade. Felt sad. Followed a raindrop as it trickled into another raindrop... then another. Followed another raindrop as it trickled... it's my birthday soon... wonder how old I'll be when I die.

Had the feeling I might be starting a cold so I swallowed an extra vitamin C tablet, sprinkled a crushed clove of garlic on my dinner and poured three dessertspoons of honey on thick slices of toast later. Thought I'd round off my plan of action with a small glass of Ben's posh whisky...

10.14 p.m. 'Ish verrry nyshe thish Glenfiddish.'
11.04 p.m. 'Jushonemore wee dram o' the finesh Sco'ish wishkee in the worl...'
11.32 p.m. Hic, 'Eashter t'morrow.'

Sunday 3rd

10.30 a.m. Christ! Feel like I've risen from the dead.
10.31 a.m. Doesn't feel like victory over death or anything though.
10.32 a.m. Gloom. Doom. Despair. I'll never ever get better. The future is shrouded in mystery. Nails of uncertainty have been hammered into my body. Thorny questions prick my conscience. God, I feel bloody cross.
10.35 a.m. Ben is groaning, my Easter bunny had too much grass last night.
10.36 a.m. Easter egg Sunday! Great! It's compulsory to eat as much choccy as possible.
10.39 a.m. Can't face chocolate today.
11.45 a.m. Water going down plug hole in sink sounds like old man belching. Feel sick.
12.30 p.m. Water crashing into bath sounds like Niagara Falls.

Weird musician friend, John-Luke, came round after Sunday mass at the local Catholic church, St. Francis. He talked about Jesus, the Last Supper, the Stations of the Cross and the Resurrection all afternoon. I asked him if he'd like an orange Judas with his sandwich and Ben wanted to know if they had Wall's Viennetta at the Last Supper because *he* always had it on special occasions; John-Luke left soon afterwards. We noticed pink and yellow squares of Battenburg cake left on his plate in the shape of a cross.

Feel guilty. I'm such a sinner, I blaspheme, I persecute Christians, I eat other people's Easter eggs and don't go to church any more. John-Luke said I need to go to confession. Oh, Lord. I'll be stuck in church all day and all night.

... she stood at the window, a speck of dark chocolate on her creamy pale cheek, her sleepy eyes staring sadly at the world outside. A knobbly brown branch, like a Matchmaker, tapped on the icy window like an accusing finger. She prayed for forgiveness...

Monday 4th

Said sorry to Ben for eating his Easter egg and saved my brachiosaurus egg to share with him this afternoon. Gave him most of it (to ease my guilt) and asked him if he knew the brachiosaurus weighed as much as fourteen elephants, was as long as a tennis court, high as a three-storey house and may have had several hearts. He said he *did* know actually; he'd read the box in Thorntons.

Tuesday 5th

Another catalogue arrived advertising a 'sensational Spring Sale'. The ten-piece towel bales brightened my morning, in navy, cornflower, yellow, lilac, cream, terracotta, mid-green and rose pink; we could do with some new ones. The Tweety air bed looked fun to sleep on and Barbie looked cool in her convertible. Quite fancied the garden furniture; a set of bistro chairs made in resin to look like cast iron, like the ones Del and Rodney sit on in *Only Fools and Horses*, but theirs are white. The stripy hammock and shade looked very comfortable, for sleepy people who need to rest a lot.

Opened an early birthday card from Artie Auntie; a painting of sunflowers by Edward Noott. I like sunflowers; they remind me of Bill and Ben, the Flower Pot Men and Little Weed. Enjoyed calming, sunny, sunflower thoughts. I am calm and peaceful, healed and healthy, I love me.

My brother's birthday card made me laugh till my ears dropped off: two penguins carrying a fridge across an ice bridge over shark infested waters, one of them was singing, 'Like a fridge over troubled waters.'

After my session with Eileen, I bought a half-price Celebrations Easter egg for Ben at the mini-market next door. Georgie is away on holiday this week with her toy boy; she told Eileen they were going to Texas. Eileen said they flew to America at the weekend, but I reckon the new man is doing up her kitchen (with Texas flat-packs) and Georgie is rewarding his efforts by letting him try out the new water bed and Jacuzzi she was telling me about the other week. Hope she'll be in a better mood when I see her next week, although I fear there will be more innuendoes than usual.

Mr. Fast-and-Furious ex-racing-driver-taxi-man, who's normally early, was nearly half an hour late picking me up tonight so I ate Ben's Easter egg to keep me calm and peaceful. Didn't mean to eat the whole egg; I really don't know how it happened. The chocolate fairies must have helped me out; I'm sure I heard a rustling in the bushes and a tiny burp. Saved the cellophane packet of miniature chocolates for Ben.

When the taxi-man finally arrived, his music was so loud it sounded like the car had a giant heart for an engine, beating fast and furiously after hours of exertion. I politely yelled at taxi-man, requesting that he turned his music down. He didn't turn it down much or apologise for being late, just continued to chew vigorously on his foul-smelling gum, pulled out in front of an oncoming car and swore a lot.

Very nearly smeared chocolatey fingers on his white shirt when I handed him four pound coins, nicely warmed in my little paws; was tempted to growl and bare my teeth too. When I'm better and full of strength and confidence, I will rub chocolatey fingers on white clothing of rude, ignorant taxi drivers and maybe growl a bit if I'm in the mood.

It's my sister's birthday today. I sent her a blue towelling whale with a sponge inside (nice and light for sending by post) I saw advertised in an animal-friendly-type catalogue. The picture on her card was a new wave painting of a whale's tail in the sea, printed on recycled paper; the envelope, a thick, recycled dark green one (that should please her). Hope the whale she adopted hasn't died or something.

Wednesday 6th

9.15 a.m. Wake up feeling anxious.

9.16 a.m. Memories of last night's dreams surface and replay in my mind's eye... it's early morning, mist hangs over a graveyard, the bright green grass dotted with purple pansies. I'm sitting on the verge, my ankles locked in medieval stocks. Stone crosses wear crowns of thorns and blood red roses entwine my body, pricking my cold, white flesh whenever I try to move. A grim priest strides up the path leading to the church door, turns his head, and informs me I will be punished for my sins.

Appearing softly out of the mist, a procession of my family and friends, dressed in black, follow the priest. Dad isn't there. Mum is smiling, dressed in yellow and carrying daffodils. Giant ants carry a coffin with a masonic apron draped over it. My sister is riding a whale, followed by my brother (helping a penguin carry a fridge) and Eileen (dressed in a Scottish Widow's cloak) with her pet haggis in his wee tartan jacket. Rose pushes a pram full of twenty screaming babies and Gail follows her on a black horse.

Psychedelic music fills the air and hippy women with hairy armpits appear dancing, swinging their love beads and munching vegeburgers. Bill wanders behind, fag in one hand, banana in the other, surrounded by young naked women. He is smiling. Ben is smiling too, www dots and witches flying around his head. Weird muscician friend rides a chocolate brachiosaurus followed by a kiwi and Artie Auntie paints the scene whilst eating a Cadbury's Flake.

I call out for help but noone hears me. Stone angels climb down from tombs, crushing the purple pansies; one of them passes me an orange mobile phone so I can ring for a taxi. Hours pass. A woman dressed in navy blue climbs out of her navy blue Renault Clio, smiles, then ignores me and searches for her navy blue handbag. An antique coffee table strolls by, stops next to the car, then lifts its leg. One of the drawers falls out; it's full of woodlice and spiders.

When the taxi finally arrives, it's in the shape of a huge, crimson, pulsating heart, the price on the meter rising at every beat. Pound coins roll down the road into the drain. The driver cannot hear me calling out for rescue; his music is too loud. I notice I'm surrounded by broken chocolate eggs and my hands are covered in chocolate. I look up to see a crowd of brown medieval mourners emerge out of a pink mist; they throw squishy tomatoes at my face, shouting, 'Murderer! Pervert! Chocolate Fiend!'

I wake up feeling anxious, checking my arms for wounds and my eyes for tomato pips.

9.17 a.m.	Still anxious *and* depressed.
9.18 a.m.	It's my birthday! I'm nearer forty than thirty now! I'm nearly forty! Oh no! I'm old!

Dear God,
Please make me better before my fortieth
birthday, I can't bear the thought of being
forty and lifeless and bored out of my skull
and having time to dwell on the years I wasted
in my thirties, while I was trying to make up
for all the time I wasted in my twenties.
Love, me x x x

9.20 a.m.   Stare into bathroom mirror.

9.21 a.m.   I'm going to drown myself in the bath.

9.22 a.m.   I am, I am, I am.

9.23 a.m.   Nobody loves me, nobody understands me, nobody cares.

9.25 a.m.   Open card from Ben. Laugh. Cartoon of two smiling fat
crocodiles lying on the sand next to a shredded jacket and
pair of glasses. There's a broken canoe and a hat floating
in the river and one crocodile says to the other, 'That was
incredible. No fur, claws, horns, antlers, or nothin'... just
soft and pink.'

Card from Jeremy. Giggle. Brightly coloured cartoon of
man and woman at a party; the man is holding a glass with
an eye in it, the woman has an eye missing.
The caption reads, 'Of all the men in the room, it was
destined that Ben should catch her eye.'
Ben's mum's card: purple pansies.
My sister's card: dolphins on recycled paper.
Mum and Dad's card – smile. Cartoon of lions with dead
zebra watching another lion pounce on a pile of
pumpkins. Caption reads, 'She's trying to make being a
vegetarian exciting.' My veggie ways are still a joke to my
parents.

9.30 a.m.   Shall I write down my dreams?

9.31 a.m.   No. Georgie will think I'm granddaughter of Salvador
Dali.

9.32 a.m.   Have surrealist thoughts... I'm sitting with a loaf of bread
on my head watching a melting television. My nose starts
to run and becomes a tap. I turn it off.

Of all the men in the room, it
was destined that Ben should
catch her eye.

	Jungle animals climb out of the telephone and drink at the watering hole at my feet.
9.33 a.m.	Decide with each birthday I'm going more off my trolley. Fancy listening to my Madness CD: sixteen classic tracks from the early eighties.
9.34 a.m.	Sit cards on TV and mantelpiece.
9.35 a.m.	Sit on toilet and listen to police car sirens. More surrealist thoughts: pigs flying down the high street.
9.37 a.m.	Decide it's time to get off the toilet and put the kettle on for birthday breakfast. Will have 'real tea' for a treat.
9.38 a.m.	Notice new frown line developing, mouth looking sulkier and eyebrows very straggly, like an old man.
9.39 a.m.	Arrange Easter cards behind birthday cards so it looks like I'm really popular.
9.50 a.m.	Tea, toast and open prezzies from Ben.
9.51 a.m.	Shame to tear pretty wrapping paper with ladybirds on. Tear carefully so can keep some of it (and forget where I've put it when I need it).
9.53 a.m.	Lovely browse through birthday books: *Understanding*

Dreams, The Paranormal and *Bird Watching by Colour* (for my new bird watching out the kitchen window hobby).

9.55 a.m.   Paranormal book is a bit scary with lots of photos of ghosties, poltergeist activity, spontaneous combustion, spectral coaches and coachmen – brilliant!

10.05 a.m.   Bird watching book looks interesting; now I know the difference between a rook, a crow and a raven.

10.06 a.m.   Will become expert, like the Birdman of Alcatraz.

10.07 a.m.   Maybe put binoculars on Xmas list.

10.10 a.m.   Eyes getting tired from reading but can't resist looking up a few things I remember from last nights dreams in my dream book:

Church exterior – augurs well for the future (goody).
Clergy – may need someone to aid or guide me (mmm).
Coffin – can signify guilt (oh dear).
Daffodils – augur a time of hope (that's nice).
Spring flowers – optimism about the future (I'm trying).
Green – a concern with health and the environment (mmm).
Crying babies – usually significant of poor health (what's new).
Watching an artist at work – you are aware, even if unconsciously, that you are wasting a good deal of time (oh, God).

10.30 a.m.   Half listened and half watched a bit of a chat show about something boring; boring-looking people asking boring questions and other boring people giving bloody boring answers.

10.45 a.m.   Put on Madness CD.

10.47 a.m.   Room's gone dark.

10.48 a.m.   Watch rain.

10.50 a.m.   Sing along to 'Grey Day'; 'In the morning I awake, my arms, my legs, my body aches, the sky outside is wet and grey, so begins another weary day, so begins another weary day!'

11.00 a.m.   Sit on loo humming to myself.

11.02 a.m.   Can't sit here all day.

11.10 a.m.   Pour hot water onto peppermint tea bag in Kit-Kat mug.

11.15 a.m.   Spot collared dove on fence through steam of herb tea.

11.16 p.m.   Would love to keep white doves; they look so calm and peaceful.

12.30 p.m.   *Bewitched* on TV.

1.00 p.m.   Birthday bath.

2.00 p.m.   Birthday books in bed.

4.15 p.m.   Bum! Have been asleep for two hours; now I'll be up for most of the night.

4.16 p.m.   Recall dreams about spontaneous combustion... all that was left of me on the kitchen floor was a hand holding a vegeburger. Ben had disappeared: www.Spont.com written on the window pane.

4.18 p.m.   Recall article in *Weekly Wife* about a woman left with a three-inch scar on her bottom after her knickers spontaneously combusted. She must have been telling lies: liar liar, pants on...

4.20 p.m.	Hungry and thirsty.
4.22 p.m.	Eat cold leftovers in fridge.
4.30 p.m.	Find three small stripy candles and candle holders in battered herb tea box, behind out of date packets of dried things and an uncooked Christmas pudding.
4.31 p.m.	Stick candles and holders in banana and look for matches.
4.35 p.m.	Find matches; only two left. Must use only one in case I forget to put them on shopping list or there's a power cut.
4.36 p.m.	Light candles. Watch candles burn down a little.
4.38 p.m.	Blow out candles and make a wish.
	Wish I were cutting into a Sara Lee Double Chocolate Gâteau.
4.40 p.m.	Worn out now.
5.25 p.m.	Mr. Boxer-face is taking antique coffee table for a walk; he stops to stroke and kiss the dog's nose.
5.30 p.m.	Remind self there are lots of people who love and care for their animals.
5.35 p.m.	Cannot watch *Neighbours*; watched it this afternoon.
	Will not be tempted to watch *Pet Rescue*. It will only end in tears.
5.36 p.m.	Start having sad cruelty-to-animal thoughts so put on Madness CD.
5.37 p.m.	Sing into large microphone-sized candle, 'It must be love, love, love...'
6.35 p.m.	Ben comes home.
6.36 p.m.	Ben urgently needs loo. Am in bathroom and have just covered hair in Flex, thick custard-like conditioner. Wrap hair in towel.
6.38 p.m.	Ben sings to music and says, 'Hey, this is Madness,' wishes me a happy birthday, hopes I liked my books, then jokes that I love my hair conditioner so much he should have bought me *The Joy of Flex*.
6.39 p.m.	We laugh and for a minute I think he's really lovely.
6.40 p.m.	Thought wears off when he passes wind, takes off his socks and says he might have to pop out tonight if Bill rings.
6.41 p.m.	Madness sing 'Welcome to the House of Fun'.
7.30 p.m.	*Coronation Street* and bottle of red wine for treat with dinner.
7.32 p.m.	Try not to think about hairy-armpit-women while eating vegeburgers, but can't face the squashy grilled tomatoes.

8.05 p.m.	Ben surprises me with a chocolate cake. Lots of birthday candles light up my face. Bill hasn't rung so he's not going out.
8.06 p.m.	He's so Wonderful!
8.07 p.m.	Watch Victoria Wood and *Ab Fab* video and get as pickled as a pickled egg.
8.30 p.m.	All pains in body and head have gone. Feel very happy. Not thinking about tomorrow.
8.50 p.m.	We share the chocolates saved from the Celebrations Easter egg; miniature Bounty, Mars and Topics...
9.15 p.m.	Life is Absolutley fabulous!

Happy birthday to me
Happy birthday to me
Soon I'll be better
Happy birthday to me

Thursday 7th

10.30 a.m.	Think I see a ghost in the bathroom mirror but, on reflection, it's only me.
10.45 a.m.	Try to focus on belated arty black and white birthday card from Gail; can't see what the picture is supposed to be.
10.46 a.m.	Gail has also sent a pocket book of spells for the Modern Witch. Adopt witchy squint, but miniature words are dancing across page like naked pagan women.
10.47 a.m.	Try to focus on hangover cures stuck on fridge.
10.48 a.m.	Drop jar of vitamin C tablets. Top comes off and they spill all over kitchen floor; cannot bend down to pick them up without head falling off.
11.25 a.m.	Spot two tree pipits in garden but suspect there is only one.
12.30 p.m.	Attempt to focus eyes on TV screen.
12.32 p.m.	Turn off TV.
2.30 p.m.	Am convinced head has fallen off and rolled down the stairs, bump, bump, bump, out the front door, into the road and under the wheels of a giant lorry.
3.12 p.m.	Squint cross-eyed at article about improving eyesight in *Weekly Wife*.
4.05 p.m.	Am never, ever drinking again. Not one slurp, not one tiny drop will pass my lips never, ever, ever. Amen.
4.22 p.m.	My brains have been removed, crushed in a garlic crusher then thrown in the frying pan to sizzle with the onions.
5.25 p.m.	Wonder what time it is; I can see what the big hand is doing but the little hand... I think that's Mr. Boxer-face lurching by and puppy dog bounding along ahead of him, chewing his lead. Or is it a lurcher on a box, chewing his master's head?
5.33 p.m.	Watch bit of *Pet Rescue*. Weep into a cushion.
6.35 p.m.	Smile bleary-eyed at Ben. Has he got a bottle of wine in that corner shop type carrier bag?
6.36 p.m.	Yes!
7.00 p.m.	Ahhh. Mmmm. Slurrrp. That's better.
7.40 p.m.	Mum and Dad visit with birthday prezzie: pretty flowery skirt from M&S.
7.42 p.m.	Flowery designs are moving on material.

7.45 p.m.	Record second half of *EastEnders.*
7.54 p.m.	Ben says he'll take skirt back for a smaller size; I think Mum was hoping I'd grow into it.
8.04 p.m.	Sister arrives. Parents leave, their sick eldest daughter looks too ill for a lot of company. It's great not to be told how well I look for a change.
8.07 p.m.	Hope Mum didn't notice the telltale red spots down the front of my sweatshirt.
8.10 p.m.	Cuddle Matthew, wearing his purple tie-dye-all-in-one.
8.13 p.m.	Feel very old, tarnished and cynical next to such soft pink beauty and pure white innocence. Hold breath so his tiny lungs won't breathe in alcohol fumes. Don't know why I bother, there's so much pollution outside, poor little mite.
8.25 p.m.	Gina gives me purple tie-dye T-shirt for birthday prezzie. The circular designs make me feel quite dizzy.
8.26 p.m.	Her green and yellow striped leggings, with orange bits in, make me feel sick.
8.31 p.m.	Matthew is sick on mummy's leggings.
8.41 p.m.	Matthew and mummy go home.
8.45 p.m.	Very achy, babies are *so* heavy.
9.03 p.m.	Drink lots of water.

Friday 8th

> *The thirsty earth soaks up the rain,*
> *And drinks and gapes for drink again.*
> **Abraham Cowley**

Sat looking out the window like a small dog waiting for his master to come home; watched the birdies like an ageing, well-fed tabby cat.

It rained cats and dogs most of the afternoon. Children splashed in poodles, wearing bright red, plastic wellies; they pussy-footed round a pile of dog poo. I curled up in the darkened sitting room reading my pocket spell book by candlelight. I cackled quietly.

Ben swam home from The Ship in Hook Lane and dripped all over the carpet before finding safe harbour under the duvet. He snored like a sleeping sailor after a stormy night at sea. I searched for a spell under **S** to stop snoring. Only found uses for sage, star anise and sandalwood, spells to cure a sore throat, make you more sensual, help you sleep better, stop smoking, build your self-esteem and heal sadness.

Saturday 9th

My eyes hurt; must have read too much ~~spell~~ small print last night; now I really am suffering from Magic Encyclopaedia.

Ben surfaced like a sailor who'd drunk the rum barrel dry. He splashed about a bit in the bathroom then crawled to the corner shop for supplies now that he was on dry land.

Rose sent me a belated birthday card: a painting of a mother sitting on the beach surrounded by her children. Does this mean she's manless again? Sweet of her to remember my birthday, with all those little stripy candles and cards she has to remember to buy for her many offspring; not to mention cakes to bake and presents to make, divorce, pregnancy, teenage traumas, toddler tantrums, ex-husband tantrums, worry about gaining pounds and where the next penny is coming from.

Early this afternoon, the teenage girl across the road stepped out of her front door into the sunlight wearing a simple white dress and flowers in her hair. Two tiny bridesmaids in pale lemon flew down the path like excited springtime fairies and the in-laws eyed a rain cloud with don't-you-dare expressions. Had a good nose at what everyone was wearing (she shouldn't wear scarlet with *her* skin problem and that suit's a bit tight round his chest) and felt sad, the bride looked so young. Hoped it wouldn't rain till after the photos; I've seen the bridegroom calling for her every evening (except Wednesdays and the odd weekend) and I think she will have enough storms to endure by the look of him.

A female blackbird, brown as a Malteser, pecked on the lawn with her mate. They ignored each other. I expect they're married.

Sunday 10th

I wonder if the teenage princess of the lemon fairies woke up today to find her prince had turned into a frog.

... the fairy princess married under a confetti tree, the breeze blew tiny pastel shapes into the air, they fluttered down gently onto small, pointy, upturned faces...

A few flakes of confetti have blown into our front garden. I picked up a blue horseshoe for luck this morning and noticed a pale pink heart on the path. A good-looking man in his thirties walked by and stepped on it; it stuck to his shoe and I wondered how many hearts he'd broken.

Gave my year-older face a treat with a face pack. When it had dried hard, I tapped it and enjoyed looking like a zombie instead of just feeling like one. Ben came into the bathroom (he didn't go to Birmingham after all, hmmm) and made me giggle. I watched my face crack and peel like the paintwork on the window frames outside; now I know how I'll look and feel when I'm Matthew's aged aunt in my baggy leggings and saggy cardigan.

Monday 11th

Rain. Rain. Rain. Rain. Rain. Rain. Rain. Rain. Sun.

A rainbow arched over the rooftops like Claude Monet's, *The Bridge*. Confetti floated on a puddle like waterlilies at Giverny. Read about waterlilies while I waited to see Eileen; their names were very inspiring...

... Mr.Cow-Lily visited Miss Fanwort, who was suffering from nymphaea odorata in her southern spatterdock; he was most concerned...

Eileen released the tension in my neck. Did she notice how cleansed and fresh my face looked after the herbal face pack? Don't think so. She said I looked more tired than usual.

Told Georgie I wasn't up to talking for long and she said a short ~~skirt~~ session suited her as she was rather ~~shagged~~ worn out herself. I asked if she enjoyed her holiday; she smiled naughtily. Didn't tell her about my weird dreams, just mentioned the ones about climbing mountains and hiding in rooms. Also mentioned the bird watching book I've been reading, thinking I'd be on safe ground. I wasn't. She said her boyfriend had a collection of books with big birds in and before she could elaborate I quickly changed the subject to my interest in homeopathy, suggesting she take belladonna for her dry barking cough. She asked if I were trying to poison her. I thought I'd better not answer that one.

Bought a half-price Kit-Kat Easter egg in the mini-market for Ben. The taxi driver was so early I wasn't tempted (didn't have time) to sample the chocolate egg and maybe discover baby Kit-Kats in a cellophane wrapper.

Mr. Ex-racing-driver-taxi-man must have watched too much *Starsky and Hutch* when he was younger; he knocked over a dustbin and a few cardboard boxes as he turned a corner. I was home before you could say, 'The Kit-Kat sat on the mat.'

Tuesday 12th

A tiny wren flitted about on the fence while I sipped my morning herbs and my favourite blue tit with a very blue hat (or crown) was busy pecking at the bird feeder.

I've discovered a goldfinch is not gold: it has a black, white and red head with brilliant yellow wing bars. There are so many birds in this country I've never seen; I'd love to spot a kingfisher close up, but usually only manage to catch a streak of blue darting over a stream, if I'm lucky. Must save for a boating holiday.

Noticed some broken Easter egg wrapped in foil in the fridge... I deserve a treat and happiness improves the immune system – where there's a will, there's an excuse.

Wednesday 13th

Woke up and consulted my dream book. I'd been riding an ostrich all night around a fairground, holding a white balloon. When I let go of the balloon, it dissolved into the clouds.

Fairground – You have probably been finding life restricting of late and would dearly love to let loose and have some fun.
Balloon in flight – Reflects a desire to rise above life's problems and escape to fantasy land.
White – Symbolic of purity, usually pointing to seeking the truth.
Ostrich – Maybe a sign that you feel restricted or have been burying your head in the sand.

Think I'll tell Georgie the ostrich turned into a merry-go-round horse. According to my dream book, riding a fairground horse has strong sexual significance; that'll make her tail wag!

Four seagulls (possibly common terns) swooped about, very white against the dark, grey-blue sky. A rainbow leapt across the heavens. I wanted to fly on the back of a white bird, over the rainbow to the land of health and happiness. Watched the rainbow fade.

Ben said he was sure he'd left some Easter egg in the fridge; I said the chocolate fairies must have eaten it.

Thursday 14th
... Stale cauliflower clouds sat in Mother Nature's vegetable rack...

This morning I studied drops of rain on the window pane in the living room, this afternoon I frowned at hundreds of little soap spots on the bathroom mirror (must clean) and this evening I peered at a gelatine-like substance on the kitchen wall. Wow! Exciting! 'Poltergeist activity,' I thought to myself, then remembered: the other day (in a fit of boredom) I'd arranged my evening primrose capsules in pretty patterns on a plate and when the excitement wore off, I rolled one between my fingers. After a minute or two, I heard the contents of the capsule squirt past my ear, but failed to see where it ended up. Now I know. Think I've been reading too much paranormalia.

Ben said I shouldn't have done that pile of washing-up. I said a house-proud poltergeist had done it and warned him they can leave messages on computers, *and* he'd better watch out next time Alex (angry, confused teenager) visits with Jeremy.

Searched for a spell to get the washing-up done under **W**. Only found uses for willow, woodruff and wheat, spells for wisdom, wealth and removing warts.

Friday 15th
Curled up in the dusty old armchair under the dirty old window, afternoon sunlight warming the back of my head and illuminating the spooky pages of my book on the paranormal. The large tome rested heavily on my lap, adding weight to the ghostly tales within.

Didn't feel like reading much, so I slowly turned the pages, studying the black and white photographs of haunted houses and churches, thoughtographs (images projected onto film or paper by mental energy alone), devastation caused by poltergeists, ectoplasm produced by a medium and a twelfth-century illustration of the torments of Hell. Couldn't finish my toast and felt sorry for the victims of poltergeists; blood spurting out of walls and things flying across the room must be terribly terrifying! I can just about cope with evening primrose oil on the wall and Sam Spider looking sinister in his web, while wrapping up a dead bug – that's enough excitement and horror for me these days.

Late this evening, while I was cuddled up in bed with teddy and engrossed in the sudden disappearance of the *Marie Celeste*, Ben crept in from his evening out with the lads and gave me such a fright! He stood menacingly, a dark figure in the doorway with two days' worth of stubble, lamplight glinting on his earring and a pirate's grin. He'd have looked quite sexy in a pirate's outfit but old jeans and T-shirt spoiled the effect.

I could say here that he'd been to The Ship in Shore Street, but he hadn't, he'd visited Morticia's Whine and Spirit Bar, Banshee Lane with Bill and Bob the Slob.

Saturday 16th

If you drop a knife on the floor, a stranger will call. I dropped a fork.

My parents called in on their way home from a trip into town. I tried to look pale and distant and move in a ghostly way as I drifted into the kitchen to put the kettle on but, as always, Dad said how well I looked. Showed him my book on the paranormal which kept him quiet for ages; Mum looked thoughtful, then asked Ben where she could buy a copy. I gave Mum a pile of *Weekly Wife* magazines and she was immediately engrossed in 'How To Cope With Divorce'.

As soon as they left, I rang my sister and told her about the book's keeping Dad quiet; she asked if she could borrow it soon. Very soon. Hope she doesn't read Matthew any bedtime stories from it!

Sometimes, I accidentally give Ben two knives or two forks with his dinner. Tonight I couldn't remember if I'd given him either, but when he picked up his pizza with his fingers, I knew the answer; I asked him anyway.

Me:	Speak now or forever hold your pizza.
Ben:	Knife and fork, please!
Me:	Why are you watching this film? It looks a bit violent.
Ben:	I've read the book.
Me:	*War and Pizza?*
Ben:	There's a sixties comedy on the other side.
Me:	Pizza and love, man! Let's watch it!

Sunday 17th

Our drummer friend, Stephen, visited on his way to a gig in town tonight. He always wears black jeans, black T-shirt, black waistcoat and black trainers; is so tall and thin he looks like a burnt-out matchstick; drinks black coffee (surprise, surprise) and likes to tap his spoon on the coffee table. If I give him two spoons, he's really happy and we enjoy a funky tattoo for five minutes.

In the days when I was first ill and couldn't see anyone, he used to bring round a posy of wild flowers from his garden and I was very touched by his thoughtfulness. OK, I complain about the way I've been treated by some doctors, family, friends and colleagues but I've also seen a lovely compassionate and understanding side of many people I didn't expect it from; very heartwarming.

Monday 18th

I suppose it's about time I took the birthday and Easter cards down. But they look so cheery... maybe one more day.

It didn't look like rain today but I searched for my umbrella just in case. Couldn't find it, so I borrowed the black one Stephen left behind. Eileen was running late tonight so I flipped through a few glossy mags at the clinic, full of adverts for make-up, perfume, cosmetic surgery, abortion, clothes to freeze to death in, serious depressing articles about women in serious depressing situations and not a lot else. But it was enlightening to discover, 'Today's skin care is wrinkle-zapping, plumping and energising. Eyes are sharp, smart and sexy, lips go liquid and spot concealers are more concealing.'

Picked up one of the children's books; *Spot the Dog and his Adventures* were much more fun.

Eileen relaxed my post-parent-visit-pains and we discussed problem parents. Georgie asked me if I'd been up to anything interesting (really hate that question). I swallowed a sarcastic reply and told her Ben had a black and white film in his camera, was taking some arty shots, and I'd taken a few myself. My third big mistake!

In an excited shrill voice (tail wagging) Georgie told me she has a friend who takes artistic photographs in the bedroom and urged me to tell her *all* about *my* artistic photography, as she leaned forward, revealing her ample cleavage, spilling out of a purple top that didn't suit her at all. I concentrated on a hole in my leggings and carefully explained I am interested in contrast, tone and textures of arranged objects in original settings. She just looked at me and scratched her left breast. It wobbled, and I was reminded of blackcurrant jelly. I nearly made up a wild, sexy story to keep her happy, but that would only get me into deeper, hotter water, so I changed the subject to the meaning behind my latest dreams. She accused me of avoidance behaviour. I wanted to accuse her of bad dress sense.

Mr. Cheerful-chatty-taxi-driver told me a joke and I fell out of the cab laughing my head off. Told Ben the joke but forgot the ending, then mentioned the arty-photo conversation to hide my embarrassment at my terrible memory. He said the bedroom was nice and warm and he wanted to finish the film in the camera. I said I had a headache. I did have a headache.

... tiredness swept over her like a polluted brown wave on Folkestone beach...

Tuesday 19th

Before breakfast, I leafed through a home and garden catalogue that arrived with the post; Robert Dyas were having a half-price sale. Think I will ask Ben to buy the garden gnome set: seven brightly coloured dwarves: Happy, Bashful, Grumpy... they'll be company for me when I'm sitting outside in the warmer weather.

My weary morning eyes followed a snow white butterfly fluttering by over the bluebell haze where the fairies live at the bottom of the garden. On the rose bush near the kitchen window, tiny pink rosebuds were beginning to peep through their green jackets, like young women showing a little femininity under their work suits. In the summer they will be whistled at by the worker bees.

Ben has bought toilet paper with pink, blue and yellow flowers and butterflies on: too pretty to use really, but gives me something attractive to look at first thing before my face sends me spiralling into a pit of misery.

Last night I had dreams I wouldn't dream of dreaming, but I'm not writing them down for Georgie's entertainment! Still in a dream-like state this afternoon, I wandered round the house lonely as a cloud of cigarette smoke at a health club.

... she wandered round the house, round the same old rooms, like a tired ride at the Folkestone fun fair...

Wednesday 20th

Didn't feel too bad today; spent ages bathing, scenting, shaving, plucking, moisurising and massaging, brushing and combing, piling my hair up and applying make-up carefully, with lots of rests in between to meditate calmly and peacefully on my split ends and stretch marks.

5.00 p.m.   Stand on bathroom scales and notice have lost three and a half pounds – must be due to all the extra stress I've endured lately. Thanks, Georgie.

5.01 p.m.   Decide stress isn't such a bad thing after all.

5.04 p.m.   Slip into the red silky undies Ben bought me for Christmas.

5.06 p.m.   Half close bedroom curtains and pull tummy in before admiring self in wardrobe mirror.

5.07 p.m.   Wish legs were longer. Wish undies were slimming black. Wish I didn't feel the need to lie down again.

5.10 p.m.   Stare at ceiling.
Mind blank.

5.11 p.m.   Search brain for positive thought. Find positive thought. After today's efforts, I am not crippled with pain and exhaustion, just tired and achy. I must be recovering. Will remind self as much as possible.

5.26 p.m.   Nibble a very small snack so tummy doesn't stick out more.

5.28 p.m.   Stare out of window. I *am* recovering. I *will* get better.
I am calm and peaceful and ever so clean and beautiful today.

5.29 p.m.   Blink
Blink
Blink
Blink
Blink
Blink
Blink
Blink –

extra effort needed due to heavily mascara'd eyelashes. Recall dreams about sad checkout girls, their eyes black and white bar codes.

5.30 p.m.	Avoid *Pet Rescue* so mascara doesn't run and make me look like a panda.
5.32 p.m.	Smile, flutter eyelashes in bathroom mirror and imagine Ben's surprise at my transformation from ugly duckling to, well, not exactly swan; Canada goose possibly, or capercaillie, or chaffinch. Will consult bird book to see which one I'd rather be... if I had to choose... which I don't... but Ben did introduce me as his bird at a party once and I may have to decide one day which bird I'd like to be in my next life. You never know; best to be prepared.
5.33 p.m.	Mascara is definitely too thick and clogged, like legs on a house spider.
5.34 p.m.	Pick bits of mascara off eyelashes. Right eye now bloodshot and watery.
5.35 p.m.	Wipe eye and spoil artistic effort with eye shadows in shades of Rose Crystal, Soft Earth and Crushed Walnut.
5.36 p.m.	Have not bothered with eyeliner; usually end up looking like ancient Egyptian priestess.
5.37 p.m.	Imagine priestess sitting at ornate dressing table surrounded by precious oils, peering into her shiny bronze hand mirror and applying make-up. Maybe she has servants to do her make-up, bring asses' milk to bathe in and then dress her... just what I need.
5.38 p.m.	I've got milk bath granules from the Body Shop somewhere in the back of the bathroom cabinet. I could find out what Egyptians ate (we've got garlic and honey for a start) paint my eyes with eyeliner and have an Egyptian Day! I could place my black cat figurine of the Egyptian goddess, Bast, from Past Times, on the window ledge, sit on the toilet and worship it. Much more pleasant to worship an exquisite feline creature than a man in his thirties, suffering and dying and dripping with blood on a cross after being tortured and persecuted. Those Egyptians got a thing or two right: they considered cats nothing less than god-like. If a household cat died of natural causes, the entire family would mourn and shave off their eyebrows as a mark of sadness. Supermodels do that now; I wonder if they're in mourning for loss of weight

or the days when big was beautiful.

If I order goods worth twenty-five pounds or more from the Cancer Research people, I will receive a golden pyramid of chocolate praline noisettes for just £2.99 (worth £5.99) with a picture of Tutankhamen on the front. The possibilities for fun are endless with all this wonderful time on my hands.

5.40 p.m.   Eyebrows look over-plucked.
            Fill in eyebrows with Coffee Bean eyebrow pencil.
5.41 p.m.   Overdone it. Rub off. Now forehead red and blotchy.
5.43 p.m.   Sit on edge of bath and swear in a feminine way as trying to get into part of pretty-lady-like-man-pleasing-girlfriend.
5.45 p.m.   Panic.
            Ben might come home early and a good laugh is not the intended effect.
5.46 p.m.   Notice under-eye shadow concealer is smudged and mixed with flakes of black mascara. Daintily wipe under eyes with cotton wool ball. Also remove a little of the Dusky Plum powder blush on cheeks because they look bruised.
5.48 p.m.   Maybe I should have dusted cheeks with Sweet Briar or Oyster Pink. Can't decide.
5.49 p.m.   Will use both.
5.50 p.m.   Looks like face has been slapped now. Remove blushers.
5.51 p.m.   Face is red now anyway.
5.52 p.m.   Lipstick is the wrong shade. Perfectly matches blood shot right eye, but not red undies.
            Wipe off Berry Treat and apply Truly Red. Too tarty. Will have to do.
5.53 p.m.   Will lower lights and light a few candles.
            Add a touch of Berry Treat to the Truly Red for my own improved shade – Truly Berry.
5.54 p.m.   Too dark, add more red.
            Starting to look like a clown now.
5.55 p.m.   *Weekly Wife* says the average woman digests one and a half lipsticks during her lifetime. Ugh, feel sick!

5.56 p.m.	Sneeze due to flimsy, inadequate and impractical clothing. Also, air is full of Sensuality body spray with oil of patchouli and sandalwood mixed with lavender and camomile and wild pansy bath essence, aroma of Dove soap and a few drops of sensuous massage oil with orange and ylang ylang for luck.
5.57 p.m.	Blow nose. Have removed spot concealer from nose and most of lipstick. Eyes runny. Spot glowing with pride at looking its best.
5.58 p.m.	Not sure about body spray, think it's gone off. May have to have another bath, but make-up will run even more and plaited wavy hair go flat in the steam and I'll become even tireder. Think I'm going to cry.
5.59 p.m.	Do female ostriches bury their heads in the sand on bad hair and make-up days?
6.01 p.m.	Pull self together, breathe deeply and peer in mirror. Pale and dark eyed, I look like Uncle Fester in *The Addams Family* now.
6.02 p.m.	Resist urge to drown self in smelly cloudy bath water. I could stick a paper bag over my head with two holes for eyes and say it's the new kinky sex craze.
6.03 p.m.	Think positive. Have probably lost half a pound with all this stress.
6.04 p.m.	Will not weigh self as just know scales will tell me I've put on a whole pound.
6.06 p.m.	Weigh self. Have lost half a pound! Must be hallucinating.
6.07 p.m.	Excitement gives me energy to repair face. Try to remeber tips from *Weekly Wife*. Errrrr... Apply concealer to lips before putting on lipstick for longer-lasting effect. Ummmmmm... Lip gloss in the centre of lips makes them fuller. Ahhhhhh... hmmm... Concealer (applied to the inner eye corners) hides shadows and white pencil applied on the inner rim makes the eye appear brighter.
6.17 p.m.	Ah ha! Perfect.
6.18 p.m.	Have forgotten to brush teeth before applying lipstick. Will keep mouth closed. That'll please him. Smile.

6.19 p.m.   Colgate Precision toothbrush isn't so precise anymore anyway, he needs to R.I.P. in toothbrush heaven.

6.20 p.m.   Put on dressing gown so do not sneeze again. Turn on heating.

6.25 p.m.   Pull out tendrils of hair round face for the 'Not tonight, Josephine' look. Practise pouting, and alluring pose.

6.27 p.m.   Leaf through bird book. Think I'd like to be a red-breasted merganser. Ben used to say I was an unusual bird with hot tits.

6.30 p.m.   Don't like to imagine what he'd say now.

6.31 p.m.   He must have caught the later train so I'll apply Flirty Flamingo nail polish to fingers and toes for the final finishing touch.

6.32 p.m.   Shaking this bottle is going to make my arm ache. I'll suffer tomorrow, but it'll be worth it.

6.33 p.m.   Oh dear, too much polish on brush.

6.34 p.m.   Ooops! Can tell I'm out of practice.

6.35 p.m.   Must let first coat dry before applying second. *Weekly Wife* suggests plunging finger tips into cold water. Mmm, good idea.

6.37 p.m.   Toenails next.

6.38 p.m.   Bit easier than fingernails.

6.39 p.m.   Don't fancy dipping toes in cold water.

6.40 p.m.   Neck and back achy, but admire effort.

6.41 p.m.   Not sure about colour now.

6.42 p.m.   What possessed me to buy it in the first place?

6.43 p.m.   Must have been present from Auntie or colour-blind friend.

6.45 p.m.   Should have chosen Romantic Red.

6.46 p.m.   Apply second coat of polish to fingers and toes.

6.51 p.m.   Remove polish from skin around finger and toe nails.

6.52 p.m.   Why do women go to all this bother?

6.53 p.m.   Flirty Flamingo looks f....... flamin' awful.

6.55 p.m.	Should have chosen Flame Red. Must remember to clench fists to hide fingernails; Ben will just think I'm excited.
7.00 p.m.	I could never have been a beautician or a make-up artist.
7.05 p.m.	Order an Indian take-away so Ben will enjoy two surprises tonight and will no longer need to desire other women. Will put on romantic music and he'll serenade me with... 'Lady in red is dancing with me...' and 'Never seen you looking so lovely as you did tonight...'
7.09 p.m.	Can't wait for him to come home; feel excited, he'll be so surprised, he's so wonderful putting up with boring old me.
7.15 p.m.	Where the hell is he, the rat bag?
7.16 p.m.	Hope he hasn't been involved in an accident; he's usually rung by now if he's working late or the trains are delayed or cancelled or something. He may die in an accident and his last memory of me will be of a pale sick hag. Shall I rush to the hospital dressed like this (not sure about wearing red shoes – *Weekly Wife* says coloured footwear makes feet appear larger) and whip off my dressing gown at his bedside so his last memory of me will be a lovely lady in red and all the nurses will think what a moving, tragic scene and cry in the canteen later?
7.17 p.m.	How can I think such stupid thoughts at a time like this? He may be lying in a gutter bleeding to death at this very moment and I'm acting like a selfish tart.
7.20 p.m.	Calm down. Calm down. I will not worry till eight o'clock. This has happened before. Will allow self to worry a lot at nine o'clock. Shall I get properly dressed? Ring his works (no, they'll have all gone home), police or hospital first? Maybe I should be worrying a lot now in case I'm told he died at seven thirty-five and I'll know I was engrossed in *Coronation Street* and will feel guilty for the rest of my life. And worse, never be able to watch *Coronation Street* again.
7.36 p.m.	Difficult to concentrate on what Vera is saying to Jack.
7.56 p.m.	Ben rings from pub (interrupting good bit in *Coro*) to say he's having a birthday drink with Simon and Delyth from work and they're going for an Indian afterwards.

Thursday 21st

Woke up wearing cold wet denim from head to foot, lead wellingtons and an old fashioned diving helmet. That's what it felt like anyway, when I dragged myself to the bathroom and sat on the toilet for a long think.

Lay on the sofa most of the afternoon with an *EastEnders* face like Bianca Butcher, muttering to myself like Pauline Fowler and feeling the need to complain about my ailments like Dot Cotton: 'Oh! me back. Oh! me stomach. Oh! me legs.' I'm not sure they can take all the extra weight I just know I've put back on.

Listened to children giggling outside and the gurgling inside my tummy. Wished I hadn't devoured nearly three platefuls of sag bhajee, chana massalla, brinjal bhajee, pillaw rice, peshwari nan, mushroom biryani, aloo gobi and tarka dahl last night. I can *feel* Madhur Jaffrey grinning on the cover of *A Taste of India*.

Ben said when he came home last night I looked very sexy asleep on the bed in my undies; he'd finished the film in the camera, and could blackmail me by threatening to send the photos to Georgie if I weren't a good girl. I informed him he'd missed the chance of a wonderful evening with his lady in red and I may not feel like a good girl again for months. I then threatened him with a plate of cold, oily, congealed, leftover Indian food for his dinner.

Friday 22nd

Removed Easter and birthday cards from the mantelpiece, TV and shelves after breakfast and felt a touch of post-Christmas-type blues.

Watched dark bodies with umbrella heads hurry past the window in the pouring rain and remembered I'd forgotten to bring drummer Stephen's black umbrella home from the clinic. Laughed to myself as I recalled the day I borrowed Dad's big black umbrella. I was at college at the time and, in those days, hid my short, fat body under a long black woolly coat, down to my ankles. With the umbrella pulled

Walking Mushroom

down over my head, the lads at college said I looked like a black mushroom gliding up the hill – wish I'd seen myself!

College days... they seem so long ago now. I spent most of my time like a canned sardine; sitting squashed up next to tired-looking commuters on a train, scribbling away at a drawing board in an over-crowded classroom, queuing in a busy canteen, squeezing into skirt or jeans in cramped dressing room of groovy boutique, sandwiched between tall people in six-foot-square room of smoky country pub (with loud music) and shivering in outside toilet of pub desperately trying to avoid insects (daddy-long-legs waiting to pounce on my bum) and spiders on walls... best days of my life! Forgot to mention horrendous Saturday jobs, and summer breaks working in a bleak factory on an industrial estate. Oh, to be young again.

... Tall, thin, worried men in long black raincoats stood in the aisle of the 6.20 from Victoria. As the train jerked into the station, the man nearest the door toppled backwards bumping into the man behind him, who also fell backwards, into her lap. She laughed; they reminded her of dominoes and she had been dreaming of a tall dark man falling at her feet...

... The taxis sat outside the station in the rain like large, black, shiny beetles waiting to pick up their prey as the men in raincoats marched past the ticket inspector...

... The beetle nearest the entrance opened its wings to let the prey enter its stomach, looking forward to its pounds of flesh. The wings slammed shut, one after the other. It flew away in the rain, antennae jerking from side to side...

Still felt awful today. Sam Spider said it served me right; he's talking to me again at last. Ben, Rick and Bill will feel terrible tomorrow. They came home from The Chinless Wine Bar, Spot Street, singing 'If I were a rich man' and opened a bottle of claret.

Rick is another drummer friend of Ben's who likes to pose (looking cool) in a tight Zildjian T-shirt, to show off his efforts at the gym. During a gig, he drapes a towel round his neck to mop his sweaty rock star brow, and lights up a cigarette whilst hitting the snare drum in the slow numbers (he needs to calm down from all the adulation after one of his divine drum solos). After a gig, he struts about like a chicken, his drumsticks moving to the beat of the jukebox as he checks out the chicks. He's always *banging* on about his latest girlfriend, the latest *hit* record in the charts and who dared to be late for his latest *bash*.

Ben fried eggs, buttered slices of toast and cut them into soldiers for their 3 a.m. breakfast. I expect Rick's favourite meal is bangers and crash.

Saturday 23rd

Found a toast soldier in a sofa trench, beer cans stood to attention in a row on the coffee table and loose change shone like gunmetal in the midday sun.

Ben took the camera film to Boots to be developed (forgot my garden gnomes) and purchased painkillers; we always seem to be running out. He also bought a carton of Sainsbury's post-Friday-fresh-orange-juice for himself and Bill, who never made it home last night and has started to build a banana and cigarette sculpture on our coffee table. Thought I'd take a photo of it, with Bill smoking in an Andy Warhol way in the background, to show people when he's famous. But there was no film in the camera.

He (Ben) couldn't face healthy Holland & Barrett so we're eating Happy Shopper thin white sliced. I'm eating it now, yum, makes me think of school days, munching slices of Mother's Pride coated in Anchor butter and Golden Shred marmalade before picking up my heavy satchel and rushing off to morning assembly. I had a blue umbrella (or was it green). It was bent and broken; the wind was often strong crossing the bridge over the railway. I remember a house near the bridge, the orange net curtains had purple spots (or was it purple with orange spots) and I longed to knock on the front door and be invited in to discover a colourful, wondrous world. I imagined artists or musicians living there; maybe they had a fruit and fag sculpture on their coffee table too.

Tore the edges off a slice of thin white sliced till it looked like Ireland. Buttered it, then spread lime marmalade all over. I was going to leave it on a plate on the doorstep for a passing leprechaun but Ben ate it.

Decided to look for energy under **E** in spell book; found a chant for raising physical energy and connecting with the goddess within.

Earth my body
Water my blood
(Make hula motion with hands at womb level)

Air my breath
(Hands reaching up)
And fire my spirit
(Pass hands above head and clap)

Repeat over as energy builds.

Oh dear! I'm not sure I have the energy to find more energy and connect with my goddess within. These pagan aerobics are too much for me. But I will try. Maybe tomorrow I will read uses for elms and eyebright instead and visualise doing the pagan hula dance.

Sunday 24th

Saw a cat-calendar-photo-type-scene as I daydreamed out of the kitchen window, waiting for the kettle to come to the boil. A silky black kitten wandered through long lime grass and sun-kissed yellow dandelions. Black cat in April. Last month I remember spotting a ginger and white cat framed by the dark green hedge... Moggy in March. Oh, and a Tabby on a toolbox, a week or two ago... Tabby in October. Think I'll keep the camera handy, I could make a calendar for feline loving family and friends... Seal-point Siamese in September... Abyssinian in August...

Wrote three short, cheerful letters to Gail, Rose and Artie Auntie, using my new recycled writing paper. I love the wide border with a bird and fish design and, although the pages are A4 size, I only have to write my address, the date, dear whoever, three sentences, lots of love and kisses in a thick italic felt pen and the page is filled up. If I write two pages, the paper is so thick when folded up in the envelope it gives the impression I've sent a very long letter. This is most useful when your hands or eyes hurt and you can't think of any jolly, witty things to say because you used them up in your last letter and all you can think is sad thoughts or you're really fed up with trying to sound positive as the years go by or the person whom you're writing to has annoyed you because they keep asking how you are every few weeks *and* expecting a detailed progress report *or* they constantly request that you visit them for a change *or* a break even though you've sent them info on your illness *because* for ages they did not seem to believe how ill you were and still do not *so* you don't feel like saying much to them *and* are sorely tempted to mention that you hope their bout of flu lasts a few more weeks *so* they have a tiny, minuscule, microscopic idea of how you are feeling – phew! As Eileen says, better out than in.

Still, I suppose I'm lucky I had pen-friends before I became ill (I'm very lucky, actually). Other friends have lost touch because I no longer come out to play and am incapable of having long chatty phone calls (really, really *really* miss them; I am a woman, after all). It must be so lonely for sufferers who've lost touch with all their friends and family. This is where the M.E. associations and support groups must help a lot – I'd like to feel well enough to attend one.

The police have dragged weird musician friend out of the river. He's still alive. He said he was trying to cleanse his soul. In the river Medway?

Drummer Stephen rang to ask when he could pick up his black umbrella. Ooops!

Monday 25th

The sun smiled on and off all afternoon like a tired bride on her wedding day. There were a few emotional tears from the congregation of clouds and leaves fluttered like pretty bridesmaid's eyelashes at the best man.

> *... the priest read the blessing, 'Cumulus nimbus non-rain-on-us.'*

I sat on the garden bench, before my bath, breathing in an after-rain-steamy-earthy smell, feeling close to nature and relieved that today's session with Georgie would be my last. Tried a little pagan aerobics but after reciting the chant twice with all the motions I collapsed on the grass. I stared up at the trees, sapped of energy. Something crawled into my ear.

Eileen and I talked about that wonderful stage at the beginning of a relationship when he listens to everything you say because he loves the sound of your voice and the way you smile and tuck strands of silky hair behind your shell-like ear and after you've been chatting on the phone for ages, neither of you wants to put the receiver down. We both sighed deeply at distant happy memories. Eileen stared out the window and forgot she was treating me. I forgot where I was. Don't know how long we stayed like that.

After my osteo-crunch, I felt great and had plenty of time before seeing Georgie to pop into the mini-market next door and buy a birthday card for Gail. I found a suitable one with a picture of a black and white cat, and a pair of earrings in the chemist next door (also black and white) like Liquorice Allsorts. Remembered Ben likes liquorice so

I returned to the mini-market to buy him a packet. It seemed as if I'd been to three shops in one day! Am recovering; I *will* get well soon. Nearly bought myself a get-well-soon card just for the hell of it.

Nearly told Georgie I'd been wandering round the house in slinky red undies doing the pagan hula dance, feeding myself Indian delights and shagging on the sofa by candlelight to romantic music. Resisted the urge to tell her I'd been dreaming about horse riding, snakes and flying because my dream book says they are believed to be related to sexuality. We talked about the importance of listening to your intuition, learning to forgive and expressing one's anger. She told me about her problems with her mother and boyfriend; I offered her a Liquorice Allsort and my good advice.

When I got home, I expressed my anger by murderously chopping up a carrot and standing on an empty upturned egg box (imagining the six cardboard egg cups as heads of certain people I used to work with) feeling it slowly crush beneath my feet – good and flat to neatly fit in the already full rubbish bin. My intuition told me to eat giant slices of cheesy pizza. Forgot to ask Eileen about the black umbrella but forgave myself; blamed my bad memory on the weather. If it had rained, I'd have remembered.

Later, I told Ben we all shelter under the same umbrella of universal consciousness. He said, 'Oh God, what have you been reading now?'

Tuesday 26th

Yesterday I stopped to talk to a dear little old man outside the mini-market. As he watched me shove my purse into my handbag, he commented that people think about money too much these days and they should be grateful if they can get out of bed in the morning and listen to a blackbird sing. He is right, and I will remember his words every morning. When I can get out of bed.

Two birds, a blackbird and a song thrush, were pecking away on the lawn early this morning (the mistle thrush prefers open fields, parks, and has greyish-brown upper parts). Every time I see a thrush, I'm reminded of Ben's sister-in-law: she has lots of freckles, a turned-up beak and small dark beady watchful eyes. Always was a bit flighty that one.

Ate three of Ben's lunchtime granary rolls full of naughty fillings. I am fed up with the anti-candida diet.

Me:	Grass on the lawn is getting really long.
Ben:	Mmm.
Me:	It needs its first haircut of the year.
Ben:	Mmm.
Me:	The dandelions are growing up fast and have started telling the time already!
Ben:	Did you eat those rolls?
Me:	No, the granary fairies grabbed them.

Wednesday 27th

... she watched thousands of tiny specks of dust frantically doing what specks of dust do in afternoon sunlight...

I was a busy speck of dust once, milling about with other specks in the great living room of life. Now the great yellow duster of chronic illness has flattened and trapped me and, like a duster that's all used up, I've been thrown in the washing machine to go round and round in circles. At the end of my cycle, I'm all limp and screwed up.

... she felt slightly crazy as she sat in the stripy deck chair on Folkestone's stony beach, staring out to sea. It started to sprinkle with rain and a chilly wind blew her hair across her mouth. Her eyes watered. She was not crying; it was the wind. She was not going to cry; someone might notice and try to comfort her and she didn't want to speak to anyone. They might also notice her thin clothing and the soggy uneaten sandwich on her lap, and think her very silly. They might say something kind or tell her off and if she started to cry she knew she wouldn't stop. Everyone had gone home now anyway...

Thursday 28th

Felt more cheerful today; must have been the sunlight and jolly apple and leaf pattern on the kitchen roll. Spent most of the afternoon flicking through a pile of old magazines, tearing out useful health and beauty tips I'll probably never read again.

5.00 p.m.	Ten seconds of pagan aerobics.
5.35 p.m.	Watch *Neighbours*.
6.01 p.m.	Turn off news.
6.02 p.m.	Listen to kitchen clock ticking tirelessly.
6.03 p.m.	Stare at the time on video recorder.
6.05 p.m.	Listen to people arriving home tired, slamming a car door followed by a front door.
6.10 p.m.	Stare at blank TV screen.
6.12 p.m.	Wipe dust off TV with new kitchen roll because dust is depressing, what with dreams of giant yellow dusters falling from the sky and squashing people and red blood seeping through the yellow. And there's no *Coronation Street* tonight.
6.19 p.m.	Remember Georgie's advice to thank my illness for giving me such a wonderful learning experience. (She was full of this sort of advice; all right for her sitting there all full of energy, free of pain and mental confusion – apparently my neck pain is caused by stubborness. Huh! How come I didn't have it before I had M.E., stupid old bag!)
6.23 p.m.	Wipe living room mirror with another piece of beloved kitchen roll and thank my reflection, not very convincingly. Pity this learning experience isn't like school, with weekends, Christmas, Easter and summer holidays to look forward to.
6.25 p.m.	Sneeze and wipe nose on dirty kitchen roll without thinking.
6.27 p.m.	Answer door to salesman and tell him, 'NO THANK YOU', after listening patiently to his spiel. Salesman asks me why I'm not interested and I want to punch him on the nose.
6.30 p.m.	Notice have dirty nose.
6.31 p.m.	No wonder salesman was smirking.
6.32 p.m.	No energy to wash nose.
6.33 p.m.	Wipe nose on sleeve and feel like scruffy schoolboy, what wiv me spots, lank hair and moody expression.

All I need is chewing gum and a football to kick around the house.

6.45 p.m.   Never mind, *Enders* on in three quarters of an hour and Martin Fowler is up to more mischief.

Friday 29th

Two catalogues and a postcard from Cornwall arrived this morning.

First catalogue: It's Spring! Time to come out of hibernation and give yourself a super, sensuous spring-clean with our new bodycare ranges – it really is the best time of year to tone-up your skin for the warmer months ahead. But hurry, hurry. These offers will only run while our spring stock lasts.

I've no energy to hurry, sorry.

Second catalogue: It's time to order the best-fitting swimsuit you've ever worn – gracious to any figure, in two torso lengths with choice of bra styles, it fits and feels as if custom made just for you. The Empire Slender Suit with Slendertex tames the tummy and hips, with three times the 'holding power' of regular swimwear fabrics. Shape and sculpt your way to an hourglass figure, with no effort on your part.

Sounds perfect. Pacific turquoise is a good colour.

Postcard from Cornwall:

> Weather V. mixed. Sun yesterday, but rain coming down like No.8 knitting needles, so hiding in caravan. Reading, writing cards and putting our feet up. Still, it won't be raining in the pub where we go for dinner....
> Love Gail and Gareth xx

> **Dear God,**
> **Please can I have time off for good behaviour. I'd love to go to Cornwall, to Mousehole where I used to stay. I want a holiday from myself. I want to splash in the sea wearing a Slendertex swimsuit. Please make me well and I promise I'll be a better person and learn to**

**think of M.E. as a wonderful learning experi-
ence. I'll stop having bad thoughts about other
people and wash my hair more often.
Lots of love xxx**

**P.S. Please let Ben come home safe. It's very
late and I'm a bit worried...**

Saturday 30th

Ben flew into the bedroom after an evening drinking Spitfire at The
Pilot last night. He zoomed out again to the bathroom then whizzed
downstairs and glided round the kitchen, cheese in one hand, bread
in the other. After making the biggest cheese sandwich in the world
and another flight to the bathroom, trailing crumbs, he made a safe
landing on the bed, fully clothed. He munched. He snored.

Covered my head with a pillow so I wouldn't breathe in cigarette and
alcohol fumes. Breathed in pillow fumes instead. Really must wash sheets.

*... in her dreams, she flew on the back of a dove to a peaceful island, Moon
Island, to recover from M.E. When she arrived, she discovered a black forest full
of gâteau bushes. In the middle of a lake, an arm appeared, holding a bottle of
champagne, the sun sparkled on the label – 'ting'. Mushroom pizzas grew in the
middle of fairy rings and Maltesers hung from the branches of trees, falling on
the ground to make lovely lumpy chocolatey piles...*

Forgot to ask Ben to buy the garden gnomes before he went out shopping this morning; must remember tomorrow.

This afternoon we sat in the sitting room. Ben slurped coffee and
studied the computer magazine resting on his tummy; I sniffed and
stared into space.

Me:	Did you know the word poltergeist is German in origin and means noisy spirit?
Ben:	Mm.
Me:	Bergamot comes from the rind of a small fruit in Italy.
Ben:	M.
Me:	Did you know Flora was the Roman goddess of flowers, the garden and spring?

Ben:	I thought Flora was a margarine, the one that keeps men in shape.
Me:	Maybe *she* kept men in shape!
Ben:	Yeah.
Me:	Her festival, Floralia, was celebrated from April the 28th to May the 3rd.
Ben:	Mmm.
Me:	That's now.
Ben:	Mmm.
Me:	It was a time of unrestrained pleasure, games and licentious revelry, where the customs of the Maypole originated.
Ben:	Mmm.
Me:	*Unrestrained pleasure! Licentious revelry! ...* Nudge, nudge... pout, pout, pout...
Ben:	Didn't you go out with a morris dancing man?
Me:	Yes, and I worked with one too. He used to show me his little Shepherds' Hey at lunchtimes... jumping up and down between the drawing boards.
Ben:	They're all barmy, playing with their bells, leaping about waving hankies and banging sticks. Like fairies with beards and waistcoats.
Me:	I *like* morris dancing. Did you know the leather strap they wear across their chest is called a baldric... like in *Blackadder!*
Ben:	Perverts... don't they wear those tapples... er, tarsles... no... tipples... tassles...?
Me:	Tatters, yes sometimes, very colourful.
Ben:	Hnngg.
Me:	I'm so bored, I want to go out singing and dancing all night... tonight... *I'm so bored!*
Ben:	Nnng.
Me:	BORED, BORED B..O..R..E..D!!!!!!!
Ben:	You should take it easy if you're feeling better and not overdo it.
Me:	HUH.
Ben:	Stick the kettle on, I'm parched.
Me:	I can't, I've got to pack. I've just decided I'm flying off to an island to meet Pierce Brosnan and Colin Firth on location.

Ben: Mmm.
Me: For lots of *loverleee* unrestrained pleasure, licentious revelry
            and *beeauutiful* bodice ripping passion... aahhh, ummm...
Ben: Don't forget to take your long nightie from Past Times and
            Chanel 007 then, dear.

Sunday 1st

9.45 a.m.　I've done it! *I've done it!! Yes, Yes, Yes, Yes, Yes, Yes!!!!*
I've survived FOUR WHOLE MOTHS of the year! And
I'm still sane (on a good day) even though my antennae
aren't at their best, my prolegs ache and sometimes I long
to return to my larva days when I fed on trees and life was
simpler.

Poplar Hawk-moth

Garden Tiger-Moth

Large Yellow Underwing

Spurge Hawk-moth

9.50 a.m.　Buzz... buzz... buzz... it's that buzzing fly in the bedroom
time of year again. An insect with a shiny blue bum is
trying to impress me with his impression of a wartime
bomber.

9.51 a.m.	I am not impressed.
9.55 a.m.	Crawl out of bed, pick up sweatshirt. Swish sweatshirt about a bit to encourage the Stuka to bomb elsewhere.
9.56 a.m.	The enemy will not be reasoned with. Name fly Adolf. Name makes me feel sick; Addy is better.
9.57 a.m.	Didn't sleep much last night, kept waking up after crash landing on Moon Island. Want to go back to sleep for a couple of hours or so.
9.58 a.m.	Whizzzzzz... Whizzzzzzz... past my ears.
9.59 a.m.	Pick up *Riders* (huge doorstep book) and throw across room. Sorry, Jilly Cooper.
10.00 a.m.	Zooooom... Zoooooom...
10.02 a.m.	Throw half an ecology loo roll and knock lamp over.
10.04 a.m.	Pick up knickers... Ssswish... Sssswish...
10.05 a.m.	Open window and accidentally throw out pair of knickers with elastic nearly gone.
10.06 a.m.	Call downstairs asking Ben to retrieve knickers from front garden.
10.07 a.m.	Peer around bedroom curtain to see if anyone is watching. The curtains twitch across the road.
10.08 a.m.	Recall a morning years ago when I was married and my husband asked for a rag to clean his car windscreen. I was in hurry to get to work, so handed him a pair of my old knickers. When he picked me up from work that evening, he held them up at my office window for all my colleagues to see. The state of my underwear became a topic of amusement for some time!
10.09 a.m.	Have used up today's mental and physical energy now.
10.10 a.m.	Will never get back to sleep. Shouldn't be throwing things about – I wouldn't hurt a fly.
10.12 a.m.	Roll up copy of *Weekly Wife* and put my *Jim Carrey with angry face* on.
10.13 a.m.	Room is silent – it worked!
10.14 a.m.	Addy is grinning at me from his perch on the rim of a Kit-Kat mug.
10.15 a.m.	It would be a pity to break a Kit-Kat mug, but it wouldn't be my fault, only self-defence.

We fancied chips tonight. While Ben piled frozen rectangles on a baking tray, I found a saucepan for the peas and made up a poem.

> **Addy the fly**
> **Is a spy**

Ben finished it,

> **Who likes his chips**
> **Crisp and dry**

Later in bed...

Me: **He likes to eat them**
            In his bed
Ben: **Better than the**
            Garden shed

I never knew life could be so exciting as one approaches middle age. Not sure I can take the pace.

Monday 2nd

Cosmic Colin tells me I'm feeling a strong desire to broaden my horizons over the May bank holiday; I'll want to get out and sock it to the world and travel far from where I am. He is right, but at the moment I'll have to be satisfied with travelling to the bathroom and picking up a dirty sock on the way.

Ben was in a good mood today; he didn't have to go to work, has a short working week and is looking forward to a trip to Birmingham next weekend. He brought home the Seven Dwarves Garden Gnome set from Robert Dyas and said they will suit my snow-white complexion. I sang, 'Hi ho, hi ho, on the window ledge we go.' I'll set them outside tomorrow, or the next day.

Me: Happy... Grumpy... ummmm.
Ben: Bashful.
Me: Errrr... can't remem...
Ben: Sneezy!
Me: Was there a Sneezy?
Ben: Not sure; I think there was one who was always sneezing.
Me: Maybe he had hay fever.
Ben: Yeah.

Me:	Yawn... Sleepy!
Ben:	Yeah, Sleepy... ahhh... umm...
Me:	That one looks like a Worried, or maybe he's Fatigued.
Ben:	Or Constipated.
Me:	That one looks like Thoughtful.
Ben:	No, doesn't sound right.
Me:	This one's got a big belly, he could be Greedy. Happy, Grumpy, Bashful, Sleepy, possibly Sneezy... Happy, Grumpy, Bashful, Sleepy... why don't you ring Bill, he might know...
Ben:	Hi Bill, howeryou?... yeah fine... yeah really busy... you?... Got a question for you, mate, can you name the Seven Dwarves?... Dwarves, yes... We've got these gnomes, you see... yeah... dwarf gnomes... yes, all seven... can you? ... yep... we've got Happy... Grumpy... Bashful and Sleepy so far... oh there is a Sneezy... we weren't sure... ah! Doc... ha, ha, ha... that's OK... cheers Bill... yeah... he is... yeah... right... yeah... six o'clock Friday... OK... cheers... bye... I will... bye.
Ben:	Bill kept thinking of Harpo, Groucho and Chico!!
Me:	Ha, ha, ha, I've got Dave, Dee, Dozey, Beaky, Mick and Titch on the brain. Doc, that's an odd one.
Ben:	Just one more to go then... They look rather sweet in their colourful little hats and jackets don't they?
Me:	Dopey.
Ben:	I'm not.
Me:	No – Dopey!
Ben:	Ah, sorry, silly me.
Me:	Happy, Grumpy, Sleepy, Sneezy, Dopey, Bashful and Doc.
Ben:	Hurrah!

This afternoon, Ben wondered where all his decent shirts were so I pointed to the little mountains of dirty clothes round his side of the bed. I also informed him that the goat moth is so called from the unpleasant smell of its larva.

Consulted my dream book after a night of moons, islands and mermaids.

Mermaid – She represents a rival of some kind, most probably for a loved one's affection. Oh dear!

Island – This can mean isolation, loneliness, escape, paradise, a firm place to be in a sea of problems, or all of these. Oh Lord!

Moon – You are likely to crave some element of romance in your life. Yes definitely.

We coughed and sneezed at *exactly* the same moment tonight; I suppose that's quite romantic. Oh! And we made up a poem together yesterday and he did pick up the knickers I threw out of the window and put them on his head to make me laugh (hope they were clean).

Consulted my pocket book for the modern witch to see if there was a spell to bring gnomes to life under **G**; there was! All I had to do was light a green candle, brew peppermint tea, then place the gnomes in a bed of mint growing in the garden. Indoors, I sat quietly visualising the gnomes talking (energy from the earth and mint bringing them to life) while I sipped the minty brew. I let the candle burn down then crept outside with a torch. The only sign of life was a large snail slithering over Sneezy's nose, but I'm sure I saw Happy wink and, as I closed the back door, there was a tiny sneeze from *that* corner of the garden. Decided to wait till morning and went to bed with fingers crossed; my *spelling* never was that good at school.

Read about uses for garlic and ginger: garlic cloves for protection and the flowers for altar offerings, ginger for love and success.

Tuesday 3rd

Seven little dwarves climbed into the kitchen through the cat flap as I was filling the kettle; I nearly fainted. They greeted me by lifting their caps and bowing, except Grumpy, who just nodded and scratched his ear. I offered them peppermint tea (when I found my voice) but they politely declined, shyly clambering back out through the cat flap and hi-ho-ing off to work down the path. Wondered if I was hallucinating; were there magic mushrooms in the peppermint tea?

Caught sight of my reflection in the kettle; definitely not the fairest of them all. Wondered if there were a spell to make one beautiful.

Baby greenfinches and sparrows were queuing next to the bird feeder on the trellis, beaks open and little bodies quivering, waiting for mum to serve dinner. They're not so fluffy now and will soon be pecking at the peanuts themselves. Ben has been buying peanut butter recently; I'm very tempted to peck at the jar with a teaspoon all day. Dipped my beak in the jar a couple of times after *Neighbours*. I might finish the jar tomorrow, it depends how depressing *EastEnders* is.

Saw my first wasp of the year. Heard it whiz past my ear before I saw it, just as I'd settled calmly and peacefully on the sofa with a teaspoon of peanut butter, poised, ready to be consumed with relish. Used up my day's worth of energy coaxing Mr. Wasp out of the kitchen, tea towel in one hand, cushion in the other – once stung, twice careful not to let it happen again. Twice stung (if you're outside and there's no handy tea towel) flap arms about madly and scream, or flap sun hat and scream madly, or if you have M.E., it's best to get someone else to do the screaming and the flapping. If you're on your own, sit under a net, like those covers to protect food from flies that granny always used, but much bigger of course.

So glad I have my tips from *Weekly Wife* for dealing with wasp and bee stings stuck on the kitchen cupboard.

1)   Scratch bee sting out instead of squeezing it.
2)   Do not rub inflamed area; this will make it more painful.
3)   Eat garlic, a natural insect repellent.
4)   A slice of raw onion draws out toxins from the skin.
5)   Vinegar reduces inflammation from wasp stings.
6)   Use baking soda mixed with water for bee stings.
7)   Lay a pack of frozen veg on the inflamed area.

My Tip: Pretend you are Julie Andrews in *The Sound of Music* and sing *fortissimo* with feeling, 'When the dog bites, when the bee stings, when I'm feeling sad, I simply remember my favourite things and then I don't feel so bad.'

If that's how they deal with pain in Switzerland, I feel very sorry for the Swiss!

Better make sure I'm in the kitchen if I'm stung this year so all the remedies are at hand. Must not close eyes for long when resting in case bee or wasp sits on nose. Forgot to take royal jelly and bee propolis today. Found spoon with peanut butter on, upside down on carpet by sofa.

Wednesday 4th

Got up in the night, glanced at my face in the bathroom mirror, and decided I might just flick through my spell book. After sitting on the toilet reading uses for basil, bay, benzoin, bergamot, betony, birch, borage, blackberry and blackthorn, I came across a beauty spell – that was lucky!

Opened the bathroom window and, making sure the moon was reflected on my hand mirror, I placed a photo of myself on the mirror. I repeated a few magical words about moonshine and starlight carried by the wind (I shivered), glow covering my body and shine covering every eye. Then I repeated a few more words (three times) asking moonshine and starlight to shape and mould my body (as a rose is granted beauty) and let me blossom in the light that grants me beauty (granting me beauty three times three). I closed the window and lit one of my candles (a pink one) letting it burn down before peering into the mirror. I looked worse, like a witch with a cold and tooth rot.

First thing this morning, I almost ran to the bathroom; thought I might look a *little* better at least, but all that stared back at me was the face of a novice witch who had inhaled too much candle smoke and cold night air. I sneezed. Think I may have used up all my power on the gnome spell, and started a cold.

A tiny bouquet of wild flowers tied with bindweed lay by the cat flap in the kitchen. I giggled; *someone* thinks I'm the fairest of them all. I laughed out loud; I have my very own seven dwarves!!!!!!!

Read a romantic story in *Weekly Wife* and decided to try and write one myself...

... she lay on the grass in the shade of a weeping willow...

No (weeping willow sounds sad)
Sycamore tree
No (helicopters might fall on her head)
Ash tree
No (don't like the word ash)
Ashtray (she could be the size of an ant)
No
Lilac tree
Yes (pleasant childhood memories)

... she lay on the grass in the shade of a lilac tree, closed her eyes and listened to the sound of birds and bees...

No bees (she might get stung)

... she lay on the grass in the shade of the old lilac tree, slowly closed her eyes and listened to a bird's song. Charlotte...

No
Emily
No (too Brontë)
Poppy
Rosie
No (too flowery)
Susan
Jane
No (too plain)
Octavia
Harriet
Imogen
No (too Jilly Cooper)
Sharon
Tracy
No (too common)
Naomi
Claudia
No (too supermodel)
Elizabeth
Victoria
No (too regal)
Shona
Saffron
Yes (groovy chick)

... Saffron must have dozed off because a sound nearby made her jump out of her skin and shriek...

No (wrong atmosphere)

... Saffron must have dozed off, a small rustling sound startled her, she opened her eyes and gazed up into sky blue eyes...

No
Sapphire blue eyes
Dark sexy eyes
Sexy blue eyes
Irish eyes
Sapphire sexy Irish eyes
No
Hyacinth blue eyes
Cornflower blue eyes
No
Kingfisher blue
Peacock blue
Periwinkle blue
No
Promises blue
Possibly
Missing you blue
Maybe
Grey blue
Greeny blue
Very blue
Blue blue
No (boring)
Prussian blue
Phthalo blue
Cerulean blue
Cobalt blue
No (too arty)
Bubble bath blue
Bubbly blue
No (too silly)
Forget the eyes.

... she gazed up to see a firm sensuous mouth...

No
Sexy lips
No
Full firm sexy lips
No
Lopsided manly grin
No
Nice teeth
Forget the lips.

... she gazed up into his smiling handsome face and trembled in anticipation of his warm kiss...

No
Soft kiss
No
Gentle kiss
No
Tingly kiss
No
Fresh and tender kiss
No
Soft as cotton wool
Feathers
Fennel leaves
Rose petals
Butterfly kiss
No
Sloppy wet kiss
No
Hot dry kiss
Forget kiss.

... anticipation of his warm body lying down next to her. He sneezed and from that moment on she knew he had post-viral syndrome...

Must work more on my endings. This writing is hard work: all the decisions! And worrying about what other people will think of what you've written and having to agonise over a single stupid comma. I'm as confident as an ant trying to hurry across Victoria station to meet his mate arriving at platform three; during the rush hour. Think I might stick to verse.

> **Moon moon**
> **They're playing**
> **Our tune**
> **I see your face**
> **Across the room**
> **Give me chocolate**
> **Pour my wine**
> **And everything**
> **Will turn out...**

...awful, try again.

> **You kiss my cheek**
> **You kiss my nose**
> **Warm as heaven**
> **Soft as rose**
> **You kiss my eyes**
> **You kiss my hair**
> **Little arrows**
> **Everywhere**

Even worse.

Thursday 5th

Found a heart-shaped potato sitting by the cat flap (another present from my little friends, I think!) and in a happy hearty mood, started to scribble a few lines...

... he noticed her lying under the lilac tree in a feminine, pre-Raphaelite way and knew she was the girl for him. The smell of herb tea emanating from a plastic cup, the Kit-Kat wrapper, neatly folded, not screwed up and thrown at nature. She was a sensible girl, but needed comfort. He knew he could comfort a body like that, those wonderful child-bearing hips and those breasts; he needed comfort too. And she baked! She had been baking bread or cakes; he noticed the

flour under her fingernails. Unless she hadn't bathed today, though he knew from her faint scent that she had. Something flowery. Floury, that's how he remembered mother's hands. Soft and floury.

He wanted to run his fingers through her long, silky, satiny, chestnut hair; not many split ends, he was pleased to see, and just a touch of make-up. Her eyebrows were plucked into perfect arches, reminding him of his beloved train set. Two buttons were undone at the top of her floaty-floral dress revealing a slight cleavage and a delicate cross and chain. Perfect, a Good Christian Girl; Mother would approve.

Taped *The Addams Family* last night and watched it this afternoon. Morticia and Gomez were *so* romantic.

Morticia: When we first met, it was an evening just like this... magic in the air... a boy.
Gomez: A girl.
Morticia: An open grave... it was my first funeral.
Gomez: You were so beautiful, pale and mysterious, no-one even looked at the corpse.

Must find my tapes with the BBC's brilliant adaptation of *Pride and Prejudice*. I can watch the best bits as many times as I like, especially that bit where... and he climbs out of the lake... oooh... and he's all wet... and he surprises Miss Elizabeth Bennet... *so* romantic...

Miss B: Mr. Darcy!
            (Thinks) Oooh, I can see his nipples through that wet shirt.
Mr. D: Miss. Bennet!
            (Thinks) Those wonderful heaving breasts in that little jacket... only three buttons...
Miss B: I did not expect to see you, Sir, we understood all the family were from home... we should never have presumed...
            (Thinks) Gorgeous dark eyes... snog me now!
Mr. D: I returned a day early... excuse me, your parents are in good health?
            (Thinks) Such fine eyes... can I shag you in my four poster?
Miss B: Ah... yes, they are very well, I thank you, Sir.
            (Thinks) I want to brush the tendrils of wet hair from his forehead.

Mr. D: I'm glad to hear it...
          (Thinks) I love to hear her sweet voice.
          How long have you been in this part of the country?
          (Thinks) How long have you fancied me?

Miss B: About two days, Sir.
          (Thinks) Oooh! that masterful voice, beat me with your riding crop, Sir!

Mr. D: And where are you staying?
          (Thinks) And where are you sleeping?

Miss B: At the Inn at Lampton.
          (Thinks) He wants to sneak up the back stairs and ravish me during the night...

Mr. D: Oh, yes of course. Well... well I'm just arrived myself... and your parents are in good health? And all your sisters?
          (Thinks) Oh God, I've already said that; she'll think I'm an idiot!

Miss B: Yes, they are all in excellent health, Sir.
          (Thinks) How sweet, he's embarrassed, I want to rip his shirt off.

Mr. D: Excuse me.
          (Thinks) I greatly desire to kiss Miss Bennet in her bonnet but I'll ruffle her splendid countenance and composure; and that would be most disagreeable.

This evening I felt inspired to write my bestest poem yet – if I'm going to be a famous poet, I'd better stop using words like bestest.

> **Her lips as red**
> **As a Kit-Kat mug**
> **Her smile**
> **As slow as a snail**
> **Her eyebrows raised**
> **In feigned surprise**
> **They twitch**
> **Like a pussycat's tail**

Pleased with effort; not sure about use of Kit-Kat mug or spelling of feigned though, or the word snail – might sound a bit slimy.

... Saffron gave him a slimy kiss and he knew, at once, she had passed her cold germs on to him; Mother wouldn't approve at all...

Sniff. Sniff. *SNEEZE!*

Friday 6th

Had an odd dream last night about clouds with a red lining, sliding across the sky at a snail's pace.

A heart-shaped leaf rested against the teapot; I laughed heartily. I made breakfast at a snail's pace. I blew my nose slimily.

There was an article in *Weekly Wife* about a writer who has sold an amazing fifty million novels around the world; she's one of the Mills & Boon best-selling authors. Now completing her eighty-eighth book, she writes about two thousand words a day and can polish off a book in five weeks. *FIVE WEEKS!* Oh Lord, I've got all this time on my hands and *all* I can manage in five weeks is a couple of paragraphs and a handful of pathetic, short poems. I couldn't write romantic fiction for love nor money – how does she do it? She says her secret is that she believes a knight in shining armour is just waiting to sweep her off her feet. Poor woman. She's probably so busy creating perfect men (disillusioning millions of women in the process) and travelling about for her research and writing away, she wouldn't notice a suitable-partner-type-chap even if he wined and dined and snogged her till her ears dropped off. Even if he were kind, understanding and thoughtful, intelligent and creative, generous and good looking, charming and fun, she'd be looking for the square jaw, masterful manner, roguish twinkle in his eye and wondering if he had a huge mansion. Mmmm, he sounds nice, wonder if he exists... oh dear, maybe I could write romance after all; but I don't believe in all this knight in shining armour rubbish: I've met too many shites in whining amour.

Anyway, the trouble with your average knight in shining armour is he's always getting you pregnant then running off to battle and you don't know if you're soon to be widowed or not. His spare suit of armour is a devil to polish, and when he comes home he's too busy nursing his wounds or you're too busy mopping his brow for any bloody romance. One of the children is always dying of some horrible illness and he's too tired to care and the place is always a mess because the vacuum cleaner and Fairy Liquid haven't been invented and your hands are rough and aged because Vaseline Intensive Care Hand and Nail Lotion hasn't been invented either. If he wins a battle and is unharmed, he's off celebrating down The Sword and Sausage or The Turnip and Trotter. Or he's jousting or hunting. Then there's the endless stag nights or he's tied up at a boar meeting and won't be home for dinner. He buys you a spinning wheel and expects you to be contented when he's away, but sitting in a chastity belt is *so* uncomfortable.

Feel sorry for Ms. Millions Novel-Writer. I hope she meets the man of her dreams one day, even if she's very old and half blind from writing thousands of books and wears pink.

Maybe she'll be literally swept off her feet by a caretaker and his broom at the local village hall after another family wedding. He'll be a fright in shining overalls with a face that must have once been handsome. She'll be waiting for her grandson to pick her up after everyone's gone home, feeling sore after sitting on a hard wooden chair. She'll lift her small feet (squeezed into smart M&S sensible shoes) so he can sweep under them and feel ever so conscious of her untidy hair and lack of lipstick (because it all came off on the plastic cup and sausage rolls). His kind watery eyes will meet her lonely watery eyes and they'll swim together for one moment in the seas of togetherness. Then he'll offer to meet her after bingo for a nice cup of tea and a cake at that quiet little olde worlde tea room in the High Street and they'll live companionably ever after.

Robert Southey on Charlotte Brontë
Literature cannot be the business of a woman's life, because of the sacredness of her duties at home.

I'd better do some blessed washing-up then!

Read without much interest about stomach disorders, about tips, tricks and trends to brighten up your home and six questions for Anthea Turner. Since Matthew was born, I'm more into, 'Better Breast Feeding', 'Relieving Colic' and 'Bach Helps Baby Sleep'.

Found a couple of CD's by Johann Sebastian Bach mixed in with the Beatles, Beethoven and the Bee Gees. Decided to make a cassette recording for my sister and wondered if Matthew would prefer concerto for two violins, strings and continuo in D minor, or possibly G major, or the Brandenburg Concerts. Left a message on Gina's answering machine mentioning the tape and later she left a message on my machine while I was sitting on the toilet humming along to an *adagio* second movement. Her message was, 'YES, PLEASE!' followed by a big yawn and the sound of healthy lungs in the background.

It was warm enough to sit outside in a T-shirt at three o'clock this afternoon. I waved Happy, Grumpy, Bashful, Sleepy and... ummm... Dozey and Sneezy and errr... Doc off to work in the garden... 'Hi ho, hi ho...'

Just before they left, Doc said a little bird had told him there was a lot of digging work at Bigger Hill so they'd be away for a few days now and again, I wasn't to worry, and they'd bring me back wonderful healing rocks. Oh goody, must ask Ben to find a book on crystals; I can pay for it with the birthday token I found, all crinkly and soft at the edges in the depths of handbag land.

I left Bach doing his thing in the sitting room while I daydreamed in the garden. Violins filled the house, pouring over the furniture like thin gravy over new potatoes. They seeped out through an open window like juice escaping from a hot fruit pie, trickled in zigzags down the pane and under the peeling paintwork on the window ledge like cream under puff pastry. Staccato notes dripped here and there like vinegar on to chips, evaporating in the sunshine into sweet light melodies like brandy on a Christmas pudding. They tangled in the strands of my hair like candy floss, lifting my spirits like a soufflé and making my eyebrows dance like popcorn. Started a diet today and of course all I can think about is food.

A breeze, gentle and fleeting as a butterfly's toenail, brushed my cheek. And thoughts, thoughts as soft and light as a strand of cotton wool caught in my eyelash, settled in my mind like a feather on a pond. Happy little thoughts and memories, like ballet dancers in the under-fives class, pirouetted across my mind's stage under a curtain of eyelashes; all baby-girl-pink and white. I sighed... I smiled... I sipped my herbs and imagined high tea in the summer garden of an English country manor; genteel conversation, delicate white china, Hobnob biscuits, lace and linen and my eighteenth-century frock fluttering in a warm wealthy breeze. Then I sneezed and spilt tea down my dirty dressing gown.

A woodlouse wandered around my foot like an old war veteran in a shiny grey raincoat on his way home from The Pilot pub, twitching his moustache.

Ben came home from The Upper Crust and Crown, very drunk and fruity. I informed him the drinker moth is so called from its habit of drinking drops of dew and when the eye hawkmoth is molested, it displays its eye marks to scare predators away. Tried flashing my eyes. He smiled with a fag in his mouth, like a toad enjoying a juicy beetle, and informed me the convolvulus hawk-moth has an extraordinarily long proboscis strongly attracted to the nectar in a tobacco plant. I flew away and locked myself in the bathroom.

Saturday 7th

9.06 a.m.   Open eyes. Vision all blurry and head moving in slow motion.

9.07 a.m.   Have been affected by dreams of cloud snails in the sky.

9.14 a.m.   Computer grey clouds float wearily past my grubby Windows 95 pane. I try not to think about Ben, halfway to Birmingham now.

9.15 a.m.   Soon he'll be hundreds of miles away. Soon he'll have forgotten I exist. He'll be enjoying the company of lively, energetic, well people.

9.17 a.m.   Try not to stare at phone. Stare at dust on phone instead and dead fly on window ledge.

9.18 a.m.   Will not sit around like pining doggie waiting for her master to call. Will allow self to glance at phone now and then because it has become a habit, like staring at clocks. Must be terrible for dogs left in kennels while the family are on holiday, not knowing if or when they'll see home again. Or worse, left in quarantine for six months in appalling conditions or abandoned and ending up in Battersea Dogs' Home, waiting to be loved.

9.20 a.m.   Happy, laughing couple bounce down the road in matching trainers and T-shirts. Together. Arm in arm. Close. Not hundreds of miles apart from each other. Side by side. Secrets. Smiles. Secret smiles.

9.23 a.m.   She shouldn't wear tight jeans with a bum like that.

9.25 a.m.   Very young couple follow behind with baby in pram. He must have got her pregnant when she was still at school, naughty boy. I expect she went to a school like mine, fashion, fags and foreplay being the main topics of conversation. I was the weirdo who read a book on her way home and bumped into lamp posts and was nicknamed Iron Knickers by the boys (maybe I wore a chastity belt in a previous life).

9.26 a.m.   I'm not going to wallow in loneliness this weekend. Will find lots of little things to do and concentrate on staying calm and peaceful. Am not going to spend every waking moment wondering what he is doing, whom he's doing it with; is Delyth flirting with him, is he flirting with her?

9.28 a.m.   Perch on side of bath wearing green T-shirt like sick budgie trapped in small cage.

9.30 a.m.   Ben forgot his toothbrush and Bad Boy aftershave; still, I expect there'll be a chemist near his hotel. I wonder if Cheryl and Candra went to the exhibition too and are staying at The Swallow with Ben, Rob, Simon and Delyth. Will they order a cosy table for six tonight?

9.31 a.m.   Candra put lots of love and three kisses on Ben's Christmas card last year. Bet her name is Sandra really, like that strange fashion designer who calls herself Zandra.

9.35 a.m.   Pull face in mirror. When I'm a famous rich poet (do poets get rich?) I'm going to have a facelift. Don't care if it hurts – I'm used to pain.

9.36 a.m.   Stretch face upwards with palms of hands to see what a facelift would do for me. Look like Japanese woman with migraine.

9.46 a.m.   Feel fat. Like budgie who's eaten too many comfort seeds. Feel very sorry for budgies transported from Australia, their wings trapped in tubes, travelling like slaves on the slave ships of the nineteenth century.

9.48 a.m.   Need huge, whole chocolate cake for breakfast.

9.55 a.m.   Toast crumbs down front of dressing gown and honey dribbling down chin.

9.56 a.m.   Slurp real tea. Will now feel extra anxious with Mr. Caffeine galloping round my arteries.

9.58 a.m.   Wonder if Jane from accounts went to Birmingham. She will soon be moving to the wilds of Scotland with her man John. Ben said they've just found a fantastic cottage – am trying not to feel too envious. Although I've never met Jane, I really like her. From what Ben has said, she's a good laugh, loves animals and always sends us a card (with badgers or bunnies in the snow) and home-made rum truffles at Christmas. Anyone who loves animals, makes truffles, and gives a box to me *must* be great! Pity it's the lovely people who move away; there's too few of them. The ones you wish would jump off a cliff stay miserably at home festering in their boring little lives.

10.00 a.m.   Long daydream about wandering in Scottish wilds.

10.06 a.m.   Remember dream where Eileen is wearing Scottish Widow cloak and carrying her pet haggis in his tartan jacket. Must tell her.

10.56 a.m.   Find self staring miserably at phone again. Tell self off. Distract self by reading letters in *Weekly Wife*.

11.09 a.m.   One letter makes me laugh, one letter makes me cry, another makes me very cross like a sparrow whose lump of Hovis has been stolen by a bad-mannered starling.

11.10 a.m.   Am an emotional wreck now.

12.12 p.m.   Fancy vege-haggis 'n chips for lunch.

12.15 p.m.	Fancy ringing someone for a good old phone moan.
12.21 p.m.	Fancy man on Gap advert.
12.22 p.m.	Does Ben fancy Delyth?
	Does she fancy him?
12.23 p.m.	Will have bath in a minute; must find energy to climb stairs. Need more food for fuel.
12.30 p.m.	Munch. Munch. Munch.
1.52 p.m.	Chirrup and splash wings about in bath water.
2.35 p.m.	Pull on yellow T-shirt. Now look like sick canary.
2.36 p.m.	One of Ben's friends at work, Paul, went to live and work in the Canary Islands last year with *his* friend Paul; they sing and play guitars in bars to entertain the holidaymakers. One of the Pauls has M.E. and is hoping the hot weather will alleviate his symptoms. Hope he's doing OK.
2.38 p.m.	Always feel a bit tearful when I think of someone else going through the same as me.
3.05 p.m.	Discover Ben rang and left a message while I was in the bath. Wish he didn't sound so cheery (girly laughter and clinking glasses in the background). Play back message three times. Play back all eight messages twice so can hear lots of human voices. Am not sad and lonely. I'm fine, I'm fine, I'm fine. Wonder where he went for lunch? What did he eat? Was it delicious? Was it expensive? Was there a good selection of veggie meals with interesting cheesy spinachy, creamy and nutty or spicy tomatoey things with side salad or chips or both? Did he have pudding? Was it very sweet and creamy and chocolaty or fruity? Who was he sitting next to? Were they laughing and joking a lot? Was the wine flowing freely and flirtily?
3.10 p.m.	Switch off questioning brain and decide to do something absorbing and creative to stop me killing myself.
3.11 p.m.	Begin to design inside cover thing for Matthew's cassette tape of music by Bach.
3.12 p.m.	Chant in a witchy way to enhance creativity...
	I create from things I find (felt pens) my own work of art as She created from herself a work of art. I call it remembrance as She provided all these treasures for our nourishment and pleasure (I should be using sticks and

plant dye). I accept the things I find. I create new worlds (a cassette tape cover?) as She laboured and played so do I remember her (no energy to do the dancing around spiralling inward and outward; flutter eyelashes instead, heavily laden with midnight blue mascara).

3.14 p.m.   Have entitled the tape 'Music for Matthew' – not very original; perhaps it should be:
Bach To Beat the Baby Blues.
Violins not Valium.
Concertos for the Cot.

3.15 p.m.   Gina won a contest to name the Radio One cat back in the eighties. I think I was married at the time and she was living with that horrible, mad biker bloke, who never worked, grew cannabis in a forest and was cruel to cats.
Anyway the Radio One cat is probably dead or very old now – I think they live about fourteen to eighteen years. Anyway... anyway, she called the moggie Meew-sic and won a few records or something. I was very proud of my little sister in her moment of fame.
I once named a gas main, installed across the Kent countryside by British Gas when I worked for them: Bloody Boring Long Heap of Uninteresting Two-Hundred-and-Fifty-Millimetre Sickly Yellow Polycthylene Pipeline Buried in Deeply Gouged Earth Disturbing and Endangering Wildlife.
They never used it.

4.02 p.m.   Quite pleased with artistic efforts on 'Music for Matthew' tape cover. I've doodled treble clefs and crotchets around my best handwriting using pink and blue and yellow felt pens.

4.03 p.m.   Mustn't smudge it. Mustn't smudge it.

4.04 p.m.   Could use toilet paper for blotting paper but will probably spoil my efforts in the process and I'm too exhausted to nip upstairs to the bathroom anyway. Wish we had a downstairs loo.

4.05 p.m.   Must find jiffy bag so I can post tape to Matthew and Mummy.

4.07 p.m.   Gina rings to ask me a favour and says she's desperate for the tape. I say it's winging it's way to her and to hang on in there (more ear piercing young lung music fills the background). She's being quite pleasant lately (will try to forget this usually happens when she wants something).

4.10 p.m.   Flap piece of artwork in front of electric fan heater to make sure design is completely dried.

4.11 p.m.   Am impatient to see what it looks like when fitted into plastic cassette case.

4.12 p.m.   Cardboard has curled a bit, have burnt my hand and cassette case is tinted brown so the colours look dingy. Will have to find plain see-through case. Problems, problems.

4.13 p.m.   Need to rest after emotionally busy day; will look for cassette case and jiffy bag later.

4.56 p.m.   Wake up to sound of man laughing heartily outside. Sounds like Ben. Think of Ben. Try not to wonder what he'll be doing tonight and whom he'll be doing it with...

4.57 p.m.   Remember Gina's request for a favour; she would like me to paint some designs on an old cot given to her by a neighbour. I didn't have the heart to say no, but explained it would take a few weeks because I can only do a little bit on good days due to muscle problems, etc. Didn't tell her how upsetting and frustrating it's going to be having to paint something over weeks that would normally take only a day or two. Books about M.E. say one should learn to say no; I haven't learnt yet. I suppose it's because I really, really want to feel useful and needed and part of things, even if it means a lot of pain. I'm so very tired of being a useless pink lump (as useful as a porcupine in a balloon factory) when I'm so used to helping others.

5.10 p.m.   **'Music for Matthew'** looks good in the clear cassette case, even though I say it myself! The case is a bit scratched but it doesn't matter: there are worse things in life, like not being able to hear music or see beautiful colours or nose at the neighbours across the road.

5.12 p.m.   Quick, quick, must *do* something before I spiral into a depression about disability which will probably wind down and down into cruelty to children and animals and war and hatred and things... write brief note to go with tape, wrap note around case and snuggly fit it into jiffy bag.

5.16 p.m.   Write address on jiffy bag and fish stamps out of purse amongst till receipts and reminder notes. Lick stamps. *Weekly Wife* says every time you lick a stamp you consume one tenth of a calorie; maybe that's how Mum fed me when I was small! I remember licking pages and pages of Green Shield Stamps and sticking them in the Green Shield Stamp book so we could have little luxuries, like an imitation Edwardian-style candelabra. Of course, I didn't know at the time it was Edwardian style but years later, I saw the same candelabra in a period drama (I wonder if theirs was from the Green Shield Stamp shop too). Just thought, maybe that's why I've got a thing about candelabras, possibly caused by Green Shield Stamp poisoning. Ha, ha. Anyway, I'd better flutter my eyelashes to work off three tenths of a calorie.

5.19 p.m.   Stamp dries while I'm thinking. Decide to sellotape stamp onto parcel, but not tape over whole stamp as man at post office will get cross, like that time four or five or six Christmases ago at our main post office when it was busy and everyone in the queue was listening... I'd sellotaped over four stamps.

5.21 p.m.   Seal jiffy bag with lots of sellotape as jiffy bag is a bit old and torn.

5.22 p.m.   Cheer up a lot. Have done good day's work. Will reward self with something yummy I discovered at the bottom of the freezer the other day. I am calm and peaceful, healed and healthy, I love me, I love herb tea; I hate chocolate, I'd hate to be a supermodel; both my socks are matching so I'm balanced. I will write better poetry, I will learn to say no, I've done something useful so I feel good about myself, my immune system is rejoicing so I'll get better quicker.

5.27 p.m.   Remember the Tesco bag full of Mills & Boon romances Rob's wife Bev has kindly lent me to inspire my creative romantic writing. Am I bored and desperate enough to read one? No, not yet.

5.30 p.m.   Fish books out of carrier bag and have giggle at the covers. All the men (usually dark action men) and women (candlelight glowing on long glossy hair) look the same, with matching perfect noses and cheekbones. Of course, only beautiful couples can enjoy wonderful romance.

5.31 p.m. You can read about the ugly ones in *Weekly Wife*.

5.32 p.m. I'm not tempted by:
A Woman of Passion
Devious Desire
Relentless Flame
Climax of Passion
Am sure titles used to be more like:
To Touch a Dream
A Moment of Magic
Loving Melody

5.41 p.m. Mr. Boxer-face walks past window.

WALKING THE DOG

Mr. Boxer-face
Walks down the street
With antique coffee table
They stride together happily
As much as they are able

5.50 p.m. Poetry not good today.

6.16 p.m. Sit at bottom of staircase. Need toilet. Cross legs and activate creative brain cells.

LUCKY ME

I have paper
On a roll
To the bathroom
Is my goal
I have soap
On a rope
And a basin
Full of hope

6.22 p.m.	Not much improvement there. Perhaps when I'm more miserable as the evening drags on and have refuelled with energy-giving carbohydrates, I will be at my most creative.
6.23 p.m.	If I eat a whole packet of chocolate Hobnobs at *that* time of the month, I'll probably write a really sweetly sensual period drama. If I devour a heap of buttery toast, maybe I'll write a romance set in a bakery – *Mother's Pride and Prejudice.*
6.50 p.m.	Blob five heaped dessertspoonfuls of mayonnaise onto enormous cheesy pizza, cooked over a *Relentless Flame.* Devour pizza with *Devious Desire* for that long lustful *Moment of Magic.* I am *A Woman of Passion* when it comes to comfort food.
7.15 p.m.	Read a paragraph out of each Mills & Boon novel so I can say I've read them, thanks-very-much-most-kind. Well, I don't *have* to say I've read the whole book, do I?
7.40 p.m.	Am engrossed in film about a woman who is stricken with a fatal illness and decides to find a replacement wife and mother for her family.
9.10 p.m.	Ben is better off without me; he will decide to replace me this weekend. He will not return home until he has found a new woman – perhaps he's found her already. I'll never see him again and he's the only one who understands me, I think; when he's listening to me. I'm going to die alone sitting at the kitchen table with my Kit-Kat mug and only a spider to say goodbye to me.
9.36 p.m.	Find a mini-stapler while searching for needle and cotton to sew up small hole in leggings.
9.38 p.m.	Sew up hole in black leggings with white cotton. Don't care what it looks like. Think about repairing heart and health and things like that.
9.46 p.m.	Sit and click mini-stapler.

Click.

Click.

Click.

Click.

Click.

Watch tiny staples drop onto lap; they look like fairy

paper clips. What would fairies need paper clips for? Oh, yes! Spells and enchantments faxed from Fairyland.

Staples run out. I keep clicking, like that bit in *Fatal Attraction* where Michael Douglas has left Glenn Close all alone and she's sitting on the floor beside the bed clicking her lamp on... off... on... off... on... off...

10.09 p.m.   Perch at top of stairs looking down at something crawling on the bottom step. I'm like an eagle at the top of a mountain pin-pointing her dinner.

10.11p.m.   Rest head against wall and watch teardrops drip onto the green carpet and soak in like starlings disappearing into a sycamore tree.

10.14 p.m.   Another teardrop splashes onto the skirting board and rolls down over bumpy paintwork – very artily sad. Imagine viewing self from above; would make good camera shot for heartbreaking Channel Four drama about loneliness; heart-string-tearing violins and grim cellos in the distance, a Kit-Kat mug all by itself on the kitchen table and a half-smoked cigarette in a grimy overflowing ashtray. One knife. One fork. A *meal for one* box on the work surface next to a small loaf of white Happy Shopper bread and two rotting bananas. *Cooking for One Is Fun*, still in cellophane wrapper (unopened bills and junk mail piled on top). A faded, dog-eared photo of a smiling couple at the seaside rests against a half-size packet of digestives, long past their sell-by date. One lonely blue toothbrush drips Sensodyne tears. The toothpaste tube is squeezed to death. Hairs rest in peace in the plug hole. Article in *Weekly Wife* lies open next to toilet: 'The Single Life is Simply Super'.

10.36 p.m.   In bed. Feel as low as a man stuck down a mine shaft with no means of escape, a winning lottery ticket in his trouser pocket.

10.38 p.m.   Sip glass of water.

Pick up pen.

I FEEL

I feel
Myself breathing
I feel
Cold glass in my hand
I feel
Water on my lips
Cold liquid
Trickling down my throat
Into my stomach
I feel
You looking at me
I feel
You look away

I am still thirsty
I want to drink you
But you are
All
Dried
Up

FEELING OLD AND FORGETFUL

I'm a crumbly
Old building
Pigeon pooh
All down
My
Face

I'm a Victorian
Old lady
Red wine
All down
My
Lace

I'm an Edwardian
Candelabra
Cobwebs
All down
My
Wax
I forgot to send
An e-mail I will have
To send
A fax

11.17 p.m. Pleased with effort – lots of feeling there. I am suffering for my art.

11.18 p.m. Peer into crystal ball to see what future holds but can only see greeny blue swirls. Crystal ball is just an old marble found in drawer (handy for fairy fortunes though).

11.19 p.m. At least I haven't lost *all* my marbles.

11.35 p.m. Has Ben gone to bed yet?
　　　　　What did he do tonight?
　　　　　Where did he go?
　　　　　Did he have a lovely meal?
　　　　　What did he eat?
　　　　　Who is he talking to at the moment?
　　　　　Has he found a woman to replace me?
　　　　　Will he be home tomorrow or Monday?
　　　　　Will I ever see him again?
　　　　　Will he ring again?
　　　　　Is he drunk?

11.36 p.m. Hear phone ringing downstairs and Ben leaving a slurry message saying he'll be home t'morrr-evenish-laytishhh. Plod downstairs to pick up receiver at same moment as he is putting it down. Squawk into receiver like an angry parrot.

11.38 p.m. Dial 1471. Ring him back but there's no answer. Squawk again and flutter off to bed, the wind screaming and rattling my cage.

Sunday 8th

When Ben rang (sounding worse for wear) to say he wouldn't be home till Tuesday (no reason), I mentioned I'd just spotted a goldfish sitting on the fence (let him think I'm going a little crazy, he may think twice about going away next time). Of course I meant to say I'd spotted a goldfinch; and when he comes home I'll tell him I saw these amazing twinkly starfish in the sky, a couple of squid in my purse, the kitchen is full of dirty crockery because there's a crocodile sitting in the sink (in a rather snappy mood) and it's a male so I don't want to mention washing-up in case he bites my head off and can he do the washing because there's a lobster in the washing machine and I don't want to move him (the lobster) because he looks so happy and in love with a red tea towel; also there's a mermaid in the bath enjoying my seaweed soap.

Sketched a few ideas for Matthew's cot: moons and stars with happy faces and Saturns. Must remember to ask Ben to buy some blue enamel paint when he comes home, if he comes home.

Monday 9th

Mr. Mills-and-Boon-cover-ex-racing-driver-taxi-man, cool as a cucumber in his tight green T-shirt, picked me up in his shiny white taxi late this afternoon. The traffic was so busy it took ages to get to the clinic. He ignored me and I couldn't wait to get out of the car; I felt so drab in baggy blue, no make-up and hair pulled back with a black scrunchie (must wash all my scrunchies; give me something exciting to do).

Eileen relieved the aches in my head, neck, hands, shoulders and back, due to too much drawing, weekend worry and seven hours of suspicious thinking. Told her my doubts and about my desperate craving for peanut butter. She was very sympathetic about everything and admitted to having a secret hoard of chocolate hazelnut spread for her monthly comfort sessions. What would I do without her; what will I do if she moves back to Scotland (she's been thinking about it lately)? It would be like losing a best buddy.

Oh, dear! I really will die alone soon. Wonder if many people will attend my funeral. If Rose brings all her children and ex-husbands that will swell the crowd; must remember all their birthdays so they don't forget me. Must start repenting for my sins so Saint Peter will let me in through the gates of Heaven. I expect there will be a Thornton's in Heaven (since 1911) and lots of exquisite little clothes shops – everything in soft white comfortable fabrics designed by Ghost; the clouds, clean and fluffy and bouncy so you can fly around all day with the angels and not get dirty. Quite looking forward to dying now!

Eileen spotted *BLACK UMB* written on the back of my left hand and laid Stephen's umbrella next to my handbag.

I was relieved Mr. Quiet-and-gentlemanly-nice-Val-Doonican-jumper-and-smile-taxi-man picked me up. When I arrived home, I placed four slices of bread under the grill and a nutty voice from a jar in the cupboard called out,

'I'm here, I'm here. You know you want me, You know you need me. I'm all yours, where are you? I'm waiting, why are you taking so long? Alright make me suffer, stick the knife in. Go On, I dare you!'

I was listening to Ben's phone message saying he would be coming home on Friday now (had decided to take unpaid leave to visit old schoolmate) and stuffing face with peanut-buttery-toast when drummer Stephen called round on his way to a gig. Hid toast under sofa and wiped crumbs off face and boobs before answering the door. He gave me a very uninterested look and complained about headaches and back pains. I gave him an understanding look, his umbrella, and told him about Eileen and her treatment. He sounded more interested but didn't stay long. I'm so boring and ugly.

After he left, I lay on the sofa picking bits of fluff off cold toast. Ate it. Cried a bit, then got down to some seriously miserable creative writing to take my mind off things.

Stephen Inglenook sat and stared moodily into the flames. His back ached. It was no good, he'd have to make an appointment to see Morag. His gardener Ted was always singing her praises and at the age of sixty-three was fitter than Stephen at thirty-six.

Bourneville Grange, dark and bitter as its new owner, was badly in need of repair. In the sitting room, the smell of damp and rotting wood was barely disguised by the sweet aroma of burning cherry logs and strong black coffee. A log crumbled, fell apart and firelight flickered in his tired eyes. He hadn't lived there long – five, maybe six weeks – but already two villagers had spoken highly of marvellous Morag, the village osteopath. It must be her. Yesterday he had asked Ted for a description of her; he'd tried and failed not to sound too interested.

He missed his faithful dog, patted the worn chair arm without thinking and wondered if she'd ever thought of him over the years. He envisaged her running happily through the fields with her long black hair and yellow dress, yellow like the buttercups. He remembered her head bent over like a sunflower when she read a book, her eyelashes thick and dark, resting on her cheek like the old yard brush leaning against the garden shed. Twenty years. Twenty long years. Twenty long, tiring years. People changed, they forgot things. Had she changed, had she forgotten him? He remembered her so well, the way she rescued a bird from the farm cat and cried when it died; nursed her sick mother through a long illness; and the day she gently cleaned a wound on his knee with cotton wool and TCP – not the most romantic of smells, but it still brought back memories.

Too Mills & Boon. Mmmm... more sinister, I think.

He thought of his own mother as he dug a sharp knife into a trout he'd caught that morning. The shiny grey head, with glassy eye, slipped onto the dirty kitchen floor covered in crumbs and onion skin. Biscuit, the ginger tom, grabbed it with eager jaws and raced out of the cat flap; a dead mouse lay at his master's feet. Biscuit thought it was a fair swap. Biscuit was a very thoughtful cat.

Starting to sound like an animal story.

Bach's violin concerto in A-minor filled the room, blending with the soft evening light. He thought of her soft voice, shiny blackberry hair, cherry lips, peachy skin, strawberry birthmark (on her inner thigh) and pretty pear shape. She had lived on Chutney Farm, near Applepie village on the Blueberry downs.

Too fruity.

Stephen forgot to take his black umbrella home.

Tuesday 10th

MILLS & BOON

When she was young, before she wed
She read her Mills & Boon in bed
And saw herself in Sven's strong arms
Complete abandon to his charms
Enjoying all the naughty bits
Was he going to touch her...

Too saucy.

NO MORE MILLS & BOON DAYS

When she was forty-something
And he walked out the door
There were no more Mills & Boon days
She couldn't read them anymore

She made a bonfire in the garden
Gave Mills & Boon a poke
All those happy endings
Going up in smoke

Too sad.

Gina delivered the cot today. Matthew had slept peacefully in the car all the way to our house so I suggested she drove all night. She was not amused.

Ben hasn't rung.

Wednesday 11th

This afternoon was warm and sunny with the promise of sunburn in June. I sat for a while in the garden admiring Ben's new fence and the blancmange pink roses; their smell reminding me of the Nulon hand-cream Mum sometimes used; the dark pink buds, like the patterns on Mum's delicate china, only brought out when Auntie Mary came to tea.

The dwarves returned from their travels, hi-ho-ing down the path. Happy handed me a pretty rose quartz crystal (for loving energy) like a huge chunk of pink Turkish delight. It felt cold and heavy but warmed in my grip; my heart sparkled. Bashful gave me a rosebud, then turned crimson. Happy laughed. Dopey gave me a splendid shiny leaf. Grumpy muttered to himself, Sleepy snored under the hedge and Doc passed Sneezy a hankie.

Wendy of *Weekly Wife* says pink is the hottest colour this summer and you'll be seeing it everywhere. I'm already seeing it everywhere. Pink is on every catwalk from New York to Milan, from the palest pink to brilliant fuchsia in a big, big way. Big deal.

Drew two smiley stars and a moon on Matthew's cot. I'm tempted to paint them pink instead of blue to please Wendy. Better not; Gina will only hit me over the head with a rolled up Greenpeace catalogue.

Still no phone call.

Thursday 12th

1.00 p.m.   Flop on duvet in middle of bed and just lie there, like an egg in flour.

1.30 p.m.	I will not be beaten.
2.00 p.m.	Draw a Saturn.
2.30 p.m.	Lie on carpet, like rolled out pastry on flat floury surface.
3.00 p.m.	Draw another Saturn.
3.30 p.m.	Lie on bed with duvet pulled over body and head, like pastry top over cherry pie.
4.00 p.m.	Stare at phone.
4.30 p.m.	There may be fault on line.
5.00 p.m.	Fancy whole cherry pie to self with gravy boat full of Bird's custard.
5.30 p.m.	No cherry pie. Make large saucepan full of custard.
6.00 p.m.	Leave burnt saucepan for Ben. Ha, ha.

Friday 13th

Half a star.
Sad poetry.
Bit of washing.

Boring film.
Nobody's rung me.
Nobody loves me.

Sometimes the stars are bright
Sometimes they are not
Sometimes memories of you
Are all that I have got

Sometimes your hankies are clean
Sometimes they're full of snot
Sometimes your dirty washing
Is all that I have got

Saturday 14th

Ben crept in late last night while I was asleep. This morning, he surprised me with breakfast in bed; not my usual boring health-shop-bread-toast and herb tea: oven-warmed croissants, chilled freshly squeezed orange juice, real tea, single red rose in a champagne glass and Thorntons chocolates neatly arranged on a tray in heart shape, followed by kisses, cuddles and compliments!! Thought maybe I'd died in the night *and* gone to Heaven already.

Decided to lap ~~top~~ up feeling spoilt and contented (like the cat who's got the bowl of Häagen-Daas ice-cream and is looking forward to a lovely long sleep in the airing cupboard) before Mr. Suspicion started whispering in my ear. Mentioned I needed a pot of blue enamel paint for my new project and my new man asked, with a wide helpful smile, 'And which shade does Madam require?'

I politely requested he take down a picture from the bedroom wall so I could inspect closely the shade of blue in the sky; it was near what I wanted but needed to be sort of darker. Then I had him rooting through a chest of drawers for a faded blue T-shirt; far too pale. After clonking around in the bathroom he returned with a blue toothbrush, sponge bag with blue fishes on, hand towel, Head & Shoulders shampoo and a whale-shaped soap. Nothing was to Madam's satisfaction, so I sent him down to the kitchen. He returned a few minutes later bearing gifts and a pained expression: oven mitts, a chequered tea towel, soya milk carton, paracetamol box, curry house take-away pamphlet and a Bird's Custard tin – 'Yes, that's near,...just a tad darker than that,... a smidgen lighter than this.'

Saw a car out of the bedroom window the exact shade I wanted and, as he ran towards the window, I said, 'Oops, you've just missed it.'

While he plodded downstairs to make a coffee, I recalled part of a conversation we had last year after Ben had seen a couple of carpets he wanted to buy and was trying to describe them: 'Well, it's a bit like the green on the lawn after rain, no, nearer the hedge but lighter, no, darker. The other one's the colour of my coffee, but a little bit darker with white bits in – Oh! You know. You're the bloody artist.'

Refreshed after his caffeine fix, Ben plonked another pile of goodies on the bed: a biro (completely wrong shade), a dictionary (too grey-blue), a Peter Pan video case (almost right shade), a candle (much too dark), a postcard from France (far too light).

He'd just slammed the front door and trotted off down the road with bits of torn labels in his wallet when I saw the perfect shade on my Wallace and Gromit mug. Sipped herbs from the mug with a naughty grin all over my face.

Ben's bathroom bag was grinning too with slightly rusty teeth as I sat in the bath admiring my nice clean fingernails. A brown eyebrow pencil like a thin cigar rested on it's lower lip. Not *my* eyebrow pencil – I would have to draw my own conclusions about this!

Like a dentist examining the molars of a man who chews garlic everyday, twice a day, I nosed inside the bag to see if there were any more surprises. There were: tweezers, gold tipped, not mine. No packet of condoms, just a suspicious looking piece of cellophane, condom packet sized. The bathroom bag laughed.

Sat on the loo and tried to work out how to broach the subject of eyebrows, and who has plucked and pencilled eyebrows at Ben's workplace. I suppose I could just turn up at the factory and squint at all the female eyebrows with a huge magnifying glass. Better not; I'll get carted off to the funny farm.

The eyebrow pencil in question is a very light shade so *she* is possibly blonde. The tweezers are gold tipped – posh tart. Mmmm, what about the rest of the make-up? Probably so pretty she doesn't need it. I hate her. She's probably very nice but I still hate her.

Decided to pluck my eyebrows to death (couldn't stop sneezing) and pencilled in a thin curved line (can't believe I did that in my teens) and thought I'd ask Ben's opinion when he came home from town. Good way to broach the subject.

He asked me why my face was all red and blotchy, had I been crying and was I thinking of becoming a clown when I'm well. So much for the weekend of compliments. I explained the problems of keeping beautifully plucked eyebrows in order to frame one's face and was just wondering, small passing thought, not that I care or anything, but did any of his female colleagues pluck and pencil the hair growing above their eyes. He didn't have a clue and asked me if I'd seen anymore goldfish sitting on the fence recently (Oh. Good! I've got him worried). Wasn't in the mood to mention the crocodile in the washing-up bowl, lobster in the washing machine and mermaid in the bath.

After sulking for three hours and forty-two minutes I showed him the tweezers and brown pencil. As he laughed, I watched his brain working overtime behind his eyeballs. Finally he came up with a convincing story about needing a pen in a hurry to write down an important phone number and his mate's girlfriend had obliged with the eyebrow pencil as her biro didn't work and he'd left his pen at the hotel;

she also lent him the tweezers to pluck out a splinter in his hand. There must have been a lot of plucking going on last week. Was tempted to ask if he'd aquired the splinter while tied to a wooden bedpost.

Think I will become a detective when I'm better, instead of a clown.

Questioned him about what he'd been doing all week and he said they'd (who's they?) been checking out the pubs and curry houses in Birmingham, as he checked his shopping till receipt without looking me in the eye. I *then* politely enquired what the pubs and curry houses were like. He laughed while unpacking a Sainsbury's carrier bag and said he couldn't remember, as he opened the fridge and carefully placed the soya milk on the top shelf and margarine in the washing-up bowl full of water! He's playing it *cool*, I thought to myself, and not realising he might soon be in *hot* water.

Me:	Did the Brummy barmaids have plucked eyebrows?
Ben:	Oh, is that the time!
Me:	Were the birianis yummy?
Ben:	I promised Rick I'd...
Me:	If you say biriani-yummy fast you get Brummy!
Ben:	Hi Rick... yeah fine mate... yeah... you OK for Monday?... great... yeah... I'll check he can make it then get back to you... Rob said he'd meet us there and Bill's coming here first... yeah... few beers... good idea...
Me:	B-i-r-i-a-n-i-u-m-m-y... b-i-r-i-u-m-m-y
Ben:	Yeah, she's OK, just going off her trolley... yeah hahaha... seeing goldfish too...
Me:	B-i-r-u-m-m-y... b-r-u-m-m-y
Ben:	OK mate, I'll get back to you... yep... bye.
Me:	Brummy, Brummy, Brummy, I've got a hungry tummy... la la la la la... money, money, money... always hungry... it's a rich man's world.
Ben:	Hello, I'd like to order a take-away please... mixed vegetables with sweet and sour sauce... yep... beansprouts... egg fried rice... mushrooms... fried onions and err... prawn crackers... yes, that's right... how much is that?... OK, can I collect about seven... OK thanks, bye.

Felt much happier with a full tummy and a pot of blue enamel paint (almost the right shade) *and* I discovered Ben's mate's girlfriend is blonde (explains light brown eyebrow pencil), is in a well-paid job (explains gold-tipped tweezers), he'd been helping his mate put up a wooden fence (explains splinter in hand), his mate hadn't paid his phone bill, so could only take incoming calls and the nearest phone box had been vandalised (explains lack of phone calls). He is a man (explains everything).

Have too much time to think; my poor man is innocent. (Surely pubs and curry houses have a phone?)

... Mrs. Suspicion pointed in her face with a shaky, veined, age spot covered hand and reminded her how worn out and satisfied her man looked. Mr. Trusting, on the other hand, smiled and said her man had merely enjoyed a break from everyday stresses but had slightly overindulged on the beer and birianies...

Sketched a moon and one and a half stars on the cot tonight while Ben downed a few cans of beer with Bill, who has been enjoying his life-drawing classes but feels he is rather too slow; he spent a whole session drawing one nipple and admiring the young model.

I'll think of one nipple everytime I see Bill now. I said, 'Bill, would you mind nipple over to the corner shop for a breast of chicken.' He replied, 'I'd rather stay in the bosom of my close friends and read your bird book.'

As I crawled upstairs for *another* bath to ease my achy bits, he shouted, 'Look Ben, there's a nice little pair of tits on this page!'

Lay in the bath with just my nipples protruding above the surface of the soapy water. Ben says my boobs look better in the bath, under the water; uplifted, not so saggy. Held a mirror above myself; he is right. Getting old is so depressing. I bet Delyth's got firm ones.

Sunday 15th

1.15 p.m.   Notice woman on advert has perfect eyebrows.
1.16 p.m.   Bet Delyth's got wild Welsh eyebrows to suit her dark, wanton looks.
2.31 p.m.   Draw a star.
2.45 p.m.   Draw a Saturn.
2.53 p.m.   Rings on Saturn look wrong shape.

2.54 p.m.	Rub rings out.
4.15 p.m.	Pencil in my eyebrows.
4.16 p.m.	Eyebrows wrong shape.
4.17 p.m.	Rub eyebrows out.
4.19 p.m.	Have another go.
4.20 p.m.	Rub them out again. Give up.
4.21 p.m.	Decide to have another attempt at rings on Saturn tonight – wonder if God had a devil of a time creating the three planar concentric rings of ice particles.
4.22 p.m.	Pluck out few more hairs above eyes.
4.23 p.m.	Wish my eyes weren't so close together.
5.45 p.m.	All women, every single one, on covers of *Weekly Wife*, with their stupid, smiley faces, have beautifully shaped eyebrows.
5.47 p.m.	Read about how five readers coped with cheating partners.
5.52 p.m.	More eyebrow spotting.
5.53 p.m.	Woman smiling after nose job has over-plucked hers. In the 'before' picture, she looks like a startled eagle.
5.54 p.m.	Mmmm, woman from *Emmerdale* has used too much eyebrow pencil in the wrong shade and has a horrible, hard face – wouldn't want to get into an argument with her.
6.30 p.m.	Staring out of bedroom window with Cathy and Heathcliff emotion – come back bushy eyebrows, I miss you.

Monday 16th

Don't know why, felt like dressing all in black today. Had this feeling of impending doom and thought I must be ovulating or experiencing a premonition; the taxi would be late picking me up from the clinic or I'd miss the first half of *Coronation Street*. My hair was straggly, a spot beamed on my nose and I gave myself dark boomerang eyebrows so I looked really witchy. It was raining bats and frogs so I was very tempted to borrow Stephen's black umbrella to match my outfit and mood. Managed fifteen seconds of pagan aerobics.

Eileen relieved my gloomy headache and fatigue while we talked about the moon, Mars, chocolate, comfortable shoes and peanut butter. She said a recent Chinese study (looking for a cure for sleeplessness) found that peanuts worked a treat. They contain two natural tranquillisers, tryptophan and vitamin B6. I *knew* my body was trying to tell me something; I need peanut butter to feel calm and peaceful. I mentioned a recent American study found that chocolate can help you live longer: it contains chemicals called antioxidant phenols that help reduce the risk of heart disease and cacao (substance from which chocolate is made) which boosts the immune system and protects against cancer.

As I was Eileen's last patient, we agreed to pop into the mini-market next door for a few essentials. I was tempted to buy bright blue eyeshadow to fill in the space between my eyes and very thin eyebrows, for the Abba look. Where's that sparkly top?

Bill, Rick, Ben and Rob went to Polly's Poppadoms to celebrate Bob the Slob's birthday.

Tuesday 17th

Spent what seemed like ages (with lots of rests) drawing a moon, star and Saturn. Wished my hands were as steady as they used to be, wished my neck wouldn't seize up like a lump of concrete forgotten on a lonely deserted building site, wished my eyes wouldn't go all cross-eyed at the slightest detail, and wished upon a star that one day I'll be able to draw all day if I want to.

> **When you wish upon a star**
> **Thinking of the peanut jar**
> **When you wish upon a star**
> **Your dreams come true**

Last night, I was a mouse on the moon. The moon was made of cheese and I was just having a little nibble when an enormouse ginger cat appeared in the sky, grinning and licking his lips from inside a spaceship. I hid under a black umbrella and he tried to pluck me out from underneath with gold-tweezer-like claws. Blue stars fell from the sky and music from the Carpenters filled the air. Then I was floating in a boat on a peanut river with an owl, a ginger pussycat and a bar of chocolate wrapped up in a five pound note. Abba sailed past singing 'Money, money, money' and a supermodel with no eyebrows steered a yacht singing, 'Her name is Rio...'

Wednesday 18th

This week's beauty tips in *Weekly Wife* included advice on plucking your eyebrows: 'If you find the experience painful, rub an ice cube on the area first.' Great, I really wanted to know that *this* week. Eileen didn't make any comment about my non-existent eyebrows on Monday; she's too polite. Mr.

Not-so-polite-miserable-as-sin taxi man asked me if I'd, 'Been-in-a-fire-or-summink-girl?' I'm willing them to grow back quickly, but I suppose a watched eyebrow never grows. Groan. Will send eyebrows a 'Grow Back Soon' card. Giggle. Recall colleagues at work once threatening to stand me in a gro-bag, I'm so short.

Felt quite excited about painting a star today and my paintbrushes (I could pull out a few hairs and glue them over my eyes) looked happy to see daylight again after years locked up in a stuffy tin with old Venus pencils, dirty rubbers and dried-up felt pens. Thought about the planet Mars where the sky is blue at sunset, while I dipped my brush in a small paint pot, then enjoyed the feeling of stroking thick liquid on wood and DOING SOMETHING!! Tried not to feel too upset when I had to rest now and again, sitting on the floor with my determined-to-finish-this-even-if-it-kills-me face on.

Tonight I wallowed in the bath trying to remove blue paint from my hands, arms, face and a few strands of hair. Blew bubbles off a bar of Pears soap. Love to watch bubbles. Feel sad when they pop.

Yesterday
All my bubbles
Seemed so far away
Now it looks as though
They're here to stay
Oh, I believe
In deodorant spray

Suddenly
I'm remembering
How it used to be
When I had
Oh so much energy
Oh I wish it
Was yesterday

Why I had to get ill
I don't know
The doctors couldn't say
I did something wrong

**Now I long for
Yesterday**

**Yesterday
Life was such
An easy game to play
Now I need my bed
To hide away
Oh I wish it
Was
Yesterday**

Hope dear John Lennon in Pop Star Heaven and Sir Paul won't mind my new version.

Thursday 19th

I sat in the warm, late afternoon sunshine humming the Beatles' song *Good Day, Sunshine*. The dwarves joined in, except Grumpy, who said he had a sore throat and Dopey, who was busy counting butterflies. I watched the birds fly in and out of the trees, then stopped to *really* listen to the bird song. I'm sure I heard a few notes of a famous melody written by one of those eighteenth-century composers; could have been Mozart's 40th symphony. Not sure. The other day I thought I heard the first few notes of the unforgettable 'Birdie Song', 'Polly Put the Kettle On' and the Beatles' walrus song. I'm so wonderfully *tuned* into nature these days, the phases of the moon and everything. I'll be hearing the stars twinkle in the night sky next.

Painstakingly painted another star with a smiley face, worried about tomorrow's visit to the doctor and read a few paragraphs of paranormal. There's a gelatinous substance that sometimes falls from the sky after a U.F.O. sighting called angel's hair. It looks like candyfloss and evaporates as it falls to earth. It's not just stars that fall from the sky then.

Friday 20th

Heavens above! I was all dizzy and fluffy-headed first thing (well more than usual, anyway). I'd been whizzing around half the night in a spaceship at a cosmic funfair while chatting to angels with candyfloss on their heads. Pink aliens and lobsters (eating Mars bars) were riding in the bumper cars; mermaids with long, yellow, flowy hair were laughing, screaming and swishing their tails on the big wheel; merry-go-round horses came alive, shook their manes, whinnied and galloped off into a blue sunset. The ginger cat was looking pleased with himself (he'd won a goldfish) and a chicken perched on my shoulder whistling the 'Birdie Song'.

On the way to the doctor's surgery, I couldn't get that blessed birdie tune out of my head so I asked Mr. Young-groovy-ex-racing-driver-taxi-man to turn up his dance music. He was *MOST* surprised. We passed an old man with a grey bushy beard and eyebrows (lucky him) and wild wizard hair, sitting on a chair at his front garden gate. I often see him on sunny Mondays. Sometimes on sprinkly rain-days he holds a tartan umbrella over his head; there's a rug to match over his knees. Wonder if he's Scottish. When the taxi slows down at the traffic lights, I give him a little wave. He waves back. Probably thinks I fancy myself as royalty. Maybe he thinks I *am* royalty; I feel like it sometimes, always riding around in a taxi with a sober expression and no money. Hope other people wave to him; I know what it's like to be lonely and so very tired.

If I sit at my front door and wave to people, they will think I've got a screw loose. At least you can get away with lots of things when you're old, like wearing purple and funny hats and a lot of clothes in the summer and sitting anywhere when you feel tired and stopping and talking to other people's children and animals and picking up worms on the pavement so they don't get trodden on and stopping to smell roses in strangers' gardens. I've always done these things (well, apart from wearing purple) but I don't feel comfortable and get stared at!

I waited wearily in the dim light of the cramped surgery with a funny smell. Sad people lined the walls, avoiding each other's eyes like prisoners awaiting trial in the same room as their victims and the victims' relatives. Wished there were some pretty pictures on the wall (misty mountains or sultry seascapes) to look at instead of depressing posters and leaflets about vaccinations, contraception and HIV.

A little boy, about four years old, wearing a red Winnie-the-Pooh jumper, gave an old lady wearing a pooh-coloured cardigan a wooden train to play with; it gave some of us prisoners a reason to smile. Someone passed wind. We all pretended not to hear. A smart, middle-aged lady with a face like a brown horse looked a bit shifty. When one patient came out and another went in, we all looked up; something to do. A fashionable young woman blushed up to her neatly curved eyebrows when her mobile phone went off. We all listened to her short conversation while we looked in another direction. She was meeting her friend at seven forty-five and they were going on to a club later and no she wasn't wearing the black one and yes Julie could borrow it. For a second I wanted to rush into town and pay the earth for a little black beaded number and join them later at Amadeus. *WHEN* I am well, I'll go out dancing a lot and get slim, make the most of having renewed energy, wear daring clothes, and everybody will think sad-old-skinny-purple-wearing-tart. And I won't give a damn – I'll be too busy *doing* instead of *thinking*.

The little boy in the Winnie-the-Pooh jumper played with a woollen Tigger and Piglet. He sat them in a yellow plastic truck and gave the toys a ride, parking between the ~~hooves~~ shoes of the smart middle-aged lady and knocking her ~~cart~~ handbag over. She flared her large hairy nostrils, rolled her dark brown eyes, and for a moment I thought she was going to throw her head back, toss her mane, whinny and gallop out of the surgery. Mummy asked William sharply to go and play quietly in the corner. I wanted to go and play quietly in the corner too with the cotton caterpillar and the duck with flappy feet, but I'm all grown up now, worse luck. When I'm old and wearing purple, I will go and play in the corner and read the rag books out loud to cheer everyone up and they won't need to see the doctor because laughter is the best medicine.

Told Dr. Downes about my slight improvement; I've been taking royal jelly for a couple of months now and feel sort of brighter with a little more energy. I repeated my usual symptoms, burped and repeated my peanut butter on toast; hoped she didn't smell it *then* said something stupid to hide my embarrassment. She said something very kind as she handed me my certificate and I nearly burst into tears.

Mr. Miserable-as-sin-taxi-man looked like death when he picked me up; he said he'd just been to a funeral. He told me lots of really awful, tragic things and I tried hard not to burst into floods again. Nearly wound down the window and screamed at the world, 'I can't stand this awful shitty life anymore!' Sat still and somehow found something soothing and comforting to say to him as I patted him on his sweaty shoulder and handed him my money with a big tip.

Closed the front door, flopped into a comfy chair, threw down my handbag and wept till *Neighbours* – saved removing my make-up. After *Neighbours*, had another cry in the bath and watched the tears dripdrop into the soapy water. After my bath, I caught sight of spiky area above my eyes, tiny hairs growing out at all angles. Had to laugh – no more tears left.

All dried off and dried up, I lay on the bed feeling better and thought of summer, feeling calm and peaceful and hopeful. Imagined my guardian angel patting my shoulder (don't think it *was* my imagination).

Ben had downed one, two or three too many at The Drum and Drunk-It down Drunkard Alley to notice my red, swollen eyes. He told me a joke that made me cackle.

Ben: What's brown and sticky?
Me: Dunno, what is brown and sticky?
Ben: A stick.

Couldn't see to paint anything tonight.

Saturday 21st

My lovely man brought four surprises home from the shops today to cheer me up (maybe he noticed my red eyes after all, bless him). The first surprise was peanut butter, 'Whole Earth Original Style' with no added sugar in a large jar from Holland & Barret, very delicious – the five hundred and ninety-two calories per hundred grams info was a bit hard to swallow though.

Surprise number two was a fresh pizza with real Italian thin pizza base, topped with spinach and mozzarella cheese on a creamy spinach and ricotta sauce (more heavenly than my guardian angel) *and* fresh herbs to sprinkle on top – I said I was surprised he had so much thyme for me, ha, ha.

Thirdly (best surprise) was a bottle of Valpolicella – light and fresh with redcurrant and cherry fruit flavours from the vineyards of Veneto in north-east Italy. What a lucky girl I am, surprises and all this time to read the labels on *everything*. Maybe if I sit on a chair at my front door reading labels on the weekly shopping with a magnifying glass (like the one I was going to use to study women's eyebrows) people in the street will feel sorry for me and make a collection to send me away somewhere spiritually healing (expensive) to recover.

My fourth surprise was an astronomy magazine tucked inside this week's copy of *Weekly Wife* with a bar of Galaxy chocolate. Discovered all about telescopes. I never realised they came in so many shapes and sizes; a big one could keep me busy all night under the stars. Read about Sir Arthur Eddington who was one of Britain's foremost astronomers and started his career at an early age: he would often try to count the stars at the age of four. Wonder how Matthew will be affected by the moons and stars and Saturns on his cot. Oh dear! He'll grow up thinking there are lots of moons and Saturns as well as stars with smiley faces.

The pictures in the astrophotography section were impressive. The shots of Saturn (with rings that span a distance of one hundred and seventy thousand miles, composed of innumerable dust and ice particles up to ten metres in size), the moon and the surface of Mars (the craters and volcanoes all red and lonely and barren) were brilliant too. I didn't feel quite so brain dead as I normally do when reading 'Best Beauty Tips', 'He Died in My Arms on Our Wedding Day', 'Fabulous Family Puddings' and 'Dressing for Two – Smart Looks for Mums-to-Be'.

There was an interesting article about evidence of water in other galaxies: well, I expect aliens get thirsty too and need a reviving wash and brush up after a hard day's night joyriding across the universe. Lay in the bath trying to imagine galaxies millions of light years away – my brain nearly exploded. Remembered another galaxy, not a million miles away. In the fridge.

Painted the rings on Saturn but they turned out a bit wobbly and my ellipses not quite right; think I'd like to see a total ~~ellipse~~ eclipse of the sun one day. Outlined two stars. Unfortunately, they look more like starflowers now (wonder if starflower oil is any good).

Weird musician friend has returned from his travels abroad to find 'THE TRUTH'. He couldn't find it, so he came home disappointed. When he called into Mr. Patel's for some fags, he came out enlightened.

A storm was brewing as he lurched out through the front door tonight complaining bitterly about the British weather. I couldn't resist pointing out that he is fortunate he doesn't live on Jupiter: the storms last three hundred years there. He asked me what planet I was on; I told him women are from Venus...

Sunday 22nd

What a stressful night! Spent most of it at a funeral for black taxi cabs. I watched them slowly lowered into huge dark square holes, wreaths of purple flowers laid to rest on their bonnets. The rain rained like a mother's tears and lightning flashed like a teenage daughter's eyes when she's told to wipe that muck off her face. Cab drivers, white and worn from working long hours, sat as still as church candles in their driving seats like captains going down with their ships. Their tragic families sat in the back, huddled together and terrified.

Woke up in a panic, lacking in drive and energy as usual, to hear Ben tapping away on his computer like a busy woodpecker making a home for her young. These days, the computer is always on when I get up at weekends and stays on all day and evening, purring away like a large square mechanical cat in its favourite corner. In the week, when Ben comes home from work, it's jacket off, shoes off, watch off, and computer on to see if anyone's sent an e-mail; then a spot of internet surfing or file copying or general fiddling, unless *Star Trek* is on. When he goes out, the computer is left on to search for aliens. The project S.E.T.I. (Search for Extra-Terrestrial Intelligence) allows people on the internet to help analyse radio signals collected from outer space. Spoooky.

Ben would sit at his computer all day and night long if he had the chance, so now I call it his life support machine. If I speak to him when he's watching the screen he either ignores me or carries on looking at the screen and grunts (have been forgetting to use www dot at the beginning of my sentences). Sometimes I get this strange feeling that I don't really exist; must check with Eileen that I'm not becoming slowly invisible; she's the most honest person I know. In my book on the paranormal, there's a story about a magician who made himself invisible except for a faint outline of his body, like a sketch. His audience could still hear his voice clearly and he was unaware he'd faded so much. Verrry spoooky.

... when Stephen opened his eyes, he was in the back of a black cab; he must have nodded off. At the traffic lights, an old man sitting in a garden with a tartan rug over his legs waved at him. There was something familiar about the old boy. He waved back, then settled into the leathery seat to watch ~~par-tridges~~ particles dancing in a shaft of sunlight. He thought about the stars, time, space and his Star Trek watch needed mending...

Finished painting Saturn and a star while I polished off the Galaxy chocolate. Started painting the outline of a smiley moon and another star.

Monday 23rd

Twinkle! Sparkle! Twinkle! Sparkle! Twinkle!

I thought a little star had landed on the fridge, but on closer inspection I found a quartz crystal, the size of an ice cube, sitting in the rays of the morning sun. I picked it up feeling its healing energy tingling through my veins and balancing my chakra system. (I've been reading the crystal book again!)

When I saw Eileen and mentioned feeling invisible, she laughed and assured me I was still solid bones and flesh and she could see me quite clearly. Breathed a sigh of relief; well, you never know, I could turn out like that magician fellow. Told Eileen about him and some other ghostly stories I'd read last night. She said the clinic was haunted; an old man has been seen sitting in front of his fire in the room she practises in. I glanced at the black fireplace, shivered, and grew lots of goose bumps as she spoke. Her workbench is placed across the front of the Victorian fireplace and apparently he's upset about this. Funny thing is, I recall many times when I've entered her room and felt like pushing her workbench (or table or whatever she calls it) out of the way. In fact, come to think of it, I find it extremely irritating where it's placed. Also, I've sometimes felt someone is watching me when I'm on my own, as I flick through magazines while waiting for my appointment; often I look up but see no-one. Ooooh! Verry, verry spoooky!

Feel sorry for Mr. Ghost; he's probably hungry and wants to toast his bread by the fire and warm his arthritic bones.

Coronation Street was good tonight, so was *EastEnders*: lots of worry and strife, deception, jealousy, torment, misery and moaning. Brilliant, cheered me up no end.

Plastered moisturiser on my spiky eyebrows to train them to march in the right direction. Weeded out a few stragglers that wouldn't get in line. Sneezed a lot. Couldn't find an eyebrow growing spell under E but found uses for eyebright, elm, and a spell for strengthening eyesight (will do when the weather is fine and I'm in the mood).

Didn't paint anything.

Tuesday 24th
Weird. Hot feet.

Woke up this morning feeling strangely happy and my feet all hot. Eileen and I and Mr. Ghost had just been sitting on her workbench, swinging our legs and warming our toes in front of a roaring fire after a bracing walk in the snow, dodging the horses and carriages. Eileen had hung up her thick tartan cloak next to mine, olive green velvet with embroidered bats and frogs. In the flickering candlelight, I read them my story about Stephen Inglenook, and they clapped; and we all laughed. My God! I had a *nice* dream! Would have been even better if we'd been eating chocolates of course. Really wish one could write down the dreams one would like to have, place them under the pillow, then dream happily all night... Bliss.

Sat for ages watching a bumble bee on the roses like an old woman rummaging at a jumble sale. Finished painting a moon and pencilled in a few tiny round planets with my newly sharpened Venus pencil.

Drummer Stephen dropped in this evening and I tied his black umbrella to his wrist with strict instructions not to untie it till he was in his car, on his way home. He said I could tie him up and be strict with him anytime – oooh, blimey!

Ben must have told him I've gone all cosmic; he left a copy of *Hitchhiker's Guide to the Galaxy* by Douglas Adams for me to read. Wish it were on tape; more than a few pages and my headaches still worsen. Oh well, at least with *Weekly Wife* I'm not tempted to read too much. Must do eyesight spell.

Wednesday 25th

Opened the curtains to see a woman hurry across the road to greet a friend outside our house. She was into divine and cosmic order in a chaotic world. I know this because I recognised her umbrella from the Past Times catalogue, covered in stained glass designs inspired by the great west rose window in Notre Dame cathedral, Paris. I bet she leaves it behind in church next Sunday and a nun from the convent next door takes a fancy to it (I can imagine a nun with an umbrella like that). The nun starts to feel guilty and leaves it on a bus and gets very wet on her way to the centre for the homeless and falls very ill and knows she's being punished by almighty God for her sins. Father McCarthy just happens to find the umbrella and sees it as gift from Him upstairs because he gave his own umbrella to a man downstairs on his luck. The woman who left her umbrella in church originally, sees him (the priest) with her property and never goes to church again on Sunday mornings, has a sinfully satisfying lie-in and feels much better for it.

Found a baby woodlouse on his back with his legs wiggling in the air, turned him over and he crawled off happily. I hope he was happy, at least he doesn't have to go to church. Wonder if woodlice feel guilt.

Painted a star. Started reading the book by Douglas Adams and longed for the day when I can read a whole book, every single page, with relish, over a weekend, saving the last few yummy pages to cheer up a miserable Monday. Very tempted to say a little prayer now but feel too guilty; I've been joking about nuns and priests.

Thursday 26th

Goldshield wrote:

'Let's Get Ready for Summer!' Advising me to safeguard my skin from UVA and UVB rays with their wonderful skin care range and 'Relax and unwind naturally' with the new comprehensive range of over forty essential aromatherapy oils. If I order any three products from the zesty fruit essential range I will pay only five pounds, saving nearly ten pounds off the R.R.P.!

The Derm-essential Cellules looked quite intriguing, the most hygenic and effective way of protecting the skin, apparently. Read about tea-tree products (used by the Aboriginal people of Australia), aloe vera (treasured for thousands of years by the ancient Egyptians, Greeks and Chinese) and evening primrose oil (dating back to the ice ages some sixty or seventy thousand years ago).

Swallowed an evening primrose capsule with my breakfast herbs while reading further about the history of how the flower came to grow in this country. It's origins lie in Mexico but it established itself as a healing herb in North America, and the seeds of the plant came to Britain accidentally in the eighteenth century with imported cotton. Mmmm, interesting.

When I next order my primrose capsules, I think I'll treat myself to a few beauty products; after all, they're real bargains, I need to feel beautiful to keep me calm and peaceful and if I order soon I'll be sent a free pot of soothing foot balm.

VERY IMPORTANT LIST

Anti-wrinkle cream
Instant facelift
Under-eye cream

Evening primrose oil shampoo
Evening primrose oil conditioner
Evening primrose oil all over moisurising lotion

Kiwi fruit moisturising bath foam

All that for only sixteen pounds! Pity they don't sell hair re-growth pills. I'm never plucking my eyebrows again. Ever. Well, perhaps the odd one. No. No. No. I'm going for the old man look: moustache, hairy chin, hairy nostrils, scowl, muttering about the youth of today while I pick the wax out of my hairy ears. I will fill in the order form tomorrow; too worn out now from the excitement of it all.

Friday 27th

A beautiful bird song blue day.

Cosmic Colin said I deserved a big beautiful treat so I filled in the Goldshield order form for lots of little treats. They will add up to one big treat. He also said I must make the most of my artistic talents, 'OK! OK! Col, I'm trying, I'm trying.'

Drew and painted a star. Played David Essex's greatest hits and sang, 'We're gonna paint ya a star ar ar.' Wiggled a bit to 'Rock On', then sang 'Lamplight' into a microphone-sized candle.

That's my painting and singing and dancing talents put to good use, just leaves the poetry...

> **A girl with a cosmic umbrella**
> **Had trouble finding a fella**
> **She relied on her stars**
> **Beauty bottles and jars**
> **And advice from her old**
> **Auntie Stella**
>
> **Buying lots of healthy capsules**
> **Was her most successful step**
> **And now she is happily married**
> **To Colin the Goldshield rep**

The other day Cosmic Colin told me to relax and daydream of what I love doing most in the summertime. So after a long hot herbally bath, I lay on the bed leafing through a summer clothes catalogue. I daydreamed; I used my imagination... I saw myself sipping long chilled drinks outside sea front cafés, the sun warming my skin and sparkling on ice cubes, feeling comfy in a pair of Indian Madras shorts, with zip fly and single-button fastening... wandering happily round seasidey gift shops, cool in a carefree cotton-rich blouse, tailored with straight collar, knife pleats at the back and a neat shirt tail hem... hunting for interesting shells and pieces of driftwood, relaxed in a striped jersey with shell layers and styled with wide shoulders for modest coverage... exploring rock pools, soaking up the afternoon sun or splashing in the shallows, looking great in flattering swimwear. Maybe a Hawaiian-inspired Bali-hai Tankini, the vest top lending extra support and the briefs giving tummy control that flatters and smoothes. Or possibly a Faille suit, the square neck drawing attention to my face while the princess seams suggest an hourglass figure... running barefoot on warm golden sand, and feelin' groovy in tropical-print cropped pants with sleek pocketless styling... strolling along a pebbly beach at Whitstable watching the sunset, casual in a ribbed revere cardigan with 'jacket appeal', three-button front, hip pockets and vertical welts... munching hot, fat chips as the evening cools, sitting on a cold sea wall, comfortable in wide-leg trousers with elastic waist and offset side pockets, in a flatteringly flowing rib knit... pottering in my garden in a pair of easy to wear, flower-print cotton capris... singing and dancing round the house in a cling-free, ribbed interlock, ballet neck tunic, the 'drop-needle' knitting creating slenderising stripes that run from ballet neckline to hip-covering hem, pre-washing making it all extra cuddly and with a loop on the left sleeve in case somebody wants to pull me closer. Mmmmm. Available in mint green, Aegean blue or dark coral. Aegean blue will do.

Colin once said I inspired others. That's nice. I think I may have inspired Ben to express his innermost feelings through sensitive, heartfelt verse:

> **I sat frowning**
> **In my own fart**
> **And I knew**
> **Deep in my heart**
> **As I lit**
> **A stinking fag**
> **Then blew snot**
> **Into a rag**
>
> **I'd eaten too many beans.**

. . . .

It's turned so bloody cold
And I feel so bloody old
And the cellar's full of mould
And it was already sold
So I'm stubbing out a stub
And I'm going down the pub.

Saturday 28th

Gina rang to ask how the cot was coming along. I told her I'd completed half a star today and felt half dead with *the monthly problems*; but it was nearly finished and I was quite pleased with the results. She said she'd just hung out half the washing, had collapsed in a chair feeling half dead too, changed Matthew, and could do with half a lager. I said, 'Would that be at The Pooh and Potty, Smellbottom Street?' She didn't laugh.

The woman into cosmic order with the Past Times umbrella trotted past again and I wondered if she *does* go to church. I thought about nuns and the dried-up disciplinarians from Hell who taught me on Saturdays. Actually, Sister Peter was OK; it was her friend who looked like a children's storybook witch and scared me silly. The convent was a horribly depressing dark brown place with a Victorian atmosphere (high windows, etc.). Rose went to school there full time in her brown uniform. No wonder she's, well, like she is, and detests the colour brown. Can't believe I wanted to be a nun once; if Gina and I were nuns (the way we're feeling) we'd be Sister Rigor and Sister Mortis.

There was a dead interesting programme on tonight about Egyptian mummies and pyramids and things; I watched the last half before attempting to climb the twelve stairs to bed. Sat on the bottom step feeling sad and creative...

... she sat at the foot of the stairs looking up like a tired, thirsty tourist contemplating climbing the pyramid in the baking hot sun after a night sampling Scarab Bite (cider and lager), Sarcophagus Surprise (musty, wood flavoured beer), Lapis Lazuli Delight (blue coconut cocktail) and Rameses' Revenge (tomato juice, vodka and Daddies Sauce)...

God I need a drink!

Sunday 29th

Bill came round looking arty with multicoloured paint spattered on his beard, jeans and shoes. We discussed Egyptian art, he admired my blue moon and stars, and said how well I looked. He told us he'd missed his life-drawing class last week and had found out the model was young and very attractive, instead of the usual wrinkly old bird. I remarked how disappointed he looked – poor Bill!

My parents dropped in on their way to visit friends and admired their grandson's celestial cot. I could tell they'd just had a big row as usual. Childhood misery filled my head, felt like getting drunk, devouring chocolate and my headache worsened.

2.05 p.m.   Dad says how well I look.
2.35 p.m.   Mum says how well I look.
7.15 p.m.   Thish Glenfiddish luverlee.
8.10 p.m.   Mush paint nother shtar.
8.15 p.m.   Ooops – big mishtake!

Monday 30th

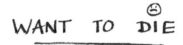

WANT TO DIE

Tuesday 31st

9.50 a.m.   Post is boring and depressing.
10.06 a.m. Spill soya milk while opening new carton.
10.07 a.m. We've run out of my beloved kitchen roll.
10.08 a.m. We've run out of clean knives.
10.40 a.m. I've run out of clean knickers.
11.06 a.m. Will have to clean streak of blue paint off cot.
11.20 a.m. House looks disgustingly dirty in sunlight.
12.30 p.m. Do bit of clothes washing (knickers, leggings and sweatshirt).
1.00 p.m.   Bit of washing-up (knife and fork).
2.22 p.m.   Bit of dusting (telephone and answering machine).
3.00 p.m.   Bath.
3.25 p.m.   Can't get out of bath.
3.28 p.m.   Let water out and lie in damp bath.

3.30 p.m.	Too drained to wash hair.
4.00 p.m.	Head feels like a ton of soya milk cartons have fallen on it.
5.41 p.m.	Taxi early. Trip on badly tied laces and fall down last two steps of stairs.
5.50 p.m.	Mr. Miserable-as-sin makes me cry again.
6.25 p.m.	Eileen says how well I look.
7.02 p.m.	Mr. Cheerful-chatty twinkly-eyes flirty-smile picks me up in his big black shiny cab.
7.17 p.m.	Un-click safety belt as cab turns into my street and search for purse in untidy handbag.
7.18 p.m.	Find purse and root around for pound coins to pay driver. Four coins fall into my lap then roll all over floor. Bend down to pick up coins as car slows down but car lurches on slopey road and I fall, curled up on my back, knees to chin, behind the driver's seat. Driver thinks I've disappeared when he turns round (I *knew* I was invisible sometimes). Hard to get up as laughing too much and car on slope.
7.19 p.m.	Pound coin has rolled down into gap between door and side of car. Open door whilst still on hands and knees laughing and fall out on to pavement. Imagine neighbours thinking I'm drunk. Turn *ever so* pink.
7.20 p.m.	Cab driver thinks I'm drunk. Difficulty paying him as laughing too much with embarrassment. Wouldn't be so bad if I were ten, but I'm a grown-up now, worse luck.
7.21 p.m.	Hobble to front door trying to look sober and composed.
7.23 p.m.	Ben says how well I look.
9.15 p.m.	Watch few minutes of medical drama.
9.16 p.m.	Patient has face covered in spots.
9.21 p.m.	Bright idea!!
9.28 p.m.	Cover face in red spots with Truly Red lipstick.
9.29 p.m.	Tell self how ill I look.
10.32 p.m.	Think I will have henna spots tattooed on my face.
10.33 p.m.	If it's good henna, they will last three months.
10.34 p.m.	Eileen was telling me last week, some of her patients have unusual tattoos in all sorts of unusual places. One large lady wears a tiny thong to show off a huge black tarantula on her bum; feel sorry for Eileen when the woman turns over on her stomach...

10.35 p.m. Terrible urge to pluck out hair above right eye.

10.36 p.m. Just three more... maybe four.

10.37 p.m. Now right eyebrow doesn't match left eyebrow.

10.38 p.m. Now left side doesn't match right side.

10.39 p.m. Just ten more.

10.40 p.m. Oh no! Plucking hell!! What have I done?

11.46 p.m. Fancy rose tattoo on ~~bum~~ arm, blood dripping from thorn as symbol of pain.

June

Wednesday 1st

9.04 a.m.   Open eyes.

Morning again.

Dark rainy world.

Rainy morning sounds.

9.05 a.m.   Car door slams.

Engine starts up.

Dog barks.

9.06 a.m.   Close eyes.

Need bathroom.

9.07 a.m.   Shouldn't have drunk all that water so late last night.

Turn over. Am staying here as long as possible.

9.17 a.m.   Sit on toilet thinking about a rose tattoo.

9.18 a.m.   Think about last night's dreams, where I found myself wandering in a sickly white world, the colour of milk going off. Lonely desperate people ambled around me dressed in sour cream with bitter crimson mouths, blood red teardrops trickling down their white cheeks. They each held a single scarlet rose, the petals falling onto snow.

9.18 a.m.   I might press the rose Ben gave me on his return from Birmingham (have a feeling it will be the last one I ever receive) but I don't like the thought of squashing the last juices of life out of something that used to be so vibrant and living.

Recall second nightmare last night set in a country manor house. The handsome Earl of Somewhere, I was married to, called me his little English rose petal. He said he loved me because I was all pink and delicate and blooming with health (the dream started off OK). One evening, while we were enjoying candlelit dinner at a table, beautifully set

233

with ornate silver (engraved with roses), plates (pink rose decoration) and pink champagne in rose-stemmed glasses, he suggested a stroll in the gardens; he wanted to pick a summer rosebud for me although he knew it would never compare to my beauty and softness.

He held me gently in his arms, presented me with the rosebud and whispered, 'I want you to stay young and beautiful always and never change, my dearest.' I was about to tell him this was impossible when he pressed me up against a gritty stone wall and I got all excited; but he kept on pressing and pressing all the life and breath out of me till I was thin and flat and dry as hand-made paper. Only then did I notice his evil satisfied expression... Unable to move or scream, I lay helpless as he framed me behind a sheet of glass surrounded by a dark mahogany frame... I was carried along dimly lit corridors... I was hung on the wall along with his ex-wives and ancestors. Visitors stopped to admire me and I desperately tried to show my desperation with my eyes but they said things like... 'She was his little English rose, how sad'... 'Bit flat-chested though'... 'She knows her place now'... 'Must go dear, *You've Been Framed* is on in half an hour and James will be ready with the car.'

9.20 a.m.   Skin feels dry and rough today; must bother to use a night cream more often.

9.21 a.m.   Arrrgh! someone has stolen my eyebrows!

9.24 a.m.   Sit on side of bath listening to rain...

Drip   Drop
Drip   Drop
Plip   Plop

9.26 a.m.   Don't know why it sounds so comforting...

Pitter   Patter
Spitter   Spatter
Spip   Spop

9.28 a.m.	Have survived *five whole months* of yet another boring year... drip... drop... drip... drop... drip... mentally pat self on back... pitter, patter... pitter, patter... I'm doing really well... plip... plop... haven't killed myself or strangled anyone for telling me how well I look... drip, drop... drip.
9.32 a.m.	Examine yellowy purple bruises on legs after Monday's minor accidents. Bruises are below my knees; I look as if I've been attacked by an angry garden gnome. Hope the dwarves visit again soon. Shoulder hurts. Rub shoulder. Pride hurts. Rub pride.
10.04 a.m.	Breakfast.
11.40 a.m.	*The Bigger Breakfast.*
12.20 p.m.	In bath having long think as usual about things.
12.21 p.m.	Cot nearly finished, just the odd tiny star needed and a small planet, size of a Smartie.
12.22 p.m.	Hope Gina will like it.
12.23 p.m.	Must sew up hem on favourite summer dress and button on cotton summer jacket.
12.24 p.m.	Must diet so can fit into stripy shorts.
12.25 p.m.	Really hate dieting.
12.26 p.m.	Really hate sewing.
12.27 p.m.	Really hate feeling sew so tired all the time.
12.29 p.m.	Pick up my collection of soaps one by one, enjoy their scents and the feel of their shape; the large oval Pears soap, creamy curved Dove soap, square seaweed soap with weedy bits in and chunky-herby-seedy one. Soaps in the bath and soaps on TV are two of the few, small pleasures that keep me sane; wonder why soaps on TV are so called. Ben says it's something to do with American soap adverts.
12.31 p.m.	Think about Ben.
12.33 p.m.	Admire colourful yellowy-greeny-purpley bruises on legs again. Studying the colour changes will give me something interesting to do; I could make a bruise chart!
12.34 p.m.	Massage Pears soap bubbles into feet and thank feet for all the plodding they've done, all the hundreds of miles they must have walked over the years supporting my heavy body. Apologise for all the tight pointy shoes and high heels then smile to self; they must be so much happier now they live in slippers all day.

12.36 p.m.	Smooooth creamy Dove soap under armpits and over boobs, apologise to boobs for ill-fitting bras over the years; smile, they must be happy now they dangle about freely. In a few years, my nipples will be in line with my hips.
12.37 p.m.	Wash naughty bits with herby-seed soap but soap has scratchy bits in. Apologise to naughty bits for lack of excitement and scratchy soap.
1.15 p.m.	Lie on bed staring at ceiling recalling days of excitement; they seem a long, long time ago now.
1.25 p.m.	Shall I do some sewing? Maybe tomorrow.
1.26 p.m.	Shall I start diet? Too late. Tomorrow.
1.30 p.m.	Rain has stopped. Sun sparkling on everything.
1.40 p.m.	When will I get my sparkle back?
1.41 p.m.	Fancy sparkly lemonade with a stripy straw.
1.45 p.m.	Want to go to a party.
1.46 p.m.	Ben is going to a birthday party tonight.
1.48 p.m.	Take quiche out of freezer to defrost. Will nibble with glass of wine tonight. Will find sparkly top and do Abba type make-up, put on seventies tape and pretend am at party and everyone has gone home exhausted... *but I'm* still dancing.
2.37 p.m.	Oooooh! Aaaaah! Pins and needles in leg, have been sitting on leg too long and am now being punished for neglecting my sewing jobs.
4.23 p.m.	Wiggle toes to 'Coolest dance summer tracks!!!' on advert. Must get in practice for tonight's party.
4.30 p.m.	The model on the cover of *Weekly Wife* is smiling at me with her, 'I've never had a period' smile, Crown-white teeth and glowing freckly skin. I bet she lives on black coffee, throws up all the time, takes drugs and her freckles are painted on.
4.31 p.m.	Admire cool blue summer dresses, laugh at stupid model leaping about all over the sand wearing very unsuitable sandals for the beach. I bet the male model smiling down at her in one of the shots hates her really because she's just run off with his best mate – she wouldn't get far in *those* sandals.

4.33 p.m.   Read all about green foods. They are brilliant for boosting energy levels as they're packed with potassium, magnesium and B vitamins. A healthy-looking blonde woman, dressed in dazzling orange, chops up colourful vegetables and grins out of the page at me. She's quoted saying, 'Salads give me loads of energy.' Really hate her; hope she chokes on her many varieties of lettuce.

4.48 p.m.   To dress for energy, colour therapists say you should wear green, violet, orange or turquoise. I've got a green T-shirt, but I look like a sick budgie in it.

4.49 p.m.   Oooh! Just noticed; I should be wearing an *accessory* in one of those colours too.

4.50 p.m.   Haven't got an accessory in one of those colours. Would love some jewellery set with lapis lazuli stones though. Mmmm, I've never owned anything orange (except a plastic mixing bowl, frisbee, water wings, reflective arm bands, clementines, satsumas and oranges). Maybe I'll chop up a few squares of orange peel (watched Delia Smith making marmalade the other day, what a palaver) make a hole in one corner of each square, dry them out and thread a piece of string through for a groovy natural necklace. Maybe not, it will only enhance my dry skin areas and the orange peel quality of my cheeks.

4.53 p.m.   For a green necklace, I could thread some green cotton through dried peas and squares of dried green pepper. I know! I'll press some herb leaves, wear real lilac in my hair and cut up Ben's turquoise T-shirt to make a purse...

4.54 p.m.   Worn out with excitement now.

4.55 p.m.   Must rest for my party.

Thursday 2nd

The sun was rather watered down today, like the beer at The Sticky Carpet Tavern, Slime Street. I pottered in the kitchen singing *Here Comes the Sun* by the Beatles; only know the chorus so I sang it over and over again (feel sorry for the neighbours).

Drew a little star. Sang a bit of 'Vincent' – 'Starry, starry night, paint your palette blue and grey...' Can't remember the rest, probably just as well. Painted a little star.

Read 'Moonlight Beauty Tips':

New Moon	Good time to have beauty treatment, electrolysis and waxing will be less painful.
Waning Moon	Willpower at its strongest so good time to start diet.
Waxing	
Full Moon	Good time to have facial or body treat as skin at its most absorbent.
Full Moon	Good time to cut hair as it grows back stronger, but don't shave legs or pluck eyebrows (oh dear). Mourned loss of eyebrows.

Friday 3rd

Mother Nature, wearing her paint-stained smock and holding a palette, made the sun more lemon yellow today. She washed out her brush then mixed up a cerulean blue for the sky and sap green for the grass.

Must find the remnants of last year's sun lotion, my Vandyke brown sunglasses and old bikinis; might try to get a bit of a burnt sienna tan this year. Must look under T for tanning, F for freckles and H for hair growth in spell book.

Ben said he'd been down The Sun tonight with Bill, Rob and Bob the Slob. He came back beaming; The Sun went down a treat.

Saturday 4th

Summer afternoon – *Summer afternoon; to me those have always been the most beautiful words in the English language.*

Henry James (1843 – 1916)

These words are written on the back of a card that arrived with this morning's post from Artie Auntie; a reproduction of a painting by Harold Harvey, entitled, 'On the Sands'. Two girls, with an Enid Blyton look about them, lie on the beach; one is engrossed in a book. The soft seasidey, bluey-cream colours and the way the artist has used light is very restful so I've placed the card where I'll see it as I make breakfast every morning to help me stay calm and peaceful.

Sat in the late morning sun thinking about the words in the English language I find most beautiful: 'blue sky, spring morning, mountain air, morning dew, rosebud, Emerald Isle, white Christmas, winter wonderland, pain relief, deep pan pizza, lots of chocolate, you have recovered...'

I asked Ben what his favourite words in the English language were. He sat and thought for a moment... 'home time, bank holiday, summer holiday, in credit, pint sir?, lunch break, sandwich lady, pretty face, nice legs'. Is he trying to tell me he fancies the sandwich lady; wish I'd never asked.

'If only' – two words I hate in the English language. I could make a very long list of *if onlys*, like most people, I guess. But I'm not going to, far too depressing. Hmmm, in ten years, time I'll probably be thinking, 'If only I'd made that list I wouldn't have made that mistake again.' Maybe I'd better make a list. No. Stop being paranoid. Another word I hate is *chronic*. Oh! And *calorie; tense* and *torture, failure* and *fatigue, vein* and *vomit*. Must stop this before I become really gloomy. Just one more then – *small print* (unless its a print left by a tiny animal).

Consulted my spell book. There were no rituals for improving a tan or growing more freckles, but I found under T, uses for thyme (wards negativity and purifies), tansy (for health) and trefoil (for luck and protection). Under F: feverfew (wards sickness), fennel, fern, foxglove and frankincense (for protection). Under H, there were uses for hazel, heather, hawthorn, hops and hyssop *and* a hair growth spell. I must collect a bowl of rain water and leave overnight in the moonlight. But I'll have to wait till after summer to collect chestnuts – to match my hair colour. Maybe I could use spices of a similar colour from Safeway; maybe not.

Found the sun lotion, after sun cream, scratchy old sunglasses and three bikinis. Tried on the bikinis. All three were far too small and tight. Decided I need new ones. Will have to order one of those catalogues that pesters you for the rest of your life, even when you're in your coffin...

Would you care to look at this year's silk linings in many shades, our most popular being Hint of Afterlife... or maybe velvet is more you... in Heavenly White, Banshee Black, Sinful Green, Cosmic Blue or... Satanic Satin in Vein Blue, Ritual Red or perhaps Vampire Crimson.

Sunday 5th

Awoke to the sound of ~~yawns~~ lawns everywhere being mowed; sinful green lawns under a cosmic blue sky. My heavenly white face shined at me in the mirror, a vampire crimson spot beamed in the middle of my chin... I stared with banshee blackness at my lack of eyebrows.

The model on the cover of *Weekly Wife* beamed at me too so I found a biro and gave her three spots and a black tooth. Felt better. Later, while watching the omnibus edition of *EastEnders*, I gave her a moustache, Dot Cotton wrinkles, thick-framed glasses and a Pat Butcher frown. Felt wonderful.

'Spring into Summer!' says Wendy, and Samantha sports a party pink leotard that looks as if it's about to split her in half. Cosmic Colin says I should be full of beans and creativity.

Ate half a can of cold beans, scribbled all over my stars and added the finishing touches to Matthew's cot. Gina came round to collect it and I worried that the paint hadn't dried properly. She said she liked the design but I don't think she did really; I should have painted blue whales and dolphins.

Still mourning loss of eyebrows.

Monday 6th

Spent the whole night with Gina and Matthew on the moon. We were happily bouncing around trying to catch blue stars with smiley faces and little creatures with with lots of bulgy eyes and stringy legs; lunar-tics, ha, ha.

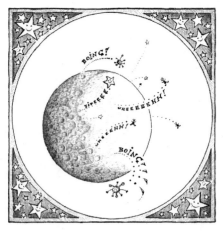

There was a knock on the front door about eleven-thirty this morning. Dragged myself from my smelly comfy corner of the sofa (will wash cushion covers again one day) and peered out of the window to see a harassed looking woman with a parcel and a clipboard. Hurried as fast as I could to the bathroom to grab a towel, to wrap up my greasy hair (I hate it when delivery people don't give you much time to answer the door before trying next door or just shoving a card through the letter box, jumping back into their vans or cars and driving off!) then sprayed Moonstone deodorant down the front of my sweatshirt so Mrs. Harassed-impatient-parcel-person (they always look on the verge of a breakdown) wouldn't smell that I hadn't washed yet today. Opened the bedroom window and yelled (as she climbed into her car), 'I'm coming!' then decided it would have been more polite to nicely shout, 'Just one moment, Madam', in my posh voice or, 'ang-onna-minute-please' in my normal squeaky voice. If I were a little old lady, I'd have said, 'I won't be long deary, it's me legs you see.' Maybe I should have called out, 'I'm gonna be ages, I'm a smelly old M.E. sufferer who always looks a mess and I'm going to cry in a minute but don't be put off dear, I can't help it, not that the doctors believe me or my friends or relatives for that matter, but don't let me burden you with my problems, though I must admit I *am* so lonely but I don't tell anyone this, in fact it's the first time I've admitted it to myself and it's so lovely to have someone to talk to when you're on your own all day – and the day is so long – even if it's only a delivery person, no offence meant of course, and I don't get many parcels, or nice letters, well, only if I write lots of replies and send off for supplements AND that's an effort I can tell you, like trying to talk on the phone, you *wouldn't believe* how hard it is to concentrate, yes really, it's quite awful and then there's my eyes, yes, the eye muscles are affected too! I can hardly read or watch telly for long without my headaches getting worse, I can see you're surprised but don't look so worried, I'm OK really, one adjusts you know after a few years of contemplating suicide, no, no didn't mean it, I'm fine really, honestly. Ooh! That's a nice tan you've got, and I love those streaks in your hair, been abroad this year? I'd love a holiday in a hot country but of course I'm just not up to the travelling though the heat would probably do me good, mind you I worry about the insects and the water and the food. Aargh! Don't look at my carpets, can't do much housework, yes, you're right, very frustrating, better go and have a herb tea now. I'm feeling worn out and my voice is going all croaky, have you noticed? Yes, it does that sometimes, I'll have a lovely warm herb tea, Mmmm you're right, a lot of them do taste bloody awful but the peppermint's not too bad once you get used to it, nothing like real cuppa is there? I have to avoid caffeine of course, yes, it's a pain, then there's my yeast problem but I won't go into that, don't want to bore you, oh! You've got to go, it's-bin-nice-talking-to-you-I'll-wave-you-down-the-road, Take care! forgot to tell you about my osteopath! would you like to hear one of my poems?!... oh... you've gone.'

My Goldshield goodies had arrived at last. Joyfully opened the large square parcel and had a brilliant day reading all the labels on the plastic pots and bottles, unscrewing their tops, sniffing the contents, and rubbing the free soothing foot balm into my feet. My feet smiled and sighed; they slept; they dreamt of walking on wet bumpy sand on Hastings beach and wading in the waves of the shallows, later curling up in comfy sandals and snoozing in that cozy little pub near the seafront.

Smoothed anti-wrinkle cream, under-eye cream and instant facelift into my dry skin with gentle circular upward movements from my chin to the centre of my forehead; then I softly ran my fingertips back to the starting point, ten times, just like *Weekly Wife* advised – well, nearly ten times, three to be more precise, and that was an effort.

Made another effort to think positively, breathe deeply and relax, calm and peacefully, from head to foot. Tried ~~paranormal paranoia~~ pagan aerobics while lying on the floor. Managed about four seconds of chanting and arm waving. Held my crystals, one by one, and meditated on their special healing powers. Felt better for five seconds. Sniffed aromatherapy candle. Sipped herbal tea. Counted the knots in the wooden shelves, counted how many candles in my collection I could see (twenty-six) started counting the CD collection but lost count because my eyes went all funny. Willed the face creams to do their job; why not, the mind is a very powerful thing.

Glanced in the sitting room mirror (deliberately forgetting the light is bad) and thought how much better and brighter and uplifted I looked; even had a bit of colour in my cheeks.

One asked me where the roses grew:
I bade him not go seek,
But forthwith bade my Julia show
A bud in either cheek.
R. Herrick

Ben's sister, Julia, is writing a book; wonder how she's getting on. He said she was having difficulty finding the time to get down to it. Feel guilty, here I am with all this time and all I can manage is the odd poem and a few lines now and then, here and there. Can't imagine writing thousands of words. I'm sure I would just keep repeating myself and make loads of spelling mistakes and get the grammar all wrong and the plot all muddled up and keep forgetting what I'd just written and say 'and' too many times. Must try to finish my short story; haven't looked at it for weeks now and I'm not in a poetry writing mood of late. I expect the seventeenth-century poet Robert Herrick wrote most days; even when he wasn't in the mood.

What can I do in poetry,
Now the good spirit's gone from me?
Why, nothing now but lonely sit
And over-read what I have writ.
R. Herrick

Nibbled cold slices of kiwi fruit to boost my blood sugar and curb my craving for unhealthy snacks; the potassium doing my blood pressure lots of good and all that wonderful vitamin C doing what vitamin C does, while I languished in the bubbles of a warm kiwi fruit foam bath. Bit later; washed my hair with evening primrose shampoo and conditioner, wrapped my *clean* hair in a towel and rubbed a little evening primrose body lotion on my elbows and legs below the knees – will do whole body when I have enough life in me. My eyebrows looked like pink cacti.

Spent ages drawing in my eyebrows with a dark brown eyebrow pencil, then dragged myself into a taxi at five past seven for my weekly bone crunch; exhausted but *very* clean, *very* pampered and *very* beautiful after my day at the beauty parlour.

Mr. Cheerful-chatty-taxi-man said I looked awful.
Eileen said I looked peeky.
Mr. Ex-soldier-taxi-man flirted with me.
Ben said I looked ill.

Beauty is in the eye of the ex-soldier.

Tuesday 7th

Today my face was pale as parsley – a sprig of parsley left in a mug on
the draining board for two weeks, drained of its vibrant green, now the
palest yellow. Dry and crinkly at the edges.

Ben bought a firm, fresh cucumber and a head of crispy lettuce
so I knew summer had arrived; the lettuce was so large and heavy I felt
as if I were trying to shove a human head into the salad compartment
of the fridge...

*... in the middle of the night she crept downstairs to remove the shelves in
the fridge so the head could grow a body and eventually push it's way out of its
metal egg during the early hours. She'd always believed in little green men and
now she would have one of her very own and take him to church on Sundays;
the priest was always saying, 'Lettuce pray', after all...*

Prepared myself a tasty salad and sat outside in the sunshine to eat it.
I was happily munching my first forkful and enjoying healthy, crunchy
thoughts when a fried egg and bacon smell wafted through the holes
in the fence and drifted evilly under my nose, exciting my nostrils.
Had to go back indoors – I may be a vegetarian but there are times...
Reminded myself that the smell of cooking pig is similar to that of
burning human bodies (a fireman told me – ugh).

I am calm and peaceful, healed and healthy; I love me and all the
little fishes in the deep blue sea. I will eat lots of lettuce because *Weekly
Wife* tells me the outer leaves are rich in vitamin C, it's a good source
of potassium, contains calcium and phosphorous, and the white latex
that oozes from the stalk when it's picked contains a natural substance
known as lettuce opium – good for promoting sleep. Can't imagine it
as a bedtime snack though.

Wrote three short letters to Auntie, Rose and Gail (big writing
with a thick italic pen on recycled paper with a very wide, colourful,

arty border) and mentioned I was doing fine, on the up, very positive, pampering self, writing poetry, painting a little, eating healthy salads, of sound mind and recovering well. Forgot to mention defacing magazines, non-veggie thoughts, ginger cats in spaceships, little green men in the fridge, catching blue stars and lunar-tics, angels with candy floss on their heads, minor accidents, exhaustion and loneliness, peanut butter cravings, pagan aerobics, dwarves, spells, chickens whistling the 'Birdie Song' and painting face with Truly Red lipstick spots.

Wednesday 8th

Peered up at the sky through my scratched sunglasses and lazily followed silhouettes of swifts, martins or swallows – had to consult bird book. House martins! Common and widespread; they were originally a bird of open country, now associated with man, building mud nests under house eaves. The sand martin is similar with obvious brown breast bar and no white rump.

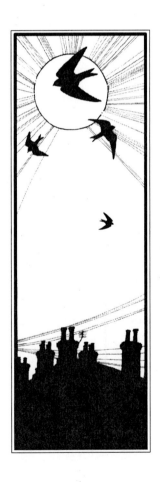

I spend a lot of time outside looking at the sky, now the weather is warmer; a change of ceiling is good for you. Happy, Bashful, Sneezy, Dopey, Grumpy and Sleepy watched the birdies or dozed in hammocks made out of ivy and bindweed, while I discussed the tawny owl with Doc. We made 'to-wit-to-woo' noises and everybody joined in. What *will* the neighbours think?

Tonight I found a fantastically beautiful blue crystal with gold and white flecks sitting on the bread bin.

Thursday 9th

Long lazy lapis lazuli blue day.

A tall thirty-something woman tip-tapped past our house in high heels this morning wearing a pretty poppy-red dress with yellow check. She was a large lady (size sixteen or eighteen I'd say; more an eighteen) and I couldn't help thinking of those old red telephone boxes with the door you couldn't open and the wind whistling through broken glass. Anyway, I noticed it was the same dress she had on yesterday; it was a bit crumpled, so was her hair and face, and she usually looks so smart whenever I see her, in slimming black or dark brown or navy. I think she's put on a bit of weight lately; maybe she's recently split up with her boyfriend, left her husband, he's left her or she's married and contented now and cooking big dinners for two. OK – back to the crumpled, poppy-red dress; hmmm, maybe she'd just left her lover's house or had been out clubbing all night and getting drunk to forget, or the washing machine has broken down and she doesn't hand wash and has run out of decent work clothes, or she has two red dresses the same (from an Evans spring sale) or her iron just broke – shall I ask her?

Freewoman catalogue arrived so I ordered myself a bright stripy uplifting bikini and a white one to show off my wonderful tan (when I've got one). I've never had a wonderful tan all over (hate sunbathing for long) but of course now I have all this absolutely fabulous time to just lie around and get absolutely fabulously golden brown. I ate lots of raw carrots last year and the bits I showed to the sun turned a gorgeous orangy brown. Must put more carrots on the shopping list this week.

Made a start on tan. Lay in the afternoon sun for about half an hour, toasting both sides under God's grill, in my bra and knickers. They were sensible-cover-all-cotton but I still noticed a disapproving glare from Mrs. Large-flowery-dress (next door but one) as she sailed past in the breeze (plucking out any unfortunate weed that dared to show its face in public) and gave Chris Evans (ginger cat) a dirty look for doing his business on the dahlias. Mr. Old-green-shirt-baggy-brown-trousers hid in his potting shed behind cobweb curtains. Sidney. Poor Sidney, I hear her telling him off sometimes. I'm afraid I might get a telling off soon too; perhaps I'll wear one of my tight bikinis tomorrow (three *minute* triangles of cotton with spots on... 'she wore an itsy-bitsy-teeny-weeny'...) and parade around a bit pretending to pluck out weeds and smile as I bend forward. That'll give her something to snort about and maybe she'll leave Sidney alone for five minutes. Maybe I'll make *his* day; these older men like a bit of flesh.

Grumpy looked very disapproving, Happy giggled and Sneezy blew his nose to hide his embarrassment. Bashful turned pink, Dopey watched cross-eyed as a bee sat on his nose and Doc removed his glasses to polish them.

Oh dear... this warm weather really... makes... me... wilt... makes me droop... like the rose in the kitchen that's been in a cup of water for days now, leaning over the rim, floppy and wrinkly with a fly sitting on it; a fly with a stripy body and crimson head.

... Sidney Fly, wearing a faded pinstripe suit, crimson face fixed on his bank statement, rubbed his hands together. He'd landed a big job, left a little deposit here and there and done the dirty on several of his competitors...

FLOWER

Some days
I feel
Like a flower
Wilting
By the hour
In need
Of a good
Shower

Consulted book on crystals: lapis lazuli inspires positive thinking (good) is a tonic to the nervous system (wonderful), can reduce pain (great) and boosts the immune system (just what I need).

Friday 10th

6.36 p.m.   Mr. Boxer-face stops to chat to Miss Phone-box-body outside No. 8. They look very friendly. Antique coffee table looks up at her, panting with his tongue hanging out, then he looks up her dress.

7.30 p.m.   *Coronation Street.*

8.00 p.m.   It's all bin 'appening at The Rovers this week... Oooh!

What's Vera going to do about Jack? It's all bin 'appening in Albert Square too!... Oooh! What's Pauline gonna do about that wayward son of 'ers?

8.03 p.m.   Nuffin's 'appenin' 'ere. Ooooh! What am I gonna do about me?

8.04 p.m.   Fink about life 'n' deff.

8.05 p.m.   Where there's life, there's soap, ha, ha.

8.06 p.m.   Watch grass growing.

Must remind Ben to mow lawn.

Will miss the buttercups.

8.07 p.m.   Watch bird flying high in pale sky. Clouds remind me of dirty cotton wool balls used to remove mascara.

8.08 p.m.   Wendy of *W.W.* says 'colour, curl and condition are the three keywords for mascara this summer' – I'd better check the latest products to suit my style then!

8.09 p.m.   An enormous cloud drifts over my head, Loch Ness monster-shaped, sort of. The cloud below is a mouse with a big head, kind of. Two small clouds are a pair of grandad slippers, if you squint a bit.

8.10 p.m.   Search for God's pipe, to go with slippers. Cool gust of wind blows roses about. They remind me of boats bobbing up and down in a harbour on a stormy night.

8.12 p.m.   Slipper clouds have gone. Couldn't find pipe. Obviously, God's given up smoking. Loch Ness monster is much thinner and longer. The mouse's head broke off and moved away.

8.13 p.m.   The bells of All Saints' church are ringing in the distance...

... she sat in the corner, quiet as a church mouse...

8.14 p.m.   Recall my wedding day; think about something else quickly before brain spirals downwards into pit of past relationship pain.

8.15 p.m.   There's a fluffy white cat sitting on the fence.

I smile like a wedge of Edam cheese.

8.16 p.m.   Cat neatly walks along fence like a radiant confident gymnast who knows she'll win the Gold. Easily.

Must find camera and take picture for my cat calendar –

'White cat in June'.

8.17 p.m.   'Hello dare pussy.'
'Here liddle pussy.'
'C'mon den fluffy.'

Cat looks at me as if to say, 'Actually, my name is Arrrabella de la Paw and sometimes I'm Dadeeez big beaudifulll princezz, not and I rrrepeat not, little pussy-woosy or fluffy wuffy thank you verrry much.'

8.18 p.m.   Feel broody. Feel ever so broody for a kitten – a whole house full of kittens. Want to hear the patter of tiny paws, feel soft fur and the tickle of whiskers, a small rough tongue on my nose and hear the sound of a rumbly purr.

8.19 p.m.   The beautiful Arabella picks her way over the lawn, trying not to get her white skirts dirty.

8.20 p.m.   Look for camera.

8.25 p.m.   Find camera.

8.26 p.m.   Cat gone.

8.30 p.m.   There's a pale rind of moon high in the sky – God's fingernail clipping.

8.31 p.m.   Recall asking God for his help this morning. Well, not exactly. I simply said, 'Oh God, help me,' when I discovered the washing machine had leaked all over the kitchen floor and I'd slipped on the water, dropped a Kit-Kat mug (of course it didn't break but I felt like I'd broken my leg) and the phone was ringing and someone was banging on the front door. Anyway, all God has given me is a fingernail clipping and a glimpse of his bedroom slippers. Maybe it's all I deserve. I expect I've broken most of the Ten Commandments.

8.32 p.m.   What are the Ten Commandments? Mmmm, let's see... Thou shalt not covet thy neighbour's wife.
That's one I *know* I've never broken.

8.34 p.m.   Mustn't take the Lord's name in vain... errrrr... and something about bearing false witness against something... ummmmm... I know! Keep the Sabbath day holy and mustn't kill. Oh! Lord. (Ooops!) Wonder if thinking about murder counts? When did I last set foot in a church? Errrrrrr...

8.40 p.m.   Small dark crescents fly across God's fingernail.

8.41 p.m.	Am expert on birdies now. Know straight away they are house martins.
8.42 p.m.	Thou shalt not be a big head; that might be another one.
8.43 p.m.	Examine fingernails. Push back cuticles on fingernails, ten tiny half moons (more like sixteenths and eighths of moons, really). Thou shalt not push thy luck, might be another one.
8.44 p.m.	Recall painting my nails dark purple when I was a teenager and the priest telling me off after Sunday mass; probably thought I was in league with the devil.
8.45 p.m.	Think about being young and silly.
8.46 p.m.	Smile at one of my seven dwarves (Dopey, with his orange hat and boots and coat the colour of lichen) and remember how excited I was when I went to the pictures for the first time and *Snow White* was on...
8.47 p.m.	Look at hands.
	Think about getting old.
	Notice cracks in path.
	And bent branch.
	Glance at fallen pink petals.
	Curling at the edges.
8.50 p.m.	Am old and silly.
8.56 p.m.	Getting chilly.
8.57 p.m.	Fed up.
8.58 p.m.	Thou shalt not feel sorry for thyself.
9.07 p.m.	Best go indoors.
11.35 p.m.	Lie in bed staring at the ceiling and cobweb on lampshade. Ben snores; an after-several-pints-and-lots-of-fags-type-snore. Whisper, 'Thou shalt not overindulge', in his ear.
11.37 p.m.	Decide the Ten Commandments need updating.

1.	Thou shalt not fancy the socks off man next door, or his wife.
2.	Thou shalt not shag best mate's girlfriend or boyfriend.
3.	Thou shalt not steal from pick and mix at Woolworths; nick pens or paper from place of work, photocopy private work or private parts.
4.	Thou shalt not spend whole lunch break on phone to Mum, best mate or partner, or gossiping in café or wine bar.

5.   Thou shalt not bare false teeth in public, boobs at a nightclub or flutter false eyelashes down the local pub.

6.   Thou shalt not be vain, e.g., plastic surgery, hair pieces, lipo, white bikini to show off wonderful tan.

7.   Thou shalt not worship pop stars or movie stars or read thy stars.

8.   Thou shalt not swear at family or work colleagues or murder them.

9.   Thou shalt not shag work colleague when married or living in sin.

10.   Thou shalt not live in sin nor covet thy neighbour's conservatory or ever-so-posh three-piece suite you saw delivered last week.

Saturday 11th

A wealthy looking busybody wearing a thick black and yellow striped fur coat tottered down the garden path mumbling to herself in the late morning sunshine. I wrote, 'honey, royal jelly and bee propolis' on the shopping list.

Ben didn't feel like shopping today. He stood in the garden smoking, a Clint-Eastwood-with-a-headache face on, watching the fence: it leaned towards next door, tired from the effort of standing upright. Then he plonked himself in front of the TV with a coffee, tired from the effort of thinking about all the little jobs that needed doing around the house. I asked him if there were anything bothering him, apart from his mental things-to-do list getting longer and longer.

He said he was having problems at work and would have to stick his neck out. I informed him giraffes have seven bones in their neck, the same number as humans, and no two giraffes have the same spot pattern. He thanked me for that little interesting piece of information and said it would be most helpful in sorting out his problems. I said I could tell him lots of other interesting facts if he liked, but he suddenly had the urge to scuttle off to www dot land (wonder if that's where Sam Spider is; haven't seen him for ages).

When Ben had been happily tapping away for a few hours, I brought him coffee and a sandwich and told him (said, 'www dot' first – I remembered!) giraffes eat in the morning and at night, rest in the afternoon and have four stomachs, like a cow. He lit a cigarette and nodded with a do-continue-I'm-really-interested expression. So I continued... ha! ha! ha!

Sunday 12th

Weird musician friend dropped in for a strong black coffee but didn't stay very long. He filled the room with gloom like a drunk finding a handy place to throw up, then wandered off to the park to find Jesus. I gave him some bread to help him feed the five thousand ducks.

Ben watched the fence, puffing away like Clint Eastwood on four hundred a day, then turned on his heel and disappeared once more into www dot land to tap away like a mallard attacking a crust before the other ducks notice it. I sunned my feathers for a while, then curled up on a pile of cushions like a nesting moorhen by the river.

Stephen stood at the kitchen window and surveyed the damage after last night's storm. He frowned and stubbed his cigarette out in a plate with toast crumbs on; the ashtray was overflowing with empty Benson & Hedges packets, banana skins, dog ends and matches. He lit another cigarette, inhaled deeply and tried to ignore the dull ache in his back as he leafed through the phone book.

Morag stared at the name in her appointment book and the world stopped for a moment as she remembered the man she had most tried to forget. For the rest of the day, she found it difficult to concentrate on her work and couldn't wait till her last patient had left; then she could drive home for a good long worry.

Monday 13th

Feel fed up, abandoned and sorry for thyself. Summer rain splashes the window pane. I notice a few people have forgotten their umbrellas; I expect they're feeling sorry for themselves too. In the distant distance, I hear the lonely sound of a train. Eileen is in Scotland and Ben is at a groovy new restaurant in town with his work colleagues. They went straight from work but Ben dropped in briefly for our parking permit so Rob could park in our street. When he dashed out again, I suddenly felt more lonely than I had all day. I hurried to the front door and opened it to give them both a cheerful little wave. They were in happy holiday spirits, Rob glanced in my direction but didn't notice me. I squeaked, 'Hello,' and Ben turned round and started walking back towards the house, thinking he'd forgotten something. I squeaked again, 'No, it's OK, I'm only saying hello,' so he turned on his heels and ran back to catch up with Rob. I wished I'd let him come all the way back to the house so I could have a peck on the cheek to cheer me up.

Everyone is out
I'm here all alone
Staring in the fridge
Staring at the phone
Staring at me feet
Staring at me face
How-I-really-wish-that-I-was-in-another-place

I want to be in Scotland
I want to be in Rome
Staring at the pyramids
Kiss the Blarney stone
Staring at a ceiling
By Michelangelo
I-want-to-be-in-Switzerland-skiing-in-the-snow

I want to be in Paris
I want to be in Spain
Give me back my energy
Free me from this pain
I want to be in Belgium
I want to be in Greece
The-beaches-of-Hawaii
For-the-beauty-and-the-peace

Tuesday 14th

A postcard arrived from one of Ben's aunties, holidaying in Cadgwith, Cornwall (on the Lizard Peninsula). I studied the photo of pink roses against whitewashed walls and sky-blue paintwork of a quaint Cornish cottage. Groaned. Sky-blue lizards eating Cornish ice-cream can crawl over whitewashed walls and throw up on the roses for all I care. I WANT TO GO ON HOLIDAY!

Was amazed to read the other day that visitors to Thailand often return home to find blue lizards in their suitcases. They are put in ~~aquamarine~~ quarantine, then sent home (the lizards not the visitors). I wonder if they really are sent home... There was a photo of a beautiful sky-blue lizard next to the article (he wasn't eating ice-cream).

Wednesday 15th

Wendy tells me bold, bright and flowery is the latest look. Thanks a bunch. Well, I've ordered a stripy bikini now, my favourite summer tops are stripy and I *like* stripes. Deck chairs and straws and seaside rock... ooooh... I can feel a verse coming on... yes... yes... YES!!

> **Stripy deck chair**
> **Stripy rock**
> **Stripy Frenchman**
> **In stripy top**
> **Stripy straws**
> **In stripy booze**
> **Strappy sandals**
> **Stripy shoes**

Later in bath...

> **Stripy shoes**
> **Stripy socks**
> **Money in my**
> **Stripy box**
> **Stripy toothpaste**
> **On my chin**
> **Stripy paper**
> **In the bin**

Looking out window at kitten on wall...

> **WRITTEN BY A KITTEN**
>
> **Stripy straw**
> **In my paw**
> **Stripy scratches**
> **On the door**

Watching trees...

WRITTEN BY A NATURE LOVER

Roads:
Deep grey scars
On soft tender skin
Of Mother Nature's
Curves

In bed, wondering when Ben will come home...

WRITTEN BY A WOMAN WHO IS MISSING HER SOLDIER HUSBAND AND FEELS THE NEED FOR A HOLIDAY IN THE SUN

Stripes upon his uniform
Wish I were in Benidorm
In a stripy bi-ki-ni
Lots of sun and sand and sea

Thursday 16th

Whenever www dot appears on the telly, I can't help thinking – Wendy, *Weekly Wife* – and of her wonderful weekly advice... This week I have a choice of walking, running, cycling, step class, aerobics, swimming, tennis and squash for my fat-burning exercise programme. Thanks again Wendy, but if you don't mind I'll just lie in the sun growing freckles and a fantastic tan and avoid fatty food. Simple.

Crunched heartily into a tasty organic raw carrot like Peter Rabbit as my mind hopped from one thought to another, before burrowing down into a dark depression about depressing things (wildlife run over on our roads and sheep in those horrible lorries on their way to the slaughterhouse). Heard someone knock on the door but by the time I'd climbed out of my burrow and hurried to the edge of the forest, the caller had gone. I twitched my nose. A card lay on the mat; my parcel was waiting to be collected at number twelve. The hours dragged by till...

Ben picked up the package before dinner and I tried on the bikinis before we ate, so my tummy would look flatter. They fitted OK and I felt happy all over. I'd managed to lose a bit of weight: two whole lovely pounds! Ben said I looked nice and I could be a model... for the shorter, fuller-figured mature woman. Huh.

I gave him the free tool kit from Freewoman catalogue (he needs a bit of encouragement) and he pretended to look ever so pleased. I pretended to look ever so pleased that he was so delighted. He pretended to look pleased that I was delighted about him being ever so pleased.

Friday 17th

Wore my marvellous new multicoloured stripy two piece; it even outshone next door's orange Marigold gloves, yellow duster and massive pink knickers neatly pegged on the washing line. Bashful turned bright red to match Doc's hat. Doc was polishing his glasses again and nudging Sleepy. Dopey blew on a dandelion and a seed got stuck up Sneezy's nose, which set him off again. A bird did a pooh on Grumpy's head and Happy laughed behind his hand.

The white bikini will look good when I've developed my gorgeous golden tan and I'm slimmer. I haven't much of a tan yet though and I must have devoured simply thousands of calories today.

Wiggled my toes and fingers and fluttered my eyelids to the beat of a band on a pop programme tonight in a desperate attempt to use up a few calories. Decided to be good, very, very good tomorrow... *When she was good, she was very, very good and when she was bad she had pizza...*

Psychologists at the Manchester Metropolitan University reckon you don't have actually to do any exercise to get energy boosting psychological benefits from exercise. If you just visualise yourself doing a workout, your brain can be tricked into thinking you've really done it. Oh, Lord! I really wish it worked in a physical way too.

Visualised running to Thorntons, purchasing a box of cappuccino chocs, eating them lustfully one by one as I wandered round River Island, Monsoon and Dorothy Perkins (offering one to anyone who looked sad) then running home. Trouble was, I kept seeing myself being arrested for covering half of Dorothy P's stock with chocolate marks. Also, I had to keep going back to Thorntons to buy more chocs because there were too many sad looking people needing a little treat – don't think I'll ever master this visualisation thing.

Ben and Bill did their weekly exercise at the bar of The Tone and Trimmit, Skinnier Street.

Saturday 18th

Late morning, I watched a thirty-something couple emerge from a Range Rover (Ben said it was a Mitsubishi Shogun) wearing matching white T-shirts and shorts, tans and trainers, sunglasses and smiles, and we-go-to-the-gym-three-times-a-week bodies. They had that we've-just-come-back-from-holiday and we're-going-into-town-to-buy-tableware to match the-garden-furniture-and-barbecue look about them. Before they locked up the Mitsubishi palace on wheels the man rubbed Ambre Solaire into the back of his neck (couldn't see which factor, fifteen I guess judging by his red hair). Then he rubbed some on the woman's nose. They smiled again.

I expect they'll pop into B.H.S. later to purchase jazzy shorts for him and bold, bright and flowery bikinis for her, for their next holiday in the sun. Then she'll spend ages in Boots and he'll pretend not to leer at the women behind the make-up counters. The women at the make-up counters, trying not to look bored out of their beautifully manicured minds, will pretend not to lust after his muscular brown body.

Sunday 19th

Cosmic Colin says the Summer Solstice is a great time for me to consider making changes to my home and image. Moved three scented candles from the top of the TV on to the bookcase, gently laid a sleeping dragon in their place, positioned my crystals on the bathroom window sill where I could enjoy light shining through them, and considered wearing blue mascara tomorrow.

Rick and Bill came round in high spirits on their way to see Rob and Bob the Slob playing with Black Pizza at The Thirsty Tongue Tavern. They wanted to know if Ben and our weird musician friend (Je Kan) would join them, but Ben wasn't in a drinking mood (the lure of www dot land was too much for him) and Je Kan hates loud music in brightly lit pubs; he'd rather lurk in a dark corner (preferably dusty and dirty) scowling into his Guinness.

Rick and Bill stayed long enough for a coffee and a listen to W. M. Friend's latest instrumental creation on cassette tape, entitled the 'Black Whole'.

Bill:	Bit dark and depressing.
WMF:	It's meant to be.
Rick:	Very slow.
WMF:	It's meant to be.
Ben:	Does it speed up?
WMF:	No.
Rick:	When do the drums come in?
WMF:	They don't.
Bill:	I could finish *The Sea Of Suicide* listening to this; can I have a copy?
WMF:	Yes.
Ben:	Nice key modulation.
WMF:	Thank you.
Ben:	I see you got the old minor seven flat five in that bit!
WMF:	Yes.
Me:	It's very... er... moving.
WMF:	Thank you.
Ben:	When are you moving, Rick?
Rick:	Well...
WMF:	Please listen, the piece isn't over yet. The violins at the end say everything I want to say.
Ben:	(Quiet voice) Did you go to that funeral?
Bill:	(Whisper) No.
Rick:	(Loud voice) Is that the time?
WMF:	It's over in twenty-seven seconds.
Rick:	(Twenty-seven second pause) Good... Great! Let's go, Bill!
Bill:	Er... can I use your loo, Ben?
Ben:	Yeah mate.
Me:	(Tiny voice) Oh God, feel like I'm at a funeral. (Whisper to Ben) What sort of music would you like at your funeral? I think I'd like something jolly... a song about angels... Abba or the Eurythmics.
Rick:	(Tactless voice) Are you going to bump off your old man then?
Ben:	Have you poisoned the pizza, dear?

Me:	(Theatrical voice, with hand on forehead) Don't tempt me!
	(Lots of manly laughter)
Ben:	Anyone for another coffee?
WMF:	Yes. Very, very black. Please.

Daydreamed in the late afternoon sunshine with my writerly head on while Ben tapped away on his computer like a... like a... I dunno... madly keen tap dancer... who can't get it right?

Sam Spider sat on the computer and thought about setting up a new web site.

... Stephen Inglenook. Morag recalled the young farmhand and how she had worshipped him from behind faded curtains, hiding behind her curtain of hair, written endlessly about him in her diary, remembering his every word and the way he grinned when she was speechless.

The day of the incident with her father and the Range Rover flashed into her mind. (Just remembered it's Father's Day today). *After that, she hadn't written in her diary anymore and her love had turned to hatred. She never thought she would see him again, ever, after he left. Never ever. She sat and stared at her appointment book... she would have to face him now... Oh God... perhaps this wasn't the same man... but somehow she knew it was... she could be wrong... but she knew she was right... just knew...*

Monday 20th

I can't believe it!! This is *REALLeee* weird. Eileen told me today she is seeing someone called Stephen! Think I must be tuned into the future or something. Also there was a bright yellow jacket hanging on the back of her chair; sunflower yellow. *SPOOKeeeeee...*

Waved to the old Scottish wizard sitting at his garden gate on my way home. Forgot to ask Eileen if she had a lovely time in Scotland. She must have, she looks the happiest I've ever seen her. Maybe she'll get married and move back to the Highlands and without her treatment, my circulation will slow down, my body seize up and I'll die in pain.

Tuesday 21st

A postcard from Gail and Gareth arrived today – a picture of the north Cornish cliffs. They were glowing in the light of a summer sunset (the cliffs, not Gail and Gareth).

Ben did his Tuesday shop on the way home from work. He bought kitchen roll with a pretty curly wave and fish pattern: really cheered me up; it's the little things.
Watched a bit of the tennis at Wimbledon.

9.00 p.m.   Wandered down the garden to relieve Tuesday boredom, after an exciting Monday evening at the osteopath. A wonderful sweet yellowy fragrance from the honeysuckle bush filled my nostrils and soft pink clouds filled the blue skies in my eyes. I sighed. I smiled. I watched tiny spiders making delicate webs in the rose bush. The daisies and buttercups were still awake; the birds singing their evensong. For a moment, I wished I were in Cornwall, on the cliffs, watching a summer sunset, but consoled myself with the thought that I was seeing life with renewed sight.

9.15 p.m.   A fly flew into my eye.

GEORGE SEAGULL
She sat before the sunset
In her summer twinset
She watched the seagull soaring
He thought her rather boring

When she fed him next day
He changed his mind

Wednesday 22nd

Turned on the TV, closed my weary eyelids and dozed, listening to the tip-tap-twangy sound of tennis balls hitting tennis rackets and spectators clapping – a rushing sound like waves on a pebbly seashore. Ever so relaxing.

Lay in the late afternoon sun for a while, clouds drifting over my head like cotton wool balls floating in Essence of Ocean bath water, the sun a perfect white disc behind the clouds. I talked about our planet with Doc and Grumpy and, glancing at the sun, we agreed that at least humans can't destroy that. It will die... one day... in five billion years' time. The sun – our star – will have exhausted its fuel. That's what the scientists say, anyway. The surface of our beautiful planet will be scorched... incinerated... become an ocean of molten rock... nothing will survive. The Earth... devoid of life... will sit in the cold emptiness of space. I expect we will have destroyed our planet in five thousand years anyway... maybe five hundred... five... Or we'll build spaceships and inhabit other planets millions of light years away and name them after countries, like we name our streets after famous artists and writers. When every country has its own planet, no doubt it will be constant Star Wars in the seas of time.

Happy and Sleepy, who were listening to our conversation, looked sad. Doc removed his glasses and wiped a tear away. Bashful sobbed behind a broken flower pot, Dopey looked confused and Grumpy kicked a stone which hit Sneezy on the nose and started him off again.

I've discovered Ben and Delyth have been sending each other e-mails – she's the biggest tart in the universe, from planet Tarty Tits! I confided in Happy.

Later, I heard a tapping noise; it sounded like Ben was on his computer, but he was at work. Intrigued, I crept upstairs to find Happy jumping up and down on the computer keys. When I asked him what he was up to, he said he was trying to get the word-window to work so he could tell Delyth what he thought of her, bless him.

Must write cotton wool and sunflower oil on shopping list and try to think happy thoughts.

SUNBATHING

I love the sun
When it shines on
My tum
And when I turn
Over
It shines on my
Bum

Thursday 23rd

Watched a tiny seed, like a miniature white chimney sweep's brush used by fairies, float across the garden path. Listened to the trees in the breeze: God rustling sweetie wrappers. Thought about Galaxy chocolate. Heard a child crying in the distance and wanted to comfort it. Listened to a shrill, monotonous sound made by a bird; wanted to tie the bird's beak up. Thought about birds trapped in cages. Counted my freckles. Used new kitchen roll with curly wave and fish pattern. Snipped off twenty three split ends and cut fingernails while listening to relaxing tennis sounds. Wiped mark off TV.

It's *that* time of the month and I'm hungry *all* the time and feeling a strong urge to shove a tart in the oven. I *desperately* want to clean the house and scrub every room *madly* from top to bottom in a *crazy* frenzy. I'm suffering from N.H.S. (Nesting Hoovering Syndrome) and S.A.D.S. (Strangle a Delyth Syndrome). I can't *wait* till Monday; Eileen's treatment will calm me down.

Wendy says, when you're bursting with ratty energy you should get some extra work done and if you're at breaking point, meet a friend or go for a walk. Great. Fine. Wonderful. I'll just sit here, thanks, and O.D. on chips, honey and primrose oil capsules, howl at the full moon, pace around like a big hairy wolf with lots of teeth and bite Ben's head off.

Lucky, *lucky, lucky, lucky, lucky* me. A weekend of crippling period pains to look forward to after two weeks of N.H.S. worsening all my other symptoms. I just love being a woman.

BEING ME

I love being me
When he tells me
I look good.
I love being me
When my hair looks
As it should.
I hate being me
When I've been
Thinking
Far too much.
When I feel locked up
In this body
Like a rabbit
In a hutch.

Friday 24th

... Barbara Bumble Bee is in love with Sidney Fly. He's invited her on a pub crawl... on a table in the beer garden of The Sun...

Listened to more tennis. Quite romantic really, they're always saying love this and love that. Sunbathed a bit. An ant crawled up my leg. Something flew up my nose and flew out again, obviously didn't like what it saw. Snot to worry. A wasp flew round my head, saw my expression and flew away again. Happy laughed and Sneezy worried about the pollen count.

Ate a healthy, salady snack then made a flower pattern on the plate with one pea and seven sweet corn nibblets. Picked three leaves from rose bush to add to decoration. Nursed scratch from pointy thorn (banished sad crucifixion thoughts). Shall I send my creation to the Tate Gallery entitled 'Bored Sick Person'?

Ben met Bill and Rob at The Cup and Saucer, Teapot Lane. They came home smashed.

Saturday 25th

Mother Nature cleaned her paintbrush, dipped it in zinc white paint then delicately stroked the pale cobalt blue canvas here and there in a confident, arty way. With a finer brush, she added three tiny charcoal-grey lines, vaguely bird shaped. She stood back to admire her master-piece, head to one side.

Curled up in bed all day with the monthly pains, wishing I were a man, not a bleedin' woman. Crawled to the toilet now and again.

Ben was in a jolly summery Saturday mood, full of life and ener-gy and hangover free. The lads didn't drink much last night – Rob had no money, Ben only had a fiver and Bill is into Minimalism. He (Ben) bought a punnet of huge, shiny, bright red English strawberries. I ate four juicy ones. Mmmmmmm. Delicious. Cleansing. Nutritious. Vitamin C. I used to tell myself that one of the most enjoyable, healthy summer experiences is eating fresh strawberries and drinking ice-cold mineral water with bright, life-giving sun shining on my face. These days, when I should be constantly thinking such healthy thoughts, all I really, real-ly want is a whole packet of Jaffa Cakes with the smashing orangy bit in the middle, their crisp, dark love-giving chocolate on my face.

Sunday 26th

A rainy summery Sunday. A girl in white holds a white umbrella over her blonde head. A distant rumble in the heavens: God moving the furniture again; perhaps he's lost his slippers. In *Blackadder* last night, Rowan Atkinson said bad weather is God's way of telling us to burn more Catholics! Hope Mum didn't see it.

Strange month, June. Mr. Miserable-as-sin-taxi-man said the other day, 'One minit it's bleedin' 'ot, next it's bleedin' cold.' Well, that's not *exactly* what he said; he mentioned sweaty parts of the male anatomy and the freezing of certain parts of male anatomy kept in trousers; a good Christian girl like me does not repeat that sort of thing.

With all this changeable weather, it's no wonder I've seen lots of people unsuitably dressed, especially these youngsters. And as for that Scary Spice girl... saw a picture of her in *Weekly Wife* with great big holes in her jeans. Honestly, you'd think with all her money she'd buy a decent pair!

The fence is swaying like a rain-soaked drunk. Ben hasn't noticed yet. Weird musician friend (Lao Tzu) has been arrested for *being* a rain soaked drunk. He was caught cleansing his soul and balancing his life energies – standing naked in the rain, practising Tai Chi, in the middle of the park.

Monday 27th

Turned the sound down and watched a black and white romantic comedy starring David Niven (while I recovered from my pre-osteopath bath) and had a giggle at his facial expressions. I expect it was a funny film; don't know; I never got round to turning the sound up and fell asleep.

Elizabeth Montgomery in the sitcom *Bewitched* has a lot of excellent extremely pained expressions, I noticed the other morning. I'm going to practise them in front of the mirror, so, when people enquire about my illness, what I'm saying will be more believable. I'll end up in a home for senile, retired actresses if I'm not careful...

... she sat quietly in the high-backed floral armchair near the window, a crochet blanket covering her small frail legs. A silent movie flickered in the corner, her favourite, Charlie Chaplin and the blind flower girl; yesterday it was Buster Keaton with the front of a house falling on him. She made dramatic facial expressions at the screen – one must keep in practise, one never knew when the perfect part would come along. She nibbled popcorn with shaky hands, her thin, scarlet lips smiling constantly, then happily scooped up ice-cream from a small round tub with a flat wooden spoon.

Popcorn crumbs lay sprinkled around her chair and every evening she giggled and remarked that someone had left the window open again and let the snow in. Her cardigan pocket was always full of wooden spoons as she shuffled off to bed wearing worn, pink, dotty slippers, to dream of seaside holidays in Hastings. The wooden spoons would come in handy one day to build sand castles and make fences around them.

Iris loved Hastings: lifting her long skirts to paddle in the waves, all that sunny sea air and sounds on the pier, the penny arcade and fish and chips wrapped in newspaper. Gordon would take her again one day. Gordon, her handsome grandson, who had her wit and smile. He had promised, and a promise is a promise. She touched the seashell necklace in her seashell jewellery box, enjoying the smooth cool feel and soft seaside colours. She recalled the sensation of cold, wet, rippling sand under her bare feet and watching tiny crabs disappear between the grains like magic. Every day she reminded nurse Susan to have her stripy blue beach bag and towel and sun hat ready, even in January, just in case – one must be prepared. Sometimes, Iris sat in a deck chair in the garden with the crochet rug over her legs – one must practise getting in and out of deck chairs, just in case. It was a splendid stripy red and white deckchair; she had her very own bucket and spade too and a hand-

ful of shells collected long ago, small stripy shells with pink insides. They'd look good on a castle made of sand. Gordon built such super sandcastles when he was a boy, shrieking with delight as the waves splashed into the moat. He built hotels now and had to travel abroad a lot. He used to send Grandma postcards from all sorts of places she'd never heard of: what an exciting life, such a lovely boy. How long had it been since she'd last heard from him? She screwed up her face; she couldn't remember. She shook her head, frustrated at her failing memory.

Nurse Susan kept a letter in a drawer in the office; a letter informing the Swansong Nursing Home of Gordon's death in the Gambia. Some sort of strange illness. He had died in the hotel he had designed and helped to construct, six years ago. He had never married; he'd never had the time. Susan didn't have the heart to tell the old dear.

Tomorrow was Iris's eightieth birthday. She didn't know. Surprise party cakes hid silently in the fridge, covered in cling film. Two railway tickets to Hastings slept in Susan's purse next to a small book of second class stamps. A packet of popcorn and a clean towel snuggled up next to a yellow sun hat in the stripy blue beach bag.

Eileen looked a bit low today, I think she's suffering from N.H.S. too. She said all the women working at the clinic (herbalist, aromatherapist, homeopath*ist*, counsellor-round-the-twist) have their period at the same time every month now. I think I've tuned in with them too, I've been attending the clinic for so long.

Men should be warned to keep away for one week every month; a collection of road signs placed around the doorway.

DANGER Keep Clear Women Close To The Edge!
WARNING Hard Hat Area Heavy Mood Swings!
HALT Hormones at work!
STOP Think before you speak!
CAUTION Agree with everything she says!

Anyway, I showed her my new variety of facial expressions to make her laugh; dead bored and miserable, ecstatically excited, terribly worried and nervous, unsure but hopeful, madly in love and starry eyed (I sighed to add to the effect). She fell about laughing but on her recovery, she still looked sad. Maybe she's split up with Stephen. Maybe she won't get married and move away now. Feel selfishly pleased. Feel guilty for being so selfish. Hope she's still with Stephen and they marry but don't move away. Feel a bit less selfish now.

OLD POET

> **There's a verse**
> **In me purse**
> **Can you get it for me**
> **Nurse**
>
> **Thank you dear**

Will send this to *Weekly Wife* and ask them to send my payment to Help the Aged. Feel better and only a tiny bit selfish.

Will buy Eileen small chocolatey present and try not to eat it myself. Am lovely person again.

Tuesday 28th

After sifting through about twenty Bonusprint and Boots envelopes full of big shiny photos (reminding me of well, energetic days, holidays surrounded by very green scenery and very blue skies, summer days scoffing ice-cream, gulping lots of alcohol, walking miles, charming villages, ugly ex-boyfriends, friendly locals in friendly pubs, parties, family, dancing, weddings of friends now divorced, babies now at school or pregnant themselves and pets that have long gone to pet heaven) I eventually found an amusing pet photo (tabby cat sitting in same pose as cat on mug) to send to *Weekly Wife*. I could earn thirty pounds!

I might also rewrite the story I've just written about Iris; maybe go into more detail about her family, the other residents in the home, her thoughts and things, and send that in too... Mmmmm... and possibly one of my better poems... Errrrr... which one... don't know... whichever makes Ben laugh the most... ? He'll have to listen to them all, ha! ha! ha!

I could make a few pennies. Maybe I won't send all the money to Help the Aged. One needs to be a little selfish to care for oneself and I *am* ill, after all, and money *does* have the magical ability to cheer one up *especially* if one is poor and feeling happy is so *essential* when one's immune system needs lots of support... I *could* try a money making spell.

Tired of feeling excited about future money-making plans, I gazed out of the window and spotted a red umbrella this afternoon – I've actually started umbrella spotting! I even pointed out an amusing one (green, with frog eyes sticking out) to Mr. Cheerful-chatty-taxi-man recently. I *even* found myself designing a pattern for one: sad, verrry saaad. It was quite good really, bright and jolly: yellow sun at the top surrounded by fluffy white clouds on a light blue background, and happy raindrops falling from the clouds onto pretty rainbows with pots of gold at the end. Large pots of gold, enough to pay for an animal sanctuary, a new kitchen, or a facelift, and extra to go to Help the Aged, the R.S.P.C.A. *and* research (non-animal) into M.E. of course.

More sad than umbrella spotting, much more sad, quite tragic really, is my fluff collection. Yes fluff. Some people collect stamps or postcards, bugs or antique jugs, china pigs or dogs or frogs; but I've got a neat little row of bits of belly button fluff, thank you very much. Not mine, Ben's. His belly button is very deep, beautifully deep, and I *do* so enjoy delving into the depths of my partner's personality. Your belly button fluff can say a lot about you, you know; just like the shape of your face, your eyes and mouth, nails and hair. Ben's fluff says he's been wearing the same old black and blue and green clothes for far too many years and he doesn't mind his partners probing into his dark private world under the bold check shirt of existence. I'm *so* lucky, this new hobby doesn't take too much out of me, or Ben! I don't have to go out hunting in antique shops or car boot sales, just happily root around in a smelly belly – suits my quiet, simple life perfectly.

The money-making spell looks complicated, a lot of effort. And my vision is too blurry to read magical chants written in small, curly, witchy writing. I'll only bring on an M.E. (Magic Encyclopaedia) attack. The spell has to be performed at 8 a.m. or 3 p.m. on a Wednesday, Thursday or Sunday, symbolising Jupiter for ~~bitches~~ riches, the sun for ~~honey~~ money and fortune, or Mercury for ~~skull~~ skill. I have to set up an altar and circle, and call up the ~~elephants~~ elementals and ~~dietary~~ deities. I must use patchouli ~~incest~~ incense on the altar for the element of air and mix herbs with ~~a flame~~ athame in a bowl; this ~~emperors~~ empowers them. The bowl should be passed through the ~~representatives~~ representations of the elements as I call upon them to charge the herbs with their power. Candle flame for fire, incense for air, salt for earth and blessed water for water.

Allspice, bergamot, ~~comfy~~ comfrey, chamomile, cinquefoil, two ~~gloves~~ cloves, nutmeg, mint and ~~magician~~ marjoram should be combined and dropped into a green candle annointed with bergamot oil and inscribed with symbols for the Lady and Lord, good fortune, victory, ~~property~~ prosperity, wealth and completion. There's lots of ~~panting~~ chanting to be done, dripping of wax and wand waving in a circular ~~potion~~ motion matching the magnetic flow of the earth. The herbs may be dropped into a simmering pot-pourri as you chant about the spell being carried away by air, the magic released by the fire and the power of the earth bringing the goal into being.

You must let the magic work for one hour, then snuff the candle and check wax for signs and symbols or blow out the candle heating the pot-pourri and read the pattern of the herbs as you would for tea leaves – more of a palaver than Delia Smith making her delicious slimy marmalade!

My spell book suggests I put my own spells together once I get a feel for it. Think I'll develop a feel for short spells for the tired witch... spells to bring chocolate to me...

Spell no. 1
Stare at the full moon and imagine it as a planet sized Malteser or Cadbury's chocolate button on its side, for seven seconds without blinking.

Spell no. 2
Hold breath and stare at the half moon for three seconds thinking of Terry's chocolate orange. Breath out and imagine placing segment into mouth.

Spell no. 3
Stare at the stars for as long as you like thinking of Galaxy chocolate, Milky Way and Mars bars.
N.B. It is dangerous to think of Black Magic chocolates for long. This darkens the soul and turns your freckles into warts, so only think of this particular chocolate for two seconds. If you find you've thought for too long, quickly imagine a room full of Milky bars, hundreds of Milky bars waiting to be devoured.

Spell no. 4

Stand in a pentagram made out of Matchmakers (your favourite flavour) if you want love as well as chocolate to come to you. For a tall dark, handsome and athletic man, who doesn't mind climbing through windows and leaping out of helicopters, think of Milk Tray. For a man at the peak of his career, think of Toblerone. Aero, for a bubbly personality. Fruit and Nut for an eccentric. Topic, for good conversation. Cadbury's Flake for a creative artist. Smarties, for intelligence. Ferrero Rocher for wealth. Minstrels for a musician. Wispa for a quiet personality and Double Decker for a bus driver!

N.B. You may concentrate on several of the above.

Spell no. 5

Lie on the sofa with eyes closed, sniffing drinking chocolate while chanting words like: divine, desirable, seductive, heavenly, luscious, velvety, exciting, smooth, rewarding, tempting, delicious, sumptuous, wicked, ecstasy, lustful, sexy, addictive, silky, fragrant, comforting, sweet, naughty, aromatic, indulgent, creamy, luxurious, tantalising, fulfilling, alluring, irresistible and unforgettable.

Spell no. 6

For health *and* chocolate, place a glass of milk with a teaspoon of honey drizzled into it, in the centre of a Matchmaker pentagram. Visualise health and chocolate.

Spell no. 7

Break the fingers of a Kit-Kat apart and lay them end to end on kitchen roll with herb pictures on. This will enable you to break free from the worry of weight gain and give you a long, choc-full life. Eat Kit-Kat, savouring every mouthful.

Spell no. 8

At eight o'clock, open a box of After Eight. Eat whole box between eight and 12 o'clock; one every eight minutes. This will improve your willpower. If you feel sick, sip peppermint tea.

N.B. A practical choco-witch can eat chocolate all day and only experience chocuphoria. You will develop this skill with practise.

Spell no. 9

If you do not possess a wand, use a Matchmaker or brown felt pen, and make circular anti-clockwise movements chanting the word ABRACADBURYABRA as many times as you like. This also improves your memory and diction.

Spell no. 10
If too tired to move or speak or lift an eyelash, visualise performing favourite spell, smile, then fall asleep.

Wednesday 29th

Oh dear! sunbathed too much today (Grumpy tutted and Doc shook his head from side to side). So easily done though, the heat eases my aches and pains and I'm sorely tempted to gain something out of all this wasted time – a splendid stewed-tea tan with golden highlights from lots of carrot munching for others to envy; however, no-one is going to envy skin cancer. Pity eating lots of chocolate doesn't turn you brown.

After reading a holiday health care checklist in *Weekly Wife* including anti-malaria tablets, mosquito net, sting relief, insect repellent, earplugs, eye drops, pain relief, travel sickness and diarrhoea remedies, I wasn't too bothered about travelling to a far away place. I look like I've been roasting on beaches and doing too much sight seeing anyway.

Couldn't do any brolly spotting today.

SUNBURN

I've done it agen
I've done it agen
Forgot to use me factor ten
I've gone and got
A nasty shock
Forgot to use me Baywatch block

I'll never look as stunning as Pam Anderson
Anyway

Thursday 30th

Happy, Sneezy, Doc, Sleepy and Bashful sat on the fence swinging their little legs and singing, 'Hi Ho Silver Lining' to the clouds. Dopey gave me a lump of citrine (yellow quartz) to bring wealth and abundance into my life and reflect the energy of the sun; lifting mild depression and anxiety, like a sunny day.

Weekly Wife fashion: 'cool white cotton knits, crisp white linens and fluid jersey shifts are perfect for whiling away summer days in style.'

Wendy would have a shock if she saw my so-called whites, they resemble pots of paint in B&Q: hint of pink, dawn mist (grey tinge) and apple white (green tinge). My favourite T-shirt is still OK because I haven't worn it yet. It's white with a picture of a cat wearing a pointy bra. Underneath the picture is written, *Madonna's Cat.*

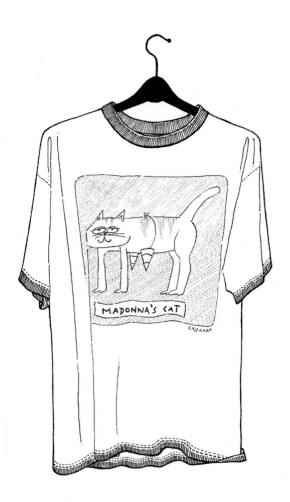

Friday 1st

Yes! Wonderful! Well done me! I've done it! *Absolutely fabulous me!* I've survived six whole months of the year! *I am great!* I'm halfway there! Six months closer to awarding myself my annual certificate of endurance! *I love me!* Think I'll have a great big chocolate cake at the end of the year with twelve stripy candles, colourful balloons and party hats. When I blow the candles out, everyone will cheer and give me presents; perhaps not – it'll only be six days after Christmas and everyone will be broke, or tired of prezzie buying, or both. They could give me their unwanted gifts though! And those boxes of chocolates they can't eat because they're starting a diet on January the first.

Tomorrow, I will start phase two of The Insect Diet and Exercise Plan: crawl about a little more, nibble what I fancy (as long as it's healthy), continue to avoid the rolled up newspaper of stress (as much as possible) and Vapona strip of life that only gets me into sticky situations. I will groom my wings more than once a week, fly into the garden to enjoy fresh air when the sun is shining, sniff flowers (aromatherapy) try not to dwell on how bored I am (stuck in this matchbox) and stop banging my head against the window.

FEELING LOONY

Outside the butter flys
The bumble tree, it stings
I lie here feeling loony
While a caterpillar sings

Saturday 2nd

VERY EXCITING DAY!!

Ben's younger brother, David, rang from Sheepwash in Devon to ask if we would give a home to three kittens: the wild cat who sleeps in the garden next door brought her litter in through the cat flap during a storm a few weeks ago. David has already given a home to four of her kittens and one of her husbands. When he moved to Devon, he had three of his own (cats, not husbands) and is now coping with a demanding job, baby son, wife with post-baby-blues, new house in need of decorating and a large overgrown garden – how could we refuse?!!

As soon as Ben put the phone down, I started making a list of things we need like litter trays, cat litter and kitten food. We have a cat basket, a cat flap in the back door, a flea comb... somewhere.

After dinner, I lay on the sofa wearing my favourite T-shirt and stroking my round belly like a contented mummy-to-be. I daydreamed of tiny paws and whiskers, mobiles with mice on and decided which corner of the nursery to put the litter tray. Can't wait!

Sunday 3rd

1.30 p.m. I'm pregnant with expectation.

1.31 p.m. Ooooh! Three little bundles will be running round the house, one black, one grey and one ginger; they all have white paws and chests and noses.

1.32 p.m. Imagine Mother Nature's cat-making factory; a conveyor belt that dips paws in white paint, a pixie who brushes white on chests and an imp who daubs a little white on the end of noses.

1.33 p.m. I've been reading too much Terry Pratchett lately.

1.34 p.m. Big grin on face.

1.35 p.m. Bloomin' fantastic to have something to look forward to.

1.36 p.m. No more umbrella spotting, staring at the walls or ceilings or collecting belly button fluff. I'm going to enjoy watching my furry bundles sleeping or feeding, grooming or running about, curling up on my lap or playing. I'll collect their discarded whiskers and make a delicate brush...

1.38 p.m. Ben is at The Blacksmith's Armpit with Bill and his new girlfriend, Natasha, who is a stripper at the G-Stringfellows nightclub. She models for his paintings but at the moment he has only managed a small sketch of her right nipple.

1.39 p.m.   The long, lonely hours when Ben is at work or the pub or in www dot land will soon be over.

2.28 p.m.   Doze listening to tennis.

2.32 p.m.   Sip water.

2.40 p.m.   Eat banana.

2.45 p.m.   Tennis players look hot, tired and bad tempered.

2.46 p.m.   Bet she could do with a nice, long bath.

2.47 p.m.   Sniff armpit; I could do with one too.

2.48 p.m.   Journey to bathroom seems like too many miles uphill and through jungle of dirty washing.

2.49 p.m.   Body like heavy rucksack full of bedding and supplies, saucepans clattering, tied on with string.

2.52 p.m.   Will have to go to bathroom soon anyway so had better think about lifting rucksack off sofa and pulling on hiking boots.

2.55 p.m.   Open pages of *Weekly Wife* (checking map before journey).

2.57 p.m.   Cosmic Colin tells me I've got bags of energy, get up and go, and will be experiencing visions of the future.

2.58 p.m.   I've got bags under my eyes and can see myself sitting on the toilet very soon.

3.00 p.m.   Wendy says I should: be wearing the brightest whites and lemons, refresh with citrus essential oils, wear citrus make-up to enhance my golden tan, wash my hair with Citré Shine and drink lemon juice to cleanse my liver and purify my system.

3.02 p.m.   Ben has bought lemon-smelling washing-up liquid and kitchen roll with lemons on. That will have to do.

3.03 p.m.   Positive thought: one day my *zest* for life will return. I will peel back the old me and discover a fresh *zingy* me.
No longer bitter.

3.05 p.m.   Interesting fact: love (when used in tennis for the score nil) is a pun on the French word l'oeuf, meaning 'the egg', the shape represented by a nought.

3.22 p.m.   Interesting fat: Catch glimpse of naked body wobbling as I head for bath.

3.24 p.m.   In fact, fat is not slightest bit interesting but, if ignored, grows slowly like hair and nails until you *have* to take notice.

3.30 p.m.	Bath too hot. Am giant pink lump of fat in bath.
3.31 p.m.	Lump of rose quartz is radiating love in the sunlight.
3.32 p.m.	Quartz and citrine bring to mind ice cubes in lemonade.
3.33 p.m.	Thirsty now.
3.34 p.m.	Lapis lazuli is the deep blue of the ocean.
3.35 p.m.	Sniff new bar of chunky Pears soap to give me a lift. Mmmm, lovely fresh fragrance of thyme, cedar and rosemary.
3.37 p.m.	Hold curve of soap against cheek; it fits perfectly and feels cool against my skin.
3.38 p.m.	Nice colour, like honey. Hold up to light. Think of insects trapped in amber for millions of years.
3.39 p.m.	Negative thought: I'm trapped. Positive thought: I still have my sight, smell and hearing, and I haven't been trapped in amber for millions of years.
3.40 p.m.	Feel shape of soap as caress between hands under the water.
3.41 p.m.	Think of large oval pebbles on seashore. Think of the sea, a relentless sculptor working day and night.
3.42 p.m.	We are like the sea, sometimes deep, sometimes very shallow.
3.45 p.m.	I'm calm as the calmest waters under a gentle blue sky.
3.47 p.m.	I'm peaceful as miles of golden sand on deserted beaches.
3.48 p.m.	My eyelashes flutter like palm trees in a tropical breeze.
3.50 p.m.	My mind is as clear as the clearest waters in a Greek lagoon where the turtles swim.
3.51 p.m.	My thoughts are golden like Pears soap.
3.52 p.m.	My spirit swims and dances with the dolphins... Flows freely with the fishes...
3.53 p.m.	*Bang! Crash! Manly Laughter, ha, ha, ha, Clatter! Rustle, rustle, BUMP, whoosh, click, CRASH!!* silly girly laughter... *clink.*
3.54 p.m.	Obviously Ben, Bill and Natasha have returned from 'The Blacksmith's Armpit' and are falling about in the kitchen making coffee and *things* on toast and Ben is laughing with Natasha and she's young *and* attractive and *a stripper,* not sick and miserable *and* ugly *and* old *and* they all sound so happy and energetic *and* full of life and... and... *and...* and...
3.56 p.m.	I'm going to drown myself. I'm going to swim away from the dolphins and fishes in the clear waters and into the

	jaws of a great big shark. I'm going to hang myself from a palm tree...
3.57 p.m.	They'll be wanting to use the bathroom soon and I'm not going to let them in.
3.58 p.m.	Stand up in bath and reach over to door to make sure it's locked. Arrrrgh.
4.00 p.m.	Have slipped and fallen in bath and am now rubbing elbow and knee. One positive thought: will have some pretty bruises to admire. One hundred negative thoughts: towards Ben, Bill and Natasha.
4.16 p.m.	
Ben:	I need the loo!
Me:	Go dig a hole in the garden!
Ben:	I'm desperate!
Me:	So am I!
Ben:	C'mon, don't be silly!
Me:	No!
4.17 p.m.	Feel guilty. Open door. Ignore sound like horse relieving itself in field and recall mini Greenpeace pop festival in someone's garden (Green Party candidate, I think) where I had to squat over wooden planks laid over a trench. There were no separate cubicles for men and women and I was terrified of falling in! Very... er... back to nature.
4.18 p.m.	Recall hairy-armpit-vegeburger-making-women at Glastonbury festival (don't want to think about toilets there, after three days in hot weather).
4.19 p.m.	And story of tomatoes growing on sewage (wonder if tomatoes grow in the Glastonbury post-pop fields after everyone's gone home). *Was* going to have vegeburgers and salad tonight.
4.20 p.m.	Oh! Must get out of bath. Bill has just requested a seat on our avocado throne.
4.22 p.m.	Under duvet, wrapped in towels, with pillow over head. Now I know how an Egyptian mummy feels.
4.25 p.m.	Can hear pulsating music, the bass drum booming up through the floorboards. Oh God, I hope *she's* not practising her craft...
4.46 p.m.	Lots of laughter, giggling and clapping.

5.07 p.m.	More giggling.
5.10 p.m.	Music turned up.
5.21 p.m.	More clapping.
5.25 p.m.	More bloody laughter and clapping.
6.00 p.m.	Ben lifts bedcovers to tell me he's going to Polly's Poppadoms with Bill, Rick and Natasha.
6.01 p.m.	Hope Natasha chokes on her chicken tikka masala.
6.02 p.m.	Hope Bill brings up his brinjal bhajee.
6.03 p.m.	Hope Ben burns his throat on his chana masala and his peshwari naan is limp and lifeless.
6.04 p.m.	Try hard not to think of vegetable biriani, onion bhajees, naan bread, poppadoms and pickles – I'm eating for four now.

Monday 4th

Wrote list of cat names while waiting for my Monday taxi.

Bill's idea:
Biriani, Pickles and Poppadom.
Rick's idea:
Ginger Spice, Scary Spice and Baby Spice.
Landlord of The Blacksmith's Armpit:
Guinness, Murphy and Beamish.
Landlord's daughter:
Whisky, Whiskers and Whiz.
Depressed landlady:
Prozac, Mogadon and Triptozol.
Pub barmaid (part-time hairdresser):
Snip, Curly and Permit.
Café owner:
Sausage, Beanz and Mr. Chips.
Car salesman:
Mercedes, Jaguar and Mini.
Naughty Natasha:
Claw, Nip and Tickle.
Rain-soaked man:
Wellington, Boots and Hatty.
His rain-soaked girlfriend:

Umbie, Rella and Mac.
Some bloke's wife:
Marmalade, Marmite and Pickles.
Two old men at bar:
Smoky, Blackey and Ginger.
Pub cat:
No comment.

Eileen:	How are you?
Me:	I'm expecting!
Eileen:	Oh really?!
Me:	Yes, three kittens.
Eileen:	Ahhh... long or short hair?
Me:	Short.
Eileen:	When are they due?
Me:	Soon, this weekend hopefully.
Eileen:	You wouldn't know to look at you; have you thought of any names?
Me:	I've started making a list, any suggestions? Can you remember the names of *The Aristocats*?
Eileen:	Ummm... no... how about Fibia, Tibia and Pelvis.
Me:	Ha, ha, Elvis the pelvis.
Eileen:	Lots of his fans travel to Graceland and get married in Elvis churches!
Me:	Really! I wonder if instead of blessing themselves, 'In the name of the Father, the Son and the Holy Spirit, Amen,' they say, 'In the name of the Burger, the Bun and the Presley Spirit, Fatmen.'

Tuesday 5th

1.20 p.m.	Pin tea towel (arrived with this morning's post) on kitchen door.
1.22 p.m.	Admire tea towel: red, yellow, green and blue cartoon cats, made by the Ulster Weavers on beautiful Irish linen.
1.24 p.m.	Notice title of picture on tea towel – Posh Paws.
1.25 p.m.	Thanks, Artie Auntie.
2.30 p.m.	Hands in washing-up water, thinking... sometimes when Ben's on the computer and I walk into the room he quickly turns it off, hmmm.

3.00 p.m.	In bath with window open singing 'Suspicion' in my Elvis voice.
3.01 p.m.	'Suspicion torments my heart, suspicion keeps us apart, suspicion why torture meeeeee.' Seven dwarves pull their hats down over their ears.
3.02 p.m.	'Ev'ry time you kiss me I'm still not certain that you love me, ev'ry time you hold me I'm still not certain that you care.' Next door's back door slams shut.
3.03 p.m.	'Though you keep on saying you really, really, really love me, do you speak the same words to someone else when I'm not there?' A fly flies into the bathroom but needs no encouragement to fly out again.
3.04 p.m.	'Doobie, doobie, doobie, la lah lah la, should meet tomorrow.'

Tiny beetle scurries under the bath mat.

'Shoobie, doobie, doobie, la lah la, someone else tonight.'

A woodlouse crawls back into the woodwork.

3.05 p.m. Sore throat.

3.35 p.m. Sip Typhoo decaffeinated tea. Fed up with herb teas.

Oh dear, I'll be slurping real tea soon and then it'll be on to the strong black coffee followed by death by hyperactivity.

4.00 p.m. Remember part of sketch by Peter Cook and Dudley Moore in *The Dagenham Dialogues*.

Pete: I may have had tea since I was tiny but I could give it up just like that.

Dud: That's what they all say. They start off on soft drinks, move on to tea for even bigger kicks and then it's downhill all the way to black espresso coffee, frothy cappuccino and a lingering death...

4.25 p.m. Flick through *Weekly Wife*.

4.26 p.m. Article about pets: pet ownership reduces blood pressure, relieves stress, reduces aggression and prevents ~~lioness~~ loneliness and depression in the elderly.

4.27 p.m. Long daydream about kittens.

4.30 p.m. Beauty tips: mash cucumber and apply to a sunburnt face to soothe and cool (could have done with that advice last Wednesday). To pluck eyebrows the same shape, draw an outline with white nail pencil and pluck outside line. (Never again!)

4.35 p.m. Posh nosh: pecan and maple syrup cookies and almond sponge with chocolate cream.

4.36 p.m. Recipes to keep: jammy coconut cake, oaty plum crumble, apple streusel cake and warm chocolate polenta cake.

4.38 p.m. Am resisting urge to comfort eat.

4.39 p.m. I'm swimming in calm waters with peaceful fishes... I'm floating, warm sun melting my body like chocolate in a saucepan... oh!

4.40 p.m. Willpower has evaporated like steam on a treacle sponge ~~pudding~~ castle surrounded by a deep yellow moat of Bird's custard.

4.45 p.m. Fancy Elvis Presley fried peanut butter and banana buttie.

4.50 p.m.	Lustful comfort session involving peanut butter, two bananas and four wholemeal rolls.
5.05 p.m.	I am calm and peanut-butterly-bananaful.
5.06 p.m.	Leggings cutting into waist.
5.08 p.m.	Read 'Ten Instant Cures for Indigestion'; cut down on fatty food, eat smaller portions, avoid tight clothes, eat raw foods, take exercise...
5.20 p.m.	Watch Mr. Boxer-face take antique coffee table for walkies; he's early tonight! Maybe he's off work today with a cold; his nose does look a bit red.
5.25 p.m.	Three starlings are feasting on discarded sandwich in the road.
5.26 p.m.	Enjoy watching them pecking madly at dinner.
5.27 p.m.	Tall, miserable man in suit strides past them. They fly away. It's OK for him. He's probably heading home for a huge dinner and doesn't give a damn he's interrupting theirs.
5.28 p.m.	Man climbs into car. He's going to reverse over bread so it's flattened into tarmac.
5.29 p.m.	He's taking his time. Lighting a cigarette. He's going to reverse over sandwich; I know he is.
5.30 p.m.	Quick birdies, enjoy your dinner while you can; it's going to rain soon and your meal will turn to mush.
5.31 p.m.	Hope whatever is in the sandwich doesn't upset their tiny tummies.
5.32 p.m.	One bird has just flown off with a crust – sensible chap.
5.33 p.m.	Man starts up car. Car reverses. Birds fly off again.
5.34 p.m.	He's... missed... the... sandwich... Hurrah!
5.35 p.m.	Birds commence pecking again.
5.36 p.m.	Woman struts past, wearing big clumpy shoes. Birds fly away.
5.37 p.m.	It's OK for her. She's probably heading home to her Lean Cuisine and Weight Watchers' rice pudding. Or if she's not, she should be.
5.38 p.m.	Birds hopping round remains of sandwich; am tempted to go out and stand guard.
5.40 p.m.	Boy rides his bike through middle of sandwich.
5.41 p.m.	Feel urge to knock him off his bike. OK for him; mum's probably cooking burgers, beans and micro-chips.
5.44 p.m.	Think birdies have given up. It's a harsh world.

5.45 p.m.	Mr. Boxer-face returns home with antique coffee table.
5.46 p.m.	Head for kitchen and feel very fortunate, I don't have to dodge tons of metal on wheels, big clumpy shoes or horrid little boys on racing bikes.
5.55 p.m.	Lots of happy starlings hopping about. All sandwich gone – goody!
6.15 p.m.	Bloke is doing Elvis impression on Channel Four, but it's not as good as mine.
7.30 p.m.	*EastEnders*, brilliant! It should be a good one tonight.
8.00 p.m.	Exhausted after ever so exciting, entertaining episode.
8.01 p.m.	Ben returns home from after-work drink and notices his new fence is leaning at an angle.
8.02 p.m.	So is he.
Ben:	(Frowns as opens mail) What's that bit in *Blackadder* where Rowan Atkinson mentions a pelican and its bill?
Me:	He says whichever way he turns, there's always an enormous bill in front of him.
Ben:	(Frowns as opens fridge) Where's all the cheese and peanut butter gone?
Me:	There are some hungry fairies about.
Ben:	(Frowns as opens empty Benson & Hedges packet) Rashid is being nasty again to the young blokes at work. I'm not going to get involved.
Me:	Watch out, the Black Mamba is a snake in the grass that holds enough venom to wipe out more than a dozen people.
Ben:	(Frown) What's for dinner?
Me:	Leftovers with mayonnaise.
Ben:	(Tighter frown) Your throat sounds bad.
Me:	Must give up trying to be an Elvis impersonator.
Ben:	(Still frowning) I'm going out for some fags.

Wednesday 6th

Wendy says I should be making simple, super, summer snacks and suppers and wearing a simple, super, shift dress in this season's floral prints.

Sat in the shade in my knickers and Madonna's cat T-shirt eating a simply, super, squashy tomato on two rounds of burnt toast. Started writing a little song to the tune of Diana Ross's 'You Can't Hurry Love'.

You can't hurry toast
No, you just have to wait
She said toast will burn easily
It's a game of grill and scrape

You can't hurry toast
No, you just have to wait
Just pace around patiently
No matter how long it takes.

Sang verses to the dwarves and they gave me a round of applause; I bowed but had trouble straightening up again. Heard small, stifled giggles. Doc put his hand over Happy's mouth and with the other hand pointed out to Dopey that it wasn't a good idea to play with a wasp. Bashful averted his eyes from my bare legs and turned pink.

David rang tonight to arrange his visit this weekend with the kittens. He said his little boy, Joshua, has a new word, 'freckle'. Their neighbours think he (Joshua) is swearing because, in his little boy voice, freckle sounds like fuckle. Sweet. I'm reminded of the help I received from doctors when I was first ill. Sweet fuckle.

Two days to go!!

Thursday 7th

Sat in the garden again leafing through *Weekly Wife*. I should be showing some shoulder this season (one-shoulder tops and halter necks are all the rage) as well as being a simply super cook, model and medical expert.

I sighed. I dozed. Sleepy blew on a dandelion to see if it was time for his next nap and Happy tied Sneezy's beard around his nose. Grumpy grumbled about the heat and the ginger cat who sprayed him yesterday.

There was a film on late this afternoon, *Easy Come, Easy Go*, starring Elvis Presley as a frogman (a frogman!) who discovers treasure in the wreck of a sunken ship. He sang a few songs along the way and I joined in, in the choruses – had forgotten how good looking he was.

One day to go!

Friday 8th

Elvis Presley was a tuna fisherman in the hip-swivelling musical, *Girls! Girls! Girls!* today. Didn't have the energy to sing along or do any hip-swivelling, so I wiggled my fingers and toes.

The cans of kitten food are advertising a free kitten care booklet. I decided to send off for one; I want to be a simply super, purrfect mother. Burnt my hand while trying to steam a label off and said, 'Oh deary me.' Dropped the can on my foot and screamed, 'Ow! Woopsie daisee, silly old me, must wear my pixie slippers at all times.' Covered my nose when Ben returned from Old Salty's Midget Gherkin and Peanut Bar, Smellbottom Street, smiled and said, 'Must you pass so much wind in the bedroom dear, and belch in my face? It's rather unpleasant.'

I'm practising moderating my language before the arrival of the kittens. And I'm still trying to remember the names of *The Aristocats*. All I can think of is Thomas O'Malley and Toulouse-Lautrec.

Tomorrow's the day!!

Saturday 9th

David arrived this afternoon just after three o'clock with Carol and her new hairstyle, Joshua and his new word and three kittens with new claws and whiskers. Twelve little legs galloped round the house like miniature ponies. Eight big legs plonked on chairs. Two small legs wriggled on Mummy's lap.

The kittens were much bigger and less nervous than I expected. Carol was much bigger and more bad tempered than I expected. David smiled in a pale, worn and weary way. Joshua threw toys at the kittens and picked them up by their tails. Carol told Joshua off. Joshua cried. Carol had a fight with David. I wanted to cry. Ben tripped over a packet of Pampers. Carol had a headache. Joshua pointed at Mummy's freckly face and said, 'Fuckle.' We laughed. Ginger kitten had a headache after being clonked on the head with a yellow toy brick. Joshua bumped head on cat basket. Joshua screamed. I wanted to scream. David and Carol argued. I had a headache. Carol was furious we had chips for tea. Noticed Slimfast in a carrier bag in the kitchen. Joshua was furious he wasn't getting enough attention. David went upstairs for a lie down to relieve his headache. Joshua tried to shut black kitten's head in door. Carol shouted. Ben shouted. Carol turned red with anger in the spaces between the freckles on her face. Joshua yelled. I trod on a small blue metal toy truck. I yelled. Carol flirted with Ben. He flirted back. Can't stand Carol. Carol can't stand me. Hope all her freckles get bigger and join up together. Seven little heads peered in through the kitchen window to see what all the noise was about. Ben knocked a glass of red wine over white baby clothes. I laughed. Carol marched into kitchen with clothes and trod in cat litter tray. Litter tray had been used... a lot. Carol repeated a shortened version of Joshua's new word eight times. Ben had a headache. The house had a headache. We ran out of ibuprofen, paracetamol and an ancient packet of Hedex I found in the depths of handbag land. Gone off children.

Kittens brilliant!!

Sunday 10th

Woke up feeling happy and actually wanted, I really couldn't wait to get out of bed; something I haven't experienced for years (feels more like centuries). Yesterday's events left me mega-fatigued and exhausted, but I comforted myself with the thought that I'd be seeing Eileen tomorrow for my weekly bone-crunching session.

Ben, David, Carol and Joshua went out early to visit relatives, thank God. The house was blissfully quiet and I found my hairy children curled up dreaming kitten dreams in a corner of the sofa. Happiness swept softly over me like an angel stroking an angora rabbit and I thought how great it was to fall in love again.

Later this afternoon, the ginger and grey kittens jumped on to my lap but the black one sat in the corner, eyes bigger than his body, and needed a bit of coaxing. He is much more timid than the other two and has only managed one little purr, whereas the other two purr all the time. I think he will need some extra love therapy.

Tonight the house was still quiet and all three kittens curled up to watch *Coronation Street* on my lap. They only just fitted on, like a colourful, furry jigsaw. Now I have a good excuse to put on more weight, hahaha.

Kittens purrrrrrfect!!

Monday 11th

Ben had the day off work and David helped him mend the fence. Bill and W. M. Friend came round to say hello and watch them work whilst smoking interesting herbs. I heard snippets of deep and meaningful manly conversation about music, women and the barriers we put up to avoid the pain in life (e.g., the neighbours).

Dopey tried to smoke a discarded cigarette butt, then attempted to eat it. Grumpy complained about ash dropped on his head, Sneezy sneezed, Sleepy snored in a flower pot and Doc commented that herbs are very medicinal. Happy deeply inhaled herby smoke drifting under his nose; he giggled and fell over with his little legs wiggling in the air.

I had a deep and meaningful bathtime. The kittens had deep and meaningful dreamtime. Carol and Joshua had Evans and Mothercare quality shopping time.

Eileen wanted to know all about the kittens, so I told her. Mr. Quiet-and-gentlemanly-taxi-man drove me home from the clinic and mentioned his wife; now the children have left home, her cats are her babies and she dotes on them. Told him all about my hairy babies; in fact we talked about cats all the way home.

Kittens make great conversation pieces!!

Tuesday 12th

Last night in bed, Ben and I discussed cat names. Ben likes Guinness, Murphy and Beamish. I said I liked the name Murphy, it reminded me of my Irish relatives but I wasn't sure I wanted to name all my furry children after alcoholic drinks. Ben thinks Pearl would suit the little grey female. His surname is Harpur so she would be registered at the vet, Pearl Harpur, ha, ha. I think Vapona suits her because she likes to pounce on flies.

Today the little black tom, Murphy, did three purrs; the love therapy must be working. He curled up with his brother and sister on the corner of a table where the sun shone though the window. They slept most of the day.

If there is one spot of sun
spilling onto the floor, a cat
will find it and soak it up.
   – Joan Asper McIntosh

David took wife, son, bags, bananas for journey and his headache home. The house sighed and smiled.

Kittens are calm and peaceful.

Wednesday 13th

The kittens are crawling with fleas: big, brown, shiny monster fleas. Must be all that country air. I told them we will have to tackle this problem from *scratch*, combed their coats using a flea comb, and dropped the fleas into a bowl of water. One by one. Murphy kept trying to fish them out again. Two by two. Later I sprinkled herbal flea powder around their necks, spines and tail ends (where the fleas bite most) then collapsed exhausted on the floor. The kittens curled up on my tummy. It was *very* relaxing listening to their rumbling engines, all running smoothly now.

LITTLE FLEA

I could do
With energy
Like you
Little flea

You jump so fast
Make your stamina last
I wish you
Were me

Kittens are hard work!

Thursday 14th

It rained cats and dogs. Hailstones chased each other round the lawn; huge hailstones, the size of cat crunchies. Rain peed on lamp posts, it pelted down for hours. Thunder growled and barked at doors; tree branches like claws, scratched windows and brickwork. The wind screamed and howled, chased litter round the dustbins and sniffed in corners.

The odd flea is still about and I'm trying hard not to scratch every time I feel the slightest tickle. The chair covers in the sitting room look like they have been sprinkled with salt and pepper: they are covered in hundreds of tiny flea eggs and flea dirt. Ben is going to get mean with the flea spray.

Kittens are little flea bags!

Friday 15th

Weekly Wife lay open on the coffee table; Paddy (ginger kitten) lay across it. Tried to finish the article I'd been reading yesterday; Paddy moved his tail and I gave up. I'm not interested in Wendy's flirty fashions any more anyway. I've got much better things to think about now.

Watched Paddy dreaming ginger dreams, his paws and whiskers twitching, while I ate peanut butter on toast. My lap is expanding nicely. I like the way peanut butter sticks my mouth together so I can't talk. So does Ben.

Later on, I read about a couple whose tiny kitten fell down the toilet and they had to dig up the sewage pipes in the garden to find it. It was still alive! We must try to keep the toilet seat down but Ben will never remember.

He came home from The Brick And Throwit looking mean and unshaven and sprayed the house with flea spray. I hid in the bathroom with the kittens; didn't dare mention the toilet seat yet.

Kittens make you feel protective.

Saturday 16th

8.00 p.m.	Everyone's at Rob's birthday barbecue. Everyone. *Everyone,* except me. I'm not going. As usual.
8.10 p.m.	Nothing I want to watch on TV.
8.11 p.m.	I know! I'll have a party. Haven't had one for years. I'll invite the dwarves and kittens. It could be a 'bring a twig party' and I'll light a fire in the grate. There's a bottle of claret under the stairs and a giant pizza with everything on in the freezer.
8.12 p.m.	Some of Ben's mates' girlfriends are so thin, he could have a bring a twig party too.
8.13 p.m.	Hmm, wonder who he's talking to at the moment. Wonder if they've started eating yet. Wonder if there's a slimming spell in spell book. Wonder if there's a spell to frighten fleas away. Wonder if there's a spell to bring a man home from a party.
8.14 p.m.	Bet food is delicious, Bev's a brilliant cook. She makes all sorts of interesting salads and veggie-pasta and nibbly things in pastry.

8.15 p.m.	Mouth watering. Everyone is there. Everyone. Except me.
8.16 p.m.	Need a drink.
8.18 p.m.	Mmmmmmm... very tasty wine... mmmmmust put pizza in oven... mmmm.
8.19 p.m.	Bill is taking Natasha to the party, Miss Skinny-stripper-slutface. Delyth will be there, Miss Lusty-leek-flirtfeatures. Why is she still e-mailing Ben? She's got her own man now, greedy cow.
8.20 p.m.	Oh dear! Drank that glass a bit quick.
8.21 p.m.	Pour another one.
8.22 p.m.	Sip. Sip. Sip. Will drink this a bit slower.
8.23 p.m.	Slurp. Slurp.
8.24 p.m.	Gulp.
8.25 p.m.	Feelin' good.
8.27 p.m.	Pizza in oven.
8.30 p.m.	Put on Bee Gees tape and light a few candles for party atmosphere.
8.35 p.m.	Invite dwarves and kittens to 'bring a twig party'.
8.36 p.m.	Dwarves and kittens excited, except Grumpy who says he hates parties, but he'll come because he's bored.
8.39 p.m.	Dopey, Sleepy, Sneezy and Bashful drag half a tree in through the back door.
8.40 p.m.	Doc asks me for a box of matches so he can light the fire.
8.43 p.m.	Happy hands me a large smooth pebble, the colour of forest ferns. He says it's malachite.
8.44 p.m.	Will consult crystal book later.
8.48 p.m.	Dwarves sit round crackling fire, smoking and singing along to the Bee Gees.
8.49 p.m.	Ooops, that glass went down a bit quick too.
8.50 p.m.	Pour glass of wine, slice a small quiche into seven sections and pour a little wine into three egg cups to be passed around like goblets.
8.53 p.m.	Grumpy complains, 'You didn't cut the quiche up into equal portions; I got the smallest piece!'
8.54 p.m.	Give crunchy treats to kittens.
9.00 p.m.	Happy calls out, 'More wine, wench!'
9.10 p.m.	Am havin' great parteee. Nearly eaten whole pizza. Burp. Smile.

9.11 p.m.   Give small square of pizza to Grumpy to shut him up but he complains, 'I've burnt me mouth now and singed me beard on the fire and the music's so loud I can't hear meself think.'

9.20 p.m.   Ish luverlee wine, feel fantashtic, no pain, lots energee, happy head, crossed eyes. Everyone's at partee 'cept me. Don't care. Rick and Heidi, Miss Match-stick-hips-hair dresser, will be there. Bob the Slob has invited three of his girlfriends, Tracy from The Thirsty Tongue Tavern, Fiona from The Fizz And Nipple and Nicole from The Frog and Beret. Oh God, Ben fancies her, I know he does. I've seen the way he looks at her perfectly made-up face. Bob will have Tracy on one arm and Fiona on the other. Ben will have two spare arms, up for grabs, because I'm not there. Everyone's there. Not me. Need more wine. More pizza. Need chocolate. If I question him about Nicole, he'll just say she was perfectly armless. Oh God.

9.21 p.m.   Cheryl, Candra, Rachel and Sara will be there too, wearing their halter neck or off the shoulder frocks in this season's floral prints. Or little tops in zingy lemon or party pink or crisp white...

9.22 p.m.   He's probably crunching cheese and onion crisps now the drink has given him an appetite. He loves cheese and onion crisps. He loves cheese. And onions. Especially pickled onions in strong spicy vinegar. I wonder if he's eating garlic bread. He loves garlic.

9.23 p.m.   Hope Nicole hates the smell of onions or garlic on breath. Oh God, she's French; the stench probably turns her on...

9.24 p.m.   That's it! *That's it!* I'm going to the party. I'll turn up and catch him out. I will. I'll phone for a taxi. Now. I'll show him.

9.25 p.m.   OH GOD! Feel too fat and smelly and my hair is all greasy and my face spotty and mascara's all clogged up and clothes so baggy and bobbly and outdated they should be in Oxfam shop and I've drunk so much wine I'll probably make a fool of myself and have to endure weeks alone remembering what a fool I made of myself and cringing into my herb tea till the memory fades and another worry even more embarrassing replaces it.

9.26 p.m.   Kittens curl up on my tummy. They think Mummy is warm and very beautiful, especially her big, squashy lap and long fingernails for scratching behind ears and under chins.

9.27 p.m.   Happy grins at me with bits of quiche stuck in his beard. Dopey and Bashful smile at me dreamily. Dwarves luff mee tooo.

9.28 p.m.   Happy sings, 'How deep is your love, how deep is your love...'

9.29 p.m.   Wonder if Ben's dancing with Delyth. Dancing with Delyth, hah, sounds like a horror movie.

9.30 p.m.   Jealousy monster is sitting on my head, filling me with suspicion. Feel an Elvis impersonation coming on.

9.31 p.m.   Kittens hiss at monster and dwarves swear in dwarfish.

9.32 p.m.   Jealousy monster slopes off in green slimy way, spitting obcenities, 'Lushty leekish flirtface fuckle features fartytar-tytights,' and dribbles out through the cat flap.

9.33 p.m.   'Suspicion torments my heart, suspicion keeps us apart, suspicion why torture meeeeee!'

9.35 p.m.

Happy: What're you singing?

Me: Elvish.

Happy: Doesn't sound like an elf song. Have you heard elves sing?

Me: No, what do they sound like?

Happy:	Seductive... but evilish.
Me:	Oh, how about pixies?
Happy:	They're great little fellows, on the whole. Would you like to meet some?
Me:	Yes, please!
Happy:	Then you shall, Madame, I shall invite them to your splendid party.
Me:	Oh goody.
Happy:	Now let me see... There's Rhizome and Woodruff from Downunderbigtree... old Umbellifer who lives under an umbrella in Herb Hill... Bract and Bogbean, the twins who reside in Gardenshed City with Whortleberry, Teazel and Figwort. Then there's young Spignel from Thornapple Mountain... urrrr... Bloodroot and Scabwort from Wormwood Tubs; no, they're trouble-makers. Last but not least Tansy and Crispum – they're gay little fellows.
9.42 p.m.	Sneezy sings, 'We dig, dig, dig, dig, dig, dig, dig the Bee Gees, hah... hah... hah... TISHOOOO!!
9.43 p.m.	Fire gone out.
9.44 p.m.	Doc carefully places six tea lights in grate, strikes a match, and the dwarves gather round again.
9.45 p.m.	Dwarfish shadows flicker round the fireplace and wispy curls of smoke in the shape of dragons disappear up the chimney. Sleepy's eyes are closing...
9.47 p.m.	Happy turns the music up and dances on the TV singing into one of Ben's cigarette lighters, 'Jive talking, you're tellin' me lies.'
9.48 p.m.	Grumpy sticks bits of kitchen roll in his ears and Sleepy wakes up with a start.
9.49 p.m.	Doc is looking at video and CD collection. He'd like to watch David Bowie in *Labyrinth* one day soon; he's heard it's brilliant.
9.50 p.m.	Happy wants to know if I've got David Bowie's *The Laughing Gnome*. I tell him I'll ask Ben to look for it on the internet; he holds my big toe and sings, 'You should be dancing, yeah!'
9.52 p.m.	Wiggle my fingers and toes to, 'Stayin' alive, stayin' alive.'
9.53 p.m.	Happy wiggles his hips... falls off TV.
9.54 p.m.	Grumpy says, 'I was waiting for that to happen.'

9.57 p.m. Sneezy sneezes again.

9.58 p.m. 'Night fever, night fever, we know how to do it oooooooh!'

10.04 p.m. Dwarves sing to me, apart from Grumpy, 'Tragedy... la la la la... tragedy... la la la la... hard to bear... la la la la la la... you're going nowhere...'

10.05 p.m. Party in fullshwing!

10.10 p.m. *Crash* from kitchen. Twelve little pixies are clambering noisily through the cat flap, followed by Happy who says, 'We're not gatecrashers but cat flap crashers, hee, hee, hee, hee.'

10.11 p.m. Pixies dance into room wearing leggings and pixie slippers like me! They bow, one by one, before me and take off their caps. I'm queen of the pixies tonight. It's wonderful to feel adored and respected!

10.14 p.m. Tell pixies I'm delighted to make their acquaintance and offer them strawberries, and lemonade poured into bottle tops.

10.17 p.m. Put on Phil Collins CD and pour *another* glass of wine. Bottle nearly empty; who drank it all? Washn'meee.

10.21 p.m. Six pixies line-dance on window ledge to 'Su su sussudio oh...oh.'

10.25 p.m. Four pixies lifting phone receiver off hook and singing into it at both ends, 'Billy don't you lose my number!'

10.26 p.m. Teazel is trying to wake one of my sleeping dragons on the mantelpiece.

10.28 p.m. Young Spignel rides round the room on Paddy's back. Paddy doesn't seem to mind.

10.30 p.m. Tansy and Crispum entertain us singing 'Two hearts livin' in just one mind' while sitting on the bookcase swinging their legs from side to side and clicking their fingers.

11.11 p.m. We all sing 'Groovy Kind of Love': 'When I'm feelin' blue, all I have to do...'

Midnight. Dwarves snoring in fireplace. Kittens curled up on my tummy. Pixies in small corners around the room, the last of the candlelight flickering on their tiny, sleeping, walnut faces.

3.10 a.m. Ben stumbles in through front door and I wake up. Kittens stir. No sign of dwarves or pixies.

3.15 a.m.   Ben snores.

3.16 a.m.   A spider crawls across a miniature pixie boot in the fire-place.

Sunday 17th

> **Back to reality**
> **Mushy pea brain**
>
> **Back to reality**
> **Headache and the rain**
>
> **Back to reality**
> **Knocking at the door**
>
> **Back to reality**
> **Wine stain on the floor**
>
> **Back to reality**
> **Dust is gettin' thick**
>
> **Back to reality**
> **Cat's bin sick**
>
> **Back to reality**
> **Pollen count is high**
>
> **Back to reality**
> **Think I'm goin' to cry**

Still trying not to scratch. Still keeping the toilet seat down. Still trying to remember the names of the *Aristocats;* Ben said the female kitten in the film was Marie or Mary.

The grey kitten, Mary, is very interested in my handcream; I noticed written on the front of the tube '35% stronger nails'. She's keeping her claws in good condition, I'm sure the carpet will agree. Found her sitting on the bathroom scales this morning; she's becoming weight conscious at an early age. According to *Weekly Wife* I must watch out for signs of anorexia in my teenage daughter. She has been staring a lot in the mirror too. Maybe she's dreaming of becoming a supermodel when she grows up, strutting down the catwalk with a superior expression.

Laid the article about the couple whose kitten was lost down the toilet on the toilet seat – hint, hint, Ben.

Kittens can be a worry.

Monday 18th
Had to cancel osteopath session; didn't have the energy to bath and dress and hurl myself into a taxi. Lay on the sofa and watched the kittens running together from room to room, over the chairs and over me; they made me laugh out loud.

It rained a lot last night but the sun smiled this afternoon; the garden looked happy and smiled back with sparkling green teeth. I watched sunbeams play on small furry bodies as they slept. And slept.

Kittens are entertaining.

Tuesday 19th
Admired my new green crystal. Malachite is a stone of balance and calms the emotions. It's also a cleansing stone, improves the quality of the blood and soothes the nervous system. I placed it with the other crystals in the bathroom, ready to meditate at bathtime.

Ben is remembering to keep the toilet seat down; he doesn't want to find himself digging up the garden. He borrowed the *Aristocats* video from Cheryl at work and we enjoyed the film with Duchess, Thomas O'Malley, Toulouse, Berlioz and Marie. I liked the names but it's too late now; the children are already used to theirs.

Kittens become family.

Wednesday 20th

The stitching is coming apart on my pixie slippers and I'm trailing several threads, multicoloured threads; I've had the slippers a long time. I'd been wondering why the kittens were following me around the house, pouncing at my heels.

Received a postcard from my sister in France.

> **Weather wet**
> **Nappies changeable**
> **Weather changeable**
> **Nappies wet**
>
> **Love, Gina, Mark and Matthew xxx**

Hope they bring me back a chocolate Eiffel Tower.

Cleaning out a litter tray is better than changing a nappy – slightly.

Thursday 21st

Received another postcard from W. M. Friend in Rome, a picture of the Vatican on the front.

> **I have found Jesus again**
> **God bless you both**
>
> **Love, Joseph**

Kittens don't go on about religion!

Friday 22nd

Ben went for a drink with Rick, who is depressed; he's just split up with Heidi the hairdresser. Bill has been *busy* with Natasha and still is...

He brought home chips for us and some fish for Paddy, Mary and Murphy. I said my prayers:

> **Hail Mary**
> **Full of plaice**
> **Murphy is with thee**

Blessed art thou amongst feral cats
Blessed is the fruit of thy womb, kitten
Holy Murphy
Brother of Paddy
Pray for us sinners
Now and at the hour of our death
Amen

Our Father
Who runs the chip shop
Haddock be thy game
Chips nearly done
Thy fish be cooked
When the batter is ready
Give us this day
Our daily cod
And lead us not into temptation
To have a large portion
Of mushrooms in batter
Delivered from the fryer
For thine is the chip shop
The huss and the coley
For ever and ever
Amen

Forgive, O Lord, my little jokes on Thee
And I'll forgive Thy great big one on me.
— **Robert Frost**

Saturday 23rd

Ben took the kittens to the vet for their cat flu injections and health check this morning. I lined the cat basket with a fluffy towel smelling of home and kissed their noses goodbye. Couldn't help feeling like a worried mother (her three infants at the doctors) and was very relieved when they were safely home again. The ordeal didn't seem to bother them much though. Think I'll let them venture into the garden soon; they're often looking out of the window.

Wish we didn't live close to so many busy roads; must teach my little ones to look right, look left, look right again, quick march, never dash. And I must suppress the urge to dress them in miniature waist-coats: Mary in pink to match her grey fur, Murphy in red to match his black fur and Paddy in emerald green because it always goes with ginger. Told Ben about my idea and how foolish I felt, and he said he knows of a woman who *really does* dress her cat in a small jacket. I thought, 'Silly woman!' then glanced sideways at myself in the mirror...

Sunday 24th

Mum, Dad, Gina, Mark and baby Matthew came round to see Mary, Paddy and Murphy. Matthew and the kittens were the centre of attention which gave me the chance to doze quietly in the corner of the sofa, until Matthew shrieked and the kittens ran off. Then Matthew started to scream and Ben started to argue with Dad; he suggested Dad bought tuna fish caught by rod and pole in order to protect the dolphins. Then my sister had a go at me about something I did when I was six while Mum asked me if I were eating properly, taking exercise and did I see Michael Barrymore last night.

Things calmed down when we had tea; everyone's mouth full of cake, and Matthew's mouth full of nipple. He was wearing a tiny blue T-shirt with green paw prints, Gina wore a red T-shirt with yellow paw prints, and I wore an off white T-shirt with *real* paw prints. I informed my family that there's an Indian myth that says the jaguar got its spotted coat by dabbing mud on its body with its paws; and if you look closely, the markings *do* seem like a paw print. They ignored me. Matthew smiled and curled one end of his top lip; Mum calls this his Elvis Presley smile. I sang the first line of 'Suspicion' in my Elvis voice. Noone took any notice.

Maybe my family care more than they show. They do seem relieved I have the kittens to care for and keep me company, and now that Dad and Gina have met two other M.E. sufferers (Marie and Jim), they are a little more understanding towards me. Thanks Marie. Thanks Jim. They've finally stopped mentioning the benefits of swimming. Thank God.

I am calm and peaceful, healed and healthy. I love me, I love herb tea. I hate chocolate, I'd hate to be a supermodel; both my socks are matching so I'm balanced. I'm wearing my pixie slippers at all times, I'm avoiding too much sun; I'm keeping the toilet seat down, I've stopped scratching. I will write better poetry, I will stop trying to impersonate Elvis, I will learn to say no. I love me, my kittens three, Ben and my famileeee.

Monday 25th

Didn't sleep much last night. Woke up about 4 a.m. trying to keep my hair on: my sister was tearing it out and shouting at me to pull myself together. We were at sea on a sailing ship with Mum and Dad, Matthew, Ben and the kittens; the sea was choppy and china blue. Silvery tuna fish leapt out of the water and hurled themselves on deck where they turned into red and yellow wind-up toy fish for Matthew to play with. Dad caught a fish by the tail and bit its head off so Ben pushed him overboard. A luminous, lime green dolphin sprang out of the sea and ate him whole (Dad not Ben). Mum laughed and danced below deck to put the kettle on for tea and make sandwiches. A gigantic turquoise octopus appeared and flung a tentacle onto the deck with a loud heavy slap. It caught my sister by the ankle and she grabbed at a mast to save herself; it pulled and she stretched thin, like a strand of cheese when a slice of pizza is removed from the pan in Pizza Hut. A large round watery eye winked at me. My sister disappeared. Suddenly the waters were calm and peaceful and Mum served tea in delicate china cups with rosebuds on. We laughed at the kittens scrambling up the ropes trying to catch seagulls, and the seven dwarves climbed the rigging dressed as pirates, ~~manning~~ dwarfing the sails. An owl sat in the crow's nest looking out to sea through an eyeglass. He'd spotted an island where Maltesers grew on trees and fell to the ground in chocolaty piles, so I suggested we drop anchor soon and row ashore for pudding.

Eileen had trouble treating me tonight. One minute she was manipulating my back, the next she was falling about laughing her head off; it's good to have an appreciative audience for one's nightmare stories. I like to make Eileen laugh because although she always has a sunny smile, there's a rainy sadness behind her eyes.

In a story-writing mood now...

... although Morag always smiled her big sunny smile, there was a rainy sadness in her eyes; lightning flashed in their depths when she thought of Stephen Inglenook.

She lived alone in her small terraced cottage, full of plants in corners like miniature jungles, colourful ornamental cats and candles in celestial candle holders. A small dragon slept on the television set, its pointy tail hanging over the middle of the screen. She didn't watch much television anyway, life was depressing enough; just sat for hours reading novels and thinking about the past whilst stroking a cat. Morag owned three large tabby cats, although they didn't consider themselves owned. Haggis, Hamish and Horace slept a lot in lumpy armchairs covered with hairy tartan rugs and, in between meals, they ate Scottish shortbread dipped in cream.

Morag felt cold and very tired tonight. Tired in body and tired in mind. It had been a long day at the clinic. She curled up on the sofa with Hamish and a herbal tea, listening to the crackling fire and comforting sound of a big rumbling purr. Later, she switched on the radio and a dusty tartan lamp to give the room a cosy feel; it illuminated a photo of her father, proud in his red and black kilt. Both her parents were dead now, although her mother looked alive in the small oil painting above the hearth, firelight flickering on her beautiful, sad features. Bill had lovingly painted it for her; how she missed Bill. He had tried to save her parents. Stephen Inglenook had not tried enough. She blamed him for everything.

Morag asked Hamish what she should do now. He pounced on a moth and killed it.

Tuesday 26th

2.30 p.m. Sit in garden with dwarves and kittens, listening to a story. Next door, Granny is reading to grandson Max, 'One day in Teletubby land it was time for Tubby toast. Laa-Laa pressed the button.'

2.31 p.m. Mmm, fancy toast.

2.32 p.m. 'The Tubby toaster began to make funny noises... boop... cholly bolly... ticker tocker... doopy doo... noggy noggy... slurpy sucky sucky.'

2.33 p.m. Must place two slices of bread under grill, maybe three.

2.34 p.m. 'There was lots of Tubby toast for Laa-Laa... lots of Tubby toast for Dipsy... lots of Tubby toast for Tinky Winky... lots of Tubby toast for Po... and lots of Tubby toast for the Noo-noo.'

2.35 p.m. Uh-oh! I smell burnt toast.

Wednesday 27th

12.00 noon. Paddy and Murphy play next door.

1.00 p.m. Max follows Granny out of the house, 'Granny, Granny, Graneee loook, loook Graneee, loook a cat with orange and yellow stripes!'

2.00 p.m. Max follows Granny up the garden path, 'Granny, Granny, Graneee loook, a black cat with white socks on, looook!'

3.00 p.m. Granny reads Max another story, 'Laa-laa tried to reach the ball. But Laa-Laa wasn't tall enough. Uh-oh! Dipsy came to help. E-oh Laa-Laa! Ball...'

4.00 p.m. Max is peering through a hole in the fence, 'Granny loook, loook Granneee, Snowite an seven dorfs.'

5.00 p.m. Max's mummy, Rachel, arrives to pick him up; he grabs the back pocket of her jeans and follows her indoors.

Thursday 28th

We ran out of cat litter so I had to use two copies of *Weekly Wife*. The kittens did their business on Madonna, Mick Hucknall, 'Ideas for your Barbecue' and 'Best Bikinis'. I hurried out into the garden so I didn't miss the beginning of today's story, 'Tinky Winky's Bag'.

Found two pawns from Ben's chess set on the lawn and a knight in shining sunlight on the path. A king and two pawns are still missing; the kittens look innocent.

> *My kittens look at me like*
> *little angels – and always*
> *after doing something*
> *especially devilish.*
>   – Jamie Ann Hunt

Doc said, 'Search every nook and cranny.' Grumpy said, 'They're lost now, you'll never find them.' Dopey peered into his pockets and Happy laughed as he lifted up a sycamore leaf. Sleepy opened one eye, looked around, then dozed off again and Bashful looked up Sneezy's large nostrils – a very bad idea.

Bill and Ben will have to use the iron, battleship, top hat or racing car from Monopoly.

Friday 29th

Found a pawn under the fridge door.

Couldn't resist peeking through the hole in the fence to see if I could see the pictures for today's story, 'The Magic Flag'. Didn't see much but Max's lovely, bright yellow, plastic swimming pool and red bucket and spade in the sandpit caught my eye. I want to be six years old again and forget my miserable adult thoughts and put all my energies into making the best sandcastle ever on the beach; collect shells, feathers and lolly sticks to make doors and windows and flags and dig a moat so the sea will fill it as the tide comes in. I want to eat soggy tomato sandwiches with sand in, paddle in the shallows feeling sand between my toes, pick pebbles out of my plastic sandals and feel ice-cream running down my hands. Sit in a stripy deckchair with stripy sunburn, listen to the sound of the penny arcades, the waves and the hungry seagulls; smell sweet sticky candyfloss and fish and chips and breathe in soft, salty, sea air and sing all the bits I know of Cliff Richard's song 'Summer Holiday' over and over again. I wish Ben would learn to drive so we could at least sit in a car and see the sea like an old couple, with a flask, Tupperware box of sandwiches and two Penguins or Kit-Kats.

After a couple of pints at The Punch and Rudey Tavern down Stripe Street with Bill (who is depressed because Rick is seeing

Natasha), Ben found himself at the chip shop. He said he only went there to buy a fish treat for the kittens but, before he knew what was happening, a large portion of chips fell into his arms. Of course we had to eat them up, didn't we.

Saturday 30th

While saturated fats gurgled around in my stomach during the night, I endured sea-sidy-nightmares. I was a puppet in a Punch and Judy show and about to enjoy a huge Cornish ice-cream with *three* chocolate flakes, when Punch hit me over the head with a red bucket. I fell into an audience of pink faces eating candyfloss; green waves engulfed me and I found myself washed up on a familiar island where gâteaux grew in a black forest and pizzas grew in the middle of fairy rings. Maltesers fell from Malteser trees and rolled down the beach into my mouth. I grew so fat that everyone thought I was a beached whale and rolled me back into the sea. Woke up feeling ill and bloated.

Stepped on another pawn as I dragged myself out of bed. Ouch.

Sunday 31st

> **Got a sore foot**
> **A fat bum**
> **A big headache**
> **As tight as a drum**
>
> **I need a bath**
> **I need a laugh**
> **I need a wizard**
> **With a magic staff**
>
> **To magic me better.**

My waistline has expanded a lot. Now the kittens fit perfectly on my lap, but they are still growing, and if I grow any more I'll become wedged in the bath. Ben will have to hide the peanut butter and honey and put a tea cosy over the jars so I can't hear them calling to me. Feeling heavier makes me feel even tireder.

Found a king lying on his side on the bathroom floor. He didn't quite make it to the throne; must have been knocked out by a heavy knight.

AUGUST

Monday 1st

Seven months, Yippeee! I've survived seven whole months. Hurrah! Lucky seven. Lucky me! I'm so calm and positive and peaceful... fat... fatigued... frumpy... nearly forty... Oh! f.....

Today I counted my calories – until 7.30 p.m., when I was reminded of Cadbury's chocolate before *Coronation Street*, either side of the comercial break and at the end of the programme. Devoured honey on toast during *EastEnders*. Later, I thought I'd liven up my dull brown hair with a henna conditioner. When I poured the liquid onto my hand, I discovered it looked exactly like chocolate sauce; nearly licked it off my palm.

Wendy of *Weekly Wife* suggests I wear smarty pants in cream and chocolate, cover my body in chocolate body paint and brush my teeth with chocolate-flavoured toothpaste. Thanks, Wendy!

At 9 p.m., Ben asked me if I'd like anything from the corner shop before he nipped out to get some cigarettes and beer; I put on my I-need-chocolate face. Today was the beginning of his two-week summer break; he's going to Do It All tomorrow so he can do it all in the next couple of weeks. Eileen is in Scotland doing it all in Edinburgh.

At 10 p.m., the P.M.T. monster crept in through the back door.

Tuesday 2nd

I did it all today. Climbed Mount Everest and swam the English Channel (climbed the stairs and had a bath), did my daily workout (worked out what I was going to cook for dinner and played with the kittens), wrote a long letter to Artie Auntie (five lines using a thick italic pen on recycled paper with a wide decorative border) and dusted around a sleeping dragon so I didn't disturb him.

After his shopping trip, Ben made a list of jobs to do around the house. He felt so tired thinking about them he had to have a fag in the garden and a sleep in an old deck chair found in the cellar while he was thinking about clearing it out. He placed the deck chair at such an angle that when he awoke, he could admire his fence.

Grumpy: Looks like he's going to get a lot of work done this week. If he thinks mending a tap is hard work, he should try digging for a living!

Doc: Humans like to have a plan of action, then sleep on it, as much as possible.

Sleepy: Sounds like a good idea to me.

Grumpy: Huh.

Wednesday 3rd

Goldshield wrote to tell me it's the busiest holiday season of the year and all about their range of popular summer essentials, available at unbeatable prices. Then under the heading, 'NOT ALL DIMPLES LOOK SEXY', they reminded me that dimples on our thighs, buttocks, lower abdomen, upper arms and even nape of neck, do nothing for our self-confidence. But cellulite could be a thing of the past with 'CELLUTRIM', a revolutionary new product that everyone's talking about. They urged me to try the amazing formulation, available at a special introductory price, for not one, but *two* months' supply! Next, under the heading 'WANT TO LOSE WEIGHT FOR GOOD?' I was told not to despair as *help is here*, for only half the normal price: 'CHITOSAN' is a fat-binding fibre in an unrivalled Triple Action Formulation of Lipobond. I like hearing from Goldshield; they give me a good laugh.

Voices from the cupboard called out to me, 'You love me, you need me, you can't live without me.' I ignored them and sat outside eating a slimming salad. Wonder if Chitosan works?

Ben walked round to Bill's house. He said Bill has just finished a six foot square oil painting of a green nipple. *That's* why he came home singing, 'There'll be one green nipple, hanging on the wall!' Green... why green...? Maybe the milk in Bill's fridge nearly always has mould growing on it, like his banana and cigarette sculptures. I wonder if the nipple is hairy, ugh! Maybe he has a new girlfriend who is a Martian, or he's red/green colour blind, or he just likes to make people think. He could have run out of paint and only had green and white left... or green is his favourite colour and nipples are his favourite... er... thing. I feel a Julie Andrews coming on.

BILL'S SONG

Paint a green nipple
Then I have a tipple
Dip toe in the bath
And it causes a ripple
Silver white splinters
The coil of a spring
These are a few of my favourite things

Girls in white dresses
With lots of paint splashes
Snowflakes, a pay cheque
Mascara'd eyelashes
Mum's apple pie
And a girl that can sing
These are a few of my favourite things

When the hangover bites
T.C.P. stings
When I've had a slap
I simply remember my favourite things
And then I don't feeeel so...

Big doors held open
With small wooden wedges
Bananas and
Buttons and
Benson & Hedges
Brown paper sculptures
And vests made of string
These are a few of my favourite things...

Thursday 4th

A couple of autumn/winter gift catalogues arrived today. I fancied the mystic stones in a blue velvet pouch: **Amethyst**, good for purification and regeneration of all levels of body and mind; **Carnelian**, a mineral healer to increase levels of concentration; **Quartz**, to dispel negativity in one's energy field; **Tiger's eye**, useful for helping you through tough and strenuous situations; **Black onyx**, alters the course of one's destiny for the better; **Adventurine**, revitalises the mind and body.

Quite liked the spirit stones too, inspired by hieroglyphic art. The frog representing happiness, the turtle for health and the dolphin for guidance.

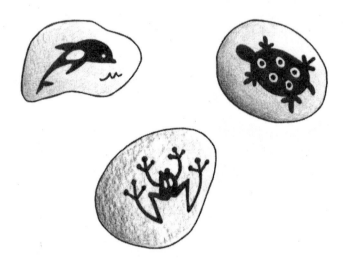

The list of 'Things To Do' is lost. Ben doesn't seem too worried. He didn't look very hard for it and spent the afternoon helping W. M. Friend move to a more spiritual home, a cottage overlooking the graveyard of a village church.

Friday 5th

Ben talked about mending the bathroom basin cold water tap and the bedroom door handle, but he needed to sort out a problem on his computer; it just happened to take him all afternoon.

Tonight he came home early from The Grin and Bear It, Sulk Street.

Ben: Got chips for us and cod for the kittens.
Me: No chips for me thanks! I'm being good. I've just had a baked potato with sweetcorn and *no marge!*
Ben: You'll weaken when you smell this lot.

Me: No I won't; I'm corn and spudful. How's Bill?
Ben: Still missing Natasha.
Me: I expect she thought he only wanted her for her nipples.
Ben: The nipple painting looks like a giant, green light switch.
Me: That reminds me, the bulb in the bedroom needs changing – number four on the 'Things To Do' list.
Ben: Oh, did you find it?
Me: No, jus' jokin'.
Ben: Mm, munch, munch, good; sure you don't want one?
Me: Jus' one then... munch, munch... jus' a couple more... are there any left in the kitchen?
Ben: Munch, munch... yep.
Me: No, I won't be tempted. I am strong, I am woman, I will provide for my children and give them their fishy treat now. I will write some verse to take my mind off soggy rectangular lumps of starch soaked in old fat and served up in paper by hairy, sweaty Greek Cypriots.

I am corn and spudful
I hate chips
A moment of madness
Grease on my lips
Two minutes of pleasure
Twenty years on my hips
Why do I bother
Reading beauty tips
Models like skeletons
Nipples like pips
I'm piling on pounds
Cutting back on my tips
They're getting expensive
These weekly Monday trips

CAPTAIN BIRDS EYE

Once upon a time
There was a man who went to sea
But on his return

He found he had M.E.
He read books on the subject
Did everything to the letter
Years went by
For Captain Birds Eye
And one day he was better

Saturday 6th

Felt ill this morning; the anti-chip verse therapy didn't work and writing gives me a healthy appetite.

Ben returned from Holland & Barrett with *the usual* and lots of nutty, oaty, sweet, crunchy and fruity treats. We had to try them all of course, as we're in holiday mood. Felt ill again.

He talked about adjusting the cooker door and getting the ignition to work, putting up a shelf and fitting a new cat flap. But more important jobs cried out to be attended to first: he wired up the new monitor for his computer, sorted his CD collection into alphabetical order, then enjoyed a congratulatory cigarette whilst admiring his fence.

Sunday 7th

W. M. Friend is helping Bill build a giant sculpture of a breast; Bill has told Joseph it's a cake with a cherry on top! There's a red light inside the nipple that needs wiring up... Ben spent the afternoon at Bill's...

A hot air balloon drifted quite low over our house this evening; I could see the jet of a flame spurting at intervals and peered through Ben's binoculars to see the people in the basket more clearly. I longed to be up there with them. Unlike many people I know, I love flying, especially over Southern Ireland. As the plane leaves Cork airport, my nose is glued to the window until we fly over where the waves break against the crinkly green coastline. We rise up high into the clouds and the world becomes white; then I'm bored and the seat feels small and cramped and the window looks tiny and I want to open it and I'm looking forward to looking down over a living map of London.

The dwarves sat on the fence, looking up.

Happy: Is it a fat dragon?
Doc: No, silly, it's a giant party balloon that carries humans off
          to parties.

Grumpy: They'll plummet to their death, mark my words.
Sleepy: Don't expect they get much sleep.

Monday 8th

Ben didn't come home till the early hours; he was celebrating the completion of the largest breast in the world with Bill and Joseph. Judging by the state of Ben this morning they were not drinking milk.

Bill has decided he wants to build a second breast in his back garden; he needs two. Ben went round to help him mix concrete, break up bricks and install a fountain which will spurt water out of the nipple.

It was good to see Eileen tonight and we had a laugh when she gave me a present from Scotland: a hairy wee haggis wearing a Tam O'Shanter. When I pressed his bagpipes, he played 'Scotland the Brave'. Loudly. She'd had a great time shopping for crafts in the old town around Edinburgh castle, visiting friends and sitting outside cafés in Leith. Wish I were going with her when she returns later this month for the Edinburgh Festival – the entertainment sounds just up my street!

I told her about Bill's nipple painting and breast sculptures, and we discussed the problems of finding a well-fitting bra. I mentioned I'd seen some comfy looking bosom halters (or over-the-shoulder-boulder-holders, as Bill calls them) in Freewoman catalogue, pretty too: for the larger lady, with firm support, three-section framed cup and deep stretch sides.

Mr. Ex-racing-driver-taxi-man leered at me in his rear view mirror (maybe I was a little breast-concious today) so I got out my little haggis and pressed the bagpipes.

Tuesday 9th

Bill is looking very thin these days so Ben invited him round for a decent meal tonight. I felt conscious of my nipples showing through my T-shirt as I laid the table and leant across to pour Bill a glass of wine, so I put on a sensible cardigan for dinner.

Tried to tell Bill that living on fags and bananas wasn't enough to keep body and soul healthy and happy. Would he listen? With his veg-esausages, peas and tomato, I gave him two round mounds of mashed potato with a pea on top of each one.

Wednesday 10th

Received a postcard from Rose. She's on holiday with her children, her friend Mandy, and Mandy's children from her many marriages. They are camping in Cornwall; fourteen children between them.

Although I'd like to be camping in Cornwall, I'm very glad I'm not in the tent next door to Rose and Mandy. On second thoughts, it might be OK. The restful sound of waves rolling upon the shore and distant call of seagulls. Children laughing gaily and a mother's gentle voice: 'Pack it in Eddie, Pack it in! Did you 'ere me?' The tap tap tapping of of tiny spades building sandcastles, families of feet crunching on pebbles, searching for a cosy spot by the breakers and a mother's soft voice: 'If you kick Tiff's castle once more, you get a smack, d'you 'ere me?' The smell of sun lotion and candy floss and the sweet call of a child: 'Mum, Mum, Mum! Emily's bin sick on the camera but it's ok, Ben's washin' it in the sea an' Oliver's bin drinkin' the Ambé Solé milk an' Katie's dun it agen, Mum! Mum! Did y'ere me?'

I am calm and peaceful, I am not thinking about rich, thick, creamy Cornish ice-cream, creamy sandy beaches, creamy cream teas, soft rolling hills, my over-sized breasts, Cornish cows' udders...

Paddy and I sat staring out of the window. Paddy watched the birdies; I watched a young Labrador, the colour of treacle poured over vanilla ice-cream, bouncing around his mistress's legs. She wore an ice-cream-coloured jacket (more a Cornish buttery colour) and her brown leggings were the two chocolate flakes.

SILLY COW

She had a touch of the shudders
He said she was carrying udders
She knew he was right
All her jumpers were tight
She wished she was one of her bruvvers

Thursday 11th

Ben read the instructions on his new shelf fittings. He opened a can of paint to check it was the right colour and took the wrapping off a paintbrush.

It's a start.

Gina rang. She mentioned a friend of hers had been admiring my designs on Matthew's cot and wondered if I'd do the same sort of thing for her little girl. Poppy (a friend of the earth) said she would like flowers, butterflies and maybe a few bumble bees on baby Daisy's cot. As Gina spoke, I decided to tell her I wasn't up to it. The kittens take up my spare energy and the frustration of painting only a little every day drives me mad; but as the words formed in my mind I said, 'Yes, OK, that'll be fine; bring the cot round whenever you like.'

6.15 p.m.	I'll ring her back and tell her I've changed my mind. I'll explain.
6.30 p.m.	Where's my notepad and pencil?
7.00 p.m.	Just do a quick sketch.
7.15 p.m.	A daisy here, a few leaves there, large butterfly with curly antennae, small butterfly with patterned wings, another daisy – bigger this time.
7.30 p.m.	I'll ring her now and tell her I'm really not up to it.
8.00 p.m.	But I *am* better than I was a few months ago; I have more good days.
8.15 p.m.	I could paint the daisies and butterflies yellow with a touch of red... bright green leaves...
8.30 p.m.	It'll do me good to work on a new project; where are my felt pens? I've put them somewhere... are they in the?... No, I moved them from there when I had a tidy up... they could be... oh I know!
9.00 p.m.	This is going to look good: bright red, yellow and green go well together... I'll just give the daisies and butterflies a little more shape... more soft and curvy... make the leaves bigger... this is going to be fun!
9.15 p.m.	Add three bumble bees.
9.30 p.m.	Oh dear, this design could take longer than the moons and stars on Matthew's cot.
10.00 p.m.	I *could* simplify the drawings. No. I'll write and explain to Gina all the reasons why I can't do it.
10.15 p.m.	She'll probably think I can't be bothered. I'd rather write than ring. She gets really scary when she's cross, especially if she's not getting her own way; more like Mum every day.

10.30 p.m. If I send the letter first class tomorrow (Ben can post it on his way to work) it won't arrive till Saturday and she's probably rung her friend Poppy already.

11.00 p.m. I know my sister; she's very crafty. She'll deliver the cot on Saturday and pretend she didn't get the letter and look all surprised if I mention it and if I refuse to take the cot, she'll get all uptight and beat me on the head with a Greenpeace catalogue or set her dogs on me to chew my hands off so I never paint again.

11.15 p.m. Want to ring her now and get it over with, but it's too late. *Why* did I agree!?

11.30 p.m. Write letter to sister. I'll pretend I'm out on Saturday if she comes round and leave the answering machine on.

Midnight. Sketch looking good.

Letter in pieces on bedroom floor. I'll ring and ask if I can take my time on the masterpiece. I am calm and idea-full... I could photograph the completed work, build up a portfolio of past commissions, make a small living when I'm more recovered and maybe do a little modelling for life classes in between; I'll have lots of interesting rolls of fat for the students to draw... Oh, God. I feel a nightmare coming on.

316

Friday 12th

Bill helped Ben clear out the cellar. They drove to the tip in Bill's old green truck and Bill found some wire fence to make a giant bra. I gave him a few pictures of bras torn out of my Freewoman catalogue; I like to be supportive.

Rang Gina. She said she was sure it would be OK to take a few weeks decorating the cot, but couldn't I try just a *bit* harder to finish it a *bit* quicker (no comment). The cot was already at her house, she had told Poppy I could do it without asking me first (typical). She's delivering it on Saturday afternoon (I knew it).

Ben and Bill met Rob, Bob the Slob and Fiona at The Fizz and Nipple tonight.

Saturday 13th

The kittens discovered the cellar and emerged with cobweb hats and tails. I discovered three little scratches on my left knee; paw-sized. Ben has discovered it's a bit late to start decorating (he doesn't seem too disappointed). He never did find the 'Things To Do' list.

Joseph came round looking arty in a technicolour dreamcoat. He'd been decorating his new home (using five brightly coloured pots of paint left by the previous owner) whilst wearing his black jacket.

Gina guzzled a coffee after plonking the cot in the sitting room. She admired her Kit-Kat mug and I was about to say she could have one when I realised I've grown quite attached to them now.

Started decorating baby Daisy's cot with a drawing of a large butterfly (curly antennae) and a tiny bumble bee.

Sunday 14th

Mary was sick on the wellingtons in the cellar – four wellies and a fur ball.

Spoke briefly to Mum on the phone tonight. She hasn't been too well lately, and must have mentioned that she was worried about me to her doctor because she (the doctor) made a few comments about my health.

I am totally astonished! Amazed!! Completely gob-smacked!! My mother's doctor has never met me and practises at a surgery at least ten miles away, but felt able to say that I am, and I quote, 'just putting it on'. Well, thanks, Doc. *Thanks very much!* That really helps my family to understand my situation. It seems there is, and I quote again, 'nothing wrong' with me either. *Great, wonderful, that's bloody fine then,* I'll just jog into town shall I and apply for a demanding physical job? No, I'll cartwheel all the way and jump for joy; after all, I'm just *putting it on.* I really do think sometimes that I'm capable of murder. I will never, EVER, be calm and peaceful again!

Monday 15th

As I'm so well *really,* I sprinted down the shops and bought a skateboard and skated along to the bus station, but felt so fit and athletic I ran behind the No. 333 bus – sometimes overtaking it and waving merrily to the passengers. After about ten minutes, I stopped to help a man change his tyre by holding up his Volvo, then borrowed his son's BMX and cycled up the steep hill just for the hell of it. I hopped on one leg as far as the health club where I dropped in to join an aerobics class for twenty minutes of flinging my arms and legs about. After lifting a few weights and trying out the rowing machine, I swam five lengths of the swimming pool and felt *so* refreshed I joined in a football match in the park and scored *three* goals for the losing team who invited me to The Slurpit and Swallow, Empty Street, to celebrate. I gulped down a pint of orange juice, burped, then did a bit of shopping at a mini-market where I grinned broadly at everyone. Carrying six pounds of potatoes with one arm and eight two-pound bags of sugar with the other, I realised time was getting on, so I skipped half a mile to the clinic for a chat and a cuppa with Eileen to discuss our skiing trip; because I don't really *need* any treatment from her, I just visit for the fun of it, because I'm only *putting it on,* there's *nothing wrong* with me. Look at me! Never felt better.

I finished decorating the cot, then carried it eight miles, on my head, to my sister's house. Her friend Poppy said she'd rather the design were in shades of pink, so I cheerfully whitewashed my masterpiece, galloped on her horse to Homebase, purchased the pots of paint and happily repainted the cot in one hour. She was thrilled and offered me six other commissions from her friends and family: one cot, two nursery wall paintings, a chest of drawers, a dresser and a Mediterranean archway view in her mother's backyard. I said, 'No trouble, I'll start my sketches right away!'

I'm looking forward to preparing a five-course meal for five hundred people at the weekend and driving up to Scotland to dance the Highland fling round Edinburgh Castle before joining in with the festival celebrations. I may swim the length of Loch Ness and say, 'Hi!' to the monster before flying home in a hot air balloon for a little rest to prepare for a week of playing squash, tennis and badminton.

Tuesday 16th

Stroked the kittens, munched a thin 'n' crispy, and leafed through a few cat books I haven't read for years, to help me stay calm and pizza-full. Eileen ironed out my murderous creases last night and Mr. Cheerful-chatty-taxi-man restored my faith in ~~humanity~~ humans 'n' tea. He said he'd been struggling to drink herb teas to please his wife but felt much better now he was back on the old Brooke Bond PG Tips. 'Lovely stuff, nuffin' like real tea, 's got a natural source of powerful antioxithings called flavowhatsits... the missus knows, she's into all that sort o'fing.'

Full of inspiration after sipping real tea and reading a verse by a French poet...

> *Come, lovely cat, and rest upon my heart*
> *And let my gaze dive in the cold*
> *Live pools of thine enchanted eyes that dart*
> *Metallic rays of green and gold.*
> **– Charles Baudelaire**

... I started scribbling away.

PADDY

Rest upon my dressing gown
Warmth and comfort softens my frown
Eyes the colour of chocolate limes
You like to sit on the *TV Times*

MARY

Your little tongue
Like bubble gum
Tiny pointy teeth
You love to purr
Upon my chest
My heartbeat underneath

MURPHY

Beautiful! Beautiful!
Bright wide eyes
See deep
Into my soul
They seem to say
This summer's day
Give me Go-Cat or else

I curled up with the kittens and read a few pages of *Cat Watching* by Desmond Morris.

Interesting Fact: In 1760 there was a story called '*The Life and Adventures of a Cat*'. In those days a male cat was known as a *ram* cat. The cat in the story was called Tom the Cat and when the story became popular people started to refer to male cats as Tom instead of ram.

Interesting Fat: My hips are getting so wide, the kittens stretch out on my lap.

Interesting Fact: Cats are believed to have more than one life because of their toughness and resilience. In ancient times, nine was considered lucky because it was a 'trinity of trinities' and therefore suited to a 'lucky' cat.

Interesting Fat: Paddy sniffed at the grill pan after I'd cooked vege-sausages.

Interesting Fact: When a cat tramples on your lap with its front paws, it's 'milk-treading'. The cat is reverting to kittenhood, going through the motions of stimulating a milk supply at its mother's breast.

Interesting Fat: Today I watched a very large man squeeze in between his car seat and steering wheel. I wondered if his wife had to pull him out when he arrived home.

Interesting Fact – for Bill: Kittens avoid squabbling when feeding from their mother because within a few days of birth, they develop an attachment towards their own personal nipple. Each nipple has a special smell, so the kittens can label them as clearly as a name-card.

Completed a small butterfly and sketched four leaves round the big daisy I drew yesterday.

Wednesday 17th

The postman delivered a small rectangular package: it was light and rattled when I shook it so I guessed what was inside. As soon as I'd removed three tubs of supplements and bubble wrap, Paddy climbed into the box and shoe-horned himself neatly inside. His fur spilling over the sides, he looked like a ginger cake in a cake tin (made with self-raising fur). I am *not* thinking about moist delicious ginger cake.

I *am* pleased with my special offer for primrose oil capsules; I expect Goldshield Healthcare Direct will continue to tempt me for the rest of the year to be more starry eyed with starflower oil, odour free with odourless garlic pearls, healthy as an eskimo with fish oil and bold, bright and fashionably bouncy with ginseng. I will need their aloe vera body lotions to smooth and elasticate the skin holding in all my bouncy fat; I wonder if they do breast reduction pills.

Ben put a new film in his camera and wanted to take a photo of me and the kittens. I asked him if he could wait till I'm slimmer but he said he didn't want to wait for ever and suggested he just photographed my face; I could show my best side. I said both sides are my worst. He gave up. Mary posed nicely for him; I think she is going to be a supermodel.

> *...Cats... never strike a pose*
> *that isn't photogenic.*
> – Lillian Jackson Braun

Thinking about my mother's doctor and coping with monthly pains made me feel miserable, so I had a good pop with the bubble wrap: Pop... pop... pop... pop... pop... pop... pop... pop... pop... That's better.
Drew one small leaf.

Thursday 18th

> *Like those great sphinxes lounging through*
> *eternity in noble attitudes upon the desert sand,*
> *they gaze in curiosity at nothing, calm and wise.*
> – Charles Baudelaire

Mary sat on the bathroom scales in sphinx position, watching the dial; Paddy slept in his cake tin again and Murphy lay in the window eyeing up the tastiest looking birds.

Ben's friend at work, Cheryl, is getting married at the weekend. He said her entire wedding list consists of the Eternal Beau collection of dinner set, tea set, place mats, bread bin, etc. I had a look through the Argos catalogue and cut out pictures of Eternal Beau plates, coasters, place mats and a coffee pot, then glued them onto a piece of card. Inside the card, I wrote, using my thick italic pen:

Wishing you both eternal happiness

Hope Cheryl has a sense of humour. I could have written *Wishing you Beau Eternal happiness,* but I only thought of it when I'd finished writing the card. Mmmm... I could make a thank you card in the same way...

Eternally grateful

A valentine card...

Eternally yours

We have an Eternal Beau side plate; I use it to feed the kittens. Cheryl would be horrified if she knew.

Only drew four small daisy petals.

Friday 19th

> *Perhaps it is because cats*
> *do not live by human patterns*
> *do not fit themselves into prescribed*
> *behaviour, that they are so united*
> *to creative people.*
> — André Norton

I completed the small daisy and painted four petals on another, then curled up with the kittens and daydreamed of English country cottage gardens.

Ben took Bill along to Cheryl's husband's stag night at The Fizz and Nipple Wine Bar. Bill found the first stripogram (with her large breasts, big wobbly bum and tiny shreds of underwear) inspiring for his creative work, but got up and walked out when the second one appeared: Natasha was wearing Rick's old school tie and knickers the size of a rubber band.

Saturday 20th

10.35 a.m.   Ben has bought kitchen roll with a pretty butterfly pattern – my morning brightens.

10.37 a.m.   Feel inspired to draw butterflies.

10.40 a.m.   Dark clouds gather over Ben's brow – he has forgotten to buy Cheryl's wedding present, can't find anything decent to wear and needs a haircut.

10.42 a.m.   I get the mad-Mitchell-brother look when I suggest he turns up at the church naked, holding the wedding card over his important little bits.

11.14 a.m.   Draw butterfly on cot.

11.19 a.m.   Butterfly wrong shape.

11.20 a.m.   Rub out butterfly.

11.31 a.m.   Read useful tips in *Weekly Wife*; how to polish your ~~cat~~ car, prevent hanger creases in trousers and cope with new shoes.

1.45 p.m.   Sprinkle a little talcum powder into Ben's new shoes to soften them and reduce the risk of chafing and blisters.

2.00 p.m.   Cut price tags off Ben's new jacket, trousers and shirt while he splashes about in the bath.

2.05 p.m.   Wish I were getting ready to go to wedding, wearing a new posh frock (in one of this season's floral prints) and strappy shoes; maybe a matching hat and handbag.

2.06 p.m.   Wish everyone would wait till I'm better to get married and have babies.

2.07 p.m.   Haven't minded missing funerals.

2.08 p.m.   Paddy curls up on new jacket.

2.09 p.m.   Must find sellotape to remove ginger kitten fur from dark grey material.

2.11 p.m.   Mary plays with discarded price tags.

2.12 p.m.   It cost that much!?

2.13 p.m.   Murphy 'helps' me wrap an Eternal Beau coffee pot in wedding paper with doves on.

2.14 p.m.   Mary 'helps' me write gift tag.

2.43 p.m.   Ben looks smart, quite fanciable, really.

2.46 p.m.	Ben climbs into taxi and waves goodbye.
2.47 p.m.	Stare out of window.
3.00 p.m.	Still staring out of window.
3.15 p.m.	Glad sun is shining on Cheryl's big day.
3.45 p.m.	Sit outside.
3.47 p.m.	Granny is telling Max a story – goody!
3.48 p.m.	'But the rainbow was far away... red... orange... yellow... green... blue... indigo... violet... what a beautiful rainbow.'
3.49 p.m.	Wonder what colour Cheryl's bridesmaids are wearing – a dark colour... crimson maybe... pastel shade... lilac... blue... or one of this season's floral prints?
3.50 p.m.	'...and the rainbow disappeared.'
3.59 p.m.	A pink rose petal flutters to the ground.
4.00 p.m.	Forgot to give Ben the confetti.
4.35 p.m.	Watch a man washing his car. I'm tempted to give him a useful tip: before polishing, apply baby oil to trim, then remove excess wax with damp cloth.
5.00 p.m.	The church service and photo session will be over now. Everyone will be eating wonderful wedding banquet, drinking champagne, smiling and laughing at the best man's speech, toasting the bridesmaids and getting drunk.
5.16 p.m.	Scrape piece of burnt toast. Time and the toast waits for no man, or woman.
5.30 p.m.	Ben forgot his camera.
5.45 p.m.	Remove cardboard tube from last sheets of kitchen roll. Slit tube in half and place over hanger bar to prevent creases in Ben's new trousers.
5.55 p.m.	Think I'll use the new kitchen roll with butterflies on in a minute – how exciting.
6.00 p.m.	What's on TV?
6.03 p.m.	Nothing.
6.05 p.m.	Cosmic Colin says the only way to fit everyone into my fabulously hectic social life is to invite them all around in one go to my place.
6.06 p.m.	Huh.
6.07 p.m.	Oh God, I'm bored.
6.08 p.m.	Watch start of boring film.
6.09 p.m.	Turn off TV.

6.10 p.m.	I know! I'll invite dwarves to watch video of *Labyrinth*.
6.20 p.m.	Dwarves excited.
6.21 p.m.	Feel cheerful.
6.30 p.m.	Feel peckish again.
6.35 p.m.	Dwarves are peckish too.
6.45 p.m.	Sitting on lawn shelling peanuts with dwarves.
7.10 p.m.	Two large pizzas in oven.
7.46 p.m.	Lying on sofa with kittens, trying not to think about Ben enjoying himself at wedding reception.
7.47 p.m.	Film has just started and dwarves are seated in a semicircle in front of TV, nibbling small triangles of pizza, their faces lit up by the screen.
7.48 p.m.	Sarah is running home in the rain with her Dulux dog: it's seven o'clock and she's late for baby-sitting her little step-brother, Toby. Dwarves are swaying from side to side in time to groovy music.
7.53 p.m.	Tired of baby-sitting on yet another weekend night, Sarah summons the goblins from her favourite book, *The Labyrinth*, to take baby Toby away.
7.54 p.m.	Dwarves laugh at goblins peeping round corners in the bedroom.
7.55 p.m.	David Bowie appears as the Goblin King and tells Sarah her baby step-brother is in his castle. He gives her thirteen hours to solve the labyrinth and reach the castle beyond the Goblin City in order to rescue Toby, before he becomes a goblin too.
7.56 p.m.	Dwarves look worried and Doc explains to Dopey what's going on.
7.58 p.m.	Sarah meets Hoggle.
7.59 p.m.	Grumpy says, 'She'll never make it.'
8.00 p.m.	Sarah enters the labyrinth.
8.01 p.m.	Happy says, 'This is exciting.'
8.06 p.m.	Goblin King is singing with the goblins in the castle. The dwarves join in, 'Dance magic dance, dance magic dance... jump magic jump, jump magic jump...'
8.07 p.m.	Is Ben dancing with Delyth? Hope he treads on her bridesmaid's dress.

Sarah is drawing arrows on paving stones with her lipstick.

8.08 p.m. Is Delyth drunk and leaning against Ben? Hope her lipstick is all smudged across her face.

8.09 p.m. Ben's probably got egg mayonnaise on his face now and is tucking into the cheese and pineapple on sticks or cheese and onion crisps or cheese straws. Is he drunk yet? Hope he throws up egg mayonnaise down Delyth's sleeve.

8.10 p.m. Hope he trips over the large handbag she always leaves in everyone's way, it falls over, a super-plus tampon rolls across the floor and Uncle Tom picks it up and lights the end.

8.11 p.m. Sarah falls down the hole of Helping Hands, they grab her and laugh at her.

8.12 p.m. The dwarves gasp!

8.13 p.m. The hands let go of Sarah and she falls to the bottom of the pit, where she meets Hoggle again. Grumpy says, 'Serves her right.'

8.14 p.m. Doc says, 'Hoggle looks like my grandfather.'

8.26 p.m. With Hoggle's help, Sarah escapes from the pit and finds a big hairy beast in distress. She recues Rudo (or Ludo), the talking beast. They become friends.

8.27 p.m. Is Ben being friendly to Cheryl's other bridesmaid, Sara?

8.29 p.m. Happy giggles, Sarah is having a conversation with a couple of door knockers.

8.30 p.m. Is Ben having a conversation with a pair of knockers?

8.31 p.m. Hope he drops fag ash down her cleavage.

8.32 p.m. Is she fluttering her bridesmaidy eyelashes? Hope they're false and one of them falls into her drink, she doesn't notice, but Uncle Tom does. He fishes it out, throws it on the floor, then stamps on it.

8.33 p.m. Jealousy monster is sitting on my head.

8.34 p.m. Head feels lighter (the dwarves laughed and frightened the monster away).

8.37 p.m. Hoggle rescues Sarah from the strange, fiery dancing creatures. They almost fall into the Bog of Eternal Stench.

8.38 p.m. Hope Cheryl is pleased with her Eternal Beau coffee pot.

8.39 p.m. Hoggle, Rudo and Sarah are trying to cross the Bog of Eternal Stench; it looks like a pond of sewage, farty noises bursting and bubbling to the greeny brown surface. Doc and Dopey are holding their noses. Sneezy sneezes and wakes up Sleepy.

8.40 p.m.   Grumpy says, 'They'll never make it.'

8.42 p.m.   Happy giggles at the talking fox with white eyebrows and moustache, dressed like a musketeer.

8.43 p.m.   Dopey grabs Doc's jacket in horror; Sarah is hanging from a branch over the bog because the bridge has broken. The hairy monster summons the rocks to help her and they all cross the bog.

8.44 p.m.   The dwarves cheer, 'Hooray!' Except Grumpy, who says, 'She'll get into more trouble, mark my words.'

8.45 p.m.   Hoggle gives Sarah the drugged peach, as ordered by the Goblin King, who is very displeased that Hoggle has been helping her solve the labyrinth.
She bites into it.
Doc says, 'Oh dear, oh dear.'
Dopey pulls his hat down over his eyes.

8.46 p.m.   Sarah falls into a deep dreamy sleep.
Grumpy says, 'That'll teach her.'

8.47 p.m.   Need a nibble, but don't fancy fruit.

8.48 p.m.   Dip spoon into peanut butter jar. Eyes glued to favourite part of film, mouth glued with peanut butter. Sarah is walking into a room full of strange fairytale dancers wearing grotesque masks. Everything's soft and dreamy and gothic – nightmarish, the music magical and lilting. She's dressed like a fairytale princess in pearly white and meets the Goblin King who dances with her; but she will not be tempted to fall under his spell.

8.51 p.m.   I'd like to have seen Cheryl in her wedding dress today.

8.52 p.m.   Sarah meets strange old woman tramp living on a rubbish tip who tries to keep her there by offering her all her old toys, but she's not distracted from the quest to find Toby and rescue him from the Goblin King.

8.56 p.m.   Sarah meets up with her friends, except Hoggle, who's hiding guiltily.

8.57 p.m.   They enter the Goblin City and a giant metal monster tries to kill them with an axe.

8.58 p.m.	Hoggle comes to their rescue. Happy shouts, 'Hooray!' Grumpy groans, 'They'll never reach the castle.'
9.00 p.m.	Everyone forgives Hoggle.
9.01 p.m.	The Goblin King is informed that Sarah and her friends have entered the Goblin City and sends his army after them.
9.02 p.m.	Dwarves stare at the screen in horror. Grumpy mumbles, 'They'll never escape now.'
9.04 p.m.	The hairy beast summons the rocks to help them.
9.06 p.m.	The rocks scare away the goblin army. The dwarves cheer and clap (except Grumpy).
9.08 p.m.	Sarah meets the Goblin King in his castle, full of strange staircases leading nowhere, like a drawing by Escher.
9.10 p.m.	Toby is crawling about on the stairs and Sarah is trying to reach him, calling his name. They both look as if they could plummet to their death at any moment.
9.11 p.m.	Happy and Dopey and Bashful cover their eyes and peep between stubby little fingers.
9.13 p.m.	The Goblin King is trying to talk Sarah out of rescuing Toby but when she finally remembers the words from her favourite book, 'You have no power over me,' the king and his castle disintegrate; normality returns, she's back at home and Toby's safely tucked up in bed.
9.14 p.m.	Dwarves are cheering and clapping and dancing around the room. Grumpy mutters to himself.
9.16 p.m.	Sarah's friends, whom she met in the labyrinth, appear in her bedroom and tell her they'll always be there for her if she needs them.
9.17 p.m.	Doc removes his glasses and wipes away a tear. Happy is happily sobbing into his beard and the others are sniffing; Grumpy marches off home.
9.18 p.m.	I pour wine into egg cups to cheer us all up.
9.20 p.m.	Big glass for me.
11.00 p.m.	Wash reallee good film... took mind off Ben at resheption... losh brill mushic... David Bowie absolutee fantashtic... losh comedee an' fantashee... marvlus characturzzz... zzzzzz.

I run a Goblin Restaurant
I cook the food in gin
That's why each diner
Has never felt finer
On the floor looking up with a grin.
— Spike Milligan

Sunday 21st

Most people are just like
cats in that if you rub them
the right way, they will purr.
— William Ross

Ben had paracetamol and coffee for breakfast; I nibbled wedding cake washed down with de-caf tea. I laid a cold flannel on Ben's brow and massaged his head; he lay on the sofa muttering, 'Never again.'

Bill came round to ask if I had any ribbon for the bow on his giant bra sculpture. I found an old pair of espadrilles that looked a bit moth-eaten, pulled off the white ribbons, washed them and hung them out in the sun to dry.

I'm still being supportive.

Completed a small daisy and drew two leaves.

Monday 22nd

The playful kitten, with
its pretty little tigerish
gambols, is infinitely
more amusing than half
the people one is obliged
to live with in the world.
— Lady Sydney Morgan

Mr. Miserable-as-sin-taxi-man had a cold; he sniffed all the way to the clinic in between sucking on a roll up, complaining about the bloody weather, bloody toothache and the bloody traffic. Tobacco fumes, exhaust fumes and enormous sweaty body fumes made me want to faint with revulsion – one of the few moments in my life I've wished I didn't have such a keen sense of smell. I hoped fervently I wouldn't catch his germs when he turned round and sneezed as I handed him a crisp five pound note. I was reluctant to give it to him; it fitted so neatly into my purse. His hand was wrapped in a dirty old stained bandage and I noticed an angry boil on his cheek, like Colin in *The Brittas Empire*. His breath stank of cabbage, garlic and teenage trainers; I tried not to breathe in as my fingers touched the bandage (ugh) and called out, 'Keep the change,' as I grabbed my bag, opened the car door, threw my legs out and hurried towards the clinic as fast as my little feet would carry me. Feeling sick as I climbed the stairs, I felt sorry for my crispy clean young fiver, crunched up next to the wrinkly, dirty old tenners, trying to breathe for all it's worth.

Enjoyed my much needed Monday treatment. Eileen seemed a bit depressed so I told her about the kittens' latest antics to cheer her up; Murphy uses the small window in our kitchen as his own personal cat flap, Paddy tries to lift the phone off the hook when it rings and Mary is still watching her weight. She laughed, but I think her heart is in Scotland.

Drew a daisy, half a flutterby and two small leaves.

Tuesday 23rd

> *You can't look at a sleeping*
> *cat and be tense.*
>   – Jane Pauley

10.00 a.m.   Open parcel from Artie Auntie and giggle – another tea towel with cats on entitled 'Cats Arrived', made in Ireland by the Ulster Weavers.

10.05 a.m.   Lay tea towel on table to admire it; the cats are mostly ginger, black and grey.

10.20 a.m.   Kittens curl up and sleep on tea towel.

1.00 p.m.   Doze in front of TV feeling calm and peaceful while Paddy and Murphy dream kitten dreams on my lap.

1.30 p.m.   Thirty seconds of pagan aerobics.

1.31 p.m.   Think about running a bath after all that strenuous exercise.

2.00 p.m.   Wallow in warm geranium and mandarin experience, the sensual scent softly caressing my senses; Mary curls up on the bath mat, whiskers and paws twitching.

2.15 p.m.   Daylight glows through Herbal Essences shampoo bottle

with extract of rosemary, jasmine and orange flower, like sunshine through the leaves of a forest ceiling.

2.17 p.m. Enjoy beauty of crystal collection.

2.18 p.m. Admire new crystal. Jade. It matches the colour of Paddy's pale green eyes.

2.20 p.m. Cold tap drips on to my big toe. Hold toe up to light from window. Feel happy – I can now see the light at the end of the toenail!

2.25 p.m. Tap still dripping. Count the ripples in the bath water, think about sound waves, time, toothpaste. Need new toothbrush; must go to the dentist. Must go on a diet.

3.30 p.m. Draw other half of butterfly.

4.15 p.m. Draw a daisy.

4.30 p.m. Doze with kittens.

4.35 p.m. Read about jade. This crystal is beneficial to the kidneys, digestive system and heart. The vibration of blue jade opens our minds to the peace within us, which makes it an excellent meditation stone.

4.40 p.m.	Search for spell to clean and strengthen teeth so one no longer needs to visit the dentist.
4.45 p.m.	Think about washing-up and preparing dinner and all the other things that need doing sometime this week... or the next... or the next.
4.46 p.m.	Stroke Mary's soft grey fur and fall asleep.

Wednesday 24th

A postcard arrived from Ben's sister, Julia, on holiday in Cumbria: a picture of Dove Cottage in Grasmere, where William Wordsworth wrote many of his finest poems. Lucky him.

Wrote three short letters to Gail, Rose and Artie Auntie and one of my worst poems.

> Dear Artie Auntie,
> Thank you for another beautiful tea towel – love the cat design! The kittens are still keeping me amused with their antics and help me relax. I've taken lots of photos and will send you one when Ben takes the film to Boots for developing.
> I've started decorating a cot with daisies, butterflies and bumble bees for Gina's friend's little girl, Daisy. I'm thinking of using bright red, yellow and green enamel paints; it will take several weeks to complete but it's nice to have a project on the go. It's great to know you are enjoying your art history lessons so much. They sound fascinating.
> Hope your back is feeling better and you're able to tend your garden again.
> Lots of love,
> Artie Niece xxx
>
> P.S. Thanks for your invite to stay for a summer break. I'm afraid I'm still not up to travelling up North.

Dear Rose,

Thanks for your postcard. Did you and the children have a great time with Mandy and her brood in Cornwall? Not too many disasters, I hope!

I'm decorating a cot at the moment for a baby girl, with daisies, butterflies and bumble bees. I'm not at the painting stage yet, but hope bright red, yellow and green will look effective.

My hairy children are doing well; they're good company and are keeping me amused on these long hot summer days.

Look forward to hearing from you soon.

Love and kisses to all,

V xxxxxxxxxxxxxx

P.S. Thanks for your invite to stay for a summer break, but I'm afraid I'm still not up to it. Maybe next year.

Dear Gail,

Sounds like you had a brilliant time in June at your usual spot in the West Country. Thanks for your invite to join you one weekend. Hopefully I will be well enough to make the journey next year – you never know!

I've started decorating a cot with daisies, butterflies and bumble bees, but don't get too excited! It's for my sister's friend's baby girl, Daisy. I'm enjoying the kittens. Paddy is trying to sit on this letter at this very moment and Mary wants to play with the pen.

I expect you will be enjoying another break soon. Hope the weather is good and all is well with you and Gareth, and Escher.

Love to all and looking forward to your next postcard,

V xxxx

P.S. The holes at the top corner of the page are Paddy's teeth marks.

P.P.S. The dirty mark is Murphy's paw print.

I enjoy writing to my pen-friends but sometimes I feel so pressured to 'GET WELL SOON'.

Drew a bumble bee.

Thursday 25th

Sat in the shade reading:

Summer's hottest looks... shells for your bathroom... body scrubs... sandals... sore feet... spots... scars... suffering... sun... sunburn... sorbets... sweet treats... sex... sea... sand... Spain... signs of senility... sentimental story... Sandie's super salads...

The salads looked delicious; I must experiment with seeds, nuts, herbs, apples, raisins and avocado pear. Sometimes I feel so pressured to 'COOK WELL SOON'.

Opened the fridge door and a huge fly flew out in a hurry; he must have got cold feet. Laid salad things out on the work surface and found a sharp knife but, as always, felt reluctant to slice into the pepper; red peppers are such a beautiful colour and shape when whole. Sandie says red peppers are rich in carotenoids and have more vitamin C than the green ones; goody, we always have red.

Café memories have just popped into my head: plastic red-pepper-shaped tomato ketchup containers in that dirty café; being ordered (as a Saturday girl) to strain the flies out of vinegar pots, and cleaning enormous smelly ashtrays full of ash mixed with strawberry milkshake and the odd chip.

Oh God, here comes another memory... being told to give customers the beer slops at the end of the evening in a pub in Maidstone. The last time I worked *there*.

Mixed red and green salad with yellow sweetcorn to go with tonight's dinner. Psychologists say brightly coloured vegetables lift your mood and make you less likely to crave unhealthy comfort food. I enjoyed the aroma of freshly sliced salad filling the kitchen; I don't know what psychologists would say about that, but I expect aromatherapists would say a salad-sniff gives you a lift.

I'm looking forward to painting the cot. Think I'll start with the green paint, I like green. No, I'll use red first: it's an energy-giving colour. Yellow is a happy sunshine vibration; I'll start with yellow. Yes. Yellow.

Nibbled red pepper and drew another bumble bee.

Friday 26th

My eyes ached today after reading too much yesterday so I flicked through clothes catalogues; Orvis arrived today. I liked the Adirondack Appliqué jacket: a pine forest on the yoke, a canoe embroidered below and the mighty moose appliquéd on the two patch pockets. I loved the stone-washed jacket, decorated with woodblock printed birds, detailed with hand-stitching, wood toggle buttons, patch pockets and wide easy-to-roll sleeves. Really fancied one of the Meadowflower waistcoats, linen-textured cotton/flax with a water-colour-like print. The other catalogues seemed boring compared, but I quite liked some of the smart cotton sweaters and skirts in Land's End.

Wendy said I should be looking cool as a choc-ice in dark choco-late brown separates with ice blue accessories. Lying about in my old white T-shirt, I felt like the ice cream that's fallen out of its cone onto the pavement – splat!

Sometimes I feel so pressured to 'DRESS WELL SOON'. Didn't draw anything on the cot today.

Bill invited Ben to The Sun to see Sally, the new shapely barmaid. Bill must do his research. Ben came home from The Sun feeling hot and bothered.

Saturday 27th

Brushed my teeth with a new toothbrush this morning; it felt more like a yard broom in my mouth. Had a good look at my teeth, wished I hadn't. Must go to the dentist. Don't want to go to the dentist. Must go on a diet. Don't want to go on a diet.

Sat on the loo and read the wrapping on an unopened packet of loo roll made from 100 percent recycled waste paper. 'During recy-cling, the paper is bleached without chlorine or chlorine containing compounds. Toxic chemicals can be produced as a by-product of con-ventional bleaching. There are two hundred and eighty sheets per roll, total area fourteen point one metres squared' – big enough for a giant's bum.

I'm learning so much. My head is full of interesting facts. Lucky me. Soon I will be well enough to give dinner parties and entertain my guests with my new-found knowledge. I'll serve up super salads, using herbs and nuts creatively, seeds and avocado pear, and lots of vitamin-rich red pepper of course. I will look sophisticated in unbleached cotton tops from a favourite catalogue and keep everyone amused with my sparkling spumanté wit. I'll have lots of energy to wash up, using my Down To Earth washing-up liquid. It says on the bottle that it respects the environment; if a little bottle of liquid without a brain can do it...

Drew a butterfly.

Sunday 28th

Exciting morning.

Ben bought three pots of enamel paint yesterday so I painted a big daisy in yellow and red. I cleaned up the mess I made using kitchen roll with a jolly green leaf pattern and Mary said her first word (mum, in cat language).

Stressful afternoon.

Mum and Dad dropped in on their way to visit Gina. They gave me a big box of Celebrations, sweet of them, but I wondered what we were celebrating – *There's nothing wrong with me? I'm just putting it on?* As usual, Dad said how well I looked and asked what I'd been up to, and had I thought of doing 'this and that' to help myself. Mum, as usual, sat quietly on the verge of a breakdown, her mouth twisted in bitterness, eyes devoid of life, after their ten-millionth row.

I offered everyone a chocolate with their cup of tea, but they didn't want one. Shame! After reading all the ingredients I should be avoiding, I ate a miniature Mars, Galaxy and two Milky Ways.

Pleasant evening.

I've always needed a drink after a visit from my parents and tonight was no exception: medicinal wine of course. Ben cooked dinner with lots of garlic and we watched a comedy film, *The Money Pit,* starring Tom Hanks – bloomin' hilarious. I don't know how I'd survive in this world if there were no comedy.

Ate three Bounty bars and dreamed of paradise. Eating chocolate on the left side of my mouth is painful; this is encouraging me to go to the dentist, not to give up chocolate.

Stormy night.

Thunder rumbled: God driving a lorry full of souls over bumpy clouds on their way to Heaven. Lightning cracked: God pulling another cracker with Mother Nature. Lightning flashed: God taking a photo of Mother Nature looking her worst, just to annoy her!

Monday 29th

10.00 a.m. Remember Eileen is at Edinburgh Festival.

10.01 a.m. Miserable. Want to be at Edinburgh Festival too.

10.02 a.m. Eat three miniature chocolates – two Bountys and a Galaxy.

10.30 a.m. Brush teeth with miniature yard broom. Consider ringing dentist.

10.31 a.m. Bad mood.

10.33 a.m. Eat Topic, Milky Way, Galaxy and a Snickers bar.

11.00 a.m. Stare out of window. Spot a blue and a purple umbrella (old habits die hard). Summer nearly over. Sad.

11.05 a.m. Munch two Mars bars, two Galaxy Caramels, a Bounty and three Malteser Teasers.

12.31 p.m. Read tragic story in *Weekly Wife*. Cry a bit.

12.33 p.m. Devour Bounty, two Mars, two Topics, three Milky Ways, a Galaxy and two Malteser Teasers.

12.35 p.m. *...Morag finished her box of Celebrations and felt much better. She hadn't been prepared for her reaction when she set eyes on Stephen at the clinic; she could tell by his face that he remembered her and everything that had happened twenty years ago. With serious eyes, he simply said, 'I'm sorry.' The young girl in her wanted to scream out, 'Sorry, sorry? You will be sorry! I will make you sorry!' then beat him with her blue and purple umbrella. But he looked so terribly tired and world-weary and in pain she just said in her white coat voice, 'Where does it hurt?'*
She treated him in silence and he left in silence. Morag had terrible nightmares that night; her parents were drowning in aromatherapy oil and she was leaning over the side of a boat with holes in it, trying to save them. She awoke to the powerful smell of essential oil of lavender; one of her cats had knocked the bottle over and the top had come off. Morag used this essential oil on her patients sometimes; it helped them to relax. She thought of one patient she would like to make relax so much that he never woke up again and knew what she had to do, apart from eating more chocolate.

6.00 p.m. Paint one small leaf.

Tuesday 30th

A postcard greeted me this morning: a photo of footprints in the sand.

We arrived Sunday and have switched off our systems already. Sitting in the village pub contemplating the menu and our navels in equal measure (menu vastly more interesting). Visiting friends for dinner tomorrow. One of their cats is expecting kittens even as I write, so they may arrive by way of cabaret between the main course and the pudding and I shall try very hard not to lay claim to all of them and end up overrun! (Escher would not be amused I'm sure...) Have been riding Beardsly along the Cornish beaches in the early morning. Hope all's well with you.

Love, Gail and Gareth xx

A gardening catalogue arrived; I wished Ben would mow the lawn.

THE RESTAURANT

Men dig into
Their steaks
Using their forks
Like rakes
Women with
Perfect hair
Sit and quietly
Stare

Wishing the men would put as much
effort into the gardening

Women pick onions
Out of their salad
And slice to the beat
Of a sixties ballad

Men with grey
And balding heads
Think of sheds
And flower beds

**Wishing the women would put as much
effort into the weeding.**

Painted a bumble bee.

Wednesday 31st

Painted two small daisies, resting every four petals.

The old couple next door (Max's grandparents) have a nice neat garden with a square of perfect lawn. A gnome in a blue hat sings to his audience of pink and purple faces. It's a very hot afternoon; the audience wilts. The other old couple at No.5 (big disapproving flowery dress and Sidney) have a perfect garden too, with a rectangle of neatly trimmed lawn. A chorus line of pansies smiles and dances to a light breeze of a melody; roses nod to the rhythm, blushing and looking romantic; there isn't a weedy soul in sight. At intervals, old men bring out refreshments in green watering cans.

The kittens like to play (and do their business) in the neighbours' gardens. Today, Paddy and Murphy galloped into the kitchen with spiky wet fur... *and it hasn't rained for days...* Murphy's black tail looked like a giant's mascara brush and Paddy looked as if he'd been combing gel through his fur. Mary sat in the kitchen waiting, looking up at me like a hopeful fan at the stage door, autograph book in hand.

All the world's a stage and some of us are not happy with the part we have been given to play. I'm sick of the same old show, day after day, week after week, month after month, year after year. Someone should have a word with the producer. And the food, well, someone should have a word with the caterer. Then there's the props: the scenery is falling down around our ears. Someone should have a word with someone. But not me.

September

Thursday 1st

Chewing-gum-grey clouds were stuck to the underside of God's desk in the sky as I stared out of the window with that dull, back-to-school feeling. Spotted three black umbrellas.

Eight months. I'm still alive after eight months of struggle. I will celebrate with a box of After Eight mints on Monday. Mmm. Good idea.

Friday 2nd

Weekly Wife says green and grey are the most popular school uniform colours and parents are spending a fortune on P.E. kit. At least I don't have to worry about *that sort of thing* with my three hairy children.

Read all about homework blues, great ideas for packed lunches, uniform solutions and stemming the tide of first-day tears. I can still remember my first day at school, and still picture the large, wooden, brightly coloured Magic Roundabout; I'd never seen anything so wonderfully fantastic. Mum was soon forgotten.

Ben had the day off work today. Bill came round and they hurried off to catch the 12.35 to Victoria; there was an exhibition at the Tate gallery, 'Breasts through the Ages'. I could say here that they had a coffee at Café C Cup, but they didn't; they had a Double D and a cheese salad roll at The Slug & Lettuce, followed by a cold shower. It rained on them. Ha! Ha!

Painted half a butterfly and three small leaves.

Saturday 3rd

Woke up worried after a nightmare night. I was standing looking up at a white sky with thin blue lines running across it, like the blank pages of a school exercise book, when words started to appear but I couldn't make out what they meant. My old school, Westlands, materialised in front of me: tired teachers staring with melancholy out of the windows. There was a sudden clap of thunder! Sharp pencils and paper darts began to rain out of the sky. They struck the school roof and smashed through the windows. My religious knowledge teacher was crucified to the notice board, the P.E. teacher harpooned to the floor of the gym. Blood everywhere. My art and English teachers escaped on the back of a spotted-dick dinosaur who waded through a custard lake, followed by children in navy blue uniforms who walked in line and turned into dark green crocodiles that swam in the thick, bright yellow custard. The rural science teacher dug a hole and hid under the turnips. The history and geography teachers sailed away on the *Encyclopaedia Britannica,* in a deep, inky-blue sea. My maths, chemistry and physics teachers clambered into a silvery spaceship, made in the chemistry lab from paper clips and set squares. They flew to a protractor moon. My art teacher threw ring doughnuts to the cookery and needlework teachers drowning in the custard; the biology teacher found he had frog's legs and leapt into the school pond. I sailed away on a magic carpet of music manuscript with my music teacher, who was playing Bach's *Toccata and Fugue in D* on his huge, shiny organ.

Ben bought *The Sun* newspaper today. Apparently Bill told him it had a really good special offer; I couldn't find it. Georgie told me she used to work for *The Sun;* that explains *a lot.*

We enjoyed a few treats from the health shop: veggie-pie and pasties with wholemeal buttery pastry. Is Ben trying to butter me up? Delyth's having a birthday party on the seventeenth. So, she's a Virgo is she, like rampant Rose and man-mad-Melanie from British Gas. Ben said I was invited too; she knows I won't come!

Must ring the dentist, but I'm worried about what he will say about my dirty teeth. I will blame the stains on peppermint tea: it stains our mugs; they look like the inside of a lock when the water has drained out, because I only have the energy to rinse them and Ben doesn't wash up very often. I use my favourite *Friends* mug all the time these days (to save washing-up). It really does look like the inside of a lock today, all dark greeny-brown with tide marks.

Brushed my teeth three times. Completed other half of butterfly.

Sunday 4th

The breeze whispered of autumn days and the cold virus. It laughed at the fence because it was a pushover, the long grass nodded in agreement. The kittens played in the grass: they looked like little tigers in a jungle, my pride and joy. I hope there will be tigers and lions left in the jungle when Matthew is a grown-up.

Read about how to achieve a whiter, brighter smile with natural remedies. Gargling with tea-tree essential oil diluted with water helps to fight bacteria and freshen breath. Chewing parsley, watercress or mint leaves, or rubbing sage leaves over teeth and gums, helps to keep breath fresh too (must remember not to eat garlic the night before dentist). Rubbing the peel of a lemon or fresh strawberries over teeth helps remove stains (must put strawberries on list). Protein is essential for healthy teeth and gums (must drink more soya milk).

Painted a bumble bee, one small leaf and half a butterfly. Fancied lots of garlic with dinner.

Monday 5th

Wendy says, 'Wear a thick chocolate-brown coat this autumn with chocolate buttons on.' I'd rather wear thick chocolate round my mouth, thanks, Wendy.

Bought a birthday card for Rose at the mini-market before my appointment this afternoon. Thought about Rose: she has wonderful olive skin with dark brown eyes and hair, so her teeth seem to glow. Everything about me is pale; life is not fair.

While choosing the card, and annoying the assistant by opening all the musical ones (and humming along to the tunes), a box of After Eight mints fell off a shelf into my basket; it couldn't have been stacked very well. I must have brushed passed it and not noticed, what with my tired blurry vision and everything. A box of *real* tea and a small stapler fell into the basket too! I don't need a stapler, but it was in the shape of a shark and I was amused that staples came out where the teeth would be.

Sat clicking my little blue shark while I waited to see Eileen and realised I should have bought some staples too: a shark isn't a shark without his pointy teeth. Recalled a boyfriend taking me to see *Jaws* when I was a teenager; can't remember his name. We ate vanilla ice-cream in a tub with a red strawberry swirl during a nasty, bloody bit in the film; I love *plain* ice-cream now. No ripple.

Struggled to remove sad shark thoughts from my mind; a couple of After Eight mints helped. I offered one to Eileen and she said she shouldn't really, so I reminded her that sugar may cause tooth decay, but chocolate is made up of elements that obstruct the formulation of plaque, so they effectively neutralise any cavity-causing potential in sugar. She said in that case she'd have another couple. We had a good moan about dentists and fillings and exchanged horror stories, and Eileen said she must make an appointment for a check up soon. Noticed her teeth looked a little Golden Virginia stained.

Mr. Cheerful-chatty-taxi-man had a broad smile and good teeth; he reminded me of the Joker in *Batman*. We laughed all the way home after he told me a brilliant joke, so I gave him three After Eights with a fifty pence tip.

I've been doing some people-watching on my journeys home lately.

PEOPLE-WATCHING POEM

A woman all dressed
In brown
With a bag and a fag
And a frown
Stood outside Boots
With a mate
And a man
At his garden gate
Sat with a rug
On his knees and
He talked to the birds
In the trees
And an old woman
Started to sneeze
As her wee scabby dog
Scratched his fleas
And a boy on a skateboard
Whizzed by
As a little girl
Started to cry
When two men in
Bright turbans and jackets
Left the corner shop
Carrying packets
Of crisps as large
As a mag
And the woman all dressed
In brown
Was looking them up
And then down
With her bag and her fag
And a frown.

Have been doing a bit of animal-watching too. Saw a cow standing in the middle of a field surrounded by sheep and was reminded of a photo in *Weekly Wife* of a female pop star surrounded by her entourage.

Cow in a field
Surrounded
By sheep
Worried men
Hover round
Little blonde-peep.

Tuesday 6th

10.25 a.m. Turn on TV. The Teletubbies are having a big hug.

10.26 a.m. I could do with a big hug.

10.27 a.m. Cuddle Paddy and nibble After Eight mint.

10.28 a.m. Toothache.

10.29 a.m. Must ring dentist.

10.30 a.m. Amazing how appealing the washing-up seems when you're avoiding making a phone call.

10.31 a.m. Must fill kittens' water bowl.

10.32 a.m. And refill water filter.

10.33 a.m. Sew on that button.

10.45 a.m. Think I'll make another cup of tea – real tea, to perk my brain up so I can concentrate on phone call.

10.59 a.m. Brush teeth.

11.00 a.m. Inspect teeth – ugh.

11.01 a.m. Stare in mirror with Emily-Bishop-concerned expression.

11.02 a.m. Really must ring dentist.

11.04 a.m. Will sew this button on first.

11.07 a.m. Search for card with dentist's number on.

11.09 a.m. Can't find it. Will look later; need to put washing in machine.

11.10 a.m. Must write that letter. Need a clear mind if I'm going to concentrate on phone call.

11.11 a.m. Need to wash and dress too.

11.12 a.m. And find pen that works.

11.30 a.m. Soak in de-stress geranium and mandarin bath.

11.33 a.m. Enjoy looking at crystals, especially new one – amethyst, in shades of the palest mauve to deep purple.

11.35 a.m. Am so relaxed, phone call will only make me all tense – maybe tomorrow.

11.40 a.m. Sniff seaweed soap and mentally dive into deep blue waters among tropical fish.

11.45 a.m.	Think about sharks. I like sharks, but I'm not sure I'd want to be face to face with one in the ocean.
12.45 p.m.	Bit of a tidy up.
12.46 p.m.	Find card with dentist's number on. As I'm standing by the phone I may as well get it over with. Right now. This minute. I can always cancel if I'm not up to it.
12.49 p.m.	Oh God, I've done it now. Next Monday is torture day.
12.50 p.m.	I've changed my mind, I'm going to ring back and cancel straight away. The stress of all that drilling will make me doubly fatigued. I could be bedridden for months and months.
12.51 p.m.	Haven't been to dentist since I became ill; don't know how it will affect me. Very scared, don't think my neck is up to it.
12.52 p.m.	Dentist's number engaged.
1.00 p.m.	Dentist's number still engaged.
1.05 p.m.	Pick up phone. Put down phone, must be brave.
1.06 p.m.	Anyway, don't want to be toothless to match long, straggly, greying hair, pointy nose and pale wrinkly face. Am witchy enough.
1.07 p.m.	Twenty seconds of pagan aerobics.
1.10 p.m.	Cover girl on *Weekly Wife* is smiling at me with sparkly, white, even teeth.
1.11 p.m.	Give her a black tooth and spot on the end of her nose, straggly hair and a witch's pointy hat.
1.12 p.m.	Feel better.
1.15 p.m.	Look under **R** in spell book for painless removal of teeth so one no longer has to visit the dentist. Find uses for rosemary, rowan, rue, and a brew to remove warts, ring-worm, roundworm, ~~rhinoceros~~ rhinitis and keep you regular.
1.20 p.m.	Drink calcium to make teeth brave and strong for Monday and crunch toast on non-achy side of mouth.
1.23 p.m.	Stare at crumbs on plate.
1.24 p.m.	Pick up crumbs by pressing finger on each one separately. One for sorrow, two for joy, three for a filling, four for an extraction...
1.30 p.m.	Granny next door is reading to Max in the garden. 'But Granny, what great big ears you've got. And the wolf said,

'The better to hear you with, my child.' Red Riding Hood began to grow more scared than she had ever been in all her life, and her voice trembled when she said, 'Oh Granny, what great big teeth you've got!'

1.31 p.m.   Crumb stuck in tooth; might go and brush teeth again. No. Gums feel sore.

1.45 p.m.   Read TV mag. Famous vet Trude Mostue likes men with nice teeth; wonder if she likes bright eyes, lots of whiskers and a shiny coat too.

2.12 p.m.   Sit clicking toothless shark stapler.

2.23 p.m.   On toilet, thinking...

Dear God,
Teeth aren't a very good creation, not your
best idea. Can I have strong pointy gums in
my next life please. Thanks.
Love, Miss V. Worried xx

2.26 p.m.   Perch on side of bath and recall once, when I was trying to explain to a doctor how exhausted I felt, I mentioned I didn't even have the energy to brush my teeth. He asked if my boyfriend brushed them for me and laughed.

2.28 p.m.   Stand in front of mirror. Sure teeth are more crooked than they used to be. Floss front teeth; 95 percent of dental disease begins between the teeth.

2.29 p.m.   Dentists recommend we brush our pearly whites for two minutes twice a day; the average person spends only thirty seconds a day. I bet the average M.E. sufferer feels delighted when they can manage it for fifteen seconds, once a day. And brush their teeth.

2.30 p.m.   My dental appointment is at 2.45 p.m. next Monday so I will book a taxi for 2.30 p.m. – tooth hurtee, ha, ha.

2.31 p.m.   Perch on bath again. My super Oral-B electric toothbrush by Braun is sitting smugly in its holder on the wall, new and clean as the day I bought it. Unfortunately, the vibration against my teeth makes me feel ill; that's twenty pounds spat down the sink with Sensodyne toothpaste. I could have bought lots of chocolate or a groovy little top in this season's floral print.

2.32 p.m.	Need someone to brush my teeth for me. The wealthy ancient Romans had special slaves to clean theirs, and experiments with toothpaste included grinding up bits of old brick and china, with terrible results – how horrible.
2.33 p.m.	Thank God for Sensodyne.
2.41 p.m.	Gaze out of bedroom window, like large, ginger Tom watching every Dick and Harry.
2.42 p.m.	Two big, jolly-looking middle-aged women are squeezed into the front seat of a Mini, chatting and laughing. The back seat is piled up with pink toilet rolls. Maybe they're happy because they're always on the go.
2.44 p.m.	Low on loo roll; must put new one out.
2.46 p.m.	Put out new loo roll.
2.47 p.m.	Sit on loo.
2.48 p.m.	Hope the taxi-man who takes me to the dentist doesn't smoke. I hate it when I have to go for any treatment stinking of tobacco when I've gone to a lot of pain and trouble to wash my hair and bathe and squirt myself with a pretty smell and wear clean clothes with a light fragrance of fabric conditioner.
2.49 p.m.	Think I'd better warn my teeth they're going to see Mr. Dentist soon. It's best to tell the whole tooth and nothing but the tooth.
2.50 p.m.	I'll be seeing a Mr. Faüel; I hope he's OK. I wonder what nationality he is with a surname like that; hope he's not German: they used to torture prisoners of war in a dentist's chair.
2.54 p.m.	Lie on sofa staring at CD collection. Think I'll listen to Bach to help me stay calm and peaceful.
2.55 p.m.	The two rows of CDs look like a mouth full of long thin teeth, with gaps in.
3.00 p.m.	File nails on left hand and push back cuticles.
3.02 p.m.	Nails look same shape as teeth now.
3.09 p.m.	Read about the healing properties of amethyst, a member of the quartz family of crystals. Until recent times, it was considered a precious and rare gem, used in the rings of kings and bishops and in the necklaces of queens. During the Middle Ages, it was more expensive than diamonds!

3.15 p.m.   Read letter from Ben's mum again...

... I've just been in the garden for a while, sitting on a low stool picking bits of bark off the gravel and throwing them back on to the flower bed. The practice of spreading pieces of bark on the beds does indeed deter the weeds, but it is an awful nuisance if it gets on the gravel. It is OK on concrete paths, of course, because you can sweep it up.

Last week, a stopping came out of a back molar, so I have a dental appointment this coming Thursday. My lady dentist is always very booked up, so I accepted this offer, but I was really meaning to go to Chatham that day. It is two months since I last went so I need to go – I must choose a different day, but can't decide which! No doubt shortly the spirit will move me and I shall set about making a shopping list.

3.16 p.m.   Wonder when they stopped calling fillings stoppings.

3.17 p.m.   Mary is curled up sleeping on my lap, paws, ears and whiskers twitching.

The smallest feline is a masterpiece
– Leonardo da Vinci

3.20 p.m.   I lightly touch her grey coat, like an artist delicately stroking a canvas.

3.21 p.m.   The room is calm and whiskerful.

3.32 p.m.   A car alarm goes off outside.

3.33 p.m.   Mary is yawning a huge cat yawn, her tiny teeth white and shiny. Must look out for signs of gingivitis when she's older.

3.46 p.m.   The model on the cover of last week's *Weekly Wife* is smiling *without* showing her teeth: a sort of 'I know *I'm beautiful"* smile. I expect she hasn't had time to have her tartar build-up removed, or a good polish, because she's too busy polishing her nails on flights between Paris and Milan. Probably hasn't had time to floss at night either: too busy partying or shagging a pop star.

4.30 p.m.   Watch fly on wall.

4.31 p.m.   Fly has flown into window and bumped his nose.

4.33 p.m.	The walls in our house could do with a splash of colour. Instead of white with a hint of sadness, cream with a hint of loneliness and toothache grey, I fancy blue with a hint of calmness, green with a hint of peacefulness and lovely lilac.
4.42 p.m.	Paint half a butterfly on Daisy's cot.
5.26 p.m.	Watch Mr. Boxer-face taking his antique coffee table for walkies.
5.27 p.m.	Really must remember not to eat garlic the night before dentist; don't want dog's breath.
5.28 p.m.	Feel sorry for dentists who have to treat patients with bad breath, body odour or dirty hair.
5.48 p.m.	A hearse drives slowly past the house.
5.49 p.m.	Where will I be when I die?
5.50 p.m.	Will I die in my sleep?
5.51 p.m.	Under a bus?
5.52 p.m.	Crushed in a crash on my way to see Eileen in Mr. Ex-racing-driver-taxi-man's car?
5.53 p.m.	Next week?
5.54 p.m.	Next year?
5.55 p.m.	When I'm sixty-four?
5.56 p.m.	How will I cope with false teeth?
6.00 p.m.	Murphy is lying on my chest rubbing his fang against my cheek; he's got beautiful kitten breath.
7.20 p.m.	Catch end of holiday programme. The Chalk Stacks, Studland, in Dorset, look just like giant teeth sticking out of the sea: one pointy shark's tooth, one human incisor.
7.40 p.m.	*EastEnders.* Actors and actresses all have sparkling celebrity choppers, ready to show off at the TV awards.
8.10 p.m.	Dinner. Vege-sausages and mash very tasty but sweetcorn niblets look like bright yellow extracted teeth.
9.00 p.m.	Thriller: *Appointment for a Killing.* Markie Post stars as a woman who suspects her dentist husband, Corbin Bernsen, may have murdered some of his unsuspecting patients.
9.06 p.m.	Ben crosses out the word killing in TV mag and replaces it with filling.
9.07 p.m.	Thanks, Ben!

Wednesday 7th

Paddy and Murphy have been sitting either side of the bird feeder with their mouths open; I'll have to stop feeding the birdies. Practised holding my mouth open for next Monday.

The model on the fashion pages of *Weekly Wife* smiled her 'I've never had a toothache' smile. I avoided reading 'My Dentist Put Me Through Agony' by dreary looking Deirdrie from Doncaster and gave the fashion page girl a green tooth. Natural Dentistry looked interesting; about non-mercuric fillings, non-adrenalin anaesthetics and homeopathy instead of antibiotics for all but the most severe infections. Mercury (from leaking fillings) released into the body can cause general ill health; adrenalin from anaesthetics stresses the heart and antibiotics can alter the whole bacterial balance of the body. Think I'll have white fillings from now on (even though they're costly) and request non-adrenalin anaesthetics.

Painted a daisy and three leaves.

Thursday 8th

Today, the clouds reminded me of the office where I used to work: cold, depressing, filing cabinet grey. I shivered at the memory of cold, depressing winter days spent drawing endless gas mains or peering into muddy trenches to measure the distance of a length of 63mm pipeline from the kerb.

Two little girls pranced happily down the street practising their dance steps, reminding me of art deco sculptures by Ferdinand Preiss. I want to be six again.
The rain danced on the lawn; it couldn't resist the groovy beat on the dustbin lid. Leaves clapped. The garden was showered with compliments, and it wasn't long before the newspaper on the kitchen floor was covered in soggy wet paw prints.

W. M. Friend (Gabriel) came round looking like a heavenly angel in his white jeans and shirt; it wasn't long before he had interesting paw patterns on his lap. He said something very un-Christian.

I noticed his teeth were yellow and black (instead of heavenly white) with a bit of cabbage on them.

Painted a bumble bee and three leaves.

Friday 9th

The sky was dark: mercury filling grey. The rain drilled into the lawn. Leaves trembled with pre-dentist nerves.

I completed the cot with two butterflies and a daisy and took a photo of my masterpiece. Rang Gina later, leaving a message on her answering machine letting her know she could collect the cot when she liked.

Ben came home soaked from The Frozen Crown, Porcé Lane.

Saturday 10th

Mother Nature tied her pinny round her waist and pulled back her long hair with a pink rose patterned scrunchie. She found her biggest paintbrush and dipped it in cobalt blue mixed with a little porcelain white. When the blue was dry, she would brush an egg-yolk-yellow blob in the middle of the large canvas.

Gina called round to collect the cot. She managed to pull her face into a half smile, so she must have been simply delighted with my wonderful creation. I hoped Poppy would show a little more joy and appreciation. Gina didn't want to disturb Matthew, sleeping like a baby in the back seat of the car, so I gazed at him through the rear window, longing to hold his warm little body and feel his soft skin.

Ben did healthy food and pet shop shopping; we are feeding the kittens Hills Science Plan diet crunchies now; it will be good for their teeth.

Watched an episode of *Only Fools and Horses* entitled 'Fatal Extraction'.

Sunday 11th

Woke up early after a ~~tortoise~~ ~~tortuous~~ torturous night, lost in the labyrinthine aisles of a huge chocolate factory. I couldn't eat any chocolates because my teeth were falling out; I held my hands over my mouth but teeth kept slipping out between my fingers. The chocolates on the conveyer belt had a molar for decoration and gallons of milk poured out from enormous nipples on massive, matronly, metallic breasts; Bill operated the machinery. W. M. Friend (in his very white heavenly overalls) poured sinister sparkly sugar out of a silver chalice.

All the chocolates melted and I started to drown in a swirly sea of Cadbury browns. I called out to W. M. Friend to help me but he dropped a large, heavy Bible on my head and I woke up.

Cosmic Colin said life is sweet and my dreams will come true; I hope not.

Worrying about tomorrow made me more exhausted and headachy than I've felt for weeks, and the thought of getting up to put the kettle on seemed like a trek around twenty shops to find comfortable, fashionable shoes when you're a size three.

Me:	My mouth is like the Waza Plain in Cameroon.
Ben:	Whyzat?
Me:	It's one of the driest places on earth.
Ben:	Oh.
Me:	I'm like the animals who gather round the empty watering holes in the dry season.
Ben:	Are you?
Me:	Yes, they wait patiently for a much needed drink.
Ben:	Nngh.
Me:	Of water.
Ben:	A coral formation, five letters.
Me:	Haven't a clue but I do know coral lives in the sea where there's *lots* of water.
Ben:	Edible part of a nut, six letters.
Me:	Kernel.
Ben:	Carve from stone, six letters.
Me:	The brain is 85 percent water, so it needs lots of *water* to make it function properly.
Ben:	Ngh.
Me:	So it can solve crosswords for its boyfriend.
Ben:	I know this! It's on the tip of my tongue!
Me:	If you had a drink, you'd lubricate the cogs of your brain straightaway.
Ben:	What *is* it?
Me:	I've got it.
Ben:	Yeah?
Me:	To form the word with my tongue, I need a lovely warm beverage.

Ben:	Oh, go on, what is it?
Me:	Not tellin'.
Ben:	Oouh, pleeze...
Me:	Alll right, I'll give you a clue. What did Michelangelo do?
Ben:	Chipped away bits of stone.
Me:	Yeahsss, what was he?
Ben:	An artist.
Me:	And...
Ben:	Sculptor... sculpt! Great! All I need now is twenty-one down, twenty-nine across and thirty-six across. Three letters: that must be 'o-n-e'. So a coral formation is 'a-t-o-l' something.
Me:	All I can think of is 'reef'. And the sea. And a lovely cup of tea.
Ben:	Twenty-one down. A-something, C-something, E-something – one with a bow and arrow.
Me:	Archer.
Ben:	Drink noisily; twenty-nine across, six letters, could be slurped, but that's seven letters and slurp is five.
Me:	I'll put the kettle on and we might get it.
Ben:	Good idea!

Monday 12th

9.00 a.m.   Wake up with headache. In my dreams, an evil dentist had been drilling through my ears all night in order to reach my back teeth and fill them with tarmac. British Gas came along and dug the fillings out again, leaving gaping holes full of wet agony.

Workmen are drilling outside this morning, why today?! *WHY!*

10.00 a.m.   Head under pillow. Like a little dormouse, I want to stay curled up in my soft warm nest. Don't want to be dragged through the dentist's spiky hedge.

10.30 a.m.   Five small cartons of longlife fruit juice with straws sit in fridge, like row of very neat Donny Osmond teeth.

11.00 a.m.   Book taxi for 2.30 p.m. Tell man where I'm going and he laughs his head off, 'Ha, ha, ha, tooth hurty, ha, ha, ha.' I'm unable to join in.

11.30 a.m.   Flower pots on window sill of house opposite look like row of old man's lower teeth with gaps in between. One pot has

	been knocked over and needs re-filling.
12.00 noon	Have bath, hair wash and brush teeth for two minutes.
12.30 p.m.	Want to be an anteater: they have no teeth.
1.00 p.m.	Too tired to go to dentist's now. Feel awful.
1.30 p.m.	Not worried at all. Feel fine. Calm and peaceful. In good humour. Ha, ha, ha. I'm telling myself jokes. An extractor fan is someone who loves their dentist after removing a painful tooth. Ha, ha, ha. Or they could have once loved tractors, but changed their mind after one ran over their foot and broke three toes – an ex-tractor fan. Ha, ha, ha. Oh God.
2.00 p.m.	Better get dressed, I suppose; taxi here soon.
2.30 p.m.	It's two thirty! Tooth hurtee, ha, bloody, ha. Where's the taxi? Where is he? Oh, hell, Mr. Miserable-as-sin is going to be late again, I just know it... Oh God... Oh good, hope he doesn't turn up... sitting around at home suddenly seems very desirable... I love it... I really do... I can watch a comedy video... Victoria Wood or maybe French and Saunders... those two white video cases look like a beaver's front teeth... wish I were a beaver building a beautiful big dam right now... oh damn... think that's the taxi arriving now...
3.00 p.m.	Open wide... arhgh!... oh od!... ahhhhhhhh!

Tuesday 13th

It's over. It's over. I've done it! I've done it! I'm so brave and wonderful! My jaw really hurts. I don't care; the world is a brighter place. Eat your hearts out *Weekly Wife* cover girls; I have a brilliant sparkly smile and two neat fillings. I deserve lots of chocolate, a chocolate bravery award, a sack full of Celebrations!!!

Wednesday 14th

> *As imperceptibly as grief*
> *the summer lapsed away...*
> – Emily Dickinson

A cold wind whistled through the cat flap and round my ankles while I sipped my morning herbs. It ran up the stairs and hid under the bed covers for warmth. Autumn begins on the 22nd of this month. Today, the wind changed its mind and decided it was best to make an early start, avoid the traffic, and make a speedy journey across the country. The trees didn't agree and held on to their be-leafs.

Eileen tied the strings back onto my wooden limbs and I told her all about the dear old widow I met at the dentist's, Ruth. She took her false teeth out (Ruth not Eileen) and showed me her lovely smooth gums; she said her sister's gums were all bumpy and for a moment I thought she was going to ask me to touch hers. I was interested to hear how she had met her husband after the war; their story sounded *so* romantic. He had to have all his twenty-six teeth removed when he came out of the army because his gums were black with quinine disease, but he was very handsome when he had his teeth in! I felt very sad when she talked about nursing him before he died of cancer. She said she was slim then from running up and down the stairs and rubbed her arthritic knee. I laughed when she mentioned the years when they lived with her parents; at bedtime there would be four sets of dentures sitting in glasses side by side on the bathroom shelf – wonder if they ever got mixed up.

Thursday 15th

Found a collection of various herb teas I'd forgotten about in the back of the kitchen cupboard and smelt each one in turn. Sweet... sickly... interesting... wet grass... earthy... stinky... aniseed... an old wardrobe. Unscrewed the top on Ben's coffee jar and had good long sniffffffff... what a beeeaaautiful aroma! I had to be strong, so I made myself a weak Earl Grey tea.

Someone once said that women are like tea bags – they don't know how strong they are until they are in hot water. Great saying. Wendy says you shouldn't discard white bras that have turned grey, but soak them in tea overnight; they will change colour to cream. How lovely. I suppose you're a bit stuck if you've only got Earl Grey. Wonder if raspberry tea creates a soft shade of pink, sort of pinky-grey like the feathers on a wood pigeon, or clouds at sunset. Maybe I've found a use for those out of date herb teas!

Ben and I had a bit of a disagreement tonight; quite a big argument really; a huge row actually. In fact, I felt well enough and angry enough to smash his computer screen with a hammer and wrap the flex of his computer mouse round his neck tightly – very, very tightly.

But, of course, I walked away as I'm a calm and peaceful, creative person now. I sipped camomile, thought about tea bags and women and hot water, and decided men were like bin liners: it's often difficult to get them to open up and when they do, you discover at the end of the day they are full of rubbish and you want to dump them. I picked up my pen and let the anger flow freely. Men are like a basin full of washing-up: when they find themselves in hot water, there's usually a scrubber involved somewhere and all the dirt comes out eventually. Men are like crockery: when they are smashed they are useless. Men are like doors: one bang, then you're shut out. Men are like cats: after walking all over you they expect love and attention in return. Men are like clothes: they look good at first, you think you're well suited, then the excuses begin to wear thin and you feel frayed at the edges. Men are like lights: they like to go out and leave you in the dark. Men are like ironing boards: if you put them up for the night, they'll never do your ironing in the morning.

Had a rest, hung my knickers on a radiator. Men are like radiators: keep you lovely and warm in the winter, but when they are cold, they become ugly and boring. Men are like fashionable knickers: they can be very attractive to look at but after a while they're a pain in the bum. Men are like exercise bikes: they look good in the bedroom, you get lots of exercise at first, then after a while they just get in the way. Men can be like sandwich toasters: they seem like a good idea at first, till the novelty wears off and you can't be bothered with them anymore.

After dinner, all my anger released, I continued – men can be like baked potatoes: tough on the outside but all fluffy on the inside and easily buttered up. Men are like pizza: when they're cut up they can still look attractive and you want to eat them all up. After my bath – men can be like a long, hot, scented bath: they can make you feel good all over.

Men are like handbags: just what you need when you go out as long as they don't get too heavy, and there's lots of colours available.

Friday 16th

W. M. Friend sent us a postcard from India; he's met a wonderful guru and has so much to tell us when he gets home. Oh dear! I wonder if he's enjoying the tea out there.

Ben went to Polly's Poppadoms with Bill to celebrate something. I can't remember what; the visit to the dentist has shaken up my brain and crossed my eyeballs.

This morning, I picked up my Body Shop mascara and read the side of the tube: fibre-free, smudge and tear resistant, contains chicken to lengthen – *chicken!* Re-read the tube: thicken and strengthen. Oh.

Read Linda's letters page. She's the beauty expert who answers all your questions.

Question: I'm getting married to an octopus. Can you recommend a mascara that will lengthen my lashes but not attract black sharks when I start sweating.

Answer: Go for a waterside massacre, then cover up. Avoid lying in ashes.

Uncrossed my eyes.

Question: I'm getting married in Cyprus. Can you recommend a mascara that will lengthen my lashes but not leave unattractive black marks when I start sweating.

Answer: Go for a waterproof mascara by Covergirl. Avoid applying to lower lashes.

Saturday 17th

7.20 p.m.   Ben has gone to Delyth's birthday party.

7.29 p.m.   I've invited the dwarves round.

7.34 p.m.   Dwarves excitedly lay Monopoly board on the sitting room carpet.

7.35 p.m.   Happy arranges the Community Chest and Chance cards in their places, Sneezy sneezes and blows them all over the board and Grumpy grumbles that the game could take hours.

7.36 p.m.   Bashful carefully places the dice in the middle of the board then runs off embarrassed, Dopey wants to know where all the little red and green houses go, and Sleepy admires the colours on the property cards.

7.37 p.m.   Doc and I are going to play the game while the others watch.

7.38 p.m.	I choose the little dog as my token to move around the board and Doc picks the boot.
7.40 p.m.	Doc gives me two £10 notes, one £5, five £1s, one £20, one £50, four £100s and two £500s.
7.41 p.m.	He picks up the dice, throws an eleven, then trots round the board to place his boot on Pall Mall. I roll the dice: nine dots face upwards and my little dog runs along to Pentonville Road.
7.42 p.m.	Doc's boot has landed on Vine Street and he decides to buy it for £200. I throw a four, land on Whitehall and can't decide whether to buy it or not. Happy says I should; it's a lovely pink flower colour. Bashful agrees and turns the same shade of pink.
7.43 p.m.	The boot is sitting on Leicester Square.
Happy:	Are you going to buy it?
Doc:	Not sure.
Bashful:	Lovely daffodilly colour.
Grumpy:	If you don't buy it she will.
7.44 p.m.	My dog is sitting on Trafalgar Square wagging his tail. I decide to buy it for £240.
Happy:	Good move, girl.
7.45 p.m.	Doc is buying Oxford Street for £300.
Grumpy:	Get the full set and stick houses on as soon as you can.
7.46 p.m.	My dog is sniffing about on Community Chest. I pick up the card and find I have won second prize in a beauty contest and will collect £10; feel quite pleased with myself. Happy claps, 'You deserve it.' Bashful nods and hides his beard. Grumpy says, 'It's only a game.'
7.47 p.m.	Doc's boot is stamping along to Mayfair; he's going to buy it for £400.
Grumpy:	Make sure you land on Park Lane, buy it, and stick a hotel on as soon as possible.
7.48 p.m.	My dog is sitting on Income Tax with his tail between his legs; I have to pay £200.
Happy:	Oh deary me.
Grumpy:	She's going to lose, I know it.

	Sneezy sneezes again and blows my money across the board.
7.49 p.m.	Doc throws a three, lands on Chance, passes Go and collects £200, picks up a Chance card and advances to Go where he collects *another* £200. The dwarves cheer, Sleepy opens one eye and Grumpy folds his arms smugly.
7.54 p.m.	Dwarves are groaning; Doc has just picked up

COMMUNITY CHEST.

GO TO JAIL
MOVE DIRECTLY TO JAIL
DO NOT PASS GO
DO NOT COLLECT £200

7.55 p.m.	Happy is trying to explain the rules to Dopey, who removes his hat and scratches his head. 'She has bought Bow Street and Fleet Street and Doc has purchased Oxford Street. All she needs is The Strand.'
Bashful:	Then a big red hotel!
8.05 p.m.	Doc is pleased with himself; he's bought Park Lane, six houses, passed Go, collected £200 and inherited £100.

8.06 p.m.	
Grumpy:	Wait till she lands on Mayfair or Park Lane; she'll lose everything, mark my words!
8.15 p.m.	My dog is standing on The Strand wagging his tail. I've bought four little green houses, placed them on Trafalgar Square, Fleet Street, Bow Street and Vine Street (I swapped it for Bond Street with Doc). Happy cheers, pats my hand and my little dog.
8.16 p.m.	I bet Ben isn't having so much fun at the party. Hope he's not taking a Chance with Delyth or one of her mates. If he is, I'll send him to Coventry Street, I won't let him pass Go or collect £200.

8.23 p.m.	Have just landed on Mayfair and paid Doc my last two £100 notes. My sad collection of fives, ones, twenties and tens look pitiful.
8.24 p.m.	The room is silent.
8.35 p.m.	There's a small sound of seven little intakes of breath; I've landed on Bond Street with one house and then picked a card telling me to go to jail, move directly to jail... at least I've avoided landing on Mayfair and Park Lane.
9.00 p.m.	Grumpy looks grim. Doc has landed on Trafalgar Square with a hotel and had to give me £1,100, which meant selling his houses on Mayfair and Park Lane, Oxford Street and Bond Street.
9.05 p.m.	Doc's boot has landed on Fleet Street with four houses and can't afford to pay me, so I've won!
9.06 p.m.	Feel a bit guilty but Doc is smiling and the dwarves are cheering.
9.07 p.m.	Grumpy grumbles into his beard, 'Sonlyabloodygame.'

Sunday 18th

Admiral Nelson is standing on his column shouting orders at the battleships on the seas of Trafalgar Square. I'm bobbing about on the waves in a giant, silver top hat, clutching my little dog and get-out-of-jail-free card. Suddenly a large wave picks us up and we're tossed into a dark, green, watery world. Down. Down. Deep. Freezing. Frightening. Next thing I know, we're whizzing along Oxford Street in a racing car, Mr. Ex-racing-driver-taxi-man is at the wheel, grinning with sparkly teeth. The dwarves are digging up the road and we stop to ask them the way; they tell us to advance to Go and collect 200 puddings. It's impossible to fit all the puddings into the boot (tied to the racing car) so I eat them and feed the crumbs to my dog. We grow big. So big and tall, we're face to face with Nelson who is very angry: nobody's listening to his orders, his boots are set in concrete and the pigeons use him as a toilet. He clonks me on the head with his eyeglass and I run away, still holding on tightly to my dog and get-out-of-jail-free card. Riot police chase me shouting, 'Go to jail, move directly to jail, do not collect 200 puddings.' My get-out-of-jail-free card is only the size of a postage stamp now and no longer valid, so I keep running.

And running. Past Piccadilly, full of yellow daffodils, Vine Street, where oranges hang from vines growing in green houses and along a dark purple lane, Park Lane. I hide in a bright, red, plastic hotel but the police find me so I grab my dog, escaping down a drainpipe; I know I'm dicing with death. The world turns black and all I can see is a luminous Monopoly board, the size of a tennis court. I pick up luminous dice and throw a seven, the dice turn into sugar lumps and fall off the board, plop, into a tea cup where dolphins swim wearing grey bras. My dog runs onto Chance. A figure wearing a black robe and holding a scythe waits in the corner, on Free Parking. I pick up a Chance card and luckily, I've won second prize in a beauty contest, the world turns pink and I'm holding a golden crown on my head. My fluffy, white, candy floss dress grows around me like a cloud and I have difficulty breathing. I wake up, my head under a pillow.

Bill came round for a game of chess with Ben but they played Monopoly instead. I went directly to my bath and did not collect 200 pizzas. When I emerged from the bathroom, Bill was creeping up the stairs in a Bill-ish way, my towel slipped a bit and I'm sure he saw my nipples! I didn't know Bill's eyebrows could lift up to the top of his forehead.

Lay on the bed and tried not to hear the sounds of Bill on the toilet. I've just remembered what Bill was celebrating on Friday: the sale of three paintings (Natasha's nipple, Natasha's birthday suit and Natasha back to nature) to a dirty old millionaire.

Monday 19th

Bill and Ben have rediscovered the joy of Monopoly. The kittens have discovered the exciting red and white box with the top left off containing lots of miniature toys to play with. I've discovered the dice, top hat, battleship and boot are missing; and probably the odd house or hotel, I've never counted them.

Another couple of Christmas catalogues full of wonderful cards and gifts shot through the letter box and nearly knocked Paddy out; they have been arriving since June! I don't want to think about Christmas until December, but I do like leafing through them, so of course, by the end of the summer, I'm nearly all decided about what to order. I mustn't let on to anyone about this; they'll think it's all I have to look forward to in life. It is at the moment but I don't want anyone to know that.

The first thing I saw when I opened one of the catalogues was a
singing toothbrush for children; the bear-shaped handle sings, 'I'm
your friendly brushy brush.' I could have done with one of those a few
weeks ago to cheer me up. Paddy wanted a cuddle after his letter box
fright. He eyed the catalogues suspiciously, then curled up on my lap
covering my black clothes in ginger fur; now I have gingervitus.

KITTENS

Paddy is the soppy one
Mary says, 'Please stroke my tum'
Murphy is a lovely snogger
Now my pen's run out oh..!

I'M

I'm a pen
With no ink
I'm a kitchen
Without a sink
I'm a kite
Without a breeze
I'm a runner
With no knees
I'm a pond
No water in it
A top with
Noone to spin it
A puppet
With no strings
I'm a bird
That never sings

I'm a drummer
With no sticks
I'm a die
Without a six

I'm a cake
Without a mix
A Magician
Without his tricks
I'm a dog
Without a bone
I'm a house
That's not a home
I'm a door
That never closes
Something's eaten
All my roses

Eileen and I discussed the problems of what to buy family and friends for Christmas; I said I'd bring one of my Christmas catalogues to the clinic next week. I asked her if she would model for Bill's next sculpture, as she'd done that sort of thing before. She said she would be happy to. Bill will be ecstatic; Eileen is very curvaceous. He has been inspired to create a sculpture of a mermaid by our reproduction of 'The Mermaid' by John William Waterhouse. I thought he might have been inspired by the sight of me emerging from the bathroom with my green towel slipping down revealingly. Ben said that was just wishful thinking.

Browsed through the Christmas catalogues again. Rose and Gail have mentioned starflower oil in their letters so maybe Rose would like the starflower filigree jewellery, starflower gift set or starflower tea towel. Gail might like the grow-your-own starflower kit, starflower thimble or diary and address book. Another name for starflower is Star of Bethlehem... Mmmm... they'll make perfect little Christmas gifts.

Ben emerged from the bathroom after his bath all pink and flaky skinned. He lay naked on the bed staring up at the ceiling, muttering computerish. I commented that *echinacea,* or purple flower cone, is a herb native to midwestern North America. It's name is derived from the Greek *Echinas* – the word for sea urchin which refers to the prickly scales of the dried seed head portion of the flower. He fell asleep as I spoke. Another name for starflower is Sleepy Dick.

Tuesday 20th

The sun was hot today for the time of year, but it won't be long before the leaves are turning paprika red and mustard yellow and Ben will be wanting to tickle his taste buds at Polly's Poppadoms every Saturday night.

Finally, the kitten care book arrived from Whisker and Tail. The kittens said, 'It's a bit late now, Mum, we're teenagers.' They answer me back all the time, waste their pocket money on scratch cards, I never know where they are, their eating habits are appalling and I let them walk all over me, treating me like a doormat.

This afternoon, Squeeze sang 'Cool for Cats' on the radio. Mary tapped her paw, moved her head from side to side and said, 'Seventies music is cool, Mum; do you remember the olden days when Tom Jones sang, "What's New Pussycat"?'

Paddy and Murphy watched cops and robbers in a car chase on Channel Four. One policeman said to the other, over his walkie talkie, 'OK Nick, keep close; we've got a tail and we don't want to lose it!' Paddy and Murphy turned to each other and nodded.

Early this evening I heard a familiar loud squawking sound. I hurried outside as fast as I could to watch the silhouettes of Canada geese flying over our house, heading south for the winter, necks outstretched; I wanted to fly with them. When I looked down on the lawn, I spotted a pair of dice like two giant white square ladybirds. I picked them up as Mary ran across next door's muddy garden to escape two large black Toms. She's having a lot of trouble with black heads and clogged paws lately; not easy being a teenager.

The dwarves sat on the fence, cloud-watching and counting geese. Happy pulled the petals off a daisy, 'She loves me, she loves me a lot, she loves me, she loves me a lot!'

Wednesday 21st

Dreamt of silhouettes of birds circling outside the windows all night and awoke feeling as if I'd been watching an Alfred Hitchcock film. Consulted my dream book: birds in flight signify a desire to escape some present situation and also an intense idealism. An eagle often reflects a concern with matters spiritual and the ancient Greeks believed that different kinds of birds symbolised kinds of people: eagles were rulers; wild pigeons were immoral women. The Hebrews believed birds were good omens. Good.

Ben rang Bill to let him know Eileen will model for his new sculpture and gave him her phone number. In my mind's eye, I visualised Bill grinning like a lizard with a full tummy. He's started making a pond, the breast fountain sits in the middle, nipple skywards. The mermaid sculpture will sit in the corner, combing her long hair. Ben said Bill's wire bra sculpture is hanging from the ceiling in the kitchen; he puts all his eggs in one cup, bananas in the other. The wire vegetable rack (in the shape of a pair of knickers) holds a shrivelled up onion and sprouting potato. Ben was too scared to look in the fridge.

He took a photo of Murphy curled up asleep in our vegetable rack and one of me searching for little green houses under the sofa; I found two houses and a hotel. I took a photo of Paddy trying to climb into the fridge, and Mary drinking from the dripping tap that was on Ben's 'Things To Do' list.

Thursday 22nd

SNAIL

I've counted the drips
From the tap
And followed the snail's
Road map

He hasn't got very far
Like me

PEA – BUG

Little bug
Rolled up like a pea
To protect yourself
From the likes of me
Your suit of armour
A perfect shell
May I borrow it please
Until I'm well

Friday 23rd

Bill and Ben met Rob and Bob the Slob at The Fisherman's Armpit, Sniffit Street. They didn't stay long: the place got up their nose, and anyway, they wanted to see Stephen playing drums with the Nice Girls, who were supporting David Blosse and The Hurlimann Band at The Drum and Drunk-It. By the end of the evening, Rob was chatting up Tarty Trish, Bob was slobbering over Pouting Pauline and Bill was sitting on Big Brenda's lap. Ben said the Nice Girls were nice and friendly; he didn't say *how* nice or *how* friendly.

Ben and Bill brought home chips. I had a bath with essential oil of lavender to relax me and mask the alluring chippy smell. It didn't work. The tiny chippy molecules knocked out the delicate lavender molecules and ran cheering up my nostrils like a winning football team.

Saturday 24th

A letter arrived from Rose thanking me for her birthday card and telling me all her news: she'd met a man on holiday, fallen madly in love, but he hasn't written and she can't stop thinking about him. Her eldest tripped over a rock on the beach and ended up in hospital, her youngest nearly drowned, she suffered terrible sunburn and peeled like a tomato in boiling water. There's been another row with ex-mother-in-law number three, ex-husband number one wants his kids for Christmas, Chastity has too many boyfriends, Honesty is telling lies and having tantrums, ex-husband number two is also having tantrums so she's changed her phone number again; she's on another diet and it's not working and she thinks she may be pregnant *again!*

My life always feels especially calm and peaceful when I hear from Rose.

After several pints at The Slurp and Swallowit, Ben and Bill lurched off to Polly's Poppadoms, Pickle Street.

Sunday 25th

Bill came round for another thrilling game of Monopoly.

I curled up with the kittens and this week's copy of *Weekly Wife* in front of the TV. Wendy informed me: 'Fashion has never been so affordable and so much fun. Snugglesoft textures and cosy knits are just some of the exciting new looks to look forward to'. Meridian were advertising kitchen roll: kittensoft, with thirst pockets. I don't need the new style kitchen roll or fun fashions: the kittens are my snuggle soft textures and cosy little thirst pockets.

Watched a ladybird crawl down the outside of the window as I wallowed in a warm, scented bath; she looked like a black raindrop. I thought about black rain and pollution and started to write some seriously depressing verse in my head, but stopped myself. Calm and peaceful people write about sparkly rainbow raindrops. Calm and peaceful pagan aerobic dancers think of colourful rainbow crystals and modern witches practise their spelling.

Ben found a miniature top hat in his jacket ~~potato~~ pocket.

Monday 26th

Eileen had a quick look through the Christmas catalogues while I undressed for my treatment. She was tempted by the twenty personalised Christmas cards (foil embossed with your message) the luxury crackers, luxury metallic gift wrap, Scottish shortbread and giant tin of Quality Street. No wonder osteopaths have to charge so much.

Eileen said Bill had rung her to arrange a sitting for the mermaid sculpture next Saturday, now all she needs is a wonder grow-fast shampoo (she won't be needing her Wonderbra) so she can look more mermaid-ish. Eileen likes swimming and she is a pisces; that's a start.

We talked about mermaid ~~tails~~ tales from the West Country, ice-cream, sunbathing, skin cancer, smugglers' caves and the reproduction posters you see on the walls of The Ship, advertising the cargo from shipwrecks.

If Bill needs a model for a wreck, I'll apply.

Found a battleship in the kittens' water bowl.

Tuesday 27th

A Help the Aged catalogue arrived today. Dad is calling in on his way to a Masonic meeting on Thursday, so I'll ask him if he wants to order anything. There's quite a few things in it I fancy for myself: a chair lift, tap turners, neck and back supports, feet and hand warmers. The Christmas cards look good too, especially the set of large square cards with a colourful Christmas pudding on. Why am I always thinking about food?

Think I'll order the Christmas pudding wrapping paper and cards. Turning taps and climbing the stairs is easier these days and my circulation is improving so I'll try not to be too tempted by all the helpful gadgets. How do old people manage? I will be much more understanding of their problems when I'm well; I may apply to be a care assistant in the future. Rose used to work in an old folks' home and had a few stories to tell. Recall stories... maybe I'll care for old animals instead.

Wednesday 28th

Lay on the sofa with a rug over my legs trying to remember what day it was. When I finally worked out it was Wednesday, I shuffled out to the kitchen, trod on a small green house then muttered to myself as I made peppermint tea to ease my indigestion. I limped back to the sofa, settling down to read more of my Help the Aged catalogue. The electronic flea comb and deceptor flea trap looked tempting. Tucked my rug in; scratched a bit and sipped herbs. Talked to myself. Talked to the kittens and told them we are going to try a flea contraceptive in their food called Program. Then I mentioned the birds and bees. The kittens said, 'We already know, birds sing, bees sting, birds are prey and bees you pray don't sting you.' They think they know it all at their age.

Thursday 29th

POEM ABOUT A DRAGON

I saw a little dragon
Sitting in my chair
He smoked all my fags
After only three drags
Then he coughed
And he frizzled my hair

Ben is trying to give up smoking: he wants to live into old age. *Weekly Wife* informs me that scientists from the University of Michigan have discovered many common vegetables contain traces of nicotine. Ben is now eating more potatoes, tomatoes and cauliflower.

Harry from Help the Aged says: 'This Christmas, treat your friends to a triple chocolate gift pack. Dark chocolate and raisin with Lamb's Navy Rum, double chocolate cream cake with cream liqueur and double chocolate blueberry pecan cake with whisky.' Harry also says, 'Chocolate lovers won't be able to resist Chocoholics Delight: a gift box containing drinking chocolate, chocolate spread, chocolate truffles and a plain chocolate bar.' Reading about heaven is hell.

POEM ABOUT CHOCOLATE

Reading about heaven
Is pure hell
Heaven is praline
The shape of a shell
Hell is a box
With one choccy crumb
Heaven is Cadburys
In my tum

Dad called in and I showed him the catalogue. When he saw it was for Help the Aged he looked offended; he retires soon. I'm always putting my foot in it.

Friday 30th

Ben had a few too many at The Dog and Turd, Squelch Street. As he crawled up the stairs, he spotted a tiny boot and asked me if I'd invited those pixies round again.

October

Saturday 1st

Nine months. I've completed three years and nine whole months of my prison sentence! Or is it four years and nine months?

> **Rain lashes my bars**
> **Wet wintry whips**
> **Thunder rumbles**
> **Lightning flashes**
> **Cold cracked lips**
>
> **There's no escape**
> **There's no escape**
> **Because of the size**
> **Of my hips**
>
> **It's all my fault**
> **It's all my fault**
> **For eating all**
> **Those chips**

Must lose some weight so I feel more energetic. Must think positive, getting-better thoughts all the time and look forward to Christmas with Ben and my three hairy children; it'll be their first Christmas.

Desperately fancied chips today: big, fat, juicy, greasy rectangles of starchy pleasure drenched in salt and vinegar. But I was strong; I listened to my body. It told me I needed chips but crisps would be just as tasty and comforting. So I asked Ben to bring home five packets of healthy crisps from Holland & Barrett. I'm now a born again Crispian.

Sunday 2nd

Rain sprinkled down on the garden like a slimmer adding just a tiny pinch of salt to her tomatoes so she doesn't retain too much water. The sky rumbled like a model's stomach that's survived all day on Diet Coke and is looking forward to a slice of Ryvita topped with a dessert-spoonful of low fat cottage cheese, garnished with two wafer thin slices of cucumber.

Next week's *Weekly Wife* will tell me how to lose seven pounds by changing my posture, wearing the right clothes and changing my hairstyle. Can't wait. I crunched spring onion flavoured organic crisps and enjoyed Dear Suzie: 'I want him – not a ring on my finger', 'He wants to move his lover in', 'We can't stop having rows', and 'My internet obsession's wrecking our marriage'.

As a born again Crispian, I think I'll enjoy crisps every weekend. Religiously. I suppose I should go to the corner shop every Sunday and sing my praises to Golden Wonder now. Chips are sinful, food of the Devil.

One of my Christmas catalogues is advertising 'Sin Soap': *'Guaranteed to wash away sins, even deadly ones; just rinse and repent. Whatever you've been up to, you'll come up smelling of frankincense, nutmeg and ginger. Family-sized bar, for sinners of all ages.'* Must order one.

Bill came round smiling devilishly; his mermaid sculpture must be going well.

Monday 3rd

A freezing wind flew in through the cat flap, grabbing my ankles with its sharp beak and claws. I pulled my dressing gown tighter round my waist, picked up a Kit-Kat mug full of steaming camomile tea and warmed my hands. I breathed in deeply. I listened to my body; it told me to turn the heating up. If I were a Siberian white fox, I would be happy in temperatures as low as minus seventy centigrade, without a sniffle or a shiver. Wish I could grow a lovely, thick, white coat for the winter. Mmmm... thinking about foxes and the cold makes me fancy a Fox's Glacier Mint.

Wore a jumper and T-shirt under my sweatshirt ready to brave the ~~elephants~~ elements tonight. Eileen and I talked about the weather, Scotland, bed socks, mountains, deer and snow. She returned my Christmas catalogues with a neatly written list of cards, wrapping paper and gifts. She smiled a lot, and mentioned the mermaid sculpture was taking shape, although she'd forgotten how difficult it is to stay sitting in the same pose for more than twenty minutes.

After my treatment and everything, I stood outside waiting for the taxi. Late again. I shivered and felt like a piece of old furniture: I'd just had a nice rub down and needed two coats.

Tuesday 4th

Read an interesting article in the medical update section of *Weekly Wife*. If the cold virus were three inches long, your nose would be the size of Wales!

Sat for ages staring out of the window, sniffing a bit and enduring paranoid thoughts... the world is full of viruses and bacteria and moulds, and they're waiting outside the house to get me. Millions of them are already hiding in the house, watching and waiting for an opportunity to jump down my throat or get up my nose (like some people I used to work with). Ben must bring thousands home from his workplace. I expect they sit in the fibres of his clothes and swing from the hairs of his skin ready to pounce on me. I'm so glad I'm taking high-potency bee propolis (antiviral, antibiotic, antifungal and anti-inflammatory) and garlic capsules (antibacterial, antifungal, antiviral and anti-cancer) every day. Outwardly, I'm calm and peaceful; inwardly I'm fighting a microscopic war, my thoughts trying not to be beaten by the enemy. I must call up more positive troops. I need a poster on my wall of a man pointing his finger at me, 'YOUR BODY NEEDS YOU!'

Wednesday 5th

A Christmas catalogue from the R.N.L.I. arrived. I was tempted by the sensational sailing sweatshirt. It looked thick and warm with a beautiful boat motif on the front. The super seaside socks with shells and fishes on a blue and jade background looked a fun present for my sister. The Cardigan Bay sweater in natural seashore colours with a dolphin and seagull design looked a fun present for me (if I could afford it). I think I'll order the enviromentally friendly coastal stationary. I need incentive to continue to write to my pen-pals. The seaside picture takes up a third of the page, so if I use up another third writing my address, the date, dear whoever and love with lots of kisses in a thick italic pen, I'll only have to write two sentences.

Lay on the sofa with the kittens and tried to think of calm and peaceful waters but rain splashed the windows and all I could think about was people trying to save lives at sea and how awful it must be to drown. I wish I hadn't read the rescue quotes on almost every page of the catalogue.

Rescue quote 1899
'After many dangerous attempts, succeeded eventually in saving one and all of us from a watery grave.'

Rescue quote 1988
'You can imagine my relief when the lifeboat arrived and hauled me to safety. Of course, we all think it will never happen to us.'

Rescue quote 1989
'When the lifeboat came, I was begging for life. It seemed as though we were in the water forever.'

I just *know* I will have nightmares tonight.

Thursday 6th

Cosmic Colin: 'If you're feeling all at sea, don't worry, this is just temporary. See it as a breathing space while your vitality is low.'

Felt a bit in the depths after spending half the night drowning in the ocean. I needed a bit of a lift, so I sniffed Ben's Original Blend, medium-roasted, ground coffee (smooth and well rounded like me), put on my uplifting bra, washed my dirty hair and curled it, using cheap eco-friendly hair curlers for big ~~girls~~ curls (toilet roll tubes). Sat in the bath. Didn't want to lie down with my head just above the water; I'd only feel in the depths again.

Gave the bathroom a little bit of a clean, here and there. Dusted some bottles within arm's reach of the toilet while I sat on it. Cleaned the toilet (because Ben never does it) and poured lots of germ killer down before the germs jumped up and bit my bum. The bath and sink will have to wait.

I'm taking extra garlic and bee propolis.

Friday 7th

I was amazed: I still had a bit of energy today and wasn't too achy. I should have rested but my mind was still in restless waters. Sorted out a few old clothes I've kept for years and years and will never wear again. There may be old deadly germs germinating in them, growing slowly over the years. You never know. Big, brown, monster germs, like the huge brown fleas on the kittens when they first arrived at our house.

Held up a shrunken black jumper to Paddy and said, 'To bin or not to bin, *that* is the question.' He played with a loose thread, then curled up on a baggy blue jumper and fell asleep; a lot of help he was. Started sneezing. Murphy and Mary looked startled. Wore myself out shoving this year's copies of *Weekly Wife* into carrier bags; the dust between the pages must have been full of paper bugs. Couldn't stop sneezing. I needed... a tissue!!... a tissue!!... a tissue!!!

Bill and Ben met Bob the Slob at The Fang and Bite It, Garlic Road. Bob spent most of the evening with Virginal Vanessa giving her love bites in a dark corner, Bill fondled his beer glass caressing the curvy bits looking creatively thoughtful and Ben talked to Vanessa's best friend, Sad Susan. He brought me home a packet of garlic-flavoured crisps. Very tasty.

Saturday 8th

Weighed down with carrier bags full of old clothes and magazines for the R.S.P.C.A. charity shop, Ben took his hangover into town. Felt *very* tired. But after sitting staring at a blank, dusty telly, I felt a desperate need to head for the duster. Comforted myself with crisps... crunch... crunch... crunch... Becoming a born again Crispian has given me the wonderful opportunity to try new and exciting flavours. Jordans make crisps called oven crisp chips. They are unlike conventional fried pota-to chips, have more crunch but are 85% fat free, with natural seasonings, no artificial flavours, colours or preservatives! Today I enjoyed sour cream and chives flavour. Delicious. Tomorrow I will sample sun-dried tomato and herb. I think I'll save the Pom-bear (teddy-shaped potato snack, gluten free and no artificial flavouring) crisps for when I'm watching the teddy cartoon in the week; if I'm up early, I may endure the Teletubbies. There's Jumpy's too, the kangaroo-shaped potato snack; they will crunch along nicely with *Neighbours* – it's quite good at the moment.

Sydney Benson's Organic Potato Crisps, made from organically grown, quality potatoes and cooked in organic oil with natural seasonings, look inviting. Think I'll save them for when I'm watching

EastEnders on Monday; that's good at the moment too. *Coro* is a bit boring, but I'll watch it. You never know, Deirdre might smile, Audrey might show a bit of tact, Gail might be written out, with any luck.

My life has so much more meaning now I'm a Crispian. Praise the Spud. I must obey the Ten Crispy Commandments.

The Ten Crispy Commandments

1. Before opening packet, read ingredients and give thanks to the Spud, for He is good.
2. If packet is difficult to open, ask for help from thy partner or thy neighbour. Consume, especially when in need of comfort and assurance that there is only one big Spud Almighty in this earth.
3. Best consumed with a fizzy drink or alcohol and good entertaining TV programme.
4. Never eat in bed, or during sex; this can put thy partner off, even if it turns you on.
5. Never eat fish or animal flavour or boast that you have a superior flavour to thy neighbour. Never covet thy neighbour's crisps, even if they're eating cheese and onion, your favourite.
6. Eat one at a time and savour, giving thanks that thy taste buds are in good working order. Suck if you want to prolong the pleasure.
7. Be generous. Offer a crisp to your partner before you try one yourself, but never more than two: there may only be seven big ones in the packet. Never steal his crisps; wait for him to offer.
8. Do not let thy partner sit on thy crisp packet; they are more fun when you can pull them out of the packet whole...
9. Give praise to Golden Wonder on Sundays, kneel outside the corner shop for five minutes. Mr. Patel might feel sorry for you and give you a box of his out of date stock.
10. Dispose of wrapper thoughtfully or if you particularly like the design of the packet, pop it in a clip frame and hang it on the kitchen wall.

Sunday 9th

When I asked Ben if he would hoover all the carpets in the house, he looked at me as if I were an alien. So I told him (in my best Martian voice) I came from the planet Vacuumalot, where men are exterminated if they fail to keep their homes dust free. He laughed and said in that case he might do it later. I said he must do it 'now!', because if orders are not obeyed right away on planet Vacuumalot the women drug their men and cut off little important parts of their anatomy while they are sleeping... and, even worse, they are banned from the crater houses, where they love to consume crates of purple beer and green crisps.

The bars are kept very clean because the locals polish off the evening with cock-tails, ha, ha.

The depression in the carpets has lifted.

Monday 10th

I was thinking it's *that* time of the year already, as I watched tiny brown helicopters flying across the lawn. The day looked cold and bright and clean, and dust free. Mother Nature is very house-proud.

It felt good to leave the house, breathe in the fresh air, close the front door and climb into a taxi; but Mr. Cheerful-chatty-taxi-man had a cold and I felt trapped in a cab-sule full of germs. I nearly climbed out again, and asked him if he would kindly stop breathing. He said, 'All right ven love but you'll 'ave to drive y'self up the massage parlour.' So I told him he could breathe if he kept his germs to himself and reminded him I was going to an osteopathy parlour! Covered my nose and said an antiviral prayer.

Eileen wore her hair up with a seahorse hair slide. I also noticed tiny delicate mother of pearl earrings (in the shape of seashells) and pearly varnish to match on her nails. She said she is sitting for Bill's sculpture in the same pose as the Little Mermaid in Copenhagen and it's all going *very* well, apart from his studio being a bit chilly and she thinks she's starting a cold. We discussed natural remedies to boost the immune system and help prevent colds: echinacea, green tea, garlic, bee propolis, shiitake mushrooms and honey.

Must lend her my Help the Aged and R.N.L.I. Christmas catalogues; she may be interested in the Ocean Mist toiletries, seahorse and dolphin jewellery, or the Sensational Ocean Cardigan to keep her warm in Bill's studio.

Eileen is smiling a lot.

Wonder if the mermaid sculpture will have goose bumps.

Tuesday 11th

Didn't feel like smiling today. Curled up in bed with monthly cramps and read the ABC of health in *Weekly Wife*. This week: M for menorrhagia, mammography and malignant. Couldn't miss the huge photograph of an orange and purple malignant cancer cell that looked like a poisonous sea creature and can be fatal. Or the enlarged electron micrograph of listeria that causes flu-like symptoms, brain inflammation, paralysis and foetal deaths during pregnancy. It was next to an advert for Parozone, a bleach that fights germs' breeding grounds. Last week's ad showed an enlarged picture of salmonella that usually causes severe food poisoning; complications can be fatal and include blood poisoning, heart problems and meningitis.

I tried to stay calm and peaceful but failed when I picked up a can of flea spray and read the instructions; a picture of a monster blood-sucking flea grinned at me, waving its ectoparasitic legs.

Wednesday 12th

After a restless night scratching and dreaming of hungry bed bugs, I dragged myself out of bed and shuffled to the kitchen to make breakfast. Later I studied the crumb-covered plate. With bleary eyes, I scrutinised my fingerprint, a tiny maze for minute germs to run around in; they must be all over the door handles and the kettle and everything. Must change the sheets but I feel so tired.

Thursday 13th

Wendy says: 'Warm up to sweater dresses; they're cosy, comfy and easy to wear!' Why didn't she just say, 'Good to wear when you want to disguise your big bum, boobs and lack of waist, under the heading, "Cover up those winter wobbles".'

Wendy also says: 'Bits of food in your mouth allow bugs to ferment and while you sleep, your mouth is teeming with bacteria.' Must brush teeth every night.

Wendy goes on a bit: 'If you buy clothes or shoes from charity shops, you are at risk of catching impetigo, verrucas or athlete's foot; and if you travel on public transport and touch door handles, then bite your nails, you'll have stomach problems.'

Wendy depresses me: 'You're at risk of getting scabies from the itch-mite if you don't wash your sheets regularly; it burrows under your skin and lays eggs.' Oh dear.

Ben sat on the edge of the bed practising his bass guitar tonight. I joined in the rhythm with different plastic tubs of supplements; we sounded quite good! Ben suggested when I'm better, we could go on tour calling ourselves The Supplements. I suggested he wash the sheets before we packed the tour bus.

> **Shake rattle 'n roll**
> **With all your heart and soul**
> **Rock to the rhythm**
> **And dig it like a mole**

Friday 14th

Wore my favourite big baggy jumper today: it's cream with brown flecks, my Horlicks jumper. Wendy would call it oatmeal, or this season's chunky natural look with rib-knit neck, cuffs and bottom. During winter, I hibernate inside it.

Ben went to see a jazz band tonight with Bill and Rob. Ben wore his jazzy jumper, Bill wore the same jumper he wears all winter with paint splashes on, and Rob modelled his wife's latest creation, red and blue guitars on a black background. Rick was drumming with the band; he has split up with Natasha, so Bill is talking to him again.

Ben:	How do you know there's a drummer at the door?
Me:	Don't know; how do you know there's a drummer at the door?
Ben:	He doesn't know when to come in!
7.15 p.m.	'Walt Disney Presents' pops up on the screen. The dwarves shuffle into a semicircle on the carpet in front of the TV, their eyes lit-up with excitement. *Peter Pan!* Hoorah!
7.16 p.m.	Dwarves hum along to dreamy music and sing, swaying from side to side. Except Grumpy, who mutters to himself. Dopey's hat falls over his eyes.
7.22 p.m.	Wendy's father is annoyed with her for telling her brothers stories about Peter Pan. He tells her mother it's about time Wendy had a room of her own; she is growing up. He tells Wendy it's her last night in the nursery and banishes Nana,

the nursemaid dog, to the garden. The dwarves look sad.

Grumpy: That's what happens when you tell silly stories.

7.23 p.m. Wendy says she doesn't want to grow up.

Happy: Nor do I.

Grumpy: You succeeded then.

7.25 p.m. Peter Pan appears on the roof of their house with Tinker Bell, while Wendy, Peter and John sleep in the nursery. He is searching for his shadow.

Sleepy: I expect he's going to wake them up now, and they're sleeping so peacefully.

Grumpy: Completely thoughtless if you ask me.

Happy: We didn't!

7.27 p.m. Tinker Bell admires her figure in a hand mirror. Bashful blushes, Happy whistles, and even Grumpy's eyes light up (a little). Doc wipes his steamed-up glasses.

7.28 p.m. Wendy is chatting away to Peter Pan and sews his shadow on to his feet.

Happy: That's clever.

Grumpy: Girls talk too much.

Tinker Bell is trapped in a drawer and can't escape through the keyhole because her hips are too big.

Me: Know how she feels.

7.29 p.m. Wendy tells Peter she has to grow up tomorrow, so he tells her he's taking her to Never Land where you never have to grow up!

Wendy tries to kiss Peter. Tinker Bell is very jealous, escapes from the drawer and pulls her hair.

Grumpy: Women, huh, always jealous of other women.

Doc: Better than being grumpy all the time.

Sneezy: And sneezing all the time.

7.32 p.m. Peter Pan picks up Tinker Bell, taps her, and shakes pixie dust over the children so they can fly.

7.33 p.m. They all fly out of the window over London. Standing on the hands of Big Ben, Peter Pan points out the second star to the right; if they go straight on till morning, they will reach Never Land.

Sneezy:	Those children are going to catch their death, flying at night without coats on.
7.36 p.m.	The evil Captain Hook is pacing about on his pirate ship, full of revenge against Peter Pan who cut his hand off and threw it to a crocodile. Hook is terrified of the crocodile because it follows the ship, licking its chops for the rest of his body.
7.38 p.m.	A fat crocodile appears on the surface of the sea: ... tick... tock... tick... tock... tick... tock...
Happy:	Why's he making that noise?
Doc:	He swallowed an alarm clock!
7.40 p.m.	A pirate accidentally shaves the feathers off a seagull's bum and the dwarves fall about laughing. Grumpy manages half a smile.
7.41 p.m.	Peter Pan has been spotted off the starboard bow, flying with the children.
Doc:	Oh dear.
Sleepy:	Those children are losing their sleep.
Happy:	But it's an adventure!
7.42 p.m.	Captain Hook fires a cannon at them, just missing, so Peter Pan asks Tinker Bell to take Wendy and the boys to a safe place on the island.
7.43 p.m.	Tinker Bell tries to get Wendy killed.
Grumpy:	Women! Riddled with jealousy, the lot of 'em. They're all the same.
7.45 p.m.	Peter Pan saves Wendy and they meet the Lost Boys. Peter says he'll show Wendy the mermaids. John marches off with Peter and the Lost Boys to find Indians.
7.46 p.m.	Dwarves sing along: 'Following the leader, the leader, the leader...'
7.49 p.m.	They're captured by the Indians. John, Peter and the Lost Boys are tied up. The Indian chief wants to know where Princess Tiger Lily is; if she is not back by sunset, they will burn at the stake. Dopey covers his eyes.
Happy:	But they don't know where the princess is!
Doc:	I know.
Grumpy:	Serves 'em right. They should have stayed in bed.
Sleepy:	They'll be gettin' tired now.
Sneezy:	And cold.

Bashful:	Feeling foolish.
Happy:	Scared.
Doc:	Hungry!
7.51 p.m.	Wendy and Peter Pan watch the mermaids, who call to Peter and flirt with him, but are very jealous of Wendy.
Doc:	Don't say it Grumpy.
7.52 p.m.	Captain Hook has captured Princess Tiger Lily and is heading for Skull Rock in a rowing boat. He ties her up in the water and demands to know where Pan's hiding place is. Tiger Lily will not tell him.
Doc:	Good on you, Tiger!
7.57 p.m.	Pan and Hook are fighting.
Doc:	Go on Pete, get him!
7.58 p.m.	Hook is chased off into the sunset by the crocodile. Pan rescues Tiger Lily.
	Dwarves cheer.
8.00 p.m.	Hook has escaped from the crocodile and is sneezing with a heavy cold.
Sneezy:	Know how he feels.
8.03 p.m.	Hook finds out that Tinker Bell is jealous of Wendy. He says a jealous woman can be tricked into anything.
Doc:	(pointing at Grumpy) Don't!
8.05 p.m.	Dwarves sing along with the Indians, 'What makes a red man red...'
8.06 p.m.	Tinker Bell has been kidnapped and brought to Hook who tricks her into telling him where Pan hides by pretending he wants to capture Wendy.
Happy:	Hm, very sly.
Grumpy:	Yeah, but you know women.
8.08 p.m.	Dwarves tie Grumpy's beard around his mouth.
8.09 p.m.	Wendy is jealous of Tiger Lily. The dwarves look sideways at Grumpy.
8.11 p.m.	Wendy is singing.
	Bashful falls in love.
	Dopey looks dreamy.
8.14 p.m.	John, Wendy, Peter and the Lost Boys are captured by Hook and taken to his ship. Pan is alone in his hideout and Hook leaves him a parcel. Tinker Bell hears Hook telling

	everyone the parcel is a bomb, so she escapes to warn him and risks her life trying to save him.
8.20 p.m.	Peter Pan appears on the ship to rescue everyone and they all fight the pirates.
Doc:	Look out Peter!
Happy:	That got 'im!
Doc:	Quick, hurry!
Happy:	Behind you!
8.23 p.m.	Pan ties up Hook and makes him admit he's a cod fish. The children cheer. The dwarves cheer.
8.24 p.m.	The crocodile chases Hook off into the horizon. Dwarves laugh.
8.25 p.m.	Peter Pan sails the pirate ship up into the sky, bound for London. Dwarves clap and cheer.
8.26 p.m.	At 11 p.m., the children's parents return home; Wendy's father has decided she doesn't have to grow up yet.
8.28 p.m.	Wendy and her parents watch clouds shaped like a pirate ship sail across the moon. Lots of lovely dreamy music and singing. Dwarves sniff a little.
Sleepy:	Perhaps the children will get some sleep now.
Grumpy:	I doubt it.

Saturday 15th

Cosmic Colin:
'Jupiter and Neptune are at war so you don't stand a chance of getting a clear picture on which to make a decision. Avoid making choices until you can judge without doubt.'

Today the world outside was overcast and chilly; even the passing lorries were grumbling, sniffing and dragging their tyred feet. Ben felt under the weather so he didn't go shopping and we couldn't decide whether to have take-away Indian or pizza for dinner tonight. I avoided making the choice. Found bits of this and that in the freezer (eight sprouts, two handfuls of garden peas, a mugful of sweetcorn niblets, five forgotten vege-sausages and half a vege-roll), a sachet of instant mash behind the dried rice, a lonely tomato sitting next to the jar of French mustard and a few sad gravy granules. Delicious.

Sunday 16th

12.03 p.m. Ben is starting a cold.

12.04 p.m. Ben is fiddling with the video.

12.05 p.m. Ben is sneezing: *Ha... ha...*
Hitachi! Hitachi! Germs are flying out of his nose at one hundred miles an hour.

12.06 p.m. I'm hiding inside my Horlicks jumper with a scarf over my nose.

12.45 p.m. Hailstones on letter box sound like someone dropping frozen peas onto a baked bean tin.

1.00 p.m. I know! We'll have Heinz beans and chip shop chips for dinner.

1.01 p.m. I'm very decisive today; Jupiter and Neptune must have kissed and made up.

2.00 p.m. Must tell Ben the ten ways to cut down on bugs this winter.

The Ten Anti-Cold Bug Commandments.

1. Take lots of vitamin C.
2. Cut back on cigarettes; they lower immunity.
3. Liquid handwash is better than soap, which can act as a resting place for germs.
4. Clean under fingernails – a good place for germs to hide.
5. Wash hands frequently.
6. Wrap up warm and 'air' the house.
7. Blow nose regularly.
8. Each person in the house should use his or her own flannel and towel.
9. Use disposable tissues. Hankies contain twenty thousand viruses after one blow.
10. Wipe door knobs, tables, kitchen taps and telephones with diluted bleach.

Monday 17th

Ben rang work to say he was too ill to come in. He did a man-size sneeze down the phone followed by a man-size blow into his Kleenex; must clean phone. The kittens looked worried by the strange noises coming out of his nose; I didn't know cats could actually look worried.

Felt terribly tired all day after being chased up and down the Brecon Beacons by three-inch viruses all night. I tumbled off a cliff, down into the vitamin seas and the R.N.L.I. tried to rescue me, but my sensational sailing sweatshirt (with beautiful boat motif) weighed me down and dragged me under the waves. In a dark olive green world, a luminous blue mermaid appeared with long hair the colour of Red Leicester cheese and large eyes the colour of green peppers. She grabbed my arm, dragged me to safety and left me on a rock off the shore of Copenhagen. Red and blue guitars rained out of the sky, music filled the air, dolphins danced and fish sang, 'What shall we do with the drunken sailor'. Peter Pan sailed past on Captain Hook's pirate ship with Wendy, John and Peter; they were eating fish and chips and throwing fish batter to the crocodile following behind... tick... tock... tick... tock. Seagulls made out of Christmas wrapping paper squawked overhead and a fox stood on a glacier in the distance. I called to Peter Pan to take me back to London but he could not hear me: the air was full of the buzz of vitamin bees. A swarm chased me and I escaped only to be chased again by the dreaded cancer crabs and salmonella salmon. Luckily, they were gobbled up by parazone piranha, but the germ-ants captured me and announced they had ways of making me tell them the secret of the killer flea spray. I offered them cheese and onion *Golden Wonder* crisps and flew away with Tinker Bell while they were busy trying to open the packet.

Eileen has a cold too, so I didn't have to ~~endure~~ enjoy my weekly bone crunch. Crunched Banshee Bones instead (Irish crisps from O'Neills) while Pat and Frank had a row on *EastEnders*. Taped *Coronation Street* because Jeremy rang at 7.30 p.m. He's obviously not a fan. It should be written into the marriage vows,

'... *in sickness and in health, till death do us part, and never interrupt any part of your partner's favourite TV soaps, or ring anyone between 7.30 and 8.30 p.m. on a Monday and 7.30 p.m. the rest of the week in case their partners are soap fans.*'

Ben went to Mr. Patel's for bread, eggs, milk, tins of soup, crisps, a few frozen things, tissues and Lemsip. Later he watched a medical thriller, *Carriers*. A deadly virus was ripping through an American city and it fell to a couple of intrepid ~~alligators~~ investigators to trace the source to the African jungle. I went to bed.

Tuesday 18th

It rained bats and frogs. Leaves flew past the window. Raindrops hopped and jumped on the window ledge.

Ben didn't go into work again. Instead, he walked up to Bill's house to see the Eileen-shaped mermaid sculpture. He said it was very lifelike; *and* there were *two* toothbrushes, a new bar of blue ocean soap (instead of a tiny, dust-covered white lump), dolphin bath pearls *and* a can of sea-spray deodorant (definitely not Bill's) in the bathroom; and the toilet, bath and hand basin were clean!

Watched *Neighbours* while munching Golden Wonder cheese and onion crisps. I tasted the initial flavour hit (as instructed) then savoured the wonderful, smooth, balanced, flavour sensation. Later (in *The Rovers*) I experienced my first taste of Spicy Tomato Wheat Crunchies with a new fuller flavour while Ken Barlow aired his views about something or other and Mike Baldwin upset the girls in the factory again.

Ben watched *Outbreak*. A doctor and his estranged wife were racing to stop a deadly disease from becoming an epidemic. I like Dustin Hoffman and Donald Sutherland but I shuffled off to bed.

Wednesday 19th

Ben is back at work. I'm not sniffing yet, fingers and toes crossed. Felt a bit lonely but cheered up watching the kittens sleeping, stretching and yawning, they really know how to Y... A... W... N... well.

More Christmas catalogues arrived from the R.S.P.C.A., World Wildlife Fund and Windrush Mill. The kittens asked me if they could have a personalised pet towel and meal mat each, and feeding bowls with paw patterns on. Do they think I'm made of money? I am tempted to order nearly everything in the catalogues though; must get well so I can return to work to earn lots of money, then spend it!

Watched leaves falling – Mother Nature spending her hard earned pennies on a white coat for the winter; after Christmas, she'll be leafing through a catalogue for flowery spring dresses.

Thursday 20th

Washing the vegetables for dinner made me very frustrated. Not only was it tiring work, I'm sure it's impossible to remove all the chemical residue left on the skins – pesticides, herbicides and growth inhibitors used in storing. Ben has trouble finding organic vegetables in our local supermarkets; sometimes he finds carrots and onions, but this week there was only a swede. I am calm and peaceful: I love me, I love herb tea, I will learn to love swede.

We will have to move to California; they have wonderful markets there full of organic fruit and veg. My head is now full of the Beach Boys' songs (with a few small changes to the lyrics)... 'I wish they all could be California veg...' 'God only knows how I'd go without fruit...' 'I'm thinking of good vibrations, we need organic plantations.'

Ben watched *Shivers*: the inhabitants of a luxury tower block were turned into sex-crazed zombies by parasites. I plodded off to bed to dream of organic-veg-crazed hippies, turned on by turnips.

Friday 21st

Amazing! I haven't caught Ben's cold! Must be all the extra garlic, bee propolis, vitamin C, and remembering the Ten Anti-Cold Bug Commandments. Ben called up the Irish whiskey troops for his cold at the new Irish pub in town, O'Neills. He came home singing, 'It's a long way to Tipperrareeeee!!' Loudlccc! And gave me a packet of Banshee Bones. I crunched them loudleee too.

It's his birthday on Wednesday. I ordered him a mouse mat with a cat picture (Fat Cat Mouse Mat) for his computer mouse weeks ago but the catalogue people have only just let me know they're out of stock. Oh bum. Fat cat bum. Big hairy smelly fat cat's bums. Bums! Bums! Bums! Really glad I ordered his other prezzies months ago; you have to be so *bleedin' bloomin'* organised when you're housebound.

Saturday 22nd

Ben: Oh God! My head!!

Me: Good night, was it?

Ben: Yeah.

Me: See lots of leprechauns, did we?

Ben: Probably.

Me: Guinness good, was it?

Ben: Very.

Me: Bet it wasn't as tasty as the Guinness in Ireland; they put it down to the water, you know! It's got a thicker head over there.

Ben: Don't talk to me about heads! Oh God!!

Me: In the pubs, they pour half a pint, then leave it to rest before pouring the other half.

Ben: You seem to know a lot about it.

Me: Well, er... I *have* spent rather a lot of time in pubs in Ireland.

Ben: I've got an Irish hangover.

Me: Poor you, the *worst!*

Ben: Mm.

Me: I prefer a Southern Irish hangover to a Northern Irish hangover though.

Ben: Whyzat?

Me: In Southern Ireland, it's calm and peaceful and the people, scenery and music are lovely, but my experiences in Northern Ireland were the opposite. For instance, I was staying in Newtownards, not far from Belfast, and at the end of merry evenings huge, menacing policemen with bullet-proof vests and guns burst through the pub doors, dead on the moment they called time at the bar; completely ruined my holiday. Mind you, it was around the

12th of July, the parades and everything; my boyfriend was in the Protestant Orange Order. I didn't enjoy the parades either – felt like I had '*Catholic*' stamped across my forehead and any moment someone would stick a gun in my face.

Ben: I could do with an orange juice.

Me: Do you want painkillers?

Ben: I've had three.

Me: I'll get you some Protestant orange juice, in a Catholic glass – that will give you indigestion!

. . . .

Me: Here you are; all you need now is a big beautiful Irish breakfast complete with soda bread, spread with lots of creamy Irish butter made with milk from Irish moo cows.

Ben: No thanks.

Me: Must go to the loo.

Ben: I wouldn't go in the bathroom for a while, if I were you.

Me: Did you open the window?

Ben: Yeah.

Me: I'll hang on a minute then. African forest dung beetles perch on leaves during foraging, instead of continuously flying, apparently waiting for dung odours to reach them.

Ben: How nice for them.

Me: Yes, they're sweet, quite remarkable really. The two sexes usually meet at the dung pat or in its close vicinity.

Ben: Like Bob the Slob meeting Saucy Sonia down The Sticky Carpet Tavern.

Me: The brood ball is often rolled together by the two partners and in some cases the female climbs into the ball and is rolled off with it by the male.

Ben: Cinderella dung beetle *shall* go to the ball.

Me: Ha, ha, yes, and during the rolling process...

Ben: Are you making any toast?

. . . .

Me:	Would you like a Banshee Bone?
Ben:	No thanks, can you crunch your bones in another room.
Me:	OK.
Ben:	With the door shut.
Me:	If you insist... 'It's a long way to Tipperareee...'

Sunday 23rd

Mum and Dad, Gina, Mark and Matthew dropped in this morning on their way to somewhere nice. For a lovely day out. Without me. I consoled myself holding and cuddling a well rounded Matthew, nine months old and growing like a big healthy marrow; hope the greenhouse effect doesn't spoil his future. Is he nine months old already? The greenhouse effect must be shrinking the years.

Curled up like a baby on the sofa and dozed with Murphy's black tail resting across my eyes, while Ben watched *The Puppet Masters*, a sci-fi film about alien parasites taking control of a Midwestern town.

Monday 24th

The N.S.P.C.C. sent me their Christmas catalogue. I fancied the cast stone cat pen holder for myself (will hold a pen in its paws on your desk or bookshelf).

Black cat fridge magnets (for Gail).
'Mine's a pint' socks (for Ben).
Children in art calendar (Artie Auntie).
Musical bear playing 'When you wish upon a star' (Matthew).
Dog breeds crackers (Gina and Mark).

Found a few ideas in the other catalogues too:

'Oh, no! not socks again' socks (Dad and Peter).
'You, me and the kids' calendar (for Rose, if she's found a man to keep her warm for winter).
'Nostalgic Days' calendar (for Rose if she hasn't found a man for winter).
Fuchsia jewellery (Mum).
Heavy duty gardening gauntlets (Dad).
Floral calendar (Auntie Mary).

Seahorse brooch (Eileen).
Paintbrush pen (Bill).
Treble clef pencil (W. M. Friend).
Flexible screwdriver (Peter).
Hedgehog brooch (Peter's girlfriend).
Star Trek watch (Ben).
The kittens have paw-marked their preferred gifts.

After my Monday treatment, I bought Ben a musical birthday card with an overflowing pint of beer on the front and one from the kittens with singing cats on. Also a big iced birthday cake, small stripy candles and sweets from the kittens. Was not tempted to eat sweets or cake as my positive visualisations are going well. I'm slim, healthy, happy herbal me and I've lost three whole pounds! I expect pre-Christmas anxiety and becoming a low fat, born again Crispian helps.

Tuesday 25th

Wrote Ben's cards and wrapped his presents: a *Star Trek* T-shirt, *Star Trek* socks, mug to match and sweets from the kittens. Was a little tempted to eat the sweets, then remembered a picture I'd seen in ACE gift catalogue this morning; a bear hanging big flowery knickers on a washing line. The caption read: *'Sweetie pickers wear big knickers.'* Another picture made me smile too, a happy pig with a garland of flowers around her neck. The caption read: *'LORD, if you can't make me skinny please make my friends fat.'*

After dinner, I fancied something sweet again and heard distant voices calling to me from the depths of freezer land, 'Eat me! Eat me! Eat me!' I listened. They were the deliciously seductive voices of Ben's cakes to take to work tomorrow: Alabama chocolate fudge cake, sticky toffee cheesecake, cappuccino gâteau and Black Forest gâteau.

I am ever so calm and sinful; I am having lustful naughty thieving thoughts...

... she crept downstairs with her torch, hunched and watchful, like a cat burglar, quiet as a thinking mouse. Blinking like an owl in the moonlight, Cathy Cakeful skilfully cracked the code on the freezer door. Click. Click. Click. Removing four square boxes, she was careful not to disturb the peas and sweetcorn. Alabama chocolate fudge cake, sticky toffee cheesecake, cappuccino gâteau and Black Forest gâteau were placed on the mat in

front of the fire to defrost. A minute passed. She removed the cakes from the boxes and sat them on plates. Her mouth watered. Another minute passed. Cathy longed to be cakeful, and started to pick chocolate flakes off the Black Forest gâteau. Two minutes passed. She dipped her finger into partly defrosted cream. Thirty seconds passed; she could wait no longer and broke off a creamy swirl with a cherry on top. It melted in her mouth. She ate another... three hours later, fingers of morning light stroked her chocolaty, crumb-covered, lower lip as she lay on the floor dreaming sweetly...

Wednesday 26th

Slowly crawled out from underneath the smelly bed-bug-ridden duvet and wrapped my flea-bitten dressing gown round my achy body. Peeped between the curtains at the world outside: it was crisp and dry like McCain oven chips. Wondered if Ben would be celebrating his birthday with Delyth and his office colleagues. Or just Delyth. Him and her. On their own. Without me. Laughing. Joking. How many kisses will she put on his card? I'll check, if he brings it home. If. Hope she eats too much chocolate fudge cake and feels sick. Delyth by chocolate.

A plastic lemonade bottle has been lying in the gutter across the road for a few days. Rolling about a bit. The yellow top and label are the same colour as the stripe painted on the tarmac. This morning I noticed it had been crushed. Flat. It bled a little lemonade down the drain. I want to get well soon so I don't have time to feel sorry for lemonade bottles.

Ben received three birthday cards from his family, a home-made card from Bill (sketch of a mermaid holding a birthday cake; reminded me of someone), a joke card from Rick (Van Gogh with his head wrapped in a bandage, a plastic ear inside and the message 'Love from Vincent'), an arty Christian type card from W. M. Friend (oil painting of angels playing musical instruments) and a large card from Rob and Bev and the kids (multi-coloured, glitter-covered guitars).

When Ben came home from work wearing his thirty-seven-year-old face, he said he was sure he'd sprouted a few more grey hairs today. After dinner, he returned to his teenage years wearing his *Star Trek* T-shirt, matching socks, Spiderman boxer shorts and drinking beer out of a *Star trek* mug. I dozed through a *Star Trek* film then lit seven stripy candles on his cake. He blew them out in one go and made a wish. I wondered what he wished for; he had his eyes closed for ages. Hoped he was wishing for my recovery, then felt selfish. Ate three pieces of cake, felt greedy. Noted four kisses in Delyth's card. Murderous.

After the film, Ben put on an *Ab Fab* video. I wore my Horlicks jumper, drank red wine out of a Kit-Kat mug, and wished him a verrrry happeeee firty-sevenf absholutlee fabirfday. He said, 'I'm stuffed full, drunk too mush, beam me up to bed, Scottie!'

Thursday 27th

Oh God, it was heaven being sinful last night but we both felt like hell this morning. I gave Ben a pint mug of orange juice and paracetamol with his coffee and toast, and he said, 'You're an angel.'

I'd love to be an angel. I didn't believe they existed till I started seeing them when I was fourteen; once seen never forgotten! In times of need I've seen them ever since, sometimes with gaps of years in between. They remind me of cats in some ways: never appear on command, unless they want to, and when they do, their calm, serene, exquisite beauty fills the room. Angel words are soft, peaceful and comforting like a big warm rumbly purr on your belly on a cold winter's night. But when they want you to sit up and listen, they don't mind yelling in your ear. A fleeting vision is sometimes all you'll see, lingering for just a moment, like curly steam rising from a Kit-Kat mug full of camomile tea. If you're in need, sometimes they'll stay, like balls of bright golden light filling the room and your heart. In deepest, darkest moments of grief and terrible, tearing sorrow they bring hope and pure powerful love.

Spoke to a cab driver once who'd had an angel experience. I expect he said something like, 'Quite nice flutri white fings ain't vey, 'elp ya in times o'stress like when v'missus left me wiv five kids. Silly caah. Vere kind o' bright but don't 'urt yer eyeballs, an' if vey giv ya some sort a message like, ya ain't goin' barmy or nuffin. Quite nice lookin' birds really, y'can't see vere tits or nuffin under all 'em floaty robes like, but vere femanin style o'fing. Ain't always got 'em big wings eiver but vey can still fly, if ya know wot I mean, like 'em spirit fings wot scares ya 'alf to def.'

A voice from the fridge shouted,

'Go on. Be a devil. You know you want me, you know you have to have me. Hey. Relax. Open up. Take as much of me as you want. Don't you think I'm the tastiest, sweetest thing you've ever seen? I'm all yours!'

Ate birthday cake for breakfast. Read Ben's stars: 'Accepting that something has outlived its previous usefulness isn't easy, use your Scorpio capacity to cut off quickly from a situation and move on.' (Hope Cosmic Colin is not referring to me.) Read my stars: 'The world is your oyster Aries, there are many pearl-white opportunities waiting for you out there.' (Oh well, I've had a trip to the dentist and now have pearly white teeth; that will have to do for now.)

Friday 28th

Saw a sleeping angel. She was in a gardening catalogue and was made of weather-proof polyresin. I'm tempted to give her a home in the corner of our garden.

Ben staggered home from The Keg and Crumpet with Bill, Rob, Bob the Slob, Rick and chips. Later they went on to O.B.C. (One Brain Cell) nightclub.

After they'd gone, I finished off the chips left in the kitchen, foraging through greasy paper for tasty looking morsels like a monkey searching for grubs in his partner's hairy coat. Wrote poor but positive poetry: my creative brain cells must be clogged together with saturated fat. Serves me right.

> **Searching for the tastiest chip**
> **Pick, pick, pick, pick**
> **Small and crispy, big and fat**
> **Fishy batter for the cat**

> **Ben celebrates with his mates**
> **Beer and chips on lots of plates**
> **Belated bumps for the birthday lad**
> **Gettin' older ain't too bad**

Saturday 29th
9.30 a.m.

Ben:	Oooooh, aaaaah, a ton of bricks must have fallen on my head last night.
Me:	Heavy night was it?
Ben:	Yeah, met a couple of old school mates; they run a new café in town.
Me:	I expect you had a lot of catching, no, ketching up to do.
Ben:	Ha, ha.
Me:	What time did you get in?
Ben:	(Head in fridge) Dunno, three or four, I'll eat up these beans.
Me:	Abyssinian wolves congregate for social greetings, but forage individually.

9.40 a.m.   Ben is still holding his head.

10.00 a.m.   Notice lemonade bottle in gutter has lost half its broken top.

10.10 a.m.   Mr. Boxer-face is walking antique coffee table. He's wearing a new winter jacket (Mr. Boxer-face, not his dog). The coffee table has longer legs and a new extended lead.

11.05 a.m.   Take self for walkies in garden. Remnants of a broken snail's shell with brown and yellow stripes (like the tank top my mum knitted for me in the seventies) crunch under my foot.

11.06 a.m.   I want to travel back in time to my seventies disco days, dancing round a pile of handbags to Tina Turner's 'Nutbush City Limits' and Mud's 'Tiger Feet', my lips covered in sticky lip gloss and eyelashes weighed down with two thick layers of mascara (because Marie Osmond said she wore two coats in *Jackie).*

11.08 a.m.   Thousands of rain droplets sparkle on the grass. I think of seventies disco frocks under flashing lights.

11.10 a.m.   A clump of large clover leaves look like palms of little green hands holding shiny silver buttons.

11.11 a.m.   A soggy tennis ball is a seventies mirror ball.

11.12 a.m.   Bashful hands me a rosebud, then hurries away.

11.13 a.m.   I come over all poetic... 'Gather ye rosebuds while ye may... something... something still a-flying... something... something... smiles today... tomorrow will be dying.'

11.14 a.m.   That's that Robert Herrick writing pretty words, telling young girls not to be coy, but while they may, go marry or they may forever tarry. If he were a cab driver today he might say, 'Go an' grab a man, get shagged an' 'ave lots o' babies before ya go all wrinkly an' ugly an' no-one fancies ya. Yoove already left it a bit late, girl, ain't ya, no offence or nuffin like, jus' bin honest, know-what-I-mean!'

11.20 a.m.	The dwarves are cloud watching.
Doc:	(Pointing upwards) That's a cottage loaf.
Happy:	(Rubbing fat belly) I'm hungry.
Sneezy:	There's a Scottie dog.
Sleepy:	Where?
Sneezy:	There!
Sleepy:	I can see a yawning hippo.
Grumpy:	It's opening its jaws; probably going to eat the Scottie dog.
11.30 a.m.	Hold my face up to warm autumn sunshine and breathe in cold fresh breeze. Think positive thought.
11.35 a.m.	Wrinkly brown leaves are hiding between blades of young green grass, like small, dirty old men after closing time, dancing with thin teenage girls at a seventies disco. Raindrops sit in pink rose petals like teardrops on a young bride's cheek, who's married a silly old man.
11.36 a.m.	Think about writing a poem about a crying rosebush, broken-hearted bride or something.
11.37 a.m.	Recall verse in kitten book:

Gather kittens while you may
Time brings only sorrow
And the kittens of today
Will be old cats tomorrow
      – Oliver Herford

11.40 a.m.	Starting to rain again.

. . . .

1.35 p.m.	Rain has stopped.
1.36 p.m.	October gardens drip... think I feel a verse coming on... no, it's gone.
1.37 p.m.	A woman is walking down the street still holding a red umbrella over her head. She's marching along, head down, her tights splattered with mud. Probably wishing she'd worn knee-

length boots or were sipping a nice cup of hot tea at home.

1.38 p.m.   The leaves on the path are the colour of used tea bags on the draining board.

1.39 p.m.   Woman in the rain
Your face is full of pain
You're marching down the street
~~Tea leaves~~
~~Leaves the colour of tea~~
Leaves stuck to your feet.

1.41 p.m.   Your umbrella is red
~~A leaf stuck to your head~~
~~Must get home quickly so the kids can be fed~~

1.43 p.m.   March, March, March
In an April rain
May, May, May
I see you once again
June, June, June
Why July to me?
Why, why, why
I'm absolutely Augusted with you!
~~September September~~
~~The fifth of November~~

2.00 p.m.   Mr. Boxer-face is on his way home, from town I guess. He's carrying a red and black plastic devil's fork and a green carrier bag full of goodies. I expect he's got those flashing devil's horns too; he'll make a good devil with those evil-looking, scrunched up features.

2.02 p.m.   Want to go to Halloween party. Got lots of black clothes, a pointy hat and broomstick. Straggly hair. Witchy spell-making stare. Long fingernails. Black nail polish (though probably turned into a solid black lump by now). Eyebrow pencil to draw spot on end of nose. Black cat. Cackle.

2.05 p.m.   Will have to make do with candlelit spooky bath using Boots Hubble Bubble Bath and Werewolf Shampoo.

2.15 p.m.   Paddy is curled up in his favourite corner like a pumpkin.

. . . .

3.45 p.m.   Raining again.

3.48 p.m.   Tall thin woman wearing brown raincoat. Green umbrella. A walking palm tree. Wonder if she works for Island Records.

4.26 p.m.   Raindrops are hanging from the branches of a rose bush like chunky jewels round a posh lady's neck.

4.27 p.m.   Murphy brushes past my leg.

4.28 p.m.   Lucky me, I have raindrops on roses and whiskers on kittens.

4.29 p.m.   Raindrops drip from rose bush like tears of posh lady whose husband has left her for a younger, prettier woman.

4.30 p.m.   Drip on end of thorn, like pointy nose of posh man with streaming cold and no dry bits left on his once clean hankie because his new mistress doesn't *do* washing.

4.31 p.m.   Feel poem coming on.

4.32 p.m.   Maybe not.

4.33 p.m.   Er...

~~Raindrops on roses~~
~~Whiskers on kittens~~
~~Posh ladies cry~~
~~Into soft sheepskin mittens~~
~~Big pointy noses~~
~~That blow with a cold~~
~~Something... something~~
~~Bitter and old~~
~~Untold~~
~~Mould~~
~~Fold~~

Mistresses that become
Bitter and cold
His family for Christmas
She's left in the ~~cold~~
~~Mould~~
~~Moulder~~
~~No shoulder~~
~~To cry on~~
~~She's left with only~~
~~The chip pan to fry on~~

4.36 p.m.   Must order Christmas presents – will take my mind off writing bad poetry.

5.00 p.m.	Very windy (the weather, not me).
5.25 p.m.	Forty seconds of pagan aerobics.
5.30 p.m.	Sit on sofa sipping herbs in silence, thinking spiritual thoughts.
6.00 p.m.	Ben says there's a path near us covered in twigs.
6.01 p.m.	How exciting! I'll ask him to collect a few in a Sainsbury's carrier bag. Then I'll spray them gold or silver, maybe dangle stars or something on the branches; after all, ASDA is reminding us to start preparing for Christmas.
6.30 p.m.	Place tea light in spooky candle holder and strike match.
6.33 p.m.	Wallow in Boots Hubble Bubble bath.

Read instructions:

Hubble bubble, toil and trouble
Pour the potion at the double
Watch it turn from green to blue
It smells of blueberries and so will you

6.35 p.m.	Admire new aquamarine crystal from my little friends. The name comes from the Latin for sea water.
6.36 p.m.	What a wonderful light blue.
6.37 p.m.	Hold over eyes, to improve vision and relieve tiredness.
6.39 p.m.	Pour more hot water into bath.
6.40 p.m.	Ideas pour into mind.
6.41 p.m.	Words bubble up, then pop and disappear.
6.42 p.m.	I will always September
	Everything you said
	It's almost October
	It's finished, it's dead
6.43 p.m.	It's now November
	It's now or never
	It's up to you
	To December
6.45 p.m.	Wash hair using Boots Werewolf shampoo.

Read instructions:

When the full moon fills the sky
And you hear a werewolf cry
Smell the dewberries in the air
Best stay in and wash your hair

6.50 p.m.	What fun! Think I'll try the Vampire Blood Bath tomorrow. Who needs parties?
7.52 p.m.	Decide to practise my spelling. Find a candle (blue for health) and carve my name on one side.
7.56 p.m.	Carve my wish on the other side.
7.58 p.m.	Lick my thumb and seal the wish and my name with my spit.
7.59 p.m.	Light the candle and meditate on my wish coming true.
8.00 p.m.	I want to be well, I want to be well...

Sunday 30th

The lemonade bottle in the gutter has disappeared; maybe it's stuck to a car tyre, or somebody felt sorry for it and picked it up. But I doubt it.

Didn't bother reading *Keep Fit For Winter*. After the last few days, I think I'll be keeping fat for winter. Weird musician friend (Elijah) called in on his way to church carrying his Bible and looking Christian. I was busy munching an enormous bag of organic crisps, made in Norfolk using carefully selected varieties of organically grown potatoes which naturally vary in colour, flavour and appearance. The sunflower oil in which they are cooked comes from the pressing of organically grown sunflower seeds, and each batch of potatoes is sliced directly into a simmering cauldron of oil, cooked by hand then lightly sprinkled with Mediterranean sea salt. I informed Elijah I'm a born again Crispian. He ignored me. Paddy trod muddy paw marks on his heavenly blue jeans. He didn't stay long.

Trick or treaters knocked on the door for the fifth time this week; we'd run out of change so Ben fired his water pistol at them. Bill turned up at the same time and got a squirting too. He swore at Ben but said a lot of nice things about Eileen.

They are watching the late night thriller *The Andromeda Strain* (the tale of a deadly virus that may have come from outer space) as I write.

Monday 31st

As I left the house for my Monday treatment, I noticed the lemonade bottle was still in the gutter, further down the road, top missing and label ripped off. I picked it up and laid it on the path before Mr. Miserable-as-sin-taxi-man drove over it. He gave me a you-silly-cow look, so I sat silently all the way to the clinic with my mad-woman-bulgy-eyed-black-angelfish face on. He was too afraid to utter a word and drove through a red traffic light, ha, ha, ha.

Eileen gave me a list of the prezzies she wanted to order from my Christmas catalogues: Ocean Mist bath oil (in a recycled bottle with real seashells), Ocean Mist luxury gift pack (with shell soaps and body balm), Ocean Mist wash bag set (soaps and things and a dolphin shaped sponge), a set of seahorse-stemmed wine glasses, a dolphin mug and a box of shell-shaped Belgian chocolates. She said a lot of nice things about Bill.

Later: enjoyed a candlelit Boots Vampire Blood Bath.

Pour the red gunge in the vat
Made from blood of toad and rat
Make sure you bathe before it's night
Or vampire fangs will start to bite

November

Tuesday 1st

Woke up feeling happy and not too achy after a night of pleasant dreams; swimming with dolphins, sitting on the seashore in a pale blue ocean mist, sipping fine wine from seahorse-stemmed glasses and eating shell-shaped chocolates.

Only two more months to go and I'll have survived *another whole year!* Another year closer to recovery. Slowly but sugarly. Shell chocolates. Mmm. I will award myself seahorse-stemmed glasses filled with bubbly champagne and lovely shell-shaped chocolates.

> **The days they be shorter**
> **The nights they be longer**
> **And soon I'll be feeling**
> **Bigger and stronger**

Wednesday 2nd

Hibernated inside my Horlicks jumper, reading *Weekly Wife*. Wendy says lips are warm this season, so I pressed my mouth against my warm Kit-Kat mug and smiled in a fashionable way. Lots of hair is out, so I pulled the hair out of my hairbrush and threw it out the window. In the wildlife section, I discovered hedgehogs have five thousand spines, their diet consists mainly of slugs, beetles and caterpillars, and they hibernate this time of year. If they are lucky, a lovely person like me will put some cat food out for them.

I wish I were a hedgehog, then I could have a proper rest from everyone and everything till March. Perhaps I could tell everyone I *think* I'm a hedgehog. Perhaps not. I don't fancy a diet of slugs, or being squashed by a car on my way to bed... or being locked up in a mental hospital.

I was feeling so much better today, but I overdid it again tonight. Now I'm like a slow, slimy slug that's about to be gobbled up by a passing hedgehog. I'm worried about the hedgehogs sleeping in the compost heaps: bonfire night is approaching.

SLUG

I'm lying here like a slug
My herbal tea in a mug
I'm feeling quite sluggish
My mug is quite muggish
I'm snug as a bug in a rug

MY HORLICKS JUMPER

My Horlicks jumper
Makes me look plumper
Some days I'm wider
Than I'm tall

My Horlicks jumper
Makes me look plumper
But I'm so tired
That's all

HEDGEHOG

I'm an actress hedgehog
With lots of pretty spines
But I've been sleeping so long
I've forgotten all my lines

Thursday 3rd

3.00 p.m.   The sky darkened and a storm blew the kittens in through the cat flap; they ran behind the sofa, under the bed and behind the wardrobe. Wind whipped the leaves. They galloped across the lawn and were tossed into the air like a football in the playground. Clouds hurried across the heavens like boys running to catch the school bus.

4.00 p.m.	Schoolchildren shrieked and shouted in the street. As I wiped muddy paw marks off the fridge and cooker top, I wondered if I should put myself in detention and write out five hundred times...

I must not overdo it
I must not overdo it
I must not overdo it
I must not overdo it
I must not overdo it...

5.00 p.m.	Curled up on the sofa with the heating turned up. Storm light filled the room and a candle flickered in the draught from a window that needs replacing. A black and white film set in a spooky gothic mansion mumbled away in the corner. Silent shapes flickered on walls.
6.00 p.m.	Stared out of the window thinking positive thoughts. I can read and watch more TV now without making myself ill, but black and white is still easier on the eye. *The Munsters, Bewitched* and *The Avengers* are good by candlelight, but I don't bother with horror films; I'm already living one. Positive thought – every film comes to an end.
7.00 p.m.	Paddy sat in the bedroom window watching the world go by, twitching his tail now and again. A street lamp illuminated his furry silhouette. I lay in the dark, just watching him and writing a verse in my head.

Every cat has a silver lining
Every tea lover should try Twinings
My velvet cloak has a lining of silk
Peppermint tea doesn't need cold milk

Friday 4th

Wrapped up warm and pottered in my November garden thinking about hedgehogs, housework and how many weeks till Christmas. Picked up a sycamore leaf, lemon yellow with splodges of pea green; then another, yellow ochre with curly Van Dyke brown edges. The dwarves were taking a smoking break, perched on upturned plant pots and rusty paint tins. As I wandered past, Doc smiled politely and said good afternoon, Sneezy waved a hankie, Sleepy winked before shutting his eyes and Happy grinned, pressing a wonderful warm red stone into my hand (carnelian). Dopey bowed, then slipped on a wet leaf; I helped him up by his small grubby hand. Bashful appeared from behind a rose bush and presented me with a beautiful bouquet of crimson, orange and chocolatey brown leaves and Grumpy managed an almost imperceptible nod before scowling into his pipe.

Indoors, I carefully placed the leaves in a cup of water and put the kettle on. Sipping rosehip tea, I recalled the day I sat by the river in my lunch hour wondering how many more years I could endure feeling ugly, unloved and drawing gas mains, when a young boy, about thirteen, ran up to me and gave me a flower. He said something about liking me before running away again. I was deeply touched and decided not to end it all in the river that day. So, *Impulse* body spray really does work! OK, he wasn't a tall, dark, handsome stranger acting on impulse with a big bunch of flowers and an invite to dinner, but it's a memory I'll always treasure and my cup is overflowing with autumn leaves.

Ben said a chap he meets on the train, John, brought his dog, Tess, into work today. Bonfire night fireworks, set off early, frighten her so much he comes home to little puddles all over the kitchen floor. We'll be keeping the kittens in tonight, and the weekend.

Drummer Stephen and his girlfriend Selena came round to pick up Bill and Ben for an evening at Morticia's Wine Bar, where Stephen's band, The Stray Bats were playing. Selena smiled at me and said hello; her bright red lips and khol-rimmed eyes peeping out through a cloud of black hair and smoke. I couldn't say much; I was too busy coughing and staring at her jumper: a thick black spider's web over a long red T-shirt, hanging from her thin, chain smoker's, nail-bitten frame. She plays bass guitar in the all girl band, Sisters of Darkness. Stephen is besotted; he says she is someone he would like to meet on a dark night.

Saturday 5th

Ben said the shops are already packed with Christmas shoppers and Christmassy things, *and* the shelves are crammed full of jars of chocolate body paint in B.H.S.

Ben: Do you want chocolate body paint for Christmas?

Me: No, I'll only sniff it out with my super chocolate sniffing nose and eat the whole jar while you are at work, especially if I'm having a bad day.

Ben: You're no fun.

Me: On second thoughts, I think it would be lots of fun eating a whole jar with a spoon and, anyway, I haven't got the energy to lick it off your body.

Ben: But I've got the energy to lick it off *your* body.

Me: I haven't got the energy to get excited.

Ben: I bought some anyway.

Me: Oh good.

Me: I'd like these earrings for Christmas. Look, they're little watering cans.

Ben: They're tablecloth weights; probably pull your ear lobes off... it's a gardening catalogue!

Me: Oh well, those wellington boots are quite nice, and the fairy garden ornaments...

Ben: Shall I get some fireworks?

Me: Oh no, definitely not, frighten our hairy children.

Ben: I forgot.

Me: Listen to this;

> 'Dear Sue,
> Should I marry him, although he is kind
> and loving, there are no fireworks.' Sue
> replies, 'Forget the fireworks, that exciting
> crazy feeling never lasts.' She should have
> said, 'If you play with fireworks, you end
> up seeing stars, burnt out, or getting your
> head blown off.'

Ben: No, she should have said,
'Do you really want to end up like a damp piece of cardboard in the flower bed? That's when old bangers look their worst: the morning after the night before.'

Me: You are wicked!

Ben: I'm off to Delyth's bonfire party tonight.

Me: Will she choose you as her Guy?

Ben: Ha, ha, ha, come on Delyth, light my fire!

Me: Hope she gets a Roman Catholic, I mean Roman candle, stuck up her nose or the volcano fountain singes her split ends.

Ben: Now who's wicked?

Me: Cosmic Colin says I'll be erupting with new-found energy next week. He's right, I can feel my energy levels improving.

Ben: I'll heat up the chocolate body paint then.

Me: I'll have eaten it by the time you get home.

Ben: I've hidden it.

Me: I know all your hiding places.

Ben: I've got a new one.

Me: Sniff sniff... sniff sniff... sniff sniff...

10.00 p.m.   I'm huddled under the bed covers with Paddy and chocolate round my chops, listening to the fireworks and trying not to think about the sounds of war, death and pain and what Ben is up to. Mary is hiding behind the wardrobe, Murphy under the bed.

The young couple who have just moved in next door are making loud oooh! and ahhh! noises in their bedroom. I expect they're watching fireworks out of the window.

Sunday 6th

Ben had Ibuprofen on toast and a pint of Sainsbury's pure orange juice for breakfast, to ease his explosive hangover.

Paddy bounced happily in through the cat flap with a wet cardboard Vesuvius in his mouth. How many times have I told him not to play with fireworks? Mary sniffed a dead rocket on the lawn and ran away; girls have more sense.

Firework parties continued this evening, the whizzing, banging and screaming, sounding like angry spirits and poltergeists evicted from their gothic mansions.

Ben angrily gulped spirits to exorcise the whizzing, banging and screaming in his head.

Monday 7th

Autumn rain drenched everything it could lay its drops on. Leaves fell like huge, rusty snowflakes. A sycamore seed hung suspended in the air, caught in a spider's web; Mr. Spider must have thought his Christmas dinner had arrived early.

Eileen: Have you sent off for my Christmas goodies yet?

Me: No, not yet, must remember to fill in those forms.

Eileen: Did you see that programme about swimming with dolphins?

Me: No, was it good?

Eileen: Yes, very; I'd love to do that, wouldn't you?

Me: Mmm, yes. Did you know their colouration provides excellent camouflage. When viewed from below, the light underbelly blends with the brighter ocean surface; when viewed from above, it blends with the darker ocean floor.

Eileen: Wonder if human hair turns grey to match our roads, roofs and pavements.

Tuesday 8th

1.00 p.m.   Curl up on sofa with monthly cramps. Read about the red crystal, carnelian: it strengthens the blood and works to increase circulation. Don't want to read about blood today.

2.00 p.m.   Stare at books I've read two or three times. Bored. It'll be dark soon. Crunch large bag of organic crisps.

3.00 p.m.   S.A.D.A.G. (seasonally affected doom and gloom).

4.00 p.m.   Stare in bathroom mirror – face like Woody Allen with stomach ache.

5.00 p.m.   Open *Concise English Dictionary* near middle.

Melancholy: gloomy, dejected, mental disease accompanied by depression.

Menstruation: approximately monthly discharge of blood and cellular debris from womb of nonpregnant woman. Discharge! Cellular debris! *Ugh, feel really ill now.*

Mesembryanthemum: low-growing plant with daisylike flowers of various colours.

Ah, that's taken my mind off my female body.

Meretricious is an interesting word; I'll use it next time Mr. Miserable-as-sin-taxi-man is being insincere. Wish I were clever and knew dead clever words. I feel like Rita in *Educating Rita. Merganser,* ah! I know that's a type of duck because I'm a born again bird expert as well as dream interpreter and born again Crispian now. *Membrane,* know that too: thin tissue in a plant or animal; now I've started thinking about my womb lining and my womb knows, pain is getting worse! *Cellular debris...* quick, turn pages... *Procreate.* Don't want to think about what that means; I'll be back to monthly discharge again. *Profligate.* That's a good one; I'll use it next time Mr. Ex-racing-driver-taxi-man is driving recklessly. Turn a few more pages. *Untrammelled.* Another good one! I want to be untrammelled and free. Turn a few more pages..... V.... W.... X. Not many words under X. *Xenogamy* is cross-fertilisation, pollination from another plant. No, I'm not going to think about bodies or menstruation or cellular debris again, my bits have just calmed down. *Xylocarp:* hard woody fruit; mmm, interesting. Not many words under Y either. *Yesterday:* day before today. Yesterday... all my troubles seemed so far away. Bored now. Z. *Zombie:* person appearing lifeless. *Zygote:* fertilised egg cell. Oh God.

Wednesday 9th

Cleaned the kitchen floor. Well, not exactly the *whole* floor, half of it; about a quarter, *really*. And it wasn't a proper clean with a mop and Flash and me standing smiling proudly at a job well done, the tiles sparkling, the enamel on the cooker twinkling, the sun shining through the window on to clear, polished work surfaces and saucepans you could use as a mirror to do your make-up. The only flashing being done was my knickers showing through a big hole in the bum of my leggings, as I crawled on my hands and knees, using damp kitchen roll (lovely autumn leaf pattern) to wipe muddy paw prints near the cat flap and crumbs near the cooker and bread bin area. I now have the energy to keep the filth at bay; I'm so fortunate. Must remember to lay fresh sheets of *Adscene* by the cat flap every time I pick up the dirty soggy pages, which isn't very often.

Late this afternoon, Murphy crept into the kitchen with wet black spiky fur; he's going through a punk phase. He'll be wanting his ears, nose and belly button pierced next, and spend all day hanging around in bin bags. Paddy told me he's going on a demonstration against testing on animals: he's joining the Feral Demo-cats; I'm very proud of my ginger son. Mary is so beautiful, she's attracting all the boy cats in the neighbourhood, but she ignores them and teeters along the fence, head held high, like Marilyn Monroe in stilettos. The boys howl outside her window at night.

Rain tapped the window pane and reminded me to lay newspaper down by the cat flap. When I left the kitchen, a gust of wind blew the paper across the floor. My teenagers padded round it, jumped onto the fridge and work tops and made pretty paw-shaped tracks for mummy to admire.

Thursday 10th

I don't know how many times I've told the furry children to wipe their feet when they come in, but do they listen? No. And they rush out of the house without a jacket or any breakfast; no wonder they always have their heads in the fridge.

Last night I dreamt I was in the middle of a field in the countryside, looking after a coach-full of children. The bright green surrounding fields were covered in red and crimson killer crabs, and they were slowly coming towards us; I had to save the children by throwing handfuls of multicoloured poisonous supplements around the coach. When

I woke up, I was surprised by the nightmares till I remembered I'd received my Save the Children Fund Christmas catalogue yesterday.

Today, I filled in several order forms for Ace cards and gifts, the R.S.P.C.A., Help the Aged, the R.N.L.I. and the World Wildlife Fund Christmas catalogues. My head, neck, back and hands ache now; the kittens told me not to overdo it, but did I listen? No.

Friday 11th

11.00 p.m. Sad. Very sad. Remember our brave soldiers who fought in the World Wars. Say a little prayer for all who suffered.

12.00 noon. Stare at postcard on mantelpiece from Artie Auntie; water colour of poppies in a field.

1.00 p.m. *In Flanders fields the poppies blow*
Between the crosses, row on row...
Recall seeing the fields. Cry a bit.

2.00 p.m. Paddy is busy digging a trench in the litter tray.

3.00 p.m. Litter tray smells rank. Trip over kitten toys on way to kitchen; the house is a minefield.

4.00 p.m. I soldier on... clean out litter tray, refill water bowl, wipe muddy paw prints off kitchen surfaces and do a bit of washing-up.

5.00 p.m. Thunder booms. The house shakes. S.A.D.A.G.W.T. (seasonally affected doom and gloom war thoughts).

6.00 p.m. Wish I had the energy to go for a long, brisk walk. Hopefully, by springtime I'll be able to take little strolls down to the river; there'll be lots of places for me to sit and rest when I'm tired. Quite looking forward to it. Rose is lucky. When she's on one of her diets (between pregnancies) she goes jogging; Gail tap dances, Eileen swims, Rick goes weight training, Gina chases her dogs round the park, Bob the Slob chases women, W. M. Friend walks miles to churches, Bill strolls round art galleries, Ben strolls to pubs with Bill, and Rob uses all his spare energies to carry the weight of his wife's latest knitting creation.

7.00 p.m. Read about Choc Express: chocolate delivered to your door! Wow! Am tempted to ring Chocline. Must be strong. Eat honey on toast instead, but write down Chocline number in case of emergency (01763-257744) next to numbers for gas escape and burst water main, etc.

8.00 p.m.	Bill, Rick, Stephen and Selena call round on their way to celebrate something at Polly's Poppadoms. Everyone is dressed in black. I ask Ben if they are in mourning for my wonderful, witty, sparkling company; he says they don't want to wear anything that shows up muddy paw prints.
9.00 p.m.	Ben has gone with them. Put oven chips on gas ~~mask~~ mark nine and invite the dwarves round to watch *One Hundred and One Dalmatians*.
10.00 p.m.	

Happy:	That Cruella De Vil is an evil old witch.
Grumpy:	A devil woman! They're all the same, you know.
Sleepy:	A nightmare!
Sneezy:	Gets right up my nose!
Me:	She's like a woman I worked with at British Gas.
Happy:	Must have been very ugly and old.
Me:	She was.
Grumpy:	And jealous of all the younger women.
Me:	You're right for once, Grumpy!
Doc:	Made their lives hell no doubt.
Me:	Exactly!
Bashful:	Did she try to make fur coats out of spotty dogs?
Me:	Probably.
Happy:	There's hundreds of 'em in this film.
Doc:	One hundred and one.
Happy:	Oh, yeah.
Sleepy:	I'd never sleep with all that barking.
Sneezy:	All that fur would make me sneeze.
Doc:	They've got short hair.
Sneezy:	Makes no difference.
Grumpy:	Millions of fleas, I expect.
Bashful:	Poor Perdita! Poor Pongo! They must be so worried about their children!
Doc:	Don't worry; I'm sure they'll rescue them.
Grumpy:	I doubt it. In all that snow and icy water, they're bound to drown or freeze to death.
Happy:	But it's a nice film; it must have a happy ending.
Me:	You wait and see!

Saturday 12th

Three pairs of leggings (black) arrived with the post from Freewoman catalogue (two sizes larger than my usual).

> Cosmic Colin:
> *'If you're feeling restricted in life, a chance to grow and expand has arrived.'*

Sunday 13th

My parents called round this afternoon and I wished Dad a happy birthday for tomorrow. Mum said he shares his birthday with Prince Charles; he always did like to spend a lot of time on the throne. Dad is a Scorpio, like Ben; I daren't leave them alone together for long in case they start raising their tails at each other.

As I watched Dad and Ben eat birthday cake with their tea, I was tempted to inform them both that scorpions, as arachnids, have mouth parts called *chelicerae* and a pair of pincer-like pedipals used for prey capture and defence. I said nothing; I didn't want them to raise their tails at me! But when Dad started being patronising, I told him scorpion venoms are complex mixtures of neurotoxins which affect the victims' *nervous* system. I hoped he'd get the message that he was getting on my nerves, but he continued.

He was a bit nicer to me when I gave him his birthday card and record token; I'm not sure which particular records he has, but I know Country and Western is his favourite. Today he wore a groovy red check shirt with jeans, a wide leather belt with a fancy buckle and cowboy boots. He's mad about Dolly Parton and Pamela Anderson, so why did he marry Mum? She's dark and petite.

Monday 14th

Rang Dad to wish him a hippo birdie *before* I went for my weekly bone crunch, in case he said something to get my back up; Eileen could get it down again. Dad said how well I looked yesterday and maybe I should think about doing a little swimming now, and had I completed any oil paintings lately, and he'd heard there was a new gym opening in my town and maybe I should join as it wasn't far from where I lived and very convenient. Mum said it would be nice to have another grandchild, a little girl this time, a cousin for Matthew to play with. Eileen did quite a lot of work on my back tonight.

Ben put a new message on the answering machine in his best posh voice... 'The master of the house is unavailable. The lady of the house is resting and does not wish to be disturbed...' pause... 'anymore than she is already.'

Ben: Do you like my message?

Me: Er... yes, it's great!

Ben: Did you hear the message from your sister about painting another cot?

Me: Yes.

Ben: I bet you've done a few sketches already!

Me: Might have... (hide pencil behind cushion).

Ben: Munch, munch, munch (cheese sandwich).

Me: Giraffes use their tongue to grab their food.

Ben: Mmmm, munch, munch.

Me: Their tongues are pink and black.

Ben: Do they eat Liquorice Allsorts then?

Me: Ha, ha, acacia trees, actually.

Ben: Acacia trees are in your shampoo.

Me: That's acacia honey.

Ben: Oh...

Me: They might eat Liquorice Allsorts.

Ben: Don't know; I've never offered one to a giraffe.
                 Munch, munch.

Me: If you dream about bread, it means material well being.

Ben: Good, burp!

Me: If you dream about cheese, it means gain and profit.

Ben: Even better.

Me: I dreamt about owls last night; means I mustn't start anything tomorrow.

Ben: Better not start work on the cot then.

Me: Oh, I'm not sure I really believe in all this dream interpretation

	stuff. It depends on the person, and what you see on TV or read in books affects your dreams. It's not all warnings and prophetic dreams.
Ben:	You just can't to wait to start scribbling.
Me:	I know; Gina's delivering the cot tomorrow. I'd like to complete it before Christmas. Baby Hollie is due on Christmas Eve.
Ben:	Not a good time to have a birthday!
Me:	Battery-operated toy for her birthday and batteries for Christmas.
Ben:	Hairdryer for her birthday.
Me:	Plug for Christmas.
Ben:	Pet rabbit for Christmas.
Me:	Hutch for birthday.
Ben:	New computer mouse for birthday.
Me:	Mouse mat for Christmas.
Ben:	Smart jacket for interview.
Me:	Trousers to match.
Ben:	Six cups.
Me:	Six saucers.
Ben:	Set of knives.
Me:	Forks.
Ben:	Expensive wedding on her birthday.
Me:	Expensive divorce at Christmas.
Ben:	Expensive medical treatment.
Me:	Expensive funeral.
Ben:	The baby's not even born yet and we've already buried her!
Me:	I need cheering up.
Ben:	I bought su'more chocolate body paint.
Me:	Wish you hadn't told me.

Tuesday 15th

9.00 a.m. The wind is bending the trees. The leaves are clinging on for dear life, like survivors from a sinking ship.

10.00 a.m. Did I fill in that form in the R.N.L.I. catalogue? Yes I did. Did I send it off? Can't remember.

11.00 a.m. Watch five leaves fall. Do fifty seconds of pagan aerobics.

12.00 noon. Leaves on the lawn are lifted by the winds. They dance a little before collapsing, like a girl with chronic fatigue who goes clubbing.

1.00 p.m.   The lawn is covered in sadness and decay. Leaves are the colour of dead skin. Think of the homeless dying in the winter cold.

2.00 p.m.   Hate camomile tea. Love teaspoonful of chocolate body paint.

3.00 p.m   Hate peppermint tea. Love two teaspoonfuls of chocolate body paint.

4.00 p.m.   Miserable thoughts growing on brain like damp mould.

5.00 p.m.   Stare in mirror. Face is the colour of lichen. Chocolate on chin.

6.00 p.m.   Sad memories creeping into my mind like ivy growing over new garden fence. Devour delicious dessertspoonful of chocolate body paint.

7.00 p.m.   Great! The cot has arrived; now I can start decorating it. Excited. New project. Will use the red, yellow, green and blue enamel paints left over from painting Matthew and Daisy's cots.

8.00 p.m.   Hollie's mum Saffron wants Christmassy designs. Draw sprig of holly on headboard of cot.

Wednesday 16th

Read a holiday special report about the island of St. Lucia in the Caribbean; the banana is their sole source of income and the locals believe bananas cure depression. I expect the beautiful beaches and warm temperatures all year round help a lot too. Ate three bananas.

Ben: Would you like some banana and cinnamon tea?

Me: No thanks, I've tried it.

Ben: It tastes better if you leave it to brew in the mug for a long time.

Me: Ten years'd suit me.

Ben: They were talking about garlic at work today; it's good for your immune system.

Me: Yes, I know.

Ben: There was nearly half a garlic in those vegeburgers we had at the weekend.

Me: That's good.

Ben: Yeah.

Ben:	I was in a wood once, wild garlic everywhere.
Me:	Who were you with?
Ben:	A male friend.
Me:	Oh.
Me:	Did you pick some?
Ben:	No, the ground was too hard.
Me:	That's a shame, I bet wild garlic tastes beautiful.
Ben:	Yeah.
Me:	It must have smelt lovely in the wood.
Ben:	It did; made me want to lie down and sleep.
Me:	A sort of aromatherapy.
Ben:	Yeah.
Ben:	Shall I sprinkle some garlic capsules on the carpet?
Me:	I've run out.
Ben:	I'll get you su'more at the weekend.
Me:	Thanks; can you get extra bananas too.

Drew a Christmas stocking, two stars and a snowflake on the cot.

Thursday 17th

Admired my nails.

They are always long these days because I don't do much house-work (the house is nodding). The kittens are pleased about this; I do a good scritch scratch behind the ear, round the neck, and behind the other ear. They would like me to do this for hours on end, but I've had to explain to them that my hands become achy after a short while and I need to save some hand energy for housework and painting the cot.

Curled up in front of another black and white film this after-noon, set in a spooky gothic house; with a spooky staircase, spooky oil paintings lit up by drippy candles, a spooky old lady wearing black lace, spooky weather thundering and flashing on spooky moors and lots of spooky spooks. Paddy's eyes glowed in the candlelight. Murphy singed a whisker. I enjoyed a teaspoon of choc body paint.

Mary admired her claws.

Friday 18th

Spotted three black, one blue, and a flowery green umbrella. Watched the clouds; they were as menacing and grey as Clint Eastwood sitting in the dentist's chair, about to have a root filling. Drew four festive bells with ribbons; can't wait to fill them in with red and yellow paint. They looked quite good so I filled my mouth with two teaspoons of choc body paint as a reward.

Rick, Ben and Bill went to see the band, Black Pizza, supported by Limp Salad: tall thin Cucumber on keyboards, who always looks a bit green after a Friday night out with the lads; Cabbage on drums, who sits in his mum's kitchen tapping saucepans when he feels a bit fed up; Beetroot, the round-faced alcoholic, on percussion; Carrot, the red-haired bass guitarist, whose playing can grate on your nerves; Tom-alto the lead vocalist; Lettuce, the flabby lead guitarist; and Celery and Cress (Sally and Chris) sing backing vocals.

Saturday 19th

Spotted an umbrella I liked in a catalogue; it was black with a yellow Winnie-the-Pooh holding on to a bright blue balloon on each panel. Fancied the box of chocolate aphrodisiacs too: six huge foil-covered chocolate oysters with delicious praline centres.

Ben took his hangover and earache to the health shop. As well as the usual bits and pieces and packets of crisps, he brought home some herbal cures. I've been reading: *Get to the Root of the Problem with Herbal Medicine*. Bill came round later with his own herbal remedy and smoked it in the garden. I heard him chatting to the dwarves.

Didn't draw anything; overdid it yesterday. Ate two bags of organic crisps during a good crisp crunching film; had to turn the sound up.

Sunday 20th

While the rain lightly tapped on the back door and asked to come in (it was fed up with the wind and cold) Ben worked away on his computer like an impatient prostitute, her long, scarlet fingernails tapping on a car bonnet.

When the rain decided to go away (it needed a break in a warmer climate) the November sun appeared and made a rainbow. Murphy sat in the window drying his fur and enjoying warm cat thoughts; I sat near the hot radiator enduring wintery human thoughts; Mary and Paddy climbed inside my Horlicks jumper and fell asleep. I looked as if I were having kittens.

Tonight Gina called round with Matthew, asked when my kittens were due and had I finished painting the cot yet! She noticed my sketch on the table for the cot paintings. She frowned. Matthew dribbled on it, then tore it in half. Gina laughed and made a comment about his improving my work. I laughed so she wouldn't see how much she hurts me. They didn't stay long as I was having difficulty keeping my eyes open and my temper shut.

Ate three large teaspoons of choc body paint.

Monday 21st

I'm having trouble staying calm and peaceful; the Christmas adverts for cakes and chocolates and booze are driving me mad. Eileen said they are driving her mad too; I've noticed her white coat is very tight around her middle lately. I gave her an article I'd torn out of *Weekly Wife*, advertising Boot's Natural Collection shower gel containing seaweed, ASDA Sea Minerals Shampoo, the Body Shop Seaweed Soap and Loofah Body Bar, and Ralph Lauren Sea Salts Scrub.

Me:	Are you a fan of the band, Ocean Colour Scene?
Eileen:	Osha what?
Me:	Ocean Colour Scene.
Eileen:	Ocean Coloured Sea?
Me:	Colour Scene.
Eileen:	Oh! Coliseum.
Me:	Er...
Eileen:	I've never heard of them.
Me:	Did you see that programme about whales the other night?

Eileen: No, was it good? I love that part of the country.

Me: Ha, ha, ha, *whales*, the big blue ones that swim about in the ocean.

Eileen: In the ocean coliseum!

Me: Yes!

Eileen: I didn't see it; was it interesting?

Me: Very, did you know their hearts are as big as a car?

Eileen: They must drive each other round the bend with love!
            We laugh.

Me: Can you see enough of my spine in these big knickers?

Eileen: They are big, aren't they, but they're fine.

Me: Oh good.

Eileen: I've got a patient who wears knickers with days of the week embroidered on them.

Me: I remember them!

Eileen: She never wears the right pair on the right day though.

Me: I could never do that; I'd *have* to wear Monday's knickers on Monday...

Eileen: Tuesday's knickers on Tuesday...
            We laugh.

Eileen: My Auntie Beryl's visiting tonight, and I'm not looking forward to it.

Me: Oh dear, bit of a pain is she?

Eileen: Mm, all mouth and apron!

Me: Beryl is a mineral composed of beryllium aluminium silicate.

Eileen: You've been reading your crystal book again.

Me: I have. Must tell you about aquamarine, it's...

Eileen: Just turn on your side.

Me: Arrrgh!

Eileen: I saw a film with Beryl Reid in last night. I like her.

Me: Oh yes, she's good, isn't she? Have you seen that Beryl Cook print in Georgie's room?

Eileen: Yes, brilliant.

Me: I was going to tell you about aquamarine, it strengthens and tones the skeleton of the body, and the organs. Improves vision and relieves tension and induces clarity of mind...

Eileen: Just turn on your other side...

Me:	Ooh.
Eileen:	You're really into crystals now aren't you.
Me:	Yes! When I picked up a local paper, instead of reading, 'CHARTERED SURVEYORS AND ESTATE AGENTS', I read 'CHAKRA SURVIVORS AND SLATE AGATES'.
Eileen:	My day's work is over in *quartz* of an hour.
Me:	Are you *azure* about that?
	We laugh.
	Drew two stars and two snowflakes. Nibbled four teaspoons of choc body paint.

Tuesday 22nd

A miserable, stormy day.

The rain drowned its sparrows. Winter willows wept, their slim shoulders shaking in a November wind. The gutter had a stream-in-cold. Mr. Miserable-as-sin-taxi-man sat in his warm smelly cab listening to Dire Straits singing about microwave ovens. He tapped his stubby, dirty fingers on the steering wheel; he was not going to bother to traipse across the road and knock on the door in this bloody awful weather. He was not going to bother with bloody Christmas cards or bloody presents this year either, but he might buy himself a microwave oven.

Told the kittens, if they're good, Santa Claus will bring them lots of presents for Christmas. They wanted to know what sort of cat Santa *Claws* was. I said he is a St. Nicholas cat, with a thick red coat (because he lives at the North Pole), white chest and paws; and everyone stares as he enters a room because he is a cat of great presents.

Drew a parcel tied up with a bow, and a Christmas tree. They turned out well so I awarded myself two teaspoons of choc body paint.

Wednesday 23rd

A bright chilly day, good for jacket spotting. A middle-aged man wearing a woolly hat, gloves and sheepskin jacket, coughed himself down the road. I wondered if he had a chest problem and tried not to think about slaughtered sheep. A blonde thirty-something woman in a fleecy, bright red jacket climbed into an equally bright red car. I thought the colour suited her and tried not to let the song 'Lady in Red' enter my head and drive me round the bend. A young man sporting a big flappy jacket with lots of pockets, poppers, zips, built-in hood and reflective trim, marched across the road looking very stressed. I imagined he worked too hard to earn lots of money to buy expensive clothes and after-shave; he looked salesmanish. Maybe he had to walk because his car was at the mender's; I mean garage. A group of teenage girls giggled and shivered past, bumping into each other like logs on a fast-flowing river, their thin denim jackets held tightly round equally thin, eager bodies. A tiny dog in a tartan jacket took his old lady for walkies. Antique coffee table took his master for walkies.

Drew a bauble and Christmas cracker, scraped the last morsels of choc body paint from the jar and made a mental note to check the mini-market next to the clinic to see if they sell any (choc body paint, not baubles or crackers); I don't want Ben to know I've devoured *another* jar. Oh dear. Oh God. Oh panic. Three days to wait till Monday! Does this mean I'm a chocbodypaintaholic now?

Thursday 24th

An umbrella spotting day.

A huge red and white golfing umbrella was a striking contrast against a world in shades of grey, like a bright flower in a muddy puddle. A man in a slate-coloured raincoat holding a black umbrella, blended in perfectly with his surroundings in order to avoid the flying tax-man monster who could descend at any time, talons outstretched. The black bailiff bird perched, hunched and hungry, on a chimney pot. He didn't notice the man.

Spotted a gust-proof umbrella in a Christmas catalogue:

> 'Its aerodynamically designed infrastructure has been wind-tunnel tested and certified to withstand hurricane-level winds up to seventy-four miles per hour without turning inside out. The one-touch automatic opening feature lets you get your defences up fast, even if one arm is otherwise engaged with a shopping bag. The sure-grip, rubber-coated handle is easy to hang on to when wet and an ample, forty-six inch arc gives excellent coverage to shield you in driving rains.'

Mmm, impressive; Mary Poppins would approve. I bought an umbrella in Ireland once (the one thing I forgot to pack) at a market. The woman who sold it to me assured me it was waterproof in her beautiful Irish accent. I love Ireland!

Drew two sprigs of holly then suffered post-choc withdrawal symptoms. Ate honey on toast, but it wasn't the same. Stared in the mirror. Felt ugly. Told myself to be calm and peaceful. Gave up. Watched an episode of *The Munsters* entitled 'The Most Beautiful Ghoul In The World'.

This time next month it will be Christmas Eve; I can see festive fear settling into the faces of passers by.

Friday 25th

10.00 a.m.   This time next month, it'll be Christmas morning.

11.00 a.m.   This time next month, all the Christmas cards will have been written and sent.

12.00 noon   All the presents will have been bought and wrapped and given.

1.00 p.m.   Read in *Weekly Wife* about the ancient belief in the healing power of ginger and how this is supported by new research. You can make ginger tea and use fresh grated root in cooking, inhale ginger oil, add drops of the oil to water for a foot soak, apply fresh-cut ginger to chilblains and take supplements. You must be careful if you are pregnant, taking prescribed medication, or have a chronic illness... decide to cuddle Paddy and inhale the odour of warm ginger fur instead.

2.00 p.m.   This time next month, I'll be wearing an orange paper hat and setting light to the Christmas pudding.

3.00 p.m.   Draw a king's crown and a star on the cot. Long for one teaspoon of sweet pleasure. Don't we all?

4.00 p.m.   Hunt for writing paper and come across my unfinished story. Read story and picture Morag intent on revenge; imagine smell of lavender oil and a figure moving about in the moonlight. Pick up pen...

... Later that night, Morag crept into the garden clutching an empty Scottish shortbread tin. An owl followed her lonely figure as she crouched down to pluck wild mushrooms from damp, dark earth; a fox caught a glimpse of her sad, beautiful face in the cold, bright moonlight. Leaves rustled; the owl hooted; a hedgehog muttered in her sleep and a snail, who had just commited a crime,

worried about covering up his tracks.

Morag hurried back into the kitchen to mix her potion. An angry spider watched her crushing and blending from his death trap in the ceiling, the strong sickly smell of lavender clung to his web. Haggis, the cat, opened one eye, grinned, closed the eye, and curled up tighter on his pile of comfy washing. The lavender relaxed him.

Days followed nights and the winter weeks shivered by. Stephen's health began to deteriorate. One day he didn't turn up for his appointment at the clinic and Morag smiled to herself as she rubbed out his name pencilled in her appointment book; she rubbed hard, like Lady Macbeth removing the damned spot.

The following day she was found dead by a neighbour in her kitchen, with a tartan scarf wrapped around her neck, the old kettle whistling on the hob, and an empty Scottish shortbread tin on the table.

How shall I end my story? Should I leave my readers wondering? Had Morag eaten herself to death with Scottish shortbread; had Stephen discovered she was poisoning him during his visits to the clinic and strangled her with a tartan scarf; had she unknowingly poisoned herself too; had she developed M.E. and decided to kill herself?

5.00 p.m.   This time next month, I'll be dozing in front of the TV with a big, full, fat tummy. Nibbling a satsuma. Or my favourite Quality Street. And wondering if there's a good film on later.

6.00 p.m.   I could say here, Ben is at The Crown, King Street.
He's not. He got drunk at lunchtime.

6.05 p.m.   Who was he with?
Was he with *her*?

6.25 p.m.   Jealousy monster is sitting in the corner singing, 'Suspicion torments my heart.'

6.26 p.m.   Throw cushion at jealousy monster.

6.27 p.m.   Muffled singing from corner, 'Suspiffon why torfure meeee?'

6.30 p.m.   I am calm and peaceful girlfriend.

6.31 p.m.   I am not suspicious.

6.32 p.m.	He was probably celebrating a work colleague's birthday – a Sagittarian.
6.33 p.m.	Don't know many Sagittarians; lots of Pisceans and Virgos and Taurians, but not many Sagittarians.
6.34 p.m.	I'm a calm and peaceful, peanut-butterful Aries. I'm not thinking fiery Aries thoughts; I'm more like a calm, watery Pisces, a little fish swimming with the flow along life's long river. Swim, swim, swim.

6.35 p.m.	He was with Delyth! I know it! He's acting all distant; he'll buy me flowers or extra crisps tomorrow or both or a copy of *New Woman* and a *Weekly Wife*.
6.36 p.m.	Need large packet of Sydney Benson's Organic Crisps. Jealousy monster will stop sitting on my head singing Elvis songs; he doesn't like the crunching noises I make or the sound of rustling packets.
6.40 p.m.	Need tablespoonful of choc body paint.
6.41 p.m.	Need whole jar.
6.42 p.m.	Has he bought *her* choc body paint?
6.43 p.m.	Hope she eats it all at once, indulges over Christmas, puts on a stone; no – three stone – and he goes off her.
7.00 p.m.	I'm calm and pizzaful.
7.05 p.m.	Jealousy is bad for your immune system.
7.10 p.m.	I've got too much imagination.
7.15 p.m.	I think about food too much.
7.20 p.m.	I think far too much.
7.25 p.m.	I think fat too much.
7.30 p.m.	Goody, *Coronation Street;* should be really exciting tonight.
8.00 p.m.	This time next month, I'll be wishing I hadn't eaten so much rich food and searching for the peppermint tea.
9.00 p.m.	I'll be glaring at piles of washing-up.

10.00 p.m. Probably eating again.

11.00 p.m. This time next month, it'll all be over.

Midnight   Wish it *were* all over.

Saturday 26th

Drew a snowflake and a star, and munched two packets of healthy crisps with the potato skins left on, to relieve my post-choc withdrawal symptoms and frighten the jealousy monster away.

Inspired by watching a falling autumn leaf I plinked on Ben's keyboards and composed a little melody entitled 'The Dying Leaf'. It was so sad, I cried. Why, why, why do I do this to myself?!

Paddy padded across the keys making up his own tune. It was rather good; much better than mine. Mary sniffed the lovely flowers Ben bought. Murphy chased the jealousy monster out of the cat flap.

Sunday 27th

If you cut your fingernails on a Sunday, the Devil will be with you for the rest of the week. Oh dear.

The carpet is suffering from deep depression again. The house is having chest problems due to too much dust. The plates are shouting, 'Unclean, Unclean!' Armies of germs are marching about on the toilet, ready to fight the Harpic monster. I try my best, but sometimes I have to admit defeat.

I asked Ben if he minded terribly doing a bit of housework. He said he had a terrible headache, and would I mind terribly if he left it till next weekend. I'll probably do most of it myself before then, and end up in a terrible state.

Drew a terrible reindeer; it looked like a cow. I rubbed it out, like Lady Macbeth at her Wednesday art class.

Drew inspiration from *Songs of Praise* at St. David's Cathedral. Found myself singing along (in a fit of boredom) with all the hymns and was surprised I quite enjoyed myself! Thought my version of 'All Things Bright And Beautiful' was an improvement on the original though. A big improvement: the kittens agreed.

> **Kittens bright and beautiful**
> **All sitting in the hall**
> **Kittens wise and wonderful**
> **The Lord God made them small**

Each little bowel that opens
Each little scratch that stings
He made them many colours
He made them without wings

All things black and beautiful
All kittens great and small
All things grey and whiskerful
The Lord God made their call

They keep you warm in winter
They soak up lots of sun
They frolic in the garden
Then curl up on your tum

All things soft and wonderful
Their purring great and small
Feline eyes so tenderful
The Lord God made them all

He gave them eyes to see us
And noses that can smell
If there's Whiskas in the food bowl
And if it's been cooked well

Kittens bright and beautiful
All sitting in the hall
Kittens wise and wonderful
The Lord God made them small

Monday 28th

The small plump assistant at the mini-market said they had run out of choc body paint as she licked her sulky lips. I bought a bag of golden choc money instead.

Eileen's silver seahorse earrings dangled as she bent over me (ready to crunch my spine) and I couldn't resist asking if they were a present from someone special. She smiled. The diamond in the seahorse's eye winked at me.

Mr. Quiet-and-gentlemanly-taxi-man who brought me home said he picks up a young girl who has M.E. and takes her to school. I felt so sad I wanted to cry; hope her family and her family doctor are understanding. He also said some very kind, thoughtful things so I gave him three golden choc coins and a pound coin tip with his fare. He laughed heartily and said, 'Thanks.' I laughed and said he was welcome, and for a moment the world was a better place to live in. Later I drew a jolly sprig of holly and awarded myself two choc coins.

Tuesday 29th

We have two packs of kitchen roll with different pretty patterns on! I have a choice between pine cones and leaves or eight varieties of herbs. Decisions, decisions.

Spotted more wonderful weather-proof wear in a catalogue. Stylish raincoats with the ultimate packing ability:

> 'Lightweight yet totally waterproof, they fold into pouches and can be tucked inconspicuously into your hand luggage. Made of velvet soft microfibre, our rainwear has a tight yet supple weave that sheds wrinkles and drapes beautifully. Unlike so many so-called raincoats, these are 100% WATERPROOF, thanks to moisture blocking and sealed seems throughout.'

The *new* weather-proof sweater jackets were just as exciting, combining a knit and woven fabric for two distinct functions! More than two colours! More than two styles! One side is a casual knit sweater for lightweight warmth, treated for drizzle protection and, when the drizzle turns to drops, the other side is tightly woven polyester which is highly water-repellent and quick drying. No matter which side is out, you can roll out the water-repellent hood, then roll it up to store in the collar. *100% wonderful!* Draw cords with barrel locks at hood and bottom hem snug up against the cold and the sweater side has two, yes *two*, patch pockets for zip security. Full front zip closure has an extended, yes, *Extended* button tab to *block* wind *and* rain.

Who needs an umbrella with such amazing raincoats available, including reversible rain hats. A hat should shield you from the elements *and* express your personality: a reversible Goretex rain hat will do both these things. Both sides are *100% Waterproof* and the breathable Goretex membrane is sandwiched in between to keep you dry in the wildest of downpours, yes, *Wildest.*

Drew a pine cone; rubbed it out like Lady Macbeth with P.M.T. Drew two stars; nibbled two choc coins like a hamster with a sweet tooth. The Devil tempted me to finish the bag; I ignored him.

Wednesday 30th

Mr. Weatherman's map showed snowflakes moving down from the North tonight. Nibbled one large choc coin. Drew one snowflake.

December

Thursday 1st

Well, Well, Well. *Well done me!* Another year almost completed. Endured. *Survived.* Eleven months. Eleven *whole* months have disappeared up the chimney, high into the sky, drifting away on the clouds of time. Eleven million raindrops have dribbled down my window pane. Eleven million memories dribbled down the drain. Eleven million tears have gently eased the pain... ooooh, here comes a poem... Yes!... *yes!* ... No... maybe not today. Where was I? Oh yes. I *will* get *well* soon, I'm still on the road to recovery. The hill to recovery. The bloody steep, slippery hill to recovery, wet from all the millions of raindrops. And I am fortunate, I am so very fortunate. Lucky me. My 'well-being' has improved with lots of creative writing. I could write a poem about a wishing well, wishing myself well, using the wonderful, happy, positive word *well* lots and lots of times, till I'm sick of it. But I'm sick of it already. Oh well.

One more month to go – 'Let it snow, let it snow, let it snow.' Painted a blue snowflake on the cot and opened the Advent calendar window with a little number one on it. Ate three choc coins.

Friday 2nd

My new (bigger-size) leggings started to feel tighter today. But I was *so* positive and *so* creative. I wrote a jolly little song to the tune of *White*

433

Christmas and worked out the melody on Ben's keyboard.

> **I'm dreaming of a tight Christmas**
> **And I would like a little snow**
> **May my long hair glisten**
> **And Ben listen, to me**
> **Though I'm talking slow**
>
> **I'm dreaming of a tight Christmas**
> **With every gift tag that I write**
> **May your tree be sparkly and upright**
> **And may all your Christmas cakes be white**

Ben forgot to open his Advent calendar window so I opened it for him. I'm very thoughtful like that. And anyway, it would have taken him ages to find the little number two on the reindeer's hoof and I had a lot of trouble picking at the cardboard square, even with my long nails. He wouldn't have had the patience. And anyway, my great efforts only produced bells. Bloody boring bells and a bow, like the ones you see on boring Christmas cards with red poinsettia on a sickly green background; if you're unlucky, there will also be two candles stuck in a log with a bit of holly. If you're very unlucky, there will be a tartan bow wrapped round the neck of a startled kitten. Last year we were unfortunate: we received five or six cards with candles, bells or holly wreaths on, and I *hate wreaths.*

In *Weekly Wife*'s quick tricks for a beautiful Christmas home, Wendy suggests achieving a modern look by spraying a holly wreath silver, spicing up your Christmas with a Mexican-style chilli pepper wreath (chilli-shaped fairy lights wrapped around willow) or jazzing up plain foliage with shiny mini-parcels in magenta and gold. As if that weren't bad enough, she raves on about Valentine wreaths with roses (would this be sent by a man 'to die for'?) Easter wreaths with sugar eggs stuck on, a lavender wreath as a welcome gift, a nautical wreath with dried baby starfish varnished and stuck on and surprise, surprise... for an unusual centrepiece for your dinner party, a vegetable wreath. Shall I write and tell her she forgot to mention pine cones?

I could say here, Ben went to The Bell on the ring road and came home wreathed in cigarette and alcohol fumes. He didn't. He drank too much at lunchtime again. Another birthday? Early Christmas celebrations? Entertaining Welsh tart?

Painted two yellow bells with jolly red ribbons. Ate two choc coins. Flushed jealousy monster down toilet.

Saturday 3rd

A comforting toasty-coffee Saturday smell drifted up the stairs, tapped me on the nose, and said, 'Good morning.' I opened the curtains to find a world finely sprinkled with snow like icing sugar on Mother Nature's Victoria sandwich. My mood lifted like a sponge cake in the oven on gas mark five for twenty minutes.

Opened my Advent calendar window to be greeted by a smiling Santa. I smiled back. He asked me what I'd like for Christmas and when I said I wanted a book to cheer me up, he handed me my favourite childhood story. The next moment I was hiding in a wardrobe full of coats and the smell of mothballs, when I felt cold air on my face... then found myself surrounded by trees. Wandering into a clearing, I noticed it was snowing and the ground felt cold beneath my slippers. I met a friendly faun under a lamppost who carried several brown paper parcels in one arm and his tail was draped over the other, which also held up an umbrella covered with snow. I told him about my umbrella spotting and he was very interested in everything I said. We walked through the snow to his cave: all warm and cosy inside, with a carpet, table, two little chairs, a dresser and a mantelpiece over the fire. Above the mantelpiece was a picture of an old faun with a grey beard and a shelf full of books. We had a wonderful tea and afterwards sat by the fire while he told me stories about life in the forest, the nymphs and dryads, dwarfs and pixies, and Aslan the Lion who cured M.E. with a touch of his huge paw and warm liony breath.

Woke up to comforting hot mince pie and satsuma Christmassy smells. Felt too sleepy all day to paint anything and had a craving for Turkish Delight.

Sunday 4th

The kittens were excited by the cold, white, wet stuff on the ground; I was not excited by the cold, wet paws on my legs. Ben is excited at the thought of two weeks off work; the house is excited about being dressed up for Christmas. The fridge is looking forward to being filled with naughty but nice foods; I'm looking forward to being filled with naughty but nice foods.

Saw a rose quartz candle holder in Ace catalogue I liked the look of: 'When lit, the stone emits a beautiful glow to restore calm and peacefulness.' Am very tempted to order it as a Christmas present for myself.'

Ben was too busy to remember little trivialities like opening an Advent window so I saved him a job by opening it for him. He'd only have been disappointed anyway by candles sitting on a bed of holly, compared with my jolly Santa and Christmas pud. Yesterday he found the Christmas decorations. Today I unravelled a set of fairy lights, draped them round the fireplace and switched them on to get myself in a looking-forward-to-Christmassy-mood. It worked. The sitting room was transformed.

We're not having a real tree this year. Wendy says the needles can become embedded in animal paws. So, before dark I ventured down to the bottom of the garden to find a few small tree branches (thought I'd stick them in wine bottles, ready to be decorated with shiny baubles and lametta – very arty). The dwarves helped me when I told them what I was up to.

Happy: What a lovely idea, my dear.
Grumpy: The kittens will tear them down, mark my words.
           There'll be broken glass and cut paws everywhere.

I invited them all to a Christmas party and asked Doc to send an invite to the pixies living locally. Dopey jumped up and down with excitement and fell in a puddle.

Happy:	(Rubbing his belly) Will there be lots of mince pies?
Grumpy:	You'll only burn your tongue.
Doc:	And Christmas pudding?
Sleepy:	Soft twinkly restful lights?
Bashful:	And mistletoe?
Sneezy:	Hope your old decorations aren't too dusty.
Grumpy:	Bound to be, and I expect the lights won't work and there'll be no spare bulbs.
Doc:	Can I pour brandy on the pudding and set light to it?
Grumpy:	Only singe your beard again and set light to your eyebrows and then the whole house, no doubt. That *will* be a happy Christmas.

Ben said my wonderful arty branches in bottles looked like dead trees. Bill called in and asked me why I was decorating last year's dead tree. Christmas is such a stressful time.

Painted six red berries and six green holly leaves. Ate six choc coins.

Monday 5th

Dear God,
I'm so much better than I was this time
last year. Thank you.
Love,
Miss Carmen Peaceful x

Dear Santa,
Please send me a book on how to speed
up recovery from illness.
Love,
Miss Carmen Pizzaful x
P.S. I've been a good girl.

Dear Thorntons,
Please send me a box of those lovely
cappuccino chocolates, my reward for
surviving another year of illness.
Love,
Miss Carmen Chocful x

Received a letter and home made Christmas card from Gail. She has invited Rose and her many children to stay this coming weekend; her designer house will not stay designerish for long. They are calling in to see me if *I'm up to it*. It's going to be quite some time before I'm up to a house packed full of noisy children and lots of catching-up-conversation, but I haven't seen my friends for a year, so how can I refuse? Visitors are always a problem this time of year; by Christmas, all I want to do is curl up and die under the Christmas tree. This year Ben will visit his friends and family, so that'll make things easier.

I admired Gail's card: a gold, glittery star with silver glitter rays on black card. All her presents will be wrapped in black and gold or silver and black, the gift tags matching perfectly with a large silver or gold bow. Next weekend, she'll be wearing black with silver or gold accessories, instead of her usual black and white.

It's years since I've been to Gail's house. I wonder if she's redecorated. I remember her dining room with an Egyptian theme: golden pharaohs paced silently and solemnly in the same direction round the walls, disappearing behind black curtains decorated with gold hieroglyphs. Statues of the Egyptian goddess, Bast, sat with feline superiority either side of a bust of Nefertiti, keeping watch over a black table and chairs from Habitat. I've no need to describe the colour of the place mats, octagonal plates, candles and ~~black-stemmed~~ glasses. Dining with Gail was elegant but rather depressing sometimes. The rest of her house was stunning, inspired by Mackintosh, Klimt, Waterhouse, Clarice Cliff and Mucha. Hopefully, I'll be well enough to visit her ~~art gallery~~ home again next year.

Eileen reminisced about her youth in Scotland and we both thought it was a shame the rain had washed the snow away. We talked about how beautiful everything looks covered in snow and how pleasant it is when the sound of the traffic is muffled. As she manipulated my leg like a rolling pin on pastry, her silver fish earrings dangled and sparkled like raindrops in the wind.

Me: Have you heard of those new bands, Aqua and the Seahorses.
Eileen: Aqualung Sauces?

As she laughed, her dolphin hair slide fell onto my stomach. As I laughed the hair slide slipped off my stomach and onto the floor.

Mr. Cheerful-chatty-flirty-taxi-man showed me his little Christmas novelty in the back of the car: a tiny Christmas tree with flashing lights. I was very impressed. A plastic reindeer dangled from a key ring, silver tinsel sparkled on the dashboard and he wore a jolly red sweatshirt to match his round smiley face. Hope he picks me up again next week.

Ben forgot to open his Advent window again so I opened it for him. A snowflake. Painted three blue snowflakes and ate three choc treats from my new bag of coins.

Tuesday 6th

A Christmas card arrived from Ben's brother, Jeremy. He's a postman and always sends his cards early, neatly addressed, with the postcode clearly and boldly written. The picture on his card was a letter box in the snow with a robin perched on the top.

A card from the post office informed me that today was the last posting date for sending Christmas cards to New Zealand; I don't think Dave and Nicky in Christchurch have ever received our card before the New Year. Decided to write their card and catch the last post. Rooted around in the Christmas decorations box, found a bundle of last year's cards, and checked the spellings. Yes; it *is* Nicky (not Nickie), Beckie (not Becky), Martyn (not Martin), Jeff and Sandie (not Geoff and Sandy), Selena (not Selina) and Lina (not Lena). David and Carol and Rob and Bev are getting divorced next year so I mustn't wish them a very happy Christmas and a joyful New Year.

Started using the new kitchen roll with a lovely Christmassy holly design. Greatly inspired, I painted a sprig of holly and a star on the cot.

Opened today's Advent window to find two little snowmen. Wonderfully inspired, I picked up my pen...

TWO LITTLE SNOWMEN

I'm having some trouble controlling
The urge to get up and go
Like when I was ten
And two little snowmen
Were calling me out to the snow

They needed some coal for their eyes
Two carrots for their noses
I wanted to play
Till the end of the day
When my fingers and toezez were frozez

Nibbled three choc coins while watching *EastEnders*.

Wednesday 7th

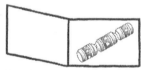

Two more cards arrived today from Jeff and Sandie in Cornwall and Ben's mum; they always send their cards early too. Jeff and Sandie's card was a cartoon of a robin throwing snowballs at a ginger cat as he emerged from a cat flap. It made me laugh so I placed it on the TV where I'll see it first thing every morning. Ben's mum's card was a Nativity scene; it's on a shelf somewhere.

The fashion models in *Weekly Wife* were prancing about in the snow like frozen fairies, wearing ~~waifer~~ wafer thin cardigans and matching camisoles, shawls as fine as a spider's web, wisps of mohair, a little cashmere here and there, and enough pure new wool to keep a beauty spot warm for the winter. I hope they're paid an allowance for Lemsip, Kleenex tissues, Night Nurse, throat lozenges, oranges and loss of earnings due to bouts of bronchitis, pneumonia, pleurisy, colds and flu.

There was a cracker in Ben's window today; must remember to put crackers on the Christmas shopping list.

Painted a cracker green and yellow and two stars blue. Ate three choc coins. The dwarves were watching me through the window so I made signals to suggest they could come in and have a look at the cot if they wanted to.

Happy:	That's lovely my dear.
Bashful:	You're ever so clever.
Grumpy:	You missed a bit, girl.
Sneezy:	Oh dear, the smell of paint is getting up my nose.
Sleepy:	I'd love a cot to sleep in.
Doc:	Keep going lass, you're doin' well.

Dopey touched the paint and grinned; now he really *did* have green fingers. The others helped me by collecting up the soggy newspaper by the cat flap and wiping the grubbiest parts of the kitchen floor with kitchen roll. I paid them each with one big shiny golden choc coin. Their faces lit up. Doc wanted to know what else they could do to help me, so I said I'd make a list of jobs. Great! Must buy lots more bags of chocolate money.

Our Hoover vacuum cleaner has stopped working. Ben is unable to find a rubber band for it in the hardware shops and we can't afford a new one at the moment so maybe my little workers will pick up the bits on the carpets for me. Doc said there's not a lot of digging work at the moment and the lads are getting bored.

Wrote a song to the tune of *Winter Wonderland* because I'm still *so* positive and *so* creative.

Oh! the carpets are dirty
And the taxi-man is flirty
Little bits are gonna snow
On the carpet it will show

We need another Hoover rubber band

Thursday 8th

The weather has turned very windy – Mother Nature rushing about doing her Christmas shopping, her plaid pull-on skirt, in shades of sage and plum, with fully elasticated waistband and functional drawstring, flapping around her ankles.

Spotted two umbrellas turned inside out (a flowery one with scalloped edge and a brown one with white spots on). In *Northanger Abbey* last night, Catherine Morland felt depressed after spotting four umbrellas; she hated the sight of umbrellas. Mrs. Allen said they were very disagreeable things to carry. In strong winds, yes, they are most disagreeable!

The windows rattled, a dried up lump of bread fell down the chimney on to material sunflowers with fluttering petals, the kittens were blown in through the cat flap (leaves stuck to their paws) and today's post shot through the letterbox, making me jump. Another could-be-a-Christmas-card type envelope lay on the mat by the front door.

I studied the card (an impressionist painting of shadows cast on snow by sunlight on trees and hedgerow) for ages. Felt very calm. Very peaceful. I placed the card on the window ledge. Thanks, Artie Auntie.

Today's Advent picture was a Christmas tree with a star on top. Recalled my bed-sit years: one Christmas Eve, I was doing a bit of food shopping after work at the local supermarket when I saw a tiny Christmas tree in a pot next to the Heinz baked beans. I had to give it a home. There was also a lonely book left in the bargain bin (for twenty pence) about the life of Barry Manilow; it needed a home too. I never read the book, but I looked at all the pictures in the middle. A few times. To get my money's worth. After Christmas, I planted the tree in my parents' garden. It's taller than me now. One year it was covered in ladybirds. I don't know what happened to the book about Barry Manilow; it's probably sitting on a shelf in the R.S.P.C.A. charity shop.

Painted a green Christmas tree in a red pot, with a yellow star and baubles. Felt sad for trees with their roots cut off, tied up, and dying outside shops. Wrote a sad poem. Screwed it up. Wrote a small pile of Christmas cards and envelopes and ate too many choc coins while I watched *EastEnders*.

Friday 9th

Had a bit of trouble locating a number nine on the Advent calendar – Ben would never have found it hidden among the presents on Santa's sleigh. It would have taken up too much of his computer time and I *did* spend *ages* picking at the little cardboard window before it opened to reveal an angel. Decided to paint an angel on Hollie's cot, her guardian angel.

Murphy dragged a wet, muddy, green glove in through the cat flap; it looked like one of Ben's. Mary batted my favourite pen under the cooker and Paddy rolled a jar of vitamin C round the dining room till the top came off. I stayed calm and creative.

> **On the twelfth day of Christmas**
> **The kittens gave to me**
> **Twelve dirty paw marks**
> **Eleven torn up tissues**
> **Ten holes in curtains**
> **Nine rips in carpets**
> **Eight laces chewed up**
> **Seven bowls need filling**
> **Six vets need paying**
> **Five chess pieces...**
> **Four dead birds**
> **Three felt pens**
> **Two muddy gloves**
> **And a bottle of vitamin C.**

I watched a man in his thirties walk past our house with four young children under the age of six; they were milling all over the pavement as Dad plodded along weighed down by carrier bags, every now and then keeping an eye on his offspring. I was reminded of a daddy swan, surrounded by his fluffy grey cygnets... is it six swans a-swimming, or seven swans a-swimming? When I was little I sang, 'four calley birds, three frenchens, two dirty doves, and a parsnip in a pear tree!'

I've run out of chocolate money, the shop only had two bags left and I had to pay the dwarves for cleaning the windows today. It was fun to watch them climbing their tiny ladders made of twigs and tied together with my garden twine; they preferred it to bindweed.

Ben went to The Barrel O'Laughs, Beer Street, with Rob and Bob the Slob.

Saturday 10th

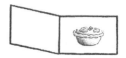

Too overhung to search for his window on the Advent calendar, Ben groaned into a steaming Kit-Kat mug. I kindly opened the window for him: a mince pie.

Read all about where to buy the best mince pies. Tesco's pies came top with 'a yummy, fruity, spicy filling and golden pastry that tastes home-made'. The best Christmas puddings came from Waitrose; with Grand Marnier 'they are perfectly moist with a refreshing orange taste'. Ate three satsumas but still had a longing for pies, puddings and Terry's chocolate orange. Read about housewives who have decided to take a holiday abroad this Christmas and forget about the usual preparations. Wrote another song to the tune of 'God Rest Ye Merry Gentlemen':

GOD REST YE MERRY HOUSEWIFE

Who's going to do the washing-up
When our bellies are full
Who's going to wrap the prezzies up
Red and green crackers pull
Who'll decorate the Christmas tree
And to the turkey see
Oh! This year it won't be me
Won't be me
Oh! This year it won't be me

Who's going to count the pennies up
And wander with sore feet
Around the endless rows of shops
For lovely things to eat

Who's going to write the Christmas cards
And postal deadlines meet
Oh! This year it won't be me
Won't be me
Oh! This year it won't be me

Who'll be rolling pastry out
With flour on her chin
Peeling sprouts and potatoes
And emptying the bin
I'll be lazing in the sunshine
With a lovely glass of gin

Oh! This year it won't be me
Won't be me
Oh! This year it won't be me

Two parcels from catalogues and two Christmas cards from relatives arrived with the post and Ben brought home a six-foot imitation Christmas tree. What a fun day! It's going to be a fun week! Advent windows to open, a Christmas tree to decorate, Christmas cards to write, a cot to paint, cards to open, presents to wrap and seven dwarves to do the housework!

The two parcels were full of Christmas gifts for Rose, Gail, Mum, Gina, Artie Auntie, Auntie Mary and Eileen; I pretended they were all for me, then wanted to keep them.

Cosmic Colin: 'Jobs around the house come to a halt this week as you turn your attention to creative matters.' Colin would have been right, as I have the urge to complete the cot, and a few poems and songs. But I have my seven little helpers now: they were busy dusting and picking bits off the carpets today while Ben was out shopping. I gave them satsuma segments and slices of mince pie but promised to pay them properly after I'd been to the chocolate money bank on Monday.

Happy: That's fine, dear.
Doc: The pie and oranges are delicious.

Grumpy: We want a Christmas bonus after all this effort.

Sneezy: Can I have a few sheets of that lovely absorbent kitchen roll?

Painted two yellow bells with red ribbons and one star.

Sunday 11th

The Advent calendar is missing. Maybe the dwarves have hidden it for a joke or the pixies have stolen it, thinking it has magic windows; I never did trust Bloodwort and Scabwort from Wormwood Tubs. Maybe the kittens have pulled it down because they wanted a turn opening a window with their tiny sharp claws. Must look under the chairs.

The dwarves came round to do the washing-up. Doc balanced on the edge of the sink lifting the bowls, plates and mugs with Happy's help. Grumpy scrubbed and grumbled about the steam and stubborn-stuck-on-bits. Bashful passed the wet crockery to Sleepy and Sneezy to dry with kitchen roll, and Dopey piled everything up precariously. They all got together to tip half the water out of the washing-up bowl so they could reach the cutlery, and Dopey fell in. Grumpy said he was waiting for that to happen and Doc said they were sorry they'd broken a Kit-Kat mug. I laughed.

I was really pleased the house looked clean and tidy when Gail and Gareth, Rose and the children arrived at two o'clock. I wasn't too tired either, although, after half an hour of chatting and everyone saying how well I looked, me saying how much the children had grown, the children tearing up and down the stairs, Emily pulling videos and CDs out of cupboards, Charlotte removing the fridge magnets from the fridge door, baby Elizabeth waking up and screaming, the twins fighting and knocking over my Christmas creations in wine bottles, Victoria having a teenage tantrum and folding her arms like her mother and little Tiffany crying because big Grant had pulled her French plait, I retreated to the bedroom and shut myself in with the excuse that I wanted to write their cards and wrap a few presents. I'd already done this, so I lay on the bed breathing deeply and massaging my fatigued shoulder muscles while Ben poured drinks for eleven, opened the Jaffa cakes and filled the oven with Mr. Kipling mince pies. I thought I might put on *The Jungle Book* video to keep the children amused, because Rudyard Kipling does write *exceedingly* good books.

Things quietened down for a while until I heard tapping on the bedroom door, whispers and giggles. I let three dear little monsters drag me downstairs and laughed at their endless questions and embarrassing comments. My large collection of coloured pencils, felt pens, drawing paper and cuddly toys came in useful, though I had visions of tying up and gagging the little darlings. But only for a second of course. I put on a video of *One Hundred and One Dalmatians* and, after cries of, 'We've seen it hundreds of times,' they finally settled down; then I had a good natter with the girls. We compared grey hairs and frown lines. Victoria unfolded her arms and nibbled the edges off a Jaffa cake, leaving the orangy bit in the middle. I wondered if she'd started counting calories and made a mental note to buy Jaffa cakes for the dwarves.

5.00 p.m.   Lots of goodbyes, kisses, hugs, good-to-see-yous, take cares, thanks for nibbles, thanks for prezzies, happy Christmasses, happy New Years, get well soons and write soons.

5.05 p.m.   Peace at last. Kittens emerge from their hiding places.

5.10 p.m.   One of the children has written 'pooh' and 'plop' on the cot. How delightful.

Monday 12th

10.00 a.m.   There's something missing from my life... what is it... oh yes, the Advent calendar. I can't find it anywhere.

10.02 a.m.   Open two Christmas cards, one with festive dolphins from Gina and a Nativity scene from my parents.

10.30 a.m.   Hooray! The dwarves have arrived to clean the carpets and wash up after yesterday's visit.

11.00 a.m.   Promise dwarves I will pay them tomorrow. Grumpy tuts and rolls his eyes.

11.15 a.m.   Excited – spot a lovely tartan umbrella.

11.16 a.m.   Think I'll go to U.S.A. (Umbrella Spotters Anonymous) next year.

11.30 a.m.   Sit on side of bath and snip off twenty-two split ends.

11.40 a.m.   I've got twenty-two more Christmas cards to write.

11.45 a.m.   Search for a spell to write Christmas cards. Can only find cures for coughs, chilblains, cataracts, catarrh and cysts.

Also uses for catnip, chamomile, cherry, cinnamon, clove, comfrey, coriander, cumin, citron and cinquefoil.

11.50 a.m. Fifty seconds of pagan aerobics.

12.15 p.m. Write out seven cards. Stamp and address seven envelopes. I only know one birthday on the 25th of December (v. famous man born in stable) but I feel as if I'm writing cards and wrapping presents for twenty-five birthdays.

12.30 p.m. The dwarves are loading the washing machine now; they're such hard little workers. Grumpy, Sneezy and Bashful are dragging the clothes down the stairs. Grumpy is complaining about the smell of Ben's socks, Sneezy sneezes as fluff and cat hairs get up his nose, and Bashful is embarrassed by my underwear. Doc is standing in the open doorway of the machine shouting orders and Happy is passing the clothes up to him. It's a dark wash and Happy keeps passing him lights! Dopey is pouring too much washing liquid into the machine and it drips on Happy's nose. Sleepy is curled up snoring on my soft woolly cardigan. Grumpy sniffs my knickers when he thinks no-one's looking.

1.00 p.m. Wash hair.
Have bath.

1.30 p.m. Dwarves are sitting on kitchen floor, watching the clothes spinning round in the washing machine, smoking and drinking dandelion and burdock out of egg cups.

1.35 p.m. Grumpy: 'Haven't you got any Black Beer or Blood Tonic?'

2.00 p.m. Dwarves load the tumble dryer.

2.30 p.m. Doc says, 'When we've washed all the clothes, we'll do the sheets, towels, throws and cushion covers. The pixies, Rhizome and Woodruff from Downunderbigtree, Bract, Bogbean and Whortleberry are dropping in to help.'

2.32 p.m. Lay back in armchair feeling like a lady of leisure.

2.35 p.m. Happy says, 'The pixies are looking forward to the Christmas party. The little gay fellows, Tansy and Crispum, are dressing up in sparkly jackets made from fairy thread. Young Spignel from Thornapple Mountain has got the flumps and needs to rest, but Teazel and Figwort are very, very excited. The lads helping with the housework are coming too; they thought your sitting room would look good decorated with holly and mistletoe. Whortleberry knows where to find holly laden with *big juicy* red berries, and Bract and Bogbean have found a log they think will make a really good coffee table. Woodruff has collected pine cones sprinkled with fairy glitter, that shines *ever so brightly* in the dark. It's going to be a lovely party, dear.'

2.40 p.m.   Really looking forward to party now.

3.00 p.m.   Mr. Boxer-face is walking antique coffee table; he must have got the day off work. Hope he hasn't lost his job just before Christmas. Saw his dad the other day, who also has a boxer dog. Four little scrunched up faces walked down the road, I was SO tempted to take a photograph.

3.15 p.m.   Kittens shelter indoors from chilly December afternoon. I stroke their cold paws and ears. Feel very calm and peaceful.

3.30 p.m.   Watch boring quiz show weighed down by three little warm hairy bodies. Whiskers tickle my nose. The odd claw pricks my flesh through my leggings. There's lots of rumbly purring.

4.30 p.m.   Write poetry.

4.45 p.m.   Paddy chews the corner of the page (his saliva making the ink run) then joyfully tears it to shreds. He's not a fan of my writing.

4.46 p.m.   I let him continue. He makes me laugh; I'm not a fan of my writing either! Sometimes I join the torn pieces together – more fun than a jigsaw.

4.50 p.m.   Mary grabs my pen with a tiny grey paw, tosses it into the air, then bats it under the sofa.

4.51 p.m.   Whenever I need a pen, I just look under a chair.

4.55 p.m.   Murphy lays across the words I've just written, swishing his long black tail over the lines I'm trying to write.

4.57 p.m.   Give up.

4.58 p.m.   Kiss Murphy on the nose.

5.02 p.m.   Paint star and snowflake on cot.

6.10 p.m.   Mr. Cheerful-chatty-flirty-taxi-man picks me up. He's wearing his bright red sweatshirt again and his little Christmas novelty flashes all the way to the clinic.

6.24 p.m.   Purchase seven bags of chocolate money and Jaffa cakes.

6.30 p.m.	Open one bag while I'm waiting to see Eileen. Eat three coins.
6.40 p.m.	Eileen is crunching my bones.
6.45 p.m.	We talk about the problems of present buying and the cost, and I ask her if she's bought anything for Bill.
6.47 p.m.	Eileen describes the jumper, shirt, trousers and book she's bought for Bill. It must be love, love, love...
7.00 p.m.	Offer to pay Eileen with a bag of chocolate money; we laugh.
7.02 p.m.	Give her the gifts she ordered from my catalogues: *Ocean Mist* bath oil (in recycled bottle with real seashells), *Ocean Mist* luxury gift pack (with shell soaps and body balm), *Ocean Mist* wash bag set (soaps and a dolphin-shaped sponge), seahorse-stemmed glasses, Belgian chocolates, festive fish gift wrap, tags and Christmas cards to match.
7.03 p.m.	I warn her they all add up to quite a few squids so she fishes around in her bag and brings out a mermaid's purse.
7.05 p.m.	Eileen thanks me for doing her Christmas shopping. I reply that it's the least I can do after all she's done for me.
7.10 p.m.	Mr. Ex-racing-driver-taxi-man whizzes me home in time to put the kettle and potatoes on before *Coronation Street* and *EastEnders*.
9.00 p.m.	Wish I hadn't finished that bag of chocolate money.

Tuesday 13th

 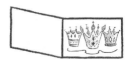

Found the Advent calendar on the kitchen floor; it had been posted through the cat flap in the night. There was a muddy paw print on Santa's face and all the little windows had been opened. From the eleventh window to the twenty-fourth, someone had tried to close them (so it looked like they hadn't been opened). But there's no foolin' an experienced Advent cal. opener like me.

Enjoyed opening three windows in one go; I've never done that before! Lucky me. Felt inspired to do lots of painting on the cot. A Christmas stocking, three crowns and a drum.

The dwarves and pixies washed and dried the curtains. I handed out mince pies, Jaffa cakes and ginger beer, and paid them three bags of chocolate money; apparently the fairies grant them all sorts of lovely wishes if they leave a pile of coins overnight in a fairy ring.

Devoured eight choc coins during a good scary bit in *EastEnders*. Wondered where the nearest fairy ring was. Ben wondered where all the mince pies had gone.

Wednesday 14th

Admired my clean curtains and windows.

Yesterday I was thinking how dirty and nicotine-stained the curtains looked in the house opposite, compared to the white frilly ones in the houses either side. Today I noticed they'd been washed. Oh dear, the people across the road have probably been thinking the same thing about my curtains, how embarrassing.

Today's Advent picture was a robin. He must have been a *him* because his breast was very bright red. I love to see robins in the snow but of course only ever see one at a time in the garden as they're very territorial. I *did* see two fighting once, which was unusual. My bird book says they're the gardener's friend but bold and aggressive towards other birds – a good description of Rick's ex-wife, who's been shagging some old boy down the allotments.

As I lay in the bath listening to the birds chirruping, the sheets and pillow cases fluttered downstairs with the pixies. Later the cushion covers and throws flew across the dining room and into the washing machine. Doc shouted orders, Grumpy grumbled, Happy laughed.

Wrote another pile of cards but didn't paint anything; overdid it yesterday. Paid the pixies and dwarves another bag of choc money but wasn't tempted to eat any myself; the slimming article, thin models in *Weekly Wife* and info about Cellutrim (the product women have been waiting for) from Goldshield made me want to count calories.

Thursday 15th

9.46 a.m.	Open Advent window. A wreath.
9.47 a.m.	Open three Christmas cards from Ben's uncle John and a couple of Ben's mates: a miserable-looking partridge in a pear tree, a bemused tabby kitten surrounded by poinsettia, and a silvery snowflake on a white background.
9.49 a.m.	I'll paint a snowflake later, maybe two.
10.36 a.m.	Paint two snowflakes.
12.33 p.m.	Sit in bath removing blue paint from hands and arms.
12.43 p.m	Admire new crystal: white onyx. Am crystal expert now, so I know this stone instills a positive outlook, lifts mild depression and combats stress.
1.00 p.m.	A church bell in the distance strikes one...

... expect the first ghost when the bell tolls one...

1.02 p.m.	As the sky darkens and the room fills with gloom, I imagine being visited by the ghost of Jacob Marley. I shiver.
1.04 p.m.	Recall playing the ghost of Christmas present in a school play. Just before the performance, I accidentally smeared red stage make-up down the front of my light green costume. Tried to cover the mark with beige No.9 but it looked worse!
1.44 p.m.	Stare at Christmas tree in box. It's about time it was up and dressed and looking lovely like me. Ha, ha.
2.04 p.m.	Take tree out of box.
2.05 p.m.	Start joining together the trunk and plastic feet and adjusting the branches. Quite hard work.
2.06 p.m.	Tree branches look so real I sniff them, for a second expecting a fresh fir tree fragrance. Feel silly. Glad no-one is looking.
2.07 p.m.	Hear little sniggers from outside.
2.15 p.m.	Tired. Must rest.
2.20 p.m.	The dwarves are sitting on the kitchen floor watching towels and dressing gowns spinning round in the washing machine. I sit with them for a while.

2.21 p.m.

Happy: I'm bringing sparkling wine to your party, made by the flower fairies.

Doc: It's similar to elderflower champagne but more delicious; after one sip you feel full of vitality and want to laugh and dance at the same time.

Me: Oh goody! The flower fairies can come to the party if they like.

Grumpy: You'll regret it, girl. There's 'undreds of 'em. They're a damn nuisance, always fluttering about, wings like flies, whispering and giggling. They talk too much and they're always up to some mischief.

Happy: They're only tiny little things, very colourful and pretty. You'll love 'em, my dear.

Bashful: They can put decorations on your ceiling and the high places.

Doc: Save you falling off a ladder or a chair.

2.25 p.m. Must ask Ben to buy fairy cakes, extra nice nibbly things, nuts and fruit. I'll tell him I'm feeling well enough to be sociable and see a few of my *little* friends. There's mushroom quiche and pizzas in the freezer; the fairies will like them. The dwarves will enjoy the brandy in the mince pies and Christmas pudding I bought at the mini-market. I've been saving the tops from my mineral water bottles; they'll make good miniature cups.

3.00 p.m. Pay dwarves last bag of choc money.

3.01 p.m. Must buy seven chocolate tree decorations on Monday.

3.05 p.m. Put on Abba tape to get me going.

3.10 p.m. 'Mamma Mia, here I go again...' Drape two sets of fairy lights on the tree.

3.12 p.m. Switch on lights to check they are working. Pixies cheer from the doorway, I didn't hear them come in through the cat flap!

3.14 p.m. Lie on floor enjoying sparkly rainbow colours in the fading afternoon light with the pixies. They're going to bring pixie pie to my party made with magic mushrooms.

3.16 p.m. We all sing, 'Money, money, money, chocolate money, it's a rich man's world.'

3.20 p.m.	Think I'll leave the curtains open so passers by can enjoy the lights. Christmas tree lights in windows always cheere me up on the way home from work on chilly December evenings.
3.46 p.m.	Drape red and gold tinsel round my neck and dance around a little to *Dancing Queen*. 'You can dance, you can jive, la la.. la la.. la la la... oooooh... see that girl, do be do, she is the tinsel queen... oooooh...' Pixies dance around my feet, they love Abba.
3.48 p.m.	Flop on sofa still wearing sparkly boa.
3.49 p.m.	Kittens charge in through cat flap and decide to rescue Mummy from big red and gold sparkly snake wrapped round her neck.
3.52 p.m.	Kittens gently deposited in back room.
4.00 p.m.	Pixies help me hang tinsel and matching baubles on tree. They stand on each other's shoulders and climb the branches.
4.10 p.m.	We admire our efforts.
4.12 p.m.	Take wooden angels playing musical instruments out of box. Pixies dangle them on the lower branches and we all sing-a-long to Abba, 'I believe in angels...'
4.14 p.m.	Whortleberry climbs to the top of the tree with the fairy over his shoulder. For a moment, I swear I see her smiling.
4.15 p.m.	Bract and Bogbean hang miniature musical instruments on the branches below her: trumpets, harps, violins, cellos and drums.
4.17 p.m.	Rhizome finds a rocking horse, a snowman, a dove of peace and a tiny Christmas pudding. He drapes them over his shoulder and climbs to the middle of the tree. Woodruff picks up a penguin in a scarf, a bell, a Father Christmas and a reindeer.
4.18 p.m.	I capture three little toy soldiers. Abba sing, 'Like a soopa troopa...'
4.20 p.m.	Pixies are giggling at their reflections in the baubles. I pull a face in a gold bauble. We all fall about laughing. Whortleberry falls out of the tree onto a soft pile of silver tinsel.
4.22 p.m.	The tree looks beauuutiful. We all cheer, HURRAH!

Friday 16th

There were seven giant snowflakes on Mr. Weatherman's map of England this morning and I was sure I could smell snow on the kittens' fur.

Two parcels arrived full of Christmas gifts. I wonder if the contents shrink in the post; they often look smaller than they appear in the catalogue. Wrapped two pairs of socks and a calendar. Wrote five Christmas cards.

Today's Advent picture was a pile of presents so, of course, I felt inspired to paint a green parcel tied with red ribbon on the cot. Gina rang to ask if she could collect it this weekend and I felt pleased I was able to say yes, as I made a quick mental note of what had to be done (a snowflake and a bell), when I could do it (if I had the energy) and were there other things more important that needed doing first. She wanted to collect it Saturday morning but I wanted to take my time finishing it in the afternoon and spend the evening preparing for, and enjoying my party. So I asked her to collect it Sunday. I've learnt to say no. And it feels good.

Saturday 17th

Mother Nature had tied her pinny round her slim waist and was sifting a little icing sugar over her chocolate log when I awoke. A dove of peace flew about in the Advent window and a reindeer with a red nose grinned out of today's Christmas card. I finished painting the cot this afternoon and, as soon as Ben had left to go to his work's Christmas dinner and dance, I began preparations for the party.

6.30 p.m. Sort out Christmas cassette tapes.
6.35 p.m. Rinse out egg cups and bottle tops, find stripy straws, cut them in half and arrange in glasses. Cut vege-sausages in

half. Place pizzas and quiche and mince pies in oven. Pour nuts and nibblies and crisps into bowls. Chill drinks. Dim lights. Switch on Christmas tree lights. Find fairy cakes and Christmas paper plates left over from last year's festivities.

7.15 p.m.   Switch kitchen lights on and off to signal to dwarves it's time to come in and help.

7.18 p.m.   Dwarves are busy cutting up food and arranging on plates, sticking cocktail sticks in vege-sausages, carrying bowls of fruit, nuts, crisps and tasty nibbles into sitting room, pouring drinks, lighting candles and lighting a fire with twigs, my screwed up poetry, and fire lighters.

7.25 p.m.   The bottles of fairy wine glow in the candlelight and sparkle like millions of microscopic fantasy fireworks.

7.26 p.m.   Food smells delightfully delicious.

7.27 p.m.   Christmas tree looks marvellously magical.

7.30 p.m.   I open the back door and Doc whistles. Pixies skip into the kitchen: Whortleberry and Teazel drag branches of holly, Woodruff's arms are laden with mistletoe, Rhizome and Figwort roll a log for use as a fairy drinks table, Bract and Bogbean carry the pixie pie with a huge golden crust.

7.31 p.m.   Tansy and Crispum show off their new jackets made from silvery fairy thread, and hand me a small sack full of pine cones sprinkled with fairy glitter.

7.40 p.m.   Tell Tansy and Crispum they look wonderful, then place pine cones in the hearth – they begin to glow like miniature luminous trees.

7.41 p.m.   Doc tells me that if I burn a pine cone in a pot before I go to bed, then sprinkle the ashes in the hearth, I will be able to make a fairy spell to heal skin problems.

7.42 p.m.   Doc sticks his head out of the cat flap and calls the fairies, then plods back into the sitting room and tells us we must sit in silence with our eyes tight shut and concentrate on beautiful flowery thoughts or they will not enter the house.

7.43 p.m.   A fairy wind rushes in through the cat flap, into the sitting room and swirls around the Christmas tree. The kittens gallop upstairs as fast as their little paws will carry them and hide. Chimes tinkle. Candles flicker. Pine cones glow brightly.

7.44 p.m.   The wind becomes a gentle breeze. The faint sound of lilting harp music reaches our ears and the scent of flowers fills the room. As we sit quietly listening, sweet melodies slowly grow closer and closer, and are joined by tiny soft voices singing. Beautiful ethereal voices singing like angels.

7.45 p.m.   Doc says it's OK to open our eyes, and what a delightful scene! Riding on the rainbow breeze are twenty, thirty, maybe fifty tiny balls of iridescent light.

7.46 p.m.   As I look carefully I can see charming fairies the size of my little finger, their translucent butterfly wings fluttering, exquisite faces laughing and singing as they dance.

7.47 p.m.   Round and round the Christmas tree they fly, sometimes stopping to smile at their reflections and check their fairy make-up in the golden baubles.

7.48 p.m.   The bright light around their bodies is gradually fading and I can see them more clearly now as they settle down to rest in the branches of the tree. They warm their hands on the fairy lights. Doc points out the Snowdrop fairy who is talking to the wooden snowman. The Colt's Foot fairy rides on the rocking horse and the Bluebell fairy plays with a bell.

7.49 p.m.   Doc tells me all their names but it's like being at a party where you're introduced to lots of people but have forgotten all their names. He says it's hard to tell them apart tonight because most of them are wearing crop tops made from spider web rinsed in moonlight dew and entwined with dandelion wool, the latest fashion from Miss Saxifrage.

7.50 p.m.   Bashful is a little pink in the face; the crop tops are see-through. Grumpy pretends not to leer.

7.51 p.m.   Put on one of the Christmas cassette tapes. The dwarves and pixies start rockin' around the Christmas tree to Shakin' Stevens. I join in.

7.52 p.m.   Fairies fly out of the tree and around the room pinning shiny paper chains to the ceiling, arranging the holly and mistletoe on shelves and singing along to Gary Glitter's *Another Rock and Roll Christmas*.

8.03 p.m.	We've all worked up an appetite and a thirst for fairy wine. Perry Como sings, *God Rest Ye Merry Gentlemen.*
8.04 p.m.	Everyone is happily munching on tasty nibbles, mushroom quiche, pizza and pixie pie.
8.05 p.m.	The fairy wine is going down well: loveliest drink I've ever tasted. Refill egg cups and bottle tops, and fill saucers up to the edges. The fairies sit round the saucers and sip wine through their tiny fairy straws.
8.06 p.m.	Cliff Richard is singing *Mistletoe and Wine.* The pixies groan; they want Abba, and the dwarves want to hear the Bee Gees. I promise to play both their requests later. Fancy singing along to David Essex myself.
8.07 p.m.	Dwarves decide to make up their own words to the songs.
Happy:	Christmas time, mistletoe and wine.
Grumpy:	Poor go hungry, lots of crime.
Doc:	Logs on the fire.
Grumpy:	Roots cut off trees.
Sneezy:	Dust from the tinsel making you sneeze.
8.08 p.m.	
Happy:	Jingle bells, jingle bells, jingle all the way.
Grumpy:	Awful noise from lots of toys.
Sleepy:	Keeping you awake.
Bashful:	Hey!
Happy:	Jingle bells, jingle bells, jingle all the way.
Doc:	Oh what fun it is to slide downhill on Grandma's tray.
Happy:	Dashing through the snow.
Doc:	In a one horse open tray.
Grumpy:	Crash into a post.
Sleepy:	In hospital all day.
Doc:	Stay in bed all week.
Sleepy:	At least you get some sleep.
Happy:	Father Christmas brings you gifts.
Grumpy:	You're not allowed to keep.
Bashful:	Hey!
8.09 p.m.	I wonder what Ben is up to, but the thought only lasts a moment, I'm having such a brilliant time. I feel *so* well and *so* happy and excited all at once.
8.10 p.m.	Fairy wine is amazing.
8.11 p.m.	Pixie pie really delicious.

8.12 p.m.   We're all enjoying the fairy cakes and mince pies (cut into tiny lumps for the fairies) pudding and fruit.

8.30 p.m.   Whortleberry and Woodruff are singing along to Paul McCartney's *Wonderful Christmas Time*. They're sitting on the mantelpiece, their legs dangling. A pixie boot drops into Grumpy's drink below; I quickly get him another one before there's trouble.

8.31 p.m.   Happy says he's heard on the bindweed that Bloodroot and Scabwort from Wormwood Tubs may try to cat-flap-crash our party.

8.32 p.m.   I have a word with Doc, who says he'll organise cat flap watch duty in the kitchen between himself and Happy and Grumpy, and if things get nasty he'll call the dragon who lives in Downunderbridge, Wood Sorrel Way.

8.33 p.m.   Hope there's no trouble. But *I would* quite like to see a dragon. I've heard he's only small and quite friendly, even though his fiery nostrils are worse than his bite if you upset him.

8.34 p.m.   Jim Reeves sings, *Silver Bells*. Teazel, Figwort, Bract and Bogbean are sitting in the Christmas tree chatting up the prettiest fairies.

8.36 p.m.   Rhizome is dozing among the presents under the tree with Sneezy, Sleepy and Dopey. Doris Day sings, *Winter Wonderland.*

8.38 p.m.   Tansy and Crispum are sitting on the TV singing along to Nat King Cole.

8.41 p.m.   With sad, solemn, miserable expressions and swaying from side to side, the dwarves (apart from Grumpy, who is on cat flap duty) sing *Lonely This Christmas* by Mud. I fall off the chair laughing.

8.45 p.m.   The fairies, pixies, dwarves and myself sing at the tops of our voices to Bing Crosby's *White Christmas.*

9.00 p.m.   The fairies love Mike Oldfield's *In Dulce Jubilo.*

9.05 p.m.   They dance a little jig round the tree, line-dance on the window ledge, cartwheel across the backs of the chairs, twist on the TV and boogie on the bookshelves.

9.10 p.m.   Sit on toilet smiling and singing to self. 'Deck the halls with something holly, fa la la la la, la la, la la; fill with food your Safeway trolley, fa la la la la, la la, la la.'

9.11 p.m.	Dwarves nip out of the cat flap to relieve themselves and hurry back in; it's a windy night.
9.15 p.m.	Woodruff and Whortleberry are dancing with the Blueberry and Bluebell fairies to Elton John's *Step into Christmas*. Teazel is teasing the Elderberry fairy and Figwort is making the Foxglove fairy giggle.
9.16 p.m.	Bract and Bogbean are playing hide and seek with the Daisy, Daffodil, Poppy, Primrose and Buttercup fairies.
9.17 p.m.	Wild Thyme and Wild Rose are annoying Grumpy by pulling his hat off and hiding it in the holly.
9.20 p.m.	David Essex is singing, *A Winter's Tale*.
9.21 p.m.	Honeysuckle is fluttering her eyelashes at Bashful and Spindleberry is tickling Sleepy's nose while he snores. Dopey has fallen truly, madly and deeply in love with the Apple Blossom fairy as she feeds him satsuma segments.
9.22 p.m.	Doc is enjoying an interesting conversation in the kitchen with the Hazel Nut, Beech Nut and Horse Chestnut fairies, as he masterfully cracks a Brazil nut for them to nibble on.
9.23 p.m.	Sneezy sneezes over the poor little Sorrel fairy as she flutters past his nose.
9.30 p.m.	Put on Abba tape. The pixies cheer and show off in front the fairies; they know all the words to *Dancing Queen*.
9.40 p.m.	Bang! Crash! Bump! Thump! Lots of shouting in kitchen! Better investigate quick!
9.41 p.m.	A dragon, the size of a dachshund, is clutching two angry, devilish-looking pixies in his talons, his nostrils pointed at their heads like the barrels of a gun. Doc orders him to put them down and they run for their life, out the cat flap and down the garden, swearing in pixish.
9.42 p.m.	Doc introduces me to Patrick Dragon, a handsome little fellow with pearly leaf-green scales the shape of shamrock. Huge golden eyes gaze up at me and I bend down to offer my hand. My fingernails have grown so long recently, we shake talons and I invite him to join the party. He flaps his small wings excitedly, wags his long pointy tail, knocks a bowl of water all over the kitchen floor, and apologises profusely in dragonish.

9.46 p.m.	Patrick is disappointed I haven't got any music by The Corrs or The Cranberries; but he quite likes Abba. He polishes off the Christmas pudding, licks his lips, then curls up on the presents under the tree.
9.48 p.m.	The fairies are taking turns sitting on top of the tree.
9.49 p.m.	Think about Ben. Wonder what he's up to. Jealousy monster sticks his head through the letter box and grins. Patrick points his gun barrel nostrils in his direction and glares. A dragon glare is *very* scary. Jealousy monster disappears. We all laugh.
9.50 p.m.	Grumpy warns us the green scaly beast will set fire to the Christmas tree and we will all burn to death. Not a nice thing to happen just before Christmas; upset the relatives and all those presents will be buried with the coffins. It'll be such a waste.
9.51 p.m.	The Groundsel fairy has taken a shine to Grumpy; she thinks he's really a sensitive softie underneath all the grump and needs a little love and understanding. Some women never learn.
9.52 p.m.	Groundsel fairy *tells* Grumpy he's going to dance with her and have a lovely time. For once Grumpy is speechless and follows her like a puppy when she takes his hand.
9.53 p.m.	We're all grinning behind our hands.
10.05 p.m.	Put Bee Gees tape on. Dwarves cheer, 'Hooray!'
10.06 p.m.	Patrick opens one eye, scratches his left nostril with his right talon, yawns like a cat and falls back to sleep.
10.07 p.m.	Sleepy is snoring happily, his head resting on Patrick's warm undulating belly.
10.08 p.m.	Pixies hurry indoors after relieving themselves and warm their hands on warm dragon belly.
10.09 p.m.	Grumpy and Groundsel fairy are groovin' to 'Night Fever'.
10.10 p.m.	There's a lot of whispering going on in the shadows.

Did you see Grumpy smile? Actually smile? Impossible! I doubt it! Could have been a trick of the light! Possibly. Or Wind. Yes. Look, is he doing it again? What? Smiling! No, are you sure? Surely not! He must be drunk. It's that fairy wine! Or the pixie pie. Maybe he's constipated. Or his teeth hurt. Or he's wetting his trousers! Or... he's in love. Surely not. He hates everyone. Look, there he goes again!

10.15 p.m. The Bee Gees sing *How Deep Is Your Love.*

10.16 p.m. *Grump's smoochin'! He's not! He is!! He's got his eyes closed and he's smiling again! He's not! He is!! He'll deny it all tomorrow. He won't! He will!!!*

10.20 p.m. We're all dancing' to *Jive Talkin'.*

10.25 p.m. Thish fairee wine is show delishh. Fantash partee. Feel like in Wall Dishnee film.

10.30 p.m. Phil Collins is singing *Invisible Touch.* I dance in a circle with the fairies.

10.40 p.m. Mush rest. Will reget'morrow.

10.45 p.m. Bee Gees sing *Tragedy.* Dwarves know all the words.

10.50 p.m. Patrick is having a dragonish nightmare. Small jets of fire spurt out of his nostrils and the dwarves light their pipes.

11.00 p.m. Bee Gees sing, *Nights on Broadway.* Feel sleepy. Jush closhe eyesh for momen.

11.30 p.m. Room is quiet, apart from snoring. Small snores. Rumbly snores. Gentle snores. Pneumatic drill snores. Fast snores. Slow snores. Throaty smoker snores. Snotty snores. Nightmare snores. Lovely dreamy snores. And a high pitched dragon snore.

11.31 p.m. The candles have burnt down. Fairy lights on the tree glow silently. Fairies sleep peacefully draped over branches of tree, cushions, bookshelves and warm dragon body.

11.32 p.m. Patrick grunts and wakes up the Elderberry fairy who strokes his shamrock scales then closes her eyes and returns to fairy dreamland, the most beautiful place to be in the world.

11.33 p.m. Pixies are asleep under the tree, under the sofa and in cosy dark corners.

11.35 p.m. Dwarves sleep or smoke in hearth round the last glowing embers of a little fire. Grumpy puffs smoke rings the shape of hearts when he thinks no-one is looking. Dopey giggles in his sleep.

1.05 a.m. Wake up. Rub eyes. No sign of fairies, dwarves, pixies or Patrick. Ben is stumbling across the floor; he doesn't notice the log fairy table, holly or mistletoe.

1.06 a.m. He probably *will* notice; the day after tomorrow when the giant grey hangover mist monster has flown off his head,

462

across the town, and rested on the roof of The Thirsty Tongue Tavern, to wait with the other monsters for the next batch of late night revellers to fall out of the front door. I'll tell him my little friends from the country visited.

1.07 a.m. Worry a bit about a hangover mist monster grabbing me in the night. Feel sad until I spy with my sleepy eye, tiny bunches of fairy healing herbs left in the hearth and a green bottle of healing fairy oil, the size and shape of a small Marmite jar. The pine cones glow for two seconds, just to let me know the magic is still there.

1.15 a.m. Ben snores. I smile. Best party in the *whole wide world ever.*

Sunday 18th

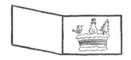

Woke up feeling great! Calm and peaceful, healed and healthy... I love me... I love herb tea... kittens three... I hate chocolate... I'd hate to be a supermodel... I throw brilliant parties... my socks match so I'm balanced... I wear my pixie slippers at all times... I've stopped impersonating Elvis... I'm better at impersonating the Bee Gees... my writing is better... my painting is better... I'm getting better... I've learnt to say no... and it feels good!

Today's window opened to reveal a Christmas cake. I opened the curtains to see Mother Nature had risen early to ice her marzipan-covered fruit cake – the plastic robin, snowman, Santa with a sack, Christmas tree and red ribbon ready for decoration.

Enjoyed a delightful bath filled with healing fairy herbs but stayed in the water too long, turning lobster pink and prunish, my seaweed face-pack green and cracked. Ben laughed, then held his head and groaned.

Me: You're your own worst enemy.
Ben: You're your own worst anemone.

Wrapped a few more presents and wrote a pile of cards. As the day wore on, I started feeling weary and the fatigue monster bit me on the neck, but he didn't sink his teeth in as deeply as usual. I think I'll be seeing a lot less of him next year. Talons crossed.

Gina collected the cot. She didn't seem very impressed with my effort but I thought it looked lovely, my best work yet. I hope baby Hollie and her mum Saffron will like it. Saffron's sister, Shona, wants me to decorate her little boy's cot; his name is Neptune. I didn't bother to ask what sort of designs she'd like, as smiley starfish, dolphins, seahorses and mermaids leaping over shipwrecks appeared on the sketch pad in my mind. I'm looking forward to my New Year project already!

Monday 19th

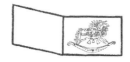

A rocking horse.

Eileen was surprised at my glowing, healthy appearance and lack of fatigue; wished I could tell her about my fantastic weekend. She told me all about her fabulous weekend visiting Seaworld, a seal sanctuary, and planning a holiday abroad where she'll be able to swim with dolphins and sea turtles. I admired her silvery seaweed earrings encrusted with seed pearls; she admired my long pearly nails. I longed to tell her I'd shaken talons with a dragon on Saturday but changed the subject to my favourite theme this time of year. Food.

Me:	I love Christmas pudding.
Eileen:	Mmm, so do I, with lots of brandy poured over before you light it.
Me:	To get a good flame, sprinkle the pudding with a tablespoon of sugar before you add the spirit.
Eileen:	Before you add spit?
Me:	Ha, ha, ha, *spirit* as in ghosties!
Eileen:	Ah, ha, ha, ha.
Me:	I like lots of cheese and crackers too.
Eileen:	I love Babybel cheeses.
Me:	I think it's cruel to eat baby cheeses, ha, ha.
Eileen:	What's cruel to baby Jesus?

I noticed a carrier bag bulging with mince pies and Christmas stockings next to her desk, a fleck of chocolate on her cheek, a sweety-type-rustle in her white coat pocket and two mince-pie-type-crumbs next to a mug with seashells on. Remembered I needed to call in at the mini-market before the taxi arrived to purchase choc tree decorations, choc money, mince pies, hair conditioner and post-Christmas-stress wrinkle cream. We exchanged Christmas cards and I gave Eileen her prezzie, a seahorse brooch. Eileen gave me a Goodfellows (1897 original) Dundee cake, baked in Scotland on the banks of the river Tay, full of luscious sultanas and tangy orange peel, and topped off with the finest split almonds. I licked my lips and smiled. We wished each other a merry one and I went on my merry way.

While I waited for the taxi to arrive, I saw a baby's woollen mitten on the path. I picked it up, placed it on a wall, and thought it seemed strange to see a black baby's mitten. Maybe grandma had run out of white or pastel shades because her fifteenth grandchild was unexpected, or mummy was a fan of *The Munsters*, a Goth, or into grunge. Felt sad. A little munster somewhere had a tiny cold hand.

A posh-looking woman with a hard face plonked her large leather handbag on the wall and rummaged through it angrily, muttering to her red-lipped self; the mitten was tossed to the ground. It lay sadly on the wet path once more where the belt of the woman's long camel-coloured coat rested in a muddy puddle. I thought, 'Ha, ha, ha,' then remembered it was the season of goodwill and quickly hoped the mud would wash off. I wondered if she'd even notice as I dreamily thought I'd look lovely in a coat just like that.

Mr. Quiet-and-gentlemanly-taxi-man with a Dustin Hoffman smile, asked me if I'd done all my Christmas shopping. Taxi drivers *always* ask you that this time of year. I told him I *had* done all my gift shopping, with a Babybel grin.

Wrote my last pile of cards and arranged the collection we'd received today on the bookshelf: robin in the snow, Canada goose with mistletoe in its beak in the snow, carol singers in the snow, and three wise men... in the desert. Found a miniature fairy slipper next to a book about Arthur Rackham and carefully placed it where I knew I'd remember to find it (in the hat brim of an ornamental wizard in a long purple gown with gold moons and stars on) in case the owner returned to collect it.

Tuesday 20th

Mistletoe.

Mother Nature looked miserable this morning; maybe she'd burnt her mouth on a mince pie like I did last night. The rain melted the snow and I couldn't get Cliff Richard's song, 'Mistletoe and Wine', out of my head. Torture!

Today's cards were boring: poinsettia, candles and bells. But Rose's card was sweet: lots of children holding hands with Mother round a huge Christmas tree, their faces lit up with joy and wonder ('Silent Night' by Viggo Johansen, 1851 – 1935). Her letter mentioned she's pregnant again and getting married as soon as possible. She's had an argument with ex-mother in law number two, a row with ex-husband number one about who's having Emily, Elizabeth and Charlotte for Christmas; Honesty has been accused of stealing at school, Chastity stays out too late with her boyfriends, and Grant gave Tiffany a black eye on her birthday because she pushed his face into her birthday cake because he blew out her birthday candles because she had lots of presents and he didn't.

Life must be like a very long episode of *EastEnders* every day for Rose. I should have given her mandarin and geranium de-stress bath oil for Christmas.

Murphy 'helped' me wrap a few presents. I arranged Christmas cards on the window ledge. Paddy 'helped' me rearrange them. Mary made neat little paw marks on the gift tags and batted my pens under the sofa. Ben 'helped' me eat up a bag of chocolate money.

Wednesday 21st

A reindeer.

Artie Auntie sent me a W. H. Smiths gift voucher for ten pounds, Auntie Mary sent me a Boots gift voucher for ten pounds, and Mary brought a mouse into the house. Now I'm rich and grey-mouse, ha, ha.

Took me ages to rescue the mouse; it ran so fast across the room every time I tried to capture it, I couldn't see where it ran to. I had all the chairs up on their sides, throws and cushions everywhere and worried about squashing the creature. One moment I nearly caught it under a sieve but it ran behind the TV bumping its nose on the video recorder on the way. Eventually found a tiny grey animal cowering behind my broomstick in a corner and, as I was making a wall of video tape cases round the broomstick to help me trap the terrified little thing, Ben walked in. I said, 'Don't ask, just don't ask.'

It felt good to release the mouse into the wild. Now I know how those wonderful workers for the R.S.P.C.A. must feel. Wouldn't want to see some of the terrible things they must have to witness though, I'm sure I'd have a breakdown after a week.

It's about time I had a little chat with my boys about bringing birds home. I once had a cat who brought home two birds at a time – naughty boy.

Thursday 22nd

A lamp.

A couple of amusing cards cheered my morning, from friends I haven't seen for a hundred years: a half-eaten Christmas pudding with a very full mouse sleeping next to it, and cartoon reindeer sitting in front of a TV looking disappointed because Santa has just said he doesn't care if it is their favourite programme, it's time to go and deliver presents.

Spotted lots of Scottish Christmas gifts in a catalogue; I'd meant to show them to Eileen but kept forgetting to bring the catalogue along to the clinic. She may have liked the traditional pot-pourri, recalling the scent of a Highland forest at Christmas, tied with a festive ribbon, for one of her relatives or herself; she strikes me as a pot-pourri sort of person. Last year she gave me a Christmas card with a tartan border, so she'd probably have fancied the set of cards bearing a joyous Yuletide greeting, the reds of the traditional tartan in the border complementing the fine art images depicting seasonal Scottish scenes. The tartan gift wrap and tags inspired by Royal Stewart (Queen Victoria's favourite tartan) is very attractive too. Then there's the Highland Christmas crackers, whisky chocolates (laced with sixteen year old Balblair single malt whisky), Scottish blend Christmas tea (a blend of Chinese keemun leaf tea, orange, ginger and cloves), marmalade flavoured with historic Scottish whisky, tie, whisky socks...

The Christmas double issue of *Weekly Wife* was ever so exciting; full of real life stories, tips for an easier life, fab winter coats, showbiz gossip, happy holiday features, slimming secrets, recipes for Christmas pudding and seasonal soups (ignored photos of cooked turkey) fantastic ideas for festive fun and decorating the home in a creative stylish way. I read, 'The Secrets of Santa's Grotto', 'My Husband Bought Me New Boobs for Christmas', 'I Married a Real Life Scrooge', 'Five Brilliant Ways to Dress your Christmas Table' and 'My Worst Christmas Ever'!! Wendy told me to go for glamour in a big big way this party season and Cosmic Colin said I was full of energy for festive parties and must hurl myself into the fun. Well, I *did* on Saturday.

Sad moment: think about thousands of poor little slaughtered turkeys, frozen in freezer coffins all over the country.

Another sad moment: think of thousands of M.E. sufferers all over the country feeling half slaughtered by illness, their minds frozen at the thought of another new year ahead.

Happy moment: imagine self running to top of mountain in Scotland. When I reach my peak, I scream, 'I LOVE YOU!' and 'I BELIEVE YOU!' to the thousands of M.E. sufferers all over the country. They hear me and have a happy Christmas.

Another happy moment: see myself joyfully descend the mountain then have a wee drop of whisky in The Spit and Sporran where I dance on the table and the landlord says I'm so beautiful I can have anything I desire. I request the head of ~~John the~~ Bernard Matthews on a plate, with all the Christmas trimmings.

Friday 23rd

A carol singer.

Woke up at midday feeling wonderfully rested, to hear the washing machine rumbling and groaning like a giant dragon with tummy ache. There was a clanking of plates and cutlery in the kitchen, and small voices were singing along to Abba, 'Dusting, dusting, dusting, we are dusting, it's a rich man's world. Money, money, money, chocolate money, it's a rich man's world...' I smiled my lady of leisure smile as I drifted downstairs to sip herbs and open today's cards.

Dave and Nicky from New Zealand sent us a card: Santa on his sleigh whizzing across the miles to England. My brother's card was a cartoon of Santa taking his shrunken red trousers out of the washing machine; and one of Ben's relatives, I've never met, sent a peaceful snowy scene 'Homeward in the Snow' by Joseph Farquarson.

Late this afternoon, as the sky darkened, the rain slapped like Santa's reins and Christmas tree lights glowed, I curled up in the warm with the kittens and pixies to watch the last in a series of Christmas craft programmes. Now I know how to: make star-shaped biscuits with glass effect-middles (made with boiled sweets); Christmas decorations using dough and all sorts of jolly wonderful pot-pourri; create enchanting and colourful wrapping paper, lanterns from recycled cans and wreaths from orange berries; display nuts in jars (painted gold and silver), decorate candles with marvellous metallic mosaic, perk up pebbles with pearly paint and stick holly in potatoes to keep it fresh.

Ben went to The Filled Stocking, Stiletto Street, with Rick, Rob, Bill and Bob the Slob.

Saturday 24th

A star over a crib.

Another calm and peaceful snow scene arrived with the post, 'Winter Sunset' by John Corcoran, and I decided we were going to have a white Christmas after all as I carefully stuck luminous snowflakes on the windows and sprayed snow spray in the corner of the window panes. I rearranged the Christmas cards so all the snow scenes were side by side on the window ledge and had just finished singing 'White Christmas' when there was a knock at the door.

Weird musician friend and his weird musician girlfriend stood on the doorstep clutching their Bibles to their hearts and smiling festive Christian smiles; they were so looking forward to midnight mass and celebrating the birth of baby Jesus. I offered them a cup of tea and a slice of cake but Saint Mary and Joseph weren't staying (thank God) as they were busy delivering Christmas cards, goodwill, and the word of the Lord. After they'd gone, I opened their card: a gruesome painting of the Holy Family by fifteenth-century artist Fra Filippo Lippi – Mary and Joseph and two ugly angels admire a fat baby Jesus.

Wrote baby cheeses on the shopping list and sat on the loo practising my Christian smile, almost as good as my Bing Crosby impression. Ben was out doing last-minute Christmas shopping for himself and his family. He returned weighed down with multicoloured carrier bags and an I-need-a-fag-and-a-coffee smile. I put the kettle on.

Me:	You've just missed weird musician friend and his weird musician girlfriend.
Ben:	Oh no! (Feigned dismay.)
Me:	I offered him his favourite, Lyons Original Battenburg and Lyons Red Label leaf tea.
Ben:	Hmm, surprised he didn't stay.
Me:	I said I was a good person and enjoyed feeding Lyons to the Christians.
Ben:	Did 'e laugh?
Me:	Er, no.

Ben:	Did you give him his Christmas card and treble clef pen?
Me:	Oh God, I forgot, their Christian smiles put me off. Pity you missed all that goodwill.
Ben:	Shame. Do you like my new shoes? I think they're a bit big.
Me:	They look very smart! Reindeer hooves are large relative to their body; they act like snow shoes.
Ben:	What about the jacket?
Me:	Nice colour, looks warm. Reindeer hair is extremely dense and an undercoat of fine woolly hair makes an efficient air trap.
Ben:	I'm all set to pull Santa's sleigh then!

. . . .

Ben:	Where's the wrapping paper?
Me:	In front of you.
Ben:	Where's the scissors?
Me:	Next to the sellotape.
Ben:	Where's the sellotape?
Me:	Next to the wrapping paper.
Ben:	Have we got any tags left?
Me:	Yes, here you are.
Ben:	Are there any cards left?
Me:	Four or five.
Ben:	They'll do; do we need any more mince pies?
Me:	Yes (blush).
Ben:	Have we got enough sprouts?
Me:	Um, I think so, I'll check.
Ben:	Did I get potatoes?
Me:	Yeah.
Ben:	I remembered the red candles, red serviettes and brandy for the Christmas pud.
Me:	Good boy.
Ben:	I forgot the cranberry sauce and crackers, I'll nip to the shops before they close.
Me:	OK, I'll wrap those presents for you. Did you buy treats for the kittens?
Ben:	Yep.
Me:	Did you buy treats for me?
Ben:	I may have (smile).

Me:	Oh goody!
Ben:	Anything else you can think of?
Me:	Um, er, extra soya milk, er... matches... and a box of those round chocolates in the see-through box with gold wrapping, a nut in the middle and a crispy nutty outside. Ooh... maybe two boxes.

Sat in the bath and worried through my list of Christmas worries. *Why, why, why* did I invite Mum and Dad for Christmas dinner? I'm really not up to entertaining yet, but Mum has been sounding ill and depressed for months and could do with a break. I'm so relieved Gina and Peter are away over Christmas; Dad wanted me to invite them too so *all* the family were together. I will try to ignore his comments about a vegetarian Christmas; he eats it all up anyway and asks for a second helping.

At eight o'clock, Ben went out for a 'quick one' at The Star, Brightlylit Street, and the dwarves came round to help me prepare the veg and set the table for tomorrow's veggie banquet. Dopey and Sleepy polished the best glasses and cutlery while I laid a red tablecloth and green Christmassy place mats neatly on the dining room table. Grumpy, Sneezy and Bashful peeled, chopped and scraped veg while Happy and Doc helped me make an enchanting and stylish table centrepiece (inspired by *Weekly Wife*) using red candles, holly, angel chimes, fairy pine cones, red and gold baubles, green glitter and gold lametta.

The peeling, chopping and scraping stopped when Sneezy, Bashful and Grumpy decided they wanted to join in with the creative fun; they said they'd nip back late tonight to finish up. Sneezy sneezed over Dopey's freshly polished glass so he gave up, and Sleepy decided the excitement was all too much and he needed a little rest under the Christmas tree; but we managed to finish setting the table before Ben came home after his 'quick one', ha, ha, at eleven o'clock. I made little 'bishops' hats with the red serviettes and placed them in the glasses, strands of curly gold lametta ever so artistically draped over them. The effect was stunning, though we said it ourselves, and Sleepy woke up when he heard all the clapping and cheering. We all celebrated with sherry and mince pies and chocolate money.

11.20 p.m. Ben snores.
11.30 p.m. Is that reindeer hooves I can hear on the roof?
11.31 p.m. No, must be the dwarves chopping veg.

11.40 p.m. Hark! Is that the herald angels singing?
11.41 p.m. No, must be the dwarves whistling.
11.45 p.m. Is that sleigh bells?
11.46 p.m. Paddy is rolling a bottle of pills round the bathroom floor.

Sunday 25th

Munch, munch, munch (Ben eating Milky Way out of Christmas stocking); nibble, nibble, nibble (me eating Kit-Kat and about to start on a Topic); crunch, crunch, crunch (kittens enjoying treats); clatter, clatter, clatter (pots and pans); sip, sip, sip (Mum with glass of sherry); sip, sip, slurp (me testing the brandy); chat, chat, stare (Ben and Dad raising their Scorpio tails at each other); ting, ting, ting (rotating cherubs in enchanting and stylish centrepiece); bang, bang, bang, bang (pulling crackers); laugh, laugh, laugh, laugh (everybody telling their cracker joke); clank, clank, clank (metal on china); natter, nitter, natter (interesting conversation: reindeer physiology is specialised to eat and digest lichen as an energy source in winter); groan, groan, groan (Dad's comments about a vegetarian Christmas); munch, munch, munch, singe, singe, singe (Dad's eyebrows too near flame on Christmas pudding); rustle, rustle, rustle (my paper hat falling off into gravy); singe, singe, singe (Murphy's tail too near flame of candle); sip, sip, sip, giggle, giggle (sparkly wine gone to my head); natter, natter (interesting comment: twice a year, coral spawn on the Ningaloo Reef lures the whale shark in for a feeding frenzy); rip, rip, rip, smile, smile, smile (Ben and parents pleased with their presents: fuchsia jewellery, gardening gauntlets, socks, chocolates, *Star Trek* watch and more socks); rip, rip, rip, smile (I'm pleased with my presents: cat books, cat nightie, chocolate, cat picture, and best prezzie: chocolate cat with three chocolate kittens); doze, doze, doze (in front of TV); munch, munch, munch, doze, doze, doze, slurp, slurp, slurp... burp... clink, clink, fizz.

Monday 26th

Groan, groan, groan (sore head); sniff, sniff, sniff (snotty nose); grunt, grunt, grunt (sore throat – good excuse to eat lots of honey poured over Cornish ice-cream); doze, doze, doze (in front of TV); purr, purr, purr (Murphy and Paddy on lap); read, read, read (*Why Can't a Man be More Like a Cat*, by Antonia van der Meer and Linda Conner – 'Cats don't leave their whiskers all over the bathroom sink. When cats get the seven-year itch, all they do is scratch it'); Bump, bump, bump (Mary rolling a raw sprout around the kitchen floor); Rustle, rustle, rustle (Ben rolling another roll-up).

Tuesday 27th

Sniff, sniff, blow (must feed a cold – good excuse to eat soft white rolls filled with creamy, full-fat cheese with herbs and garlic); doze, doze, smile (Mary Poppins, 'A spoonful of sugar helps the medicine go down'); Slurp, slurp, slurp (a spoonful of honey helps the soya milk go brown); Munch, munch, munch (chocolate); peel, peel, peel (juicy clementines); roll, roll, bump (Mary with chocolate money); roll, roll, tinkle (Paddy with Christmas toy); sip, sip, sip (Lemsip); crunch, crunch, crunch (Murphy with Christmas treats); blip, blip, blip (Ben with computer chess); munch, munch, munch (deep-filled mince pies); sniff, sniff, blow (deep gloom-filled thoughts about returning to healthy diet in New Year).

Wednesday 28th

Sniff, read, sniff, read (*Weekly Wife* suggests I take more zinc to shorten length of cold symptoms); sniff, read, sniff, read (reasons to enjoy chocolate this festive season: 'plain choc is a good source of iron, dark choc contains magnesium needed for nerve and muscle functioning and is good for countering P.M.S.'). Munch, munch, munch (plain chocolate); doze, doze, doze (watch *Last of the Summer Wine*); slurp, slurp, slurp (last of the Christmas ginger wine); sniff, sniff, groan (ecology loo roll is rough on a red nose); sniff, sniff, think (did Rudolph the reindeer have a cold?). Sniff, sniff, groan (cruel of *ITV* to show *Pretty Woman* at this time of year).

Thursday 29th

Knock, knock, knock (Bill at front door with red nose); sniff, sniff, blow (Bill pulls wet hankie out of pocket); laugh, laugh, laugh (Bill likes his paintbrush pen prezzie); rustle, rustle, rustle (Ben and Bill roll roll-ups); sing, sing, sing (Ben puts Bill off his next chess move by singing 'Rudolf the Red Nosed Reindeer'); munch, munch, slurp (tea and mince pies); peel, peel, peel (satsumas); tap, tap, tap (chess pieces on chess board); peel, peel, munch (liqueur chocs); tap, tap, tap (chess pieces sticky now); sniff, read, sniff, read, sniff (I read *A Cat's*

Little Instruction Book, by Leigh W. Rutledge, to the kittens: 'Never yawn half-heartedly, always clean between your toes, make the world your scratching post...') tap, tap, tap (checkmate).

Friday 30th

Shuffle, shuffle, slam (Bill and Ben hurry to The Filled Stocking where Natasha is a stripper). Tap, tap, clank (jealousy monster creeps in through the cat flap); bump, bump, bump (throw satsumas at jealousy monster); sniff, cough, sniff (want to go to The Filled Stocking: Naughty Natasha sent Ben a Christmas card with lots of kisses on and I want to stick a sprig of holly on her chair; I like to get to the bottom of things). Sniff, groan, sniff (holiday adverts getting up my nose); cough, sniff, cough (I will learn astral travel; it's less painful); shiver, shiver, shiver (Mr. Weatherman says stormy winds and snow are on the way); cough, sniff, cough (curl up on sofa full of germs, food and New Year's resolutions; surrounded by sleeping kittens, smelly satsuma peelings, plates with crumbs on, empty foil mince pie dishes, soggy tissues, choccy wrappers, half a mug of cold Lemsip and mouldy post-Christmas feelings).

Saturday 31st

Ben went to an *all*-day, *all*-evening, Christmassy New Year family gathering, somewhere lovely. I sat *all* alone. I nibbled a lump of hard cheese and cold Christmas pudding, feeling sorry for myself. *All* the chocolate was gone: not even one choc coin left. I sniffed a liqueur choc wrapper. Found one minute crumb of chocolate. Ate it. Watched boring TV *all* afternoon while I cracked *all* the nuts and peeled *all* the satsumas. Paddy was sick, with tinsel in it, *all* over next year's calendar and the cat books. Murphy trod on a pile of dirty plates sending *all* the glasses and cutlery crashing to the kitchen floor. Used up *all* my energy cleaning up the mess. Used up *all* the tissues blowing my nose and had to make do with rough ecology loo roll. Decided to have a bath with fairy oil. *All* evening.

5.55 p.m.   Pour clear fairy oil into warm bath water.

6.00 p.m.   Swirly sixties-style pinks and purples begin to appear on the surface; the scent of roses and lavender fills the air.

6.02 p.m.   Lie in bath with eyes closed, inhaling deeply.

6.05 p.m.   Open my eyes. Wow! Amazing! Rose petal pinks and parma violets are changing to shades of magenta crimson and geranium scarlet.

6.06 p.m.   Tiny orange dots rise to the surface, expanding by the second. There's a sweet aroma of peaches and mandarins.

6.07 p.m.   Close my eyes... This is fun! Slowly breathe in and out, feeling energy seeping into my veins, enjoying the luxury of peace and warmth and all the time in the world to relax.

6.08 p.m.   Start to feel strong and positive as the fresh fragrance of spring daffodils lifts my spirits and makes me feel alive!

6.09 p.m.   Watch in wonder as bright yellows and oranges swirl and blend together to become soft marigold and pale lemon. The air is now lightly scented with honeysuckle.

6.10 p.m.   Thousands of lime green bubbles rise to the surface like champagne bubbles in a glass and pop, releasing a deliciously appley aroma. Leafy green steam curls and twists and turns into the shape of miniature dragons; they flap their wings and fly around the ceiling three times before dissolving like candle smoke.

6.11 p.m.	Close my eyes again. I'm lying on a grassy forest floor looking up at the sun shining through a ceiling of leaves, many shades of glowing green. I can *feel* life and growth and the trees reaching for the stars, and fairies smiling, and the angels singing.
6.12 p.m.	Oooh, itchy back. Scratch back. I've been getting a lot of dry skin lately – too many hot baths. This water feels lovely and soft and moisturising though, and cleansing and comforting.
6.13 p.m.	Spiralling shades of mistletoe and forest green are slowly permeated with peacock and periwinkle blues.
6.14 p.m.	Azure blue bubbles are appearing on the surface and popping to release essence of hyacinth and bluebells.
6.15 p.m.	Close my eyes... I'm dancing with the fairies.
6.16 p.m.	I'm flying high above the clouds.
6.17 p.m.	Like Peter Pan.
6.18 p.m.	I'm free as a bird... my wings outstretched... higher... and higher...
6.19 p.m.	I'm in heaven with the angels.
6.20 p.m.	I'm at one with the universe... I touch the stars.
6.21 p.m.	Ooops! Must have dozed off. The bath water is now white, snow white, with silvery sparkles, and huge iridescent bubbles are rising to the surface.
6.22 p.m.	Bath is overflowing with millions of pearly bubbles. It's the bubbliest bubble bath I've ever seen!
6.23 p.m.	The room is delicately perfumed with lily of the valley and snowdrops.
6.24 p.m.	Bubbles the size of tennis balls rise into the air and float around the bathroom. Inside each one are spirits of dancing fairies, birds and flowers.
6.25 p.m.	The birds and fairies are singing, even the flowers! Magic! This is fairy magic!!
6.26 p.m.	The air is thurified with the scent of many flowers.
6.27 p.m.	I close my eyes and I'm standing in the middle of the local Interflora shop.
6.28 p.m.	I've just nipped next door to Thorntons.
6.29 p.m.	I'm removing the cellophane wrapper... I'm... Oh no! All the bubbles are disappearing. As each one pops, a fairy

song ends. A bird song ends. A flower song ends. Flowery fragrances are fading like a winter sunset. The bath water is cooling.

6.30 p.m. Bath water is clear.

6.31 p.m. Bathroom is silent.

6.32 p.m. Bum.

6.33 p.m. Harp music. I can hear beautiful harp music... yes, that's definitely harp music... I'm not imagining it... and sweet lilting fairy song... definitely fairies singing... they're at the bottom of the garden... and coming closer... up the path... closer and closer.

6.34 p.m. Must get dried and dressed! Feel excited! Elated! Extraordinarily exuberant! Extremely extrovert! Exhilarated! Extraterrestially exfoliated!!

6.35 p.m. I can hear clanking in the kitchen, sounds like someone's doing the washing-up. Hope it's the dwarves.

6.37 p.m. Doc calls up the stairs, 'You can't come down yet!'

6.38 p.m. Mm, wonder what's going on.

6.39 p.m. Maybe the fairies are helping with the housework. Or they've brought fairy wine.

6.40 p.m. Could do with a drink.

6.41 p.m. Peckish too.

6.42 p.m. Knock! Knock! Knock!
'You can come down now.'

6.44 p.m. SURPRISE!!!!

6.46 p.m. Oh brilliant!! Everyone, absolutely everyone, is here. All the fairies, all the pixies, and the dwarves. Even Patrick is already curled up under the tree. He's brought his mate, Jimmy, the tartan dragon, who is busy lighting a fire in the fireplace. Phew! The whisky fumes from his red breath are rather strong.

The room is all tidy and cosy and Christmassy. There's pixie pie with a giant crispy golden crust, *real* fairy cakes with sparkly hundreds and thousands, and candlelight is flickering on a whole crate of bubbly fairy wine. Everyone, absolutely *everyone*, is wearing bright colourful party hats and popping party poppers and the Bee Gees are singing, 'You Should be Dancin' Yeah!' So we all dance!!